The Confessions of Sherlock Holmes

THE THEOLOGICAL ODYSSEY OF THE GREAT DETECTIVE

Volume 4

The Woman

Irene Adler
and the
Journey to America

THOMAS MENGERT

BLUE FORGE PRESS

Port Orchard, Washington

The Woman: Irene Adler & the Journey to America
Copyright 2024
by Thomas Mengert

First eBook Edition June 2024
First Print Edition June 2024

ISBN 979-8-89439-012-3

For information about film, reprint or other subsidiary rights, contact: blueforgegroup@gmail.com

Blue Forge Press is the print division of the volunteer-run, federal 501(c)3 nonprofit company, Blue Forge Group, founded in 1989 and dedicated to bringing light to the shadows and voice to the silence. We strive to empower storytellers across all walks of life with our four divisions: Blue Forge Press, Blue Forge Films, Blue Forge Gaming, and Blue Forge Records. Find out more at www.BlueForgeGroup.org

Blue Forge Press
7419 Ebbert Drive Southeast
Port Orchard, Washington 98367
blueforgepress@gmail.com
360-550-2071 ph.txt

Acknowledgements

The Confessions of Sherlock Holmes has, for all of its primary theological intent, a subtext that emerged in the course of the writing. That subtext is the decline and fall of the British Empire and of the imperial family structures that once supported it. The three Holmes brothers each manifest the end result of the system of primogeniture and the conflict present between art and reason in their blood. Each brother in his own way manifests the conflict entailed in finding a place and an identity in opposition to their father and his estate.

The character of the Holmes father remains distant and perhaps finally indecipherable. As the reader will discover in the course of reading the book the parental figure looks beyond his own sons in order to find an image of a substitute son that would meet the requirements and the pattern that the father needed each of them to represent. Unfortunately, each son manifested instead a diluted solution of traits that drew more from their artistic mother and her French heritage than from their stern father and his code. The individuality and character of the brothers manifests a freedom from convention that the father perhaps wished that he could have claimed for himself, but to see it present in his sons seemed both indulgent and a betrayal of his own strict principles. He valued rebellion, but not within his own house and among his own progeny. For this reason both Mycroft and Sherlock are comparative exiles, while Sherringford is saddled with maintaining Sigerside, the Holmes estate. If the Christian religion can be seen as the process of overcoming exile from God as Father through the sacrifice of a Son, the parallels will be immediately apparent.

I doubt that I would have been able to compose this book if it were not present as a reflection of the dynamics of my own family. So for this reason I dedicate this book as with all my efforts in life to my parents and grandparents and especially to my two grandmothers who each nurtured my early love for literature with their deep love and affirmation.

The support of my parents made my life possible in every way imaginable.

To my Father's mother, Tilly, who read me Longfellow's poetry on sunny afternoons.

To My Mother's mother, Gerda, who gave me the Doubleday Edition of The Complete Sherlock Holmes.

To my Father's father, Otto, who shared his library with me and taught me the value of family heritage.

To my Mother's father, Fred, who instilled in me a love of the sea and for his humor and love of stories.

To all of these my everlasting thanks.

"What is the meaning of it, Watson?" said Holmes, solemnly, as he laid down the paper. "What object is served by this circle of misery and violence and fear? It must tend to some end, or else our universe is ruled by chance, which is unthinkable. But what end? There is the great standing perennial problem to which human reason is as far from an answer as ever."

—From *The Adventure of the Cardboard Box*

"There is nothing in which deduction is as necessary as in religion," said he, leaning with his back against the shutters. "It can be built up as an exact science by the reasoner. Our highest assurance of the goodness of providence seems to me to rest in the flowers. All other things, our powers, our desires, our food, are really necessary for our existence in the first instance. But this rose is an extra. Its smell and its color are an embellishment of life, not a condition of it. It is only goodness which gives such extras, and so I say again that we have much to hope from the flowers."

—From *The Adventure of the Naval Treaty*

"The greatest schemer of all time, the organizer of every deviltry, the controlling brain of the underworld, a brain which might have made or marred the destiny of nations – that's the man!"

"Barker beat his head with his clenched fist in his impotent anger. 'Do not tell me that we have to sit down under this? Do you say that no one can ever get level with this king devil?' 'No, I don't say that,' said Holmes, and his eyes seemed to be looking far into the future. 'I don't say that he can't be beat. But you must give me time—you must give me time.' We all sat in silence for some minutes while those fateful eyes still strained to pierce the veil."

—From *The Valley of Fear*

Preface

Readers of the previous volumes of The Confessions of Sherlock Holmes will notice an altered preface for this present volume in the series. The initial preface that was included in the first three volumes was designed to act as a base and to prepare the reader for the unique style and methodology employed in this multi-volume retelling of the final decades of the life of the great detective, Sherlock Holmes. Many avid Sherlockians have awaited a synthesis where many loosely connected threads in the original tales of Sir Arthur Conan Doyle begged for a comprehensive solution. It was this need that The Confessions of Sherlock Holmes was written to fulfill.

When the series was initially written it was composed sequentially so that even in its formation the twin narratives could not anticipate what would happen next. In this sense the entire series was dictated by Holmes and Watson rather than being imposed upon them by an outside voice. The overriding intent was to write the ultimate Sherlock Holmes adventure while simultaneously answering some of the most challenging questions posed by theology and philosophy, while addressing the deeper questions raised by human beings during the course of their lives.

Such an ambitious project had not been attempted since the writing of two major works by the modernist literary figures

Marcel Proust and Robert Musil who together served as models for the present work. Each of these authors envisioned a multi-volume work that would contain every aspect of human life during a significant historical period, one that was very close to the time period chosen for The Confessions of Sherlock Holmes—the end of the 19th century and the period after the *fin de siècle* leading up to what is now called World War One.

When the entire series was completed and initially published in 2014 in a separate edition its length was just over 830,000 words. The present edition with its extensive revisions now includes an eighth volume sequel and contains over one million words in 20 Books printed in 7 volumes (plus the 8th volume sequel). This places the series among the longest fictional narratives written in any language. Its length was in keeping with the complexity of the subject and the example set by *In Search of Time Lost* (formerly translated as *Remembrance of Things Past*) by Marcel Proust and *The Man without Qualities* by Robert Musil that was left incomplete by the author's untimely death. Both of the latter works belong to the tradition of the philosophical novel that includes Thomas Mann's, *The Magic Mountain* and two novels by Herman Broch: *The Sleepwalkers* and *The Death of Virgil.*

The ultimate dream of every author committed to the great treasury of literature is to devise a new form to communicate the deepest human truths. Recent parallels in this effort embrace musical composition as the inspiration. The Confessions of Sherlock Holmes with its sequel may together be thought of as analogous to a symphony. The first volume forms an overture to the whole symphony. The second and third volumes form the 1st movement of the symphony. The fourth and fifth volumes represent the 2d movement of the symphony. The sixth and seventh volumes represent the 3d movement of the symphony, and finally the eighth volume represents the climatic 4th movement of the symphony.

The astute reader will notice that a resolution is sought to many of the institutional problems confronting the Catholic Church, and theology in general today, as anticipated in the debates of Holmes and Moriarty. Various echoes of Kierkegaard, Nietzsche, Feuerbach, Sartre, Heidegger, the post-modernists, and various textual and linguistic theorists such as Jacques Derrida and Ferdinand de Saussure will appear. The present Volume 4 is significant because the long preparatory period is coming to an end and Sherlock Holmes and Professor Moriarty are about to meet in volumes 5 through 7, face to face, and to begin their long-awaited battle of wits over the nature of human existence and the quest for a solution to what philosophers refer to as "the problem of evil.

In the remaining volumes of the series other characters are introduced to expand the scope of the debate. Sherlock Holmes, Doctor Watson, and the woman who accompanies them face an expanding circle of challenges as they review their lives and examine the events and relationships that have defined their separate identities and set the stage for all their hopes and dreams. Finally, the eighth volume sequel, entitled *The Testament of Sherlock Holmes,* alters the format of the series while being an uninterrupted continuation of the previous seven volumes. There the saga reaches the 20th century and the haunting omnipresence of the Great War of 1914-1918 as well as the peace settlement that followed its termination. The final volume of the series embraces the retirement years of the great detective as he assumes a greater role in the overarching events that still cast their shadow over the present world.

The Woman

Irene Adler
and the
Journey to America

THOMAS MENGERT

Book Nine

Sherlock Holmes' Reunion with Irene Adler, "The Woman"

Dr. Watson's Narrative Continues

To Sherlock Holmes Irene Adler, whose acquaintance he made in a tale that I entitled, "A Scandal in Bohemia," was always spoken of as "the woman." I believe that Holmes admired her more for her wit than for her beauty as an actress and adventuress of European fame. No portrait of Sherlock Holmes can afford to ignore the question of his relations with the fair sex. His comment that women bias the judgment was his own claim to immunity in regard to the enchanting power of woman and the role that women play behind the scenes in world affairs. He often spoke reverentially of his mother who was of French extraction. I never knew him to pursue either romance or to yield to the blandishments and charms of the demi-monde. For Sherlock Holmes his own unique interests left little time for the demands of courtship or for dissipation. Yet for all of this Holmes possessed a charm and gallantry towards the women who consulted him that gained their immediate trust and confidence. He had little patience with cads and scoundrels who prey upon women and on at least one occasion threatened one of these men with a sound horsewhipping. Holmes little thought that he would ever encounter Irene Adler after her marriage. She still played a silent role in his life however and he cherished the picture that she gave him as a parting gift. The ways of fate are strange though and "the woman" will appear now and again in the course of this narrative.

I closed the previous volume with a sense of peace and confidence, less because I expected these emotions to continue as we sailed towards our adventure in America than because the desire for premature closure is an innate human characteristic. Every event whether tragic or comic has a sequel. In the present volume the horizon of events begins to open up as a reward for those readers who have persisted thus far in what I believe will be the final and conclusive account of the last years of the partnership that I shared with Sherlock Holmes.

I wish as we begin to emphasize the following selections from Holmes' journal that I read on the night of our first day at sea because I found within them a synthesis of his methods and a unity of thought between science, politics, and religion. Therein could be seen much of that grand synthesis that had been his quest for so many years. We were sailing towards a land whose early settlers had approached religious matters in their own particular fashion. America had its beginnings in various forms of Protestantism with the exception of Maryland that was settled by persons of the Catholic faith. Certain colonies were formed primarily to foster a degree of religious freedom and community that was unknown in England. The first colonies in turn soon developed their own stringent orthodoxies and standards of belief over time that resulted in the formation of off-shoot additional colonies such as Rhode Island and Pennsylvania that would tolerate greater doctrinal diversity among their residents.

The desire for ever greater religious freedom soon encompassed a desire for political freedoms as well that resulted in the colonies making common cause and eventually creating a common republic that would serve to unite them into a single nation. That republic in turn had now spread from sea to sea and promised to take the lead in the practical development of the sciences and a pragmatic approach in business affairs that may someday make it a nation possessing more wealth and influence than any other on earth.

We still speak pejoratively of the Americans as a provincial people, but its energy and vigor are an example to the world. Will America find its limits or will its very development make it lose sight of those ideals that it embraced after its own early servitude to England? These were my preoccupations at the time and events since then have left the final issue of these speculations regarding the ultimate fate and importance of America still undecided. There will be more commentary on these matters as we proceed, so let us return now to Montpellier, France where Sherlock Holmes was deeply engaged in a scientific assessment of the practical uses of the coal-tar derivatives.

From the Journal of Sherlock Holmes

July 9, 1892
A Discourse on Method

I am deeply immersed in my work at the school of medicine at the university. Although it is premature even to state the course that my experiments may follow, I believe though that I may at least outline my general approach. It is essential to have some goal in mind at the beginning of any research. My ultimate goal of course is to discover a specific agent that will prove toxic to the tubercular bacillus which will not be so toxic that it will damage the patient or result in death. Another key criterion is that the agent must be capable of success in most cases in order to justify its use. If a side-effect is to weaken the body's natural defenses while promising only a slight chance of recovery, then it may serve to shorten lives rather than providing the desired cure of the disease.

Just as in dealing with the moral being of man, any proposed healing must proceed gradually and within measure of the degree of grace granted by God, so in dealing with the human body one must not presume upon the efficacy of sudden and radical action if a more gentle approach may allow the body to adapt to the new environment. Any intervention brings risks as well as benefits. Even if ideal health could be procured by the imposition of a sudden force, that interposition might so disrupt the rhythms of life upon which daily survival depends that other organ systems of the body that have adapted to the presence of the disease might be thrown into confusion and disarray. The imperfection and interconnectedness of the world entails that no change is possible without introducing certain correlative effects that cannot be calculated and provided for in advance. Change must therefore be gradual and its initiation must be cautious. I must first find a chemical agent that perhaps will be more virulent than meeting the desired end of practical treatment and thereafter to buffer those effects so that the new agent will be tolerable to the human body. An optimal regimen of dosages will then allow for health to gain ascendance and be established over time and for the dysfunctional elements to fall away by degrees. Violent or extreme intervention is seldom the best approach in creating a new balance within the organism unless life is in imminent danger.

I am not beginning my studies in a vacuum. I have thought long about the nature of the chronic in both disease and in life itself. Just as grafting virtue to a resistant soul is only an invitation to hypocrisy, so is it folly to presume to cure a chronic disease overnight. Health of both soul and body require the presence over time of life-enhancing agents and the elimination of those habits that detract from the full functioning of the entire human being. I hope that this, my brief prolegomenon, may guide me as I proceed with my research.

The next question of course is the specific one of why coal-tar, among the many substances that I might have hoped would provide the specific that I seek, is my choice for a potential cure? It may be only an intuition, but I believe that the key to the organic should be sought within the organic compounds. Since I must avoid a general toxicity, I must stay away from the metallic elements. What I am seeking is a concoction that will be noxious to the bacillus while having only marginal effects upon the host organism. There is also the consideration of the sheer variety posed by the various mutations of the coal-tars. The number of substances obtainable will have perhaps other beneficial effects and uses so that should I fail in my quest for a cure for consumption, my labors shall at least not have been in vain. Finally there is the question of cost. If the drug that I am able to synthesize is not such that it may be generally available to all who suffer from consumption, then my discovery will create an artificial class-distinction in an area where all sufferers from the disease should be equal.

The basic means of life such as food, water, and health-care should not be treated as luxuries for which each must pay, but instead should be regarded as among the essential rights of men and women. A society that cannot provide these basic measures of justice may only persist through the threat of force to retain the loyalty of those who are in effect condemned to death by the lack of these essential elements to preserve life.

I believe that God favors the common ownership of the benefits of the earth. Indeed many governments use the word commonwealth in reference to themselves in recognition that certain goods of the earth are a common possession and may not be appropriated to private ownership and use. I believe also that there is an underlying aesthetic in the universe and that God gives mankind most of what is most necessary by making them beautiful and readily available while giving only fragments or occasional appearance to those things that are merely ornamental in nature. It is, for instance, a common observation that most human faces are lacking in beauty and symmetry. Indeed, beauty is arresting precisely because it is rare and even among the beautiful it is a possession of no long-standing. The ravages of time swiftly blur and displace the facial features and only extraordinary efforts may sustain the appearance of youth beyond its proper season. At last we become scarecrows, even to ourselves.

Life begins to leave the body even while it is still living and the grave asserts its vested dominion over us long before it gains final possession. For this reason St. Paul asked, "Who will deliver me from this body of death?" The Chinese poet, Li Po, says, "The joys of the world do not last. Of old all things have flown with the eastward flowing river." Some have said that Christianity exalts suffering and death and is therefore morbid; but whoever reads the literature of the world will discover that the poets always concentrate their efforts on the great truths of life and death. It is folly to presume that we may avoid the path of mortality, but this does not imply that we must suffer life's inevitable decline without hope.

But to return to my theory of the commonwealth, it is simply stated: God bestows in abundance what is most to our benefit and gives sparsely what is only ornamental. For this reason bread is common and caviar is scarce. Iron is common and gold is scarce. Youth is short and age is long. Diamonds are rare but coal is plentiful. If coal had the beauty of diamonds who would not find it profane to feed his furnace with it. We cherish that which is easily marred by neglect. Life is designed for hard usage so it is proper that most faces are prepared to be so used. We cherish the occasional actress or ballerina and we clothe them in silks to preserve the rare flower of their beauty, but we prefer the strong arms of the milkmaid or the laundress for life's daily tasks. Where would civilization be if we were awash in prima donnas? How would industry ever thrive if the bulk of the human population were like the poet Li Po and lived in solitude upon a mountain?

The Church itself needs few monks and priests and many lay-people so that even spiritual rarity shows that God for the most part loves the common folk whose simple worship, although often lacking in a fully realized theology, is sincere and hence adequate. Also if God desired only liturgical praise as the primary mode of service, why did He not end the process of creation after making the Seraphim? Surely, if God chose men and women of dust and ashes, then He must find a unique enjoyment in what is finally only clay. The Incarnation of Jesus Christ shows the pleasure of God in men and women.

Some of the angels apparently found this to be a perverse dishonor to God's own majesty. Some have said that the sin of Satan was that he refused to serve the Second Person of the Trinity if He chose to assume a union with human nature as Jesus. Satan found such a love to be degrading to the Trinity and so turned away in rebellion and disgust. It must be recalled that in eternity there is no time in the sense of sequential decisions. Every cause is therefore coterminous with its effect. Man had therefore not completed his first sin in Eden before the intention of God to redeem him was already fully formed. Our sins are foreseen and forgiven, while they are still in contemplation within us.

In the year 1270 A.D. a Council of the Church stated as dogma that no change of heart is granted after death. The reasons for this conclusion were not explained in detail at the time, but I have come to believe that this formulation merely recognizes that in eternity no further contingent choices are possible. All data is simultaneously present and thus the decision made in death is dispositive for the destination of the soul. But is life here ever anything but a series of contingent choices. In this sense all sins are mere rehearsals for that final test when the soul faces God. Similarly, virtuous acts if they are undertaken with hesitation and resentment and solely in contemplation of a reward in heaven are unlikely to attain eternal validation after our death. For this reason we are all told to hope for salvation but to never to be presumptuously assured of it, because we cannot know in advance the ultimate choice that we will make in that dread hour of our death and the meeting with the Divine Judge. We are advised by Jesus to try and enter heaven by the narrow gate for many will try to enter by the wide gate and will be unable to enter. The baggage of life is such that it is misplaced in the courts of heaven. We enter the presence of God, in the state of fundamental equality and without property or status, and those who lack a fitting response to love, as the wedding-garment of grace, must quail before the Holiness of God and veil their faces to the Presence in Purgatorial remission of sin.

Failing the great and final test that is referred to in the gospels is what we daily pray to avoid. The Lord's Prayer says, when it is properly understood in operational terms, that we should pray that the Lord will not abandon us to temptation, but rather will spare us the full rigor of the test of choosing anything contrary to God's loving will for us, to avoid finding more loyalty in ourselves and to created things than in our God, in whom all things find their proper value, but only in relation to God. This is to say that anything divorced from God degrades and vanishes so that its own inner nature is changed into the nothingness from whence it initially came into being.

St. Paul expressed this truth when he said that all things are permitted to us in God, but not all things are profitable for us. We can grasp the true nature of angelic evil and its topsy-turvy point of view if we recall that Satan desired to act as God in his temptation of Jesus by stating that the human nature of Jesus might attain all things if it would only turn from God and worship the Evil One. This was the ultimate lie because precisely the opposite is true: in God all things find their proper place and order; so to love God is really to love all things and to despise God is to find that even victory is really the source of ultimate defeat. We must picture the despair of the Evil One as consisting in this: that to truly be the lord of this world without God is to embrace ultimate nothingness.

God allows the devil this dominion that he seeks and even allows it to tempt and to deceive men and women.   Even the human nature of Jesus was not spared this process although He was not burdened as we are with Original Sin. None of us can be spared temptation for it lies within the strange logic of evil to seek to forget the origin of all being in God. We see the merits of Christ in His categorical rejection of the specious reasoning of the devil and why it is that only in Jesus, as ultimate cause, that salvation is possible all of humankind.

Unaided by divine grace our choice is a foregone conclusion made by our original sin in Eden, which thereafter determined the course of our human nature. We felt in Eden our nakedness and hid from the face of God and we have been hiding ever since our eyes were opened and we knew ourselves as we actually are, as contingent creatures subject to evil. Only God can see within that nakedness of ours the goodness of His original intent and through the life and death of Jesus Christ God bestows that primal innocence upon us once again. "Oh grave where is thy victory, oh death where is thy sting."

Restored human nature is already intact and secure from the side of God and all that remains is our willing surrender to the rule of grace in order to enjoy the benefits of this final covenant between human beings and God, sealed with the Blood of Jesus Christ on His Cross as the Son of Man, acting for the benefit of the entire human race.

There is nothing exclusive or restrained in this gift. It was not made for some narrow elect group, nor was it meant to be a fruitless gesture, but was instead the equivalent of the act of creation itself, a vast totality that will embrace all things and draw them into God as their origin and end so that God may be all in all, the Alpha and the Omega, the beginning and the end. With God all things are possible and we interfere with the will of God when we attempt to define how God will attain his ends by narrowing them to our own conception of what is possible.

July 10, 1892

A Discussion of the Scope of Private Moral Action

For all of the ways that Catholic doctrines may have existed in a latent state after the Ascension there can be little doubt that the primary belief structures of Christianity only took stable form over the course of time and the under the guidance of the ordained clergy. As the structures of orthodox belief gelled and solidified and as the generations of believers passed one after another from the earth mingling their dust in the catacombs the church grew in power and influence until it became coextensive with European culture as a whole.

Repentance and conversion are put forth as the entry point of a covenant with God with paradise as the reward. This was surely an elaboration and extension to the individual level of the promises of old made to Israel as a nation. John the Baptist and Jesus of Nazareth came announcing that the Kingdom of God was at hand. At the present moment we are almost two millennia later and neither the exaltation of Israel nor the return of Jesus has yet to occur. Atheism grows upon us daily and Christianity is fragmented into any number of separate and mistrustful sects, while the Catholic Church under Pope Pius IX is reduced to being governed from an area of a few square kilometers centered upon the Vatican. The Pope considers himself to be a prisoner abandoned by the crowned heads of Catholic France and Austria, while it is still at odds for centuries with Eastern Orthodoxy and beset by heresy in England and Germany.

Daily the progress of science puts forth a view of physical creation and of geological time that dwarfs all human aspirations with the result that any direct action of God seems to be reduced to sacramental grace in a world where sacramental action appears to be little more than the drama of liturgical solemnity and the pageantry of the priesthood. Historical and textual criticism act like waves on the seashore clawing ever deeper into an unstable shoreline of faith.

Secular rules and ethics pay little attention to Christian doctrines or mandates so that Christianity begins to play a secondary role compared to the spread of Islam across Asia and into the far eastern regions. America although outwardly religious is little more than an amorphous conglomeration of people sharing a type of hysterical Pentecostalism based upon the political doctrine of Manifest Destiny. When repentance and conversion are not forthcoming the inquisition and warfare have usually taken their place. The entire question of noxious agents recalls to my mind the question of how we are to deal with human evils without appealing to a religious base drawn from a common culture.

There has been a profound shift in the power that religion exercises in the practical affairs of human life, at least in modern European civilization. Catholicism has always spoken of three primary enemies of the rule of God: the world, the flesh, and the devil. The central idea appears to be that of detachment from the only direct experience that we possess outside of prayer so as to give precedence to the Kingdom of God that we will only experience in its fullness after death. For years the monastic ideal was able to counsel spiritual perfection while simultaneously generating wealth in a primarily agrarian economy.

This is no longer the case in an economy based upon manufacturing and trade and is even less likely to pertain in the future. To ignore the world while living in a state of contemplation now appears to be a case of willful self-indulgence. As for the flesh, Catholicism has exalted all manner of penitential practices to curb concupiscence under the supposition that normal human desire should be confined to the narrowest possible extent consistent with the survival of the species. As for the devil, his title of "Prince of this World" presumes that God has given evil primary title and sovereignty to govern the world so that everything is essentially tainted or at best should be approached with suspicion as an occasion of sin. Images of battle have been grafted into much spiritual writing. This implies a degree of violence towards the self and towards others as the only road to salvation.

Much of human life is spent in seeking retribution and revenge. What society does not maintain prisons and jails or reformatories? Watson has recorded many instances when I have taken it upon myself to render a personal acquittal or even condemnation and execution that may not have been the decision of a judge or jury if the question gad been put to them. It has always been my desire to imitate the sentiments of Shakespeare's character, Portia, by maintaining that, "the quality of mercy is not strained."

I can however recall at least one instance when I took it upon myself to render judgment upon a fellow mortal, Dr. Grimsby Roylott of Stoke Moran. My argument with Colonel Moran deprecating direct action as a means of ridding the world of human evil may seem inconsistent with my singular course of action as applied to Dr. Roylott. I would like therefore to supplement here the record of Dr. Watson as it was recorded in "The Adventure of the Speckled-Band."

It will be recalled by those who have read that account that it was my act of beating upon the bell-rope that caused the poisonous snake, a swamp-adder, to recoil upon Dr. Roylott who had used it once already to murder one of his step-daughters and to make an attempt on the life of the second. It is no small part of my life as a detective that I have trained myself to read character swiftly. It is a necessary skill for one who spends time among thieves and cutthroats in some of London's less savory districts. My encounter with Dr. Grimsby Roylott had shown me that I was dealing with a man who had to all intents and purposes severed the bonds of the social contract as described by Rousseau and had made himself a lord over life and death. There was the example of the beating death of his servant in India followed by the death of the innocent young woman entrusted to his care by his late wife who had provided ample means for his sustenance and support. Instead of appreciating the trust that had been placed in him he had murdered her daughter so as to prevent the loss of the portion of his income that he would forfeit if she married.

A local coroner's jury had failed to adequately investigate the circumstances of her death out of fear of the man combined with a strange loyalty to the last of the descendants of the ancient Anglo-Saxon estate of Stoke-Moran. It was foreseeable that such a vicious man, one that even the ties of adoption could not restrain, would take other lives in due course. He had so placed himself that night that a defensive response on my part would turn his evil agent back upon its host. Rather than leave him at liberty to work his malice upon other victims or to repeat the chance that a local jury who had acquitted him once would do so again, I decided to act on the spot. The result was that he had felt the fangs of the reptile at his own throat. We had entered his room, with his final scream still echoing in our ears, to find the speckled-band coiled about his head, a loathsome diadem of his evil.

The whole event had seemed to me at the time to be emblematic of the proper fate for men who make of themselves noxious agents to their fellowmen, even as does the tuberculosis bacillus in its own way unconscious way. Still, I questioned whether it was my province to kill him? Did the indirect method by which I inflicted death upon him absolve me of all guilt? I said at the time that the death of Dr. Grimsby Roylott was unlikely to trouble my conscience, but I was younger then and the years since then have often raised doubts in my mind. Can an individual accomplish what the mechanisms of society cannot? Has he the right to do so and if so by what authority does he act? I know that there are certain individuals who have so left behind the common orbit of our mutual affections and morals that they are like barren asteroids wandering about in empty space. Can such individuals be summoned back to the path of humanity and resume their former orbit?

I am afraid that I concluded that the Doctor was beyond such reclamation. Circumstance had placed him in my hands and I alone decided that he should not escape and that God alone could provide a means beyond the bounds of death for his conversion. Was this an act of faith or of despair? I often find in dreams his face rising up before me, seamed and yellow with the passions of the tropic sun of India. He haunts me now more than he ever did when he entered my rooms In Baker Street and threatened me, calling me "a Scotland Yard jack-in-office." He warned me then to keep myself out of his grip, little imagining that he was already within mine. He found that my grip was indeed not more feeble than his own. I straightened out more than the bent poker that he had hurled into our fireplace in Baker Street when I bent it straight again and determined to address the situation at Stoke-Moran and in consequence hurled him into an eternity that maintains its own fireplace.

His death is done now with that finality of events that cannot be recalled and I must live with the result. His second step-daughter, Helen Stoner, has herself since passed on, her life no doubt shortened by the early loss of her beloved sister at his hands. The last eddies of the events at Stoke-Moran have been joined in the larger river of events and all is forgotten now. The ancient house is now a museum of an extinct lineage and has been turned into a refuge for unwed mothers in the district. It is just in this fashion it seems to me that evils finally resolve themselves into some measure of good. As to the part that I played at the time, was it an example of good or evil? How shall my divided emotions of pride and remorse be divided at the end of my own sojourn upon the earth?

July 12, 1892

A Brief Discourse on Warfare

My reflections above regarding the august responsibility of taking a human life will indicate at once the absurdity of military actions. By what possible authority may any man order another man to become a killing machine and to simultaneously risk his own death in battle? Is a general more than a man when he presumes to do so? Can mere lines on maps or the property designations they signify justify men lying dead along the borders of these lines. The disproportion of using up men like cattle or as mere resources rather than as individuals should long since have made organized warfare impossible, yet it continues and is even considered honorable.

How can it be that such waste and squalor has not been condemned universally; if not for its folly, then at least for its absence of adequate justification in most instances? The ultimate causes of wars are for reasons of state. Politicians and diplomats use war to cover their failures and to endorse their aims under the guise of patriotism. The result is that warfare in many respects results in the periodic culling of the human race. A review of maps over the centuries will show how inconsequential in general population dynamics and the borders of linguistic groups the many European Wars have proven to be.

I confess that I have no patience for the parade and panoply of the whole military business. Surely a war will finally come that will be sufficiently extensive and horrible in its effects for the mass of mankind so that they will come to share my present views, but I hope that I will never live to see it. The technical progress of mankind in weaponry has devised such implements that whole companies and regiments may be dispatched.

How can the mere seconds of survival embody the sustained valor and endurance of a soldier in the face of efficient killing-machines that mow them down by the hundreds? The result is a naked onrush of flesh against steel. The soldier and his cause are dwarfed by the sheer extent of the slaughter, so that whereas entire campaigns were once decided by a difference of hundreds, now it will take thousands and even higher multiples of bodies to decide the course of battles. This increases the general cost to populations to wage war with the impact upon the surviving populations as they attempt to rebuild a civilized society again out of the ashes. All of this takes no account of the worth of each soul with its unique individuality or the labor required bringing each young man to adulthood. If those who dispose so readily of these young lives bore in their own flesh as a mother does the legacy of birth would they cast so many lives adrift like so many dried leaves to fall to earth?

Dr. Watson's Narrative Continues

On our third day at sea I asked Holmes how he intended to proceed after we landed in New York. We were walking at the time on the course of our twice daily shipboard constitutional. The salt-spray cast off by our bow left tiny droplets in my tweed overcoat and I could smell the freshness of the new summer day at sea. The sun was overcast now and again by large cumulus clouds in the east, but before us there stretched the great uninterrupted vision of the great plain of the ocean. Holmes was in excellent spirits that day. We had left the Inspector playing a game of whist with our ship companions of the night before who had shared our table in the dining salon.

"We will arrive in America unannounced Watson," he began. "I think it imperative that we travel about a bit at first and get something of the national temper regarding the canal prospects in various regions of influence. Since Baron Maupertuis has already published his copies of the Murillo Papers the Americans have been embarrassed as a nation. The slave-labor used by certain companies to build the railroad in Costa Rica during the 1880's and the thousands of deaths by Yellow-Fever and Dysentery at the time made any canal project seem untenable. The cost of the project now will be immense and the American nation has only recently recovered from the economic panic of 1893. The recent election was a bitterly contested one between those who supported retaining the gold standard and those who favored a policy of free-silver and a bi-metallic currency. That monetary issue divided the western farming states and the manufacturing east. A nation that has once known a civil war has no desire to provoke another second regional conflict of such a magnitude so soon."

I protested that I was somewhat vague on the subject of the bi-metallic controversy and its possible regional manifestations. I was aware that the Democrats under William Jennings Bryan favored silver and gold whereas the Republican, William McKinley, favored a gold-backed currency that had become the world standard since its endorsement by England, which was then the primary trading power in the world. Holmes assured me that it was a fascinating subject, but one best addressed over a whisky and soda as the wind was then freshening and we had already circled the deck several times. We retired to the oak paneled saloon of the vessel and finding a table in the corner where we might discuss matters without interruption, he began his discourse.

"To begin, I should explain that at any given moment a nation as large as America is at best an uncertain union. Its very freedom is an unending invitation to secession, as the world observed in the years ending in the defeat of the Confederacy in 1865. Since then and particularly since 1877 the face of America has changed. The America that was once a land of pioneers and of small enterprises has been succeeded by the frenetic growth of various business combinations such as the great corporations and trusts which now dominate the nation's economic interests."

"The result has been the development of a concentration of wealth in the hands of a minority of the population. This would be bad enough, but the centers of wealth have proven to be geographically centered as well. Certain regions of the nation exist as de-facto internal colonies of the northern manufacturing and transportation interests. The resentment engendered by this trend led in its first manifestations to the American War conducted between the States. To call that conflict a civil war was always a misnomer for there was no intention by the south to change the general government of the remaining states of the union. The desire of the South at the time was only to withdraw as sovereign states from the national government at the will of the majority of the citizens in the withdrawing states. Since it is an axiom that sovereignty in America rests with the people, it has always seemed to me to be an absurdity to bind states to a commonwealth when the people wish to escape it. To maintain that the voice of the dead should perpetually bind the living seems to fly in the very face of the Declaration of Independence, which as a declaration of fundamental principles of legitimate government had once justified the American Revolution in the first place. Surely, if President Lincoln was correct and secession should be met by force in order to restore the union, then by that same reasoning the former colonies as a whole should still be part of England!

But let us set that aside for now. The point at issue is the present fact that farmers in the newly admitted western states are in debt for loans to banks that are dominated by eastern interests. The decline in value of crop prices in recent years has led to massive foreclosures on those very farms and this process in turn has led to great unrest in a section of the country that looks only to the markets in the east as a reason to remain in the United States. This unrest in the rural areas is matched by the sufferings of the laboring classes who have watched as wages have declined even as the great American fortunes have combined into the formation of massive trusts and corporations. The price-fixing of railroad rates is common and the practice has driven many farmers out of business and into farm foreclosure."

"Meanwhile the far-western states, such as Nevada and Colorado, are virtually awash in silver bullion. So much silver has been found there and mined that the price of the metal is in decline. Miners and mine- owners alike would prefer that the excess silver be bought by the treasury for coining purposes. This would cause an instant increase in the money supply and the increase in available money would in turn lower interest rates and thus favor debtors who would then be able to repay their loans with the inflated money supply of silver currency or secure loans with lower interest rates. This policy would prevent many bankruptcies and act as a general fiscal stimulus to the national economy. Of course it would also break the stranglehold of the eastern banks and the rail, oil, and shipping monopolies of men like Gould, Rockefeller and Vanderbilt. The free-silver movement is being fiercely resisted by those vested interests. "Big Money" has spoken and with President McKinley in office the gold standard will be safe for now, but it has left a bitter taste in sections of the country."

"America is in no mood for further taxation now to support a canal project. The publication of the Murillo Papers has raised an outcry against the methods of big business. Many workers have no doubt identified with those who died in building the railroad in Costa Rica during the reign of Don Juan Murillo. Only the primary role of the bi-metallic issue has kept the Central America canal issue from being a *cause célèbre* in the national discourse. Baron Maupertuis has stepped into the fray by so positioning himself as to give the Americans a run for their money regarding which nation will ultimately build a canal in Central America."

"The European conscience is far less sensitive to the plight of workers from foreign lands. Where for instance would England be in South Africa if it were not for the brutal methods of men like Cecil Rhodes, who may someday be placed in company with King Leopold of Belgium among the primary agents of the many deaths of poor Africans in the Congo that have occurred in this century? Our task then is to revive in America the will to build a canal thus defeating the aspirations of Baron Maupertuis. If it is revealed that

Baron Maupertuis has published forgeries to obtain an advantage in building a European financed canal, I believe that the present Republican majority in the country will react with outrage at those 'European machinations.' The citizens will line up again in support of the canal project by American interests. The proposed struggle and renewed competition will in turn cause a swift and disastrous fall in the price of the shares in the Greater Dutch Canal Company, now owned almost entirely by Baron Maupertuis and he will be ruined in the process."

I realized perhaps only now the genius of Holmes' plan, now that it was about to obtain possible fruition at last. Thus far all had happened as Holmes had predicted. I did have one significant concern though and I shared it immediately. "But Holmes," I protested, when the real papers are published by us, they are as damning to American interests as the forgeries sold to Baron Maupertuis. Will not the country still resist building an American canal when the real papers are made public?"

"You have touched on a delicate point," answered Holmes. "I admit that it was my first intention to have the papers published and thus embarrass and perhaps unseat various business tyrants in America. I even went so far as to assure Professor Moriarty that we would publish them, but I am afraid that I may perhaps yield on that point; I must keep the main chance in view. Our first obligation is to bring about the ruin of Baron Maupertuis not to embarrass certain American business tycoons. If the publication of a full version of the atrocities in Costa Rica under Murillo will jeopardize achieving that end, then we must keep the details revealed in those documents secret for now. Instead, we may sell the papers to the U.S. Department of State and we shall leave it to them to disclose what they wish in the interests of the American people. They will no doubt keep secret any resemblance between the forged copies and the originals as secrets of state. The documents then will disappear into some government vault or be destroyed. Our main end will have been achieved though and we must I am afraid be satisfied with that fact. We cannot rid the world of every scoundrel at once, but may at least disarm one of the worst villains that the world has ever known, Baron Maupertuis."

"If that alternate course is to be utilized, then eventually we must go to Washington in the District of Columbia," I observed. "But you wish first to sample the opinions of the nation Holmes. Where then do you propose to go?"

"We shall of course tour New York City, but then I propose to go up to Newport, Rhode Island for it is there that we will have some exposure to the elite of America's ruling class. The town has become a virtual American Versailles. From there we will proceed by railroad through Pennsylvania and visit the oil fields and the mining districts there. Only after that will we proceed to Washington D.C. where we will meet with President McKinley."

"Will that be all?" I enquired.

"No Watson, I intend to visit another place in answer to a vow that I made in France many years ago. It is a place that I hold sacred, more sacred perhaps than Khartoum, which I visited because it was the place where General Gordon met his end. Each man has places that speak to him deeply and this place speaks specially to me."

"I would have thought that Rome or Palestine would claim that primacy of place," I remarked.

"No, I think not," Holmes murmured thoughtfully. "Those places are where one would expect to find God, forgetting for a moment that God exists within us all or not at all. God's presence is not specific nor is it confined to any one place, yet certain religious shrines do exist and are sacred. In this case I wish to pay a visit in order to bear witness to a great crime and to offer some measure of restitution if I may in the name of those who should have behaved quite differently. There are certain crimes it seems to me require universal expiation. It is the role of the Catholic Church to offer a daily sacrifice in the Mass for sins and certainly love covers a multitude of offenses. What is committed by one is in a sense committed by all, and all may seek pardon from God for that collective offense. It is the very *raison d'être* for the existence of the penitential orders in the Church such as the Carmelites and the Cistercians. We may each participate in the benefices of their members enacted as the daily fulfillment of their penitential vows. Let us go now. I think that we should see how our friend, Inspector Hopkins, is doing over his game of whist. Perhaps he will leave his cards and join us for lunch."

Over lunch I took the opportunity to inquire why we would be visiting the industrial regions of America as well as patrician New England on our visit. I had always wished primarily to visit certain places connected with the intellectual development of America, particularly the small town of Concord, Massachusetts that was the home of Emerson, Thoreau, and Hawthorne and also to visit Pittsfield where Herman Melville had once owned a farm. When I suggested this to Holmes rather than visiting the dreary coal mining sites of the Appalachians he made a surprising revelation.

"We are visiting the region in order to honor an old promise made by me to Professor Moriarty when I returned from my long pilgrimage in 1894. The Professor insisted that I see firsthand the conditions of the American coal mines. You will recall that one of our most significant encounters with the Professor, during the course of his criminal career, involved the matter of the murder of the man, Douglas, at the hands of a secret organization called the Scowrers. At the time I took a dim view of their activities for I had been led to believe that they were simply a band of thugs engaged in extortion under the threat of violence directed towards honest mine-owners. I am afraid that at the time I was still in sympathy with my brother Sherringford, who was making every effort to maintain our family's coal holdings in Northumberland. It is not an easy matter to break with one's natal sympathies and loyalty to one's class is inculcated in us from youth. I have come lately to entertain more democratic sympathies."

"You will recall, Watson, certain spirited discussions that we once had in Baker Street when you wanted to place a portrait of Henry Ward Beecher on our walls. Although I always felt a most hearty condemnation for slavery, I always felt that the Confederate states had a right to secede. I thought John Brown was a fanatic and could not sympathize, as you once did, with the writings of those abolitionists of the time who could justify any violence to end what was admittedly a manifest evil, African slavery. I was willing therefore to resist violence in the coalfields and to lend my aid to defeat the Scowrers of Pennsylvania and similar organizations such as the Loyal Hibernians. The Popes had condemned secret societies and as a Catholic I needed to consider the moral principles embodied in their encyclicals. At the same time I have come now to recognize and to condemn with even more severity the violence and terror practiced by the established orders of the day to curtail legitimate dissent among the working class. Surely whenever dissent is silenced by tyranny we should not blame those who take the only other means left to them and associate together in these clandestine labor unions without which action they would be powerless to meet the economic forces arrayed against them."

"One of the reasons that I have pursued my study of early English Charters is to show the gradual process through which power is made to yield to right. The historical trend of the world is generally toward increasing the moral right of recognition of all people to the right to basic access to the means by which to better their lot in life. The law though always moves slower than the needs of the people who constitute a nation. The rights of property are slow to yield to the general conscience of a republic. Even today many cases sounding in tort are dismissed because there is no privity of contract between the injured party and the one responsible. How many have died through the consumption of tainted drugs and unwholesome food!"

"Then there is the question of the debtors' prisons in England and the scandal of the workhouses. The poor are often treated as mere grist for the mills of commerce. How many children die by being exposed to unguarded machinery? How many textile workers perish of lung diseases worse than consumption through the inhalation of various fibers? Professor Moriarty asked me to consider, before condemning his actions and those of Colonel Moran, how many innocents die without redress at the hands of the established order and how many rich property owners have lives free of condemnation by both state and church because no law but the forgotten mandate of universal charity forbids their actions. There are some things that must be witnessed first-hand, so that the conscience, after shedding its illusion that our way of life is a benevolent and peaceful one, may face the structural violence that exists everywhere among us.

Many a drawing-room in Pall Mall camouflages an underlying jungle and many a crocodile hands his top-hat and walking-stick to the usher at his London club. The struggle of opposed principles, each claiming to be an absolute, is the history of mankind. Only by broadening our loyalties to embrace each man and woman can we be sure that we are not governed by a moral provincialism that is not Christian. I trust that someday there will be issued by the powers that be a Charter for all of Humankind to which all nations will bear allegiance. Perhaps then wars will finally cease."

This was our conversation that day as our ship sped towards the first great democracy of the modern world; although only just having celebrated its first centennial, America in the

1890's bid fair to become the greatest industrial power the world has ever known. Would its initial insights be broadened to endow all nations with life, liberty, and the pursuit of happiness as a universal creed, or would America become in time the new Rome and perish, as had that long ago empire, in an attempt to subdue all other nations with the far-flung web of its extended legions? Having displaced the land's original inhabitants and only recently emerged from the institution of slavery imposed upon abducted Africans, the nation had much for which to atone.

While I had been in Rome in February I had read of the destruction of the battleship Maine in the English Papers. Ever since then a clamor of nationalistic sentiment had been rising in America demanding action in Cuba. I could only ask myself that day if Holmes and I were heading into a storm of violence that would long defer Holmes' dream of a charter of universal rights. In the following days I sought refuge from the storm clouds ahead by reading more of Holmes peaceful sojourn in France.

From the Journal of Sherlock Holmes

August 1, 1892
College of Medicine
Montpellier, France

I confess that I have been remiss in the writing of entries in my journal of late. My only excuse is that I have been busy every day in the laboratory. It is no small matter to adjust to living again a settled life. There is something intoxicating in travel. The discipline of science must come as a burden to one accustomed to the far-flung horizons of mountain and desert. Though Montpellier is an exciting city with sunny vistas and an impressive past, it is not Mecca with its seething crowds, nor is it Bombay. How I had longed on my journey to return to my beloved France and now having attained again the comforts of civilization I hunger again for the sway of a camel beneath me and a breakfast of dates and dried meat.

Is it my destiny to be always dissatisfied? What if I had been condemned to live my life in an English provincial village speaking a dialect known only in that region? How I was laughed at when I first went down to Cambridge when my fellow students heard my speech, tainted by a Yorkshire accent and colloquial phrases! It was then that I vowed to see the world through no particular and regional lens but to speak as a universal man. I thought science would allow me to do so, but science also has its various regionalisms and provincial prejudices.

This is why science progresses so slowly. Often one generation must pass away so that a new vision that calls into question the old truisms may at last attain a hearing and acquire influence. Perhaps science is only a discourse among many of the mind of man speaking in diverse and irreconcilable soliloquies across the centuries. Is there any real nexus between our science and the nature it attempts to study, or is science only a contract with an inscrutable outer world, the ultimate nature of which we shall never know? In the last analysis science is a dialogue with a presumed outer reality. We pose various questions to nature by our activities and we receive a response. Nature is always speaking in the language of events, the plants and animals, the stones and the weather. Its voice is mediated by a living world.

We live encased in the organic. Even our individual digestive process requires the presence of bacteria within us. For this reason, there is no greater illusion than the separation of man and nature. We are a part of all that surrounds us. We can never climb out of our skin and find a point of reference void of all pre-existing commitments and presuppositions. The effort by men such as Rene Descartes to find such an absolute and independent vantage point from outside the system will always be a vain pursuit. What we call the objective order is really an exercise in selective blindness. We take pride in being objective and by this means we hide from ourselves our own prejudices. We cannot even speak except from within a pre-established frame of reference. Even our language conditions our attention and our collection of data because it will already have focused and defined what is relevant to any pending inquiry.

To conclude for instance that medicine is a simply mechanical process is to misunderstand that spirit so interfuses our material being that any intervention must be resonant with the organism as a whole if any true healing is to take place. If I take this insight as my guide, then I am led further to the concept of consumption, not simply as s host and an invader, but as a dance between two organisms, the germ and the host that harbors it. The conflict between them is such that this dance is one where the total triumph of one or the other will result in the death of the other.

The definition of consumption as a disease is the result of the lack of any advantage conferred on the human body by the presence of this particular bacillus. The relationship is one of predation rather than exchange of mutual benefit. It is true that the bacillus kills slowly, but the fact that it incapacitates and kills is the final criterion that makes its presence noxious. To uproot such an evil from among us we might isolate its victims to prevent further incidents of contagion, but since its presence is well nigh universal the disease cannot simply be allowed to run its course and become extinct. A cure must be found that will spare the individual body while selectively targeting the bacillus. The agent I seek must be at least tolerable for the body and its appending colonies of useful bacteria. A universal agent of death would destroy them as well. To be a true medicine the agent of change must alter the balance for a sufficient time so that the forces of health are allowed to repair the community of cells so that the general balance of the human body on which life depends is restored.

I have now at my disposal a great variety of potential agents so my task is to shift from the techniques of synthesis to that of an experimental dialogue with tubercular patients. I must apply the agent to the organism in its pure state, first to separate those agents that retard growth and finally destroy the tubercular bacillus from those agents that have no effect or perhaps even enhance its growth by weakening the body while bestowing no relative advantage in the struggle. When I discover that specific agent I must then see if it can be tolerated in the requisite dosage within the human body for a period adequate to kill the tubercular organism or at least to cause it to retreat sufficiently so that the body's own immunity will be adequate to keep further progress of the disease at bay.

August 6, 1892
A Political Exegesis

In reading over my last entry I noticed certain parallels, which I think should be explored between my research protocol and the requisite political action to create a more just society. Since all of life demands upon cooperation, the vision of any final victory or perfectly just state of affairs within any given society is an illusion. Cooperation requires a mutual yielding to obtain a shared benefit. Any opposition based upon finding the maximum number of mutual incompatibilities will only yield further conflict. To attempt to remove all evil from our midst is to become that which one fears and abhors.

For this reason, violence is always a sign of failure in the one who employs it. Change must be gradual and based upon mutuality and to a consensus, when this eventually becomes possible. Revolution may have its place on occasion, but only when it returns as swiftly as possible to some sort of balance. To truly defeat a political enemy one must always stop short of final humiliation and extinction once the noxious force is subdued. Since all human conflict proceeds under the guise of justification, there will usually be found a residue of goodness even in a defeated enemy. To stop short of complete victory may seem to invite later resurgence and reprisals, but it may mean no more than a recognition that the borders of civility have been reached and to pursue victory further is to be have switched places with the enemy. The ancient Chinese classic, "The I-Ching or the Book of Changes" explains how at the edge all things become the opposite of what they just were. The proper balance in human affairs implies the acceptance of the necessity of internal adjustment to the opposition and constant alterations in the circumstances and situation of the prevailing world.

Christianity in contrast is less systematic and refers the believer to prayerful discernment of the will of God in any situation. Since God alone is goodness with no admixture of evil, He alone is the origin and the destination of all things. We may not arrogate to ourselves a perfection we do not possess so as to judge God. Human goodness is always derivative. We can at best approximate that which is all goodness in itself. This implies a continual act of self-questioning and repentance as appropriate for man. When we are most sure of ourselves, then it is likely that we will have crossed over from virtue to vice.

For this reason I abhor all crusades and find it best when the cross is always held before us, rather than being seduced by the illusion of premature glory and victory. To snatch victory from the jaws of defeat is to assume that one will always bear victory well and few human beings ever do so. I am content to recommend resistance over initiating counter-aggression as a means to achieve lasting social change and the establishment of a more just order.

That said, there are moments of crisis and fever in human events when aggression may be the course required, just as it says in the hexagram of "The I-Ching" entitled "Biting Through. The action must always be proportionate to the cause and endure no longer than is required to make its wisdom manifest. The tides of the universe seek always a mean and once an artificial stasis is ended all will proceed to a new resolution point in a new hexagram. Nature will heal itself and the divine wisdom will reassert itself from within the onward course of events, variety be restored, and a new balance will prevail for a time.

Each generation is an impatient one though. The desire to see the end of days seems to be a universal one. It will be recalled that the early Christians believed that Jesus would return before the last apostle died. They believed that the mission of Christ was to announce an imminent fulfillment to all that the prophets had foretold. This energy was present from the first in the mission of John the Baptist. The Apostles asked Jesus when He went up to Jerusalem to face his passion and death if it was at that very time that He would restore the kingdom to Israel. Jesus' answer was that His Kingdom was not of this world and that the Father had reserved the time of the consummation of all things to Himself.

This seeming indifference to our wishes and the frustration of our expectations forced the early church to review the words of Christ while He was personally among us and to discern a role for itself that would be one devoted to preparation and waiting. This placed the church in precisely the position formerly occupied throughout history by the Jewish people and constituted the church as a people to whom the promises were now extended universally to all who believed in Christ.

In this way what was presumed to be an end, the coming of the Messiah, was really only another beginning. Still, the desire for an imminent fulfillment was such that groups have perpetually arisen who have assumed that they might constitute that elect group who will witness the Second Coming of Christ and to be spared death. Such groups have assumed that their virtues were such that God would see that all had been accomplished and thus the end would come at last.

Such presumptions have always been disappointed however. Instead, the church has remained to offer, as it alone may, the comfort of the cross and that alone. The Catholic Church bears witness to the death of Christ and celebrates it daily at mass as the path of redemption from sin. The fulfillment of that redemption though remains as it always has in hope alone. Christians are taught to so use grace that they will embody something of the Kingdom of God even now through active charity in a most imperfect world.

Each Christian becomes as it were another Christ and knows in turn the desolation of the cross and the seeming abandonment of God. The church is and must remain a living contradiction to precisely that desire that would bring about the Second Coming of Christ through human efforts rather than simply to act under the impulse of grace and leave the rest to God. For this reason Christianity must always proceed along the edge of complete darkness and it must mourn even in its joy.

This is a great task but it is the only one that corresponds with the words and actions of Jesus Christ. If the Church is to be true to itself it may not claim to be greater than its Master, as Jesus once said. If the comfort of the Holy Spirit is found to be inadequate and if one desires to see his reward before death, then the one who desires this victory will have already ceased to be Christian.

Christian history then is the record of Christian failure to witness the apocalyptic age. The many struggles in the church have always been about who will be greatest in the Kingdom of God. To that question, one once posed by the Apostles themselves, Jesus had but one answer: the one who would be greatest is the one who would be like a little child. The last will be first and the first will be last. A skeptic may say that such a teaching is a perverse reversal of all human expectations and as such is finally meaningless. But to the man or woman of faith there is great wisdom in this teaching, because it shifts the locus of power beyond us to God and by doing so it reverses the presumption of the sin of Eden, that man and woman can know their own end and may stand equal to God in defining it as good or as evil.

Instead we are asked to entertain the possibility that even our deepest insights and powers are wholly inadequate to the problem posed by our own existence so that we must rely utterly upon that which will strip all things away from us at death. We go naked into the nether world. All that we have been becomes dust and ashes. Just as there is no fate worse than death, there is no greater way of estimating our own inadequacy before time which plows us into the ground. It is this final cruelty, that having once been beautiful, we must watch our own decay before we die, to realize our kinship with the mindless elements of which we are composed. We who were once capable of thought and design will someday be rendered silent in the grip of death.

So horrible is this vision of utter cessation that history is the record of its common denial. Each generation leaves the ruins of its splendor to be observed by later generations who will in turn share their fate. Even lovers know that others have loved before, kings know that other kings have ruled, the sea has been cleaved by other ships, and the tombs of the great were preceded by other tombs. We abjure the dead because they are scandalous to us. What have we to do with them? Thus, we live our brief season with passion and fury and imagine that we will be the great exception to the universal design.

I have read that the American Indians sought solace in the face of death in another way and have come to see the world about them as penetrated with spirit so that even crows and bison may speak of what is beyond all things. They refer to God as Wakan-Tanka or the Great Spirit. It occurs to me that these people who abide with comfort upon the earth and do not despise it may be closer to God than we to whom the promises of salvation have been entrusted. Surely these people are like those children spoken of by Jesus who will accept the Kingdom as a little child.

I have read much of their fate at the hands of the Americans and of that last bitter day at Wounded Knee in the Dakotas when the last resistance came to an end. I do not know if time will allow, but I hope to make a pilgrimage there someday. I believe it is in its own way a sacred site akin to Golgotha and I wonder if these people do not know more of the standard of the cross than those who claim to bear its message to them.

The Americans are the first people to have formally claimed that sovereignty is not traceable to God or in a representative of God such as a divinely ordained King, but within the people themselves. America promises life, liberty, and the pursuit of happiness and assumes that these ends may be obtained by their own will as manifested in each citizen. Is such a belief anything but a vast presumption? We have no life but in God, no liberty but to do the will of God, and our happiness rests with God alone.

It is said that Americans are an impatient people, a hungry people, and one whose rapacity is such that they have claimed a continent that was not theirs as their rightful inheritance and have killed an entire race that has dared to oppose them. Can any nation raised upon the bones of the Indian people prosper, or will it not in turn know a dreadful fate one day, one brought on by its own arrogance and presumption?

If our own British Empire is an affront to God, as I am coming to believe, then how much greater will be that of the Americans who imagine that they are scaling the walls of Jericho and establishing a new Israel, when in reality they more resemble the forces of the Kings of Babylon of old. The blood of those original inhabitants killed unjustly will cry from the soil and Christ will be seen first by those who fell as victims to a blasphemous cross-continental crusade and those who hoped to see Him and called themselves Christian may be those to whom Jesus finally says, "Depart from me you evildoers into the fire prepared for the devil and his angels." To presume from a mere familiarity with Christian doctrines that one is truly a Christian is among the oldest of "Christian" mistakes.

August 12, 1892
The Cathars

Slaughter among Christians is not a new story. I am taking advantage of the university library by doing some reading on the history of the region. Perhaps it is the beauty of Languedoc that was responsible for the religious movement known as Catharism. Its initial manifestation was a call to renewed piety and in this manner might have been embraced by the church if not for its doctrinal divergences. The Cathars drew a distinction between those capable of living the full life of virtue mandated by the Gospels whom they termed, "the Perfected Ones," and the great majority who were only capable of occasional virtue.

The next step was to assign the difference to the order of grace in such a way that human effort and human freedom were denied. By obtaining a ready explanation for the differences in degrees of sanctity and by erecting a firm barrier between the two orders of human nature, the Cathars attempted a mechanical solution to the ambiguity and mystery of human nature. Evil is not defeated by putting it within an artificial enclosure and by finding classes of men and women who are either definitively saved or definitively exempted from moral struggle.

The church immediately saw that what masked itself as a movement where at least some might attain heroic sanctity was in its true nature leading to the undermining of human dignity and the universal call to holiness and salvation for all men and women. Furthermore Catharism distorted the nature of grace and of God's will to bestow it to all people. There is a direct promise in the Gospels that if we ask for anything in the name of Our Lord Jesus Christ, it will be given to us. This passage is a guarantee that adequate grace will be forthcoming to meet any necessity.

Providence is like the air around us that however waved

aside closes again around us and is accessible like air to be breathed; one need only inhale. It will be said of course that just as lung capacity varies among people, so does the moral capacity to profit from the grace of God. However, salvation is an absolute category whereas the degree of merit may vary. This means that grace is always available sufficient to secure entry into heaven, but thereafter we are assigned a place in heaven according to our merits. Providence always leans towards abundance and any constriction of the flow and degree of efficacy of grace is our responsibility alone. In this dialogue of grace with free-will the soul rebels by demanding a greater place in heaven or an identity with the life-course of another soul. Each soul takes its own path in recognition of its individual circumstances and only God may judge the degree of cooperation with grace that is present in any individual instance.

The teaching of the church is to designate and map those broad channels of morality that lead to growth and to identify those swampy regions where the soul may meet its peril. The function of the church is always pedagogical and apostolic. The church is only a faithful guardian of what it has received. It may not innovate and create a new Gospel, nor may it reconcile all contradictions through a comfortable reduction to simplicity.

However the moment that such distinctions become too clear, heresy is at hand. Salvation must always remain essentially a mystery to us. The borders of faith and hope fade at the edges into the all-abiding mercy of God. No faith in God is so absolute that it contains no proper measure of healthy residual questioning. Doubt and fear preserve a healthy humility within us. To deny this fact is to claim a certitude based upon a fallacious estimate of the knowledge denied to the mind of man. Similarly, no hope is so secure that we cease to find within ourselves ample grounds to assume that we are far from what God has called us to become and thus to doubt that we may ever be worthy of heaven. There is also no charity that does not contain some slight admixture of base elements within itself of pride and arrogant self-satisfaction. Therefore, if we wait for clarity in these matters we will never make a beginning as a Christian and if we depend upon their perfect realization in our lives we will die in the doubt and fear rather than surrendering ourselves gratefully and in trust to the mercy of God, without certainty but yet with hope.

Catharism was a threat to the church and to the individual soul that embraced its teachings. But unfortunately the response of the church manifested that very crusading spirit that manifests a mistrust in God who knows best how to allow the truth to become manifest over time. It is a false zeal for souls that requires violence to secure the mandates of the church. The shepherd does not beat his sheep although the sheepdog might at times nip at the heels of those sheep that go astray. I suggest that the sheepdog's role is that played in a functional state by the fallen angels and by temptation. The discomfort of temptation is the best evidence of the emptiness of any false good and the satisfaction that it promises. Over time all things become manifest and in death all will be seen in its proper order and degree. If one has lived his or her life in an upside-down universe that particular moral astigmatism will be seen in all of its baneful nature when finally illumined in the true light of God. We live our lives in the shadow of eternity, curtailed by time from seeing things in all of their manifold relations. The chain of events is seen only a few links ahead and for this reason momentary advantages seem to be completely persuasive and ultimate ends as so remote as to be irrelevant.

To be "spared the test" (for which deliverance we should daily pray) is to live so that there will be a minimal divergence between our position at death between what grace would have embodied within us had we not resisted its role and our actual position. If there should be a too great divergence so that God is looking for us as it were in the place that we might have occupied, whereas we are through our own machinations found at the moment of death in quite another place, then we must hope all the more that we are not in that peripheral area of hesitation but will be prevented by the angels from sinking into the morass of our own poor prior judgments. We may be pulled out of that abyss at the last moment through the intercession of the Saints, so that some part of the collective riches of the communion of souls in the church may be applied to remedy any deficiency in our merits and supplement our account before God.

Perhaps purgatory allows us the opportunity to make some final effort to repay what has been so freely given to us. At least the redeemed soul will desire to do so and will lament and yet rejoice in that necessity and will lament all the occasions where it missed any occasion that it might have known in life to add to that blessed treasury by its own efforts while still alive. But in any case that treasury of grace is infinite through the merits of Christ. It matters little to add a cup of water to the sea, yet by doing so one cannot deny the sea is the fuller for that meager cup.

In its anxiety over its mission the church has often made itself privy to the ambitions of men. The Albigensian Crusade to rid southern France of the menace of heresy was a prime example of this misconstruction of its mission by the church, even in its exalted role and at the height of its power and influence under Pope Innocent III. The promise of Jesus Christ made to St. Peter and to his successors that they would exercise primacy over the Catholic Church was always predicated upon the assumption that the Pope would cooperate with grace. Many Popes have failed to live up to the demands of their high office, but this fact does not detract from their calling and commission.

The infallibility of the Pope may never be divorced however from the integral role of the entire Body of Christ. The head must always have a body in order to be complete. The witness of the faith lies in the sense of the faithful and in the Universal Magisterium of the Bishops as a Divine College with the Pope at its head. For this reason the Pope is always curtailed in any pronouncement he may choose to make and in any action he might perform by the tradition of the church, which is the record of grace written in the hearts of all people who have ever followed Jesus Christ in the corporate body of the Catholic Church. For this reason it is proper to say "the Catholic Church teaches" never "the Pope teaches." The role of the Pope is not *in personem* then but always coming from and within and among all the faithful, even as its head. The task of the Pope is to confirm the faithful in what has always been believed in the church and in what is becoming clearer over time under the guidance of the Holy Spirit.

Many Popes have been admonished to return to that role that is befitting to the dignity of their office or to correct a misapprehension before it can be codified into doctrine through a premature formalization. The office of the Papacy is not mechanical. The Pope is not a mere puppet of God. For this reason the personal sins of the Pope are occasionally magnified, so that what appears to be a solemn teaching is deficient in some manner, because it lacks the solid base provided by the tradition of the Church, the witness of Holy Scripture, or the consent of the enlightened conscience of the entire church over a period sufficient to forestall any impetuous and unfounded conclusion. The Church is infallible for this very reason: that under the tutelage of the Holy Spirit that dwells within the church as a whole, all intemperate movements will be defeated and every short-sighted ambiguity will be made clear.

The Church lives its life over centuries. Doctrine is not the development of a day nor can such majestic pronouncements be comprehended in a phrase. There is no element of doctrine that may be grasped in isolation from the entire message of Jesus. Seeming contradictions only show the integral scope of what must be mediated upon and tested in order to be understood. We may understand but never completely comprehend faith because our knowledge of it, though adequate for salvation, is never so complete that Christianity may be viewed as just another system of thought, to be evaluated upon its earthly merits and measured by some outside standard. Since the church awaits the application of the standard of God's own judgment, there is always an element of incompleteness in Christianity. To join the Catholic Church and to exist within it is an act of will to live in faith. No previous knowledge is adequate to reduce faith to certitude by the application of an outer standard of truth because the church's standard of truth is the person of Christ Himself and the inner dynamic of its interior life of prayer and liturgy.

This means that the Church does not first find the truth and then live it, rather it lives and out of that life of grace the truth becomes manifest out of that life that it is living. The life of the Catholic Church always remains before it in what it is becoming. Tradition is the foundation upon which the church rests. As it moves forward in time and even if it stumbles, it soon regains its balance and moves onward in its pilgrimage to God.

August 21, 1892
Reflections

My journal has assumed a pattern of more dispersed entries made necessary by the demands of my research. I will not transcribe here the contents of my laboratory notebook. My intent has been to record here a record of my own musings so that in after years I may see the course of my spiritual journey. In addition I have hoped to build up an arsenal to use against the views that Professor Moriarty may have and to convert him from his prior manner of life. I have been asking myself how I shall approach him when the day of our meeting arrives. I must admit that I dread that encounter for if I fail and he carries out his threat all of England will suffer. Though I have come to look askance at the British Empire, I love England and its people are my own. I must trust that Moriarty will honor our wager for he has done so until this day and hour, but how long can I put him off?

I have agreed to keep Colonel Moran advised of my location and progress. He in turn is in contact with the Professor as I am with Mycroft. My link with Moriarty is such that I feel his presence from afar and I feel that he must have a similar intuition of my own thoughts. Dare I hope then that he dreads my homecoming as much as I dread meeting him? Each of us believes that he will prevail. Each of us is willing to give the other time in which to bring his plans to maturity. If this is true I may count on another year or two of grace to live the life I have barely known, encased as I have been in London, that great beehive of human activity. Having broken the chains of my captivity I am loathe to resume my former way of life, to risk a return to the occasional artificial stimulus of cocaine and to the coal-smoke shrouded streets of vile London with its everlasting rain and its foul drains.

The sheer habit of living a routine existence can cause the years to slip away and suddenly there is no time for those brave endeavors outlined upon the counterpane of one's bed as a youth. In that season of springtide anything seems possible and the entire world too small for our confident aspirations. As Andrew Marvell once said, "Had we but world enough and time, this coyness, lady, were no crime ... But at my back I always hear time's winged chariot hurrying near and yonder all before us lie deserts of vast eternity." I feel that my life thus far has been at best a preliminary essay towards an uncertain end. All that I would do is still before me.

I sympathize with the impatience of a man like Colonel Moran, that great beast, slashing his way through life. I on the contrary have felt that I must review all of human thought, to delay my opening moves until I should arrive at certainty so as to make no mistakes. The many problems that I have addressed in the course of my consulting practice as a detective were preliminary sallies into the enemy territory to gage its strength, but I have thus far refused to deploy my full forces for I wondered if my strength and wisdom should prove adequate to the task.

It is no wonder that I find "The I-Ching" to be a book containing a philosophy compatible with my own views. Its purpose is to curtail any precipitate action until that time when the entire universe is so aligned with one's situation that progress is furthered and there is no blame. But who can ever afford to wait for complete certainty before embarking on a quest? Should one not rather leap into the fray at all costs and do what one can? The great synthesis of all thought that I have always pursued implies a final victory, whereas the wise men of China knew, as did Heraclitus, the great Greek philosopher, that all is change.

Change is congenial to the Chinese mind, whereas the west has always dreamed of the millennium as a point where change ceases and everything returns to the One God. God's unity is presumed to be static. Similarly, having arrived in heaven the soul is spoken of as being at rest in the peace of God. Heaven is viewed as the absence of change and change is regarded as a sign of the degradation of the world due to sin. This vision of heaven then assumes that God will gather up the toys of creation as a child gathers up its toys at the close of its play to put them back in the box. This was the manner of speaking chosen by Thackeray at the end of his book, "Vanity Fair." But will God proceed in this manner to close the story of creation?

The Apocalypse of St. John, spoken of as the Book of Revelation, speaks not of an end, but of a new beginning, a new heaven and a new earth, for the old will have passed away. How different is this conception from that popular but static vision of a heaven filled with harps and angels that however it may stimulate the visual artist who must contain heaven within the four corners of a canvass, may be exceeded by a writer whose medium is words. Words open into vistas of meaning not confined to the eye. Thus it is that Sacred Scripture promises what even words cannot convey. They only beckon towards an infinite expanse that will never cloy the appetite nor dwarf into insignificance the individual. God will satisfy but not overwhelm us. It is said in Holy Scripture that no man may see God and live. I have always believed that it might have been clearer and more in tune with the intent of the sacred writer if it had been made clear that God does not bring about death, but rather that one may not see God and live as one has always done. God's essence is to be transformative by nature and to see God is to be united with Him in His divine life.

Who then will see God? We have an answer from the lips of Jesus in the Beatitudes, "Blessed are the pure of heart for they shall see God." The dread of God that makes us flee him is our own true death, not the death of the body which must come in any case, but the death to what we once were. Grace brings about a way of life that exceeds but does not contradict human nature. Grace in eternity perfects what time cannot bestow. Sin dreads the face of God because of that very tendency of grace, of the life of God, to purify all that it touches.

The fire of purgatory is none other than the full intensity of God's love applied without any intermediary to the human soul. In purgatory there is no shade. The shadow of our sins will melt away and only our longing to retain them is painful. The long screech of damnation is simply the despair of a soul that finds the presence of God's love to be intolerable. It will take any means to escape it, even by creating its own misery for eternity and erecting a vast and insuperable gulf between its will and that of the soul's Creator.

After the state of being represented by the Doctrine of Purgatory there will remain only God's presence to the purified soul. All other things will have melted away. It is then that God will sustain the promises of old as told in Holy Scripture, but what that shall mean in detail, we cannot say. At this point all theology becomes metaphor and the mind of man must rely upon the preconditions for the promise rather than upon a clear view of the promise's fulfillment. The prerequisite is that we be found to be pure of heart for it is those who are pure of heart that will see God.

Who shall bestow that purity but God Himself if we petition him to do so? That petition is our constant prayer and the reason for the sacramental order of the Church, as well as for all of the actual graces bestowed upon us throughout our lives. If the sacraments of the New Testament are the equivalent to the Sabbath in the Old Testament, then actual grace may be thought of as that which suffices for the ordinary weekdays of our lives. In spite of its denomination as "ordinary time" in the sacred liturgy, there is no time that is really ordinary and many a soul is saved, not during the high points of sacramental intervention, but through the action of grace that abounds most where it is least expected and seeks out the lost sheep wherever that lost sheep is to be found, even if God must climb the stile and traverse coarse bracken to do so. If God were bound by forms even of his own institution He would be untrue to the vision of Jesus who did not avoid any indignity even to the washing of the feet of his apostles and finally by undergoing the crucifixion.

The church has been washing feet ever since in imitation of Jesus. St. Peter, whose very excesses were beloved by Jesus, asked that if foot-washing was necessary, why not wash everything? Jesus answered Peter's complex question with two answers.

First, he assures Peter that only the part that is most stained requires washing, i.e. the feet, thus showing that God is pleased with our virtues however small they may appear to be to us and that any cooperation with grace is efficacious for the soul's salvation. God thus honors the goodness found in man and woman and the myth of man's total depravity is an insult to his Creator.

Second, he explains to Peter that even in that assembly of apostles not all were clean, because Judas had already determined to betray Jesus with a kiss. In this way Jesus acknowledges the reality of sin and that Jesus allowed its presence even among the faithful assembly of His closest followers on that sacred night preceding the passion. God does not then defeat sin by destroying it, but rather by allowing it to do its worst, even if that worst is preceded by a gesture that seems to imply love and acceptance of God's will, the kiss of betrayal. Sometimes the greatest evils are seen within the company of Christians, because they do not assault Jesus as did the Roman soldiers but instead betray Him with a kiss. By their fruits they are known.

September 1, 1892
Further Reflections

Jesus told Judas that to betray the Son of Man is so heinous that it would be better for that man to have never been born. This is not a statement of vengeance but a simple statement of fact, that to choose other than the life of God is to have missed the point of creation, a sad fate to anyone that would ever so choose. I like to think that this statement was a final admonition of mercy to Judas so that even as the noose of his despair tightened about his throat in his final desperate act, Judas might yield to grace and accept forgiveness.

Even Judas had taken the first step in that direction by admitting that he had done wrong by confessing his betrayal to the high priests. Perhaps in spite of their malice they may have served the function of their office and though rejecting his penitence by saying, "What is that to us," God would have witnessed that partial turning of Judas and since where sin abounds, there grace super-abounds, have gone so far as to reach out in forgiveness even to Judas. The function of Judas then is to remind us of the gravity of sin, not alone in Judas, who has gone his way already, but to us who have yet to make our own final choice. It is utter folly then to populate hell with our own candidates for ultimate punishment. We have enough to do to take care of our own final disposition. If even to call a man or a woman a fool is forbidden, how much less can we presume by our own estimation that anyone is cut off from God for all Eternity!

As for the fate of the devil and his angels, Origen dared to hope that even they might be saved. It must be born in mind that a warning to avoid a non-predetermined event allows the possibility of its non-fulfillment. The question then must remain open until all events in time are completed before a final disposition may be said to occur. The fate of the devil and his legions may depend upon the final disposition of our own contingency; unless perhaps from the vantage point of eternity everything has already occurred, then the decision of the devil and his angels would be definitive and the self-exclusion from God for them would be final.

Eternity is incomprehensible from the perspective of time so that I must apply my famous dictum to Watson, "It is a capital mistake to theorize without data." We are caught in the metaphysical contradiction that what is known by God may still appear to us to rest in suspension with the final decision's outcome remaining undetermined. Since the purpose of Holy Scripture is the pragmatic one of catechesis and since the role of the church is pastoral and since the sacred writers were not Greek metaphysicians but rather writers in the Judaic Tradition, the words of Holy Scripture must be heard as they were addressed to their immediate audience and not as they would mean to an audience of our own day.

It is not the words of Sacred Scripture that change, but rather how we are to understand those words grows clearer as we escape the faulty and incomplete manner of our former understanding as we pose new questions to the Sacred Texts. The church understands as it is disposed thereto by the culture and the times of its hearing. This task is ongoing in nature. The essential message is eternal but it is the task of the Church to give it voice through the ongoing action of the life of the Holy Spirit who dwells within it. If the text of Scripture lives, it is because words may exceed their bounds of denotative meaning. The discerning body of the faithful in the dully constituted Catholic Church will discover what is true, for Jesus promised to be with the church until the consummation of the age, which is to say until the end of time.

With these reflections stated above I feel that I have summed up as well as I may what I believe regarding the church. I have no intention of relying upon any other supposed source of morality to convince the Professor when at last we meet. To stop short of the ultimate destination to which my own quest has led me would be disingenuous and inauthentic. The Professor will demand truth and truth I must give him. Truth however is seen always through the distorting lens of personal passion and prior commitments. If this was not so then religious uniformity would already be the rule of all mankind. Men and women of good will reach various estimates of religious truth due to the force of culture and at other times because of their personal values and life experience.

September 5, 1892
My Mission

I dare not fail with Professor Moriarty for I know that if the British Empire is destroyed then the entire world will be in chaos for a time. Any world-order, no matter how unjust it may be, has at least the benefit of being predictable. Economic dislocations are costly to world trade and the disruption usually breeds violence and war between the dominant nations. For this reason, though I would wish for changes in British policy, I know the danger inherent in revolutions.

But how shall I manage my case as I place it before Professor Moriarty? Shall I merely give him this journal to read? Are my own reflections as here recorded adequate to convince anyone but myself?   The very lack of system may make these entries a poor catechism and the potential catechumen must be drawn to embrace faith by the appeal of God at last, since only God can procure a true conversion of heart. The study of texts alone is like a candle unlit in the final analysis. Professor Moriarty is of all men the least likely to surrender to the demands of a superficially imposed faith.

The final source of his philosophy and world-view eludes me. Perhaps I should shift the burden of proof then and ask him to convince me that his views are correct. No specific terms of our wager were made at the time, so I must return with a pedagogical means to convince the Professor to abandon his former life. But how am I to do this? Until that question is answered I must remain abroad to delay the final struggle between us.

My research provides a temporary excuse for my absence from England. I am sure that if the Professor desired to pressure me to return at once that he would have communicated that desire to Colonel Moran and that redoubtable gentleman would now be at my side haunting me with his saturnine presence. As it is I have received only one letter since our parting and that was only to brag about his success at baccarat and to speak in lurid and suggestive detail of how attractive the ladies of Monte Carlo are and of his particular popularity with a certain Polish Countess who is spending the winter at Monte. There was even talk of chartering a boat in the spring to tour Corsica and Sardinia. So it appears that the New Year of 1893 will extend my sabbatical.

If I am free I may take this time to live the life that I find to be most in tune with those reserved intentions that all men harbor. Each man keeps a list of places to see, books to read, and actions to take that will complete whatever saga he proposes to make of his life, a heroic one at least to himself. What man is there who does not see his life as a heroic quest? The life of a woman on the other hand is often confined by the many strictures and limitations applied to her sex. From youth she is groomed to take her place before hearth and home. Upon her devolves all of the mundane requirements of sustaining the human race. She must bear the children. Her very body is adapted to the ends of the comfort and nourishment of a family. Her emotions are so ordered that she may readily respond to the small tragedies of life so that she will be a patient and enduring mother.

When death comes, it is the women who lay out the corpse. In life it is they who prepare the food and provide a center, not for the home alone, but for the entire civilization. The earliest discernible sculptures are of woman. The most basic objects of the useful arts are designed to aid her in her domestic tasks. What are baskets or cauldrons, or even the urn that holds the ashes of the dead, but an image of the womb? When we look for beauty does not woman first come to mind? When we speak of nations are they not called the motherland?   Indeed, woman is so much the substance of life that she is taken for granted. The dignity of her labors is diminished because these seem prosaic, but only because they are so essential.

The restless mind of man dreams instead of the superfluous, of kingdoms, wars, empires, voyages, conquests, and all that will keep his unique name alive beyond his mere relation to wife and children.

I am not immune to these vain desires and Watson's narratives have catered to my own need for fame. I confess to that most preposterous of vanities. If the only worthy quest is to serve God alone, then personal fame becomes the very coveting of the divine prerogatives of veneration that might be held to be the most characteristic feature of Adam's sin in Eden. Adam looked to woman to explain his sin and to excuse his own presumption. The situation would be humorous if its results were not so severe. Adam even attempts to shift the blame of his sin to God. Rather than thanking God for woman, Adam implies that she is the source of the retribution that will now descend upon him, the retribution actually not however proceeding from God, the God who actually preserves his life from the full results of his act.

God had given the earth freely, but now man must work for his bread. What might have been accepted as a gift must now be extracted through labor. Men go the hard way round to achieve every goal. What may have been mere curiosity in Eve was presumption in Adam. The gentle servant of life given to him for company now becomes the very goal of his ambition. He does not cherish her; she becomes, as does the earth itself, the field for his conquest. No hearth can ever contain such lust. Woman herself becomes then a commodity and the first of slaves. What slave but is first made a eunuch so that he may pose no threat to his master? The essence of man thus became ordered to conquest and we suffer from its effects each day. What is history but a long trail of dynasties, each meant to be the final reign of the world?

"My name is Ozymandias king of kings: Look on my works ye mighty and despair!" So says Percy Bysshe Shelley in his exquisite poem which mocks this universal state of mind in all who seek power. Woman then is bound to nature. Woman and nature alike will be obstacles to man until man learns again to cherish both as gifts and to thank God for the superfluous beauty that both manifest.

The beginning of virtue lies in the humility that is so often the product of the defeat of our aspirations. Far from dreading that the forces of the universe seem arrayed against us, perhaps we should rejoice in their recalcitrance and lack of subjection to our will. The problem of evil lies not outside of us then but inside ourselves; we imagine that the workings of God in nature are evil and that He must account for them, because we assume that if God loved us He would not so thwart our multitudinous designs.

We pray for victory and never for defeat because we assume that we know after all what is best for us. We wish to design our own ends and employ all means to attain them. We even go so far as to imagine that God approves of our crusades and our expeditions and our empires. We use the gospel to pave the way to conquest. As missionaries we bring God to the remote regions of the earth, not dreaming that God is already there, latent among the people we seek to convert.

One need think only of the plains of America, so recently divested of the great bison and of the inhabitants whose lives depended upon the bison's presence as the primary source and basis of their economy and culture. If I ever go to America I shall visit as a sacred shrine that last place of vain resistance when the flame of their independence was crushed in the bitter snow at Wounded Knee.

I shall visit the place where the bodies of the dead lay frozen in their accusation of the soldiers who slew them: women, children, old men. Those who went into exile in their own land are analogous to the remnant of Israel after the sack of Jerusalem by the Romans. When I go to America, I will remind those I meet that in defeat lies the only victory reserved to man by God. Surely the innocent dead stand before the throne of God, while the laurels of seeming conquest wither on the brow of the conqueror until he also becomes ashes to be blown away with the wind.

Dr. Watson's Narrative Continues

J closed Holmes' journal and looked out to sea. The days of our voyage had passed swiftly and we hoped to enter New York harbor on the following day. I must admit to a sense of being excited to witness at first hand the dynamism of American life. The Old World stood in awe of the produce and innovation of this multitudinous population drawn from many lands, each striving to exceed their neighbors and to grasp some share of what is deemed to be the fruits of freedom. If to Holmes America appeared as a site of pillage and exploitation, many others saw there the hope of escape from the complex strata of social privilege prevailing in the Old World. If the original inhabitants of these shores were made to yield to the newcomers and those far flung spaces of mountain and valley were to be forced to accept the plow of cultivation if only to feed the expanding population, this has always been the course of history and of the relative strength of the conquered to the conqueror.

The conquest of America may avoid the over-population of the earth prophesied by Thomas Malthus for a time but only for a time. Surely mankind must finally meet the limits of its expansion. Only then will mankind create an order of affairs that will be truly just. Until that time arrives technology seems to have proclaimed an era of new youth to the world when everything seems possible. It may be a pleasure to drink that heady brew while it still froths over fresh from the keg that would contain it, but experience curtails most of such sanguine expectations. America has to date lagged behind the rest of the world in its colonial ambitions. The present state of tension between America and Spain however may transform all of this. If so, this may further our present purpose if Spain is defeated. America will then succeed to the title over the former Spanish colonies in Cuba and the Philippines as Holmes intimated to me yesterday in a conversation that touched upon this topic.

"Do not be surprised Watson," said he, "If war is the outcome of these events. Even as we speak the question of the sinking of the Maine in Havana Harbor is being debated in Congress and the Americans are demanding that the government intervene by sending an expeditionary force to Cuba. The Battleship Oregon has been dispatched from San Francisco and is speeding round South America on its way to Cuban waters. Can America long resist the demand for a canal that will allow the American naval forces to swiftly adapt to needs that may arise upon either of its coasts? If war should break out and if America should prove victorious then our mission will ride along upon the fruits of that victory. We will make public the news of the forgery of the Murillo Papers and imply that those papers were only a ruse to deter the legitimate right of Americans to police their own hemisphere by building a canal through Central America."

"The indignant Americans will perceive that the European hope was to get a jump on America by building a canal that would be under the control of the European Banks in the person of Baron Maupertuis. We will thus turn the national temper in favor of a canal to be built by the United States of America. We will restore the full force of the Monroe Doctrine in all of its pristine vigor. The Americans will demand that the canal should be built at once with such vehemence and alacrity that the Baron will be left with a shell of a company which, when facing such determined competition to build the canal will need to resort to every extremity if it is to survive."

Holmes pondered before continuing further, "I do not expect the Baron to give up easily though. This project has now taken deep root within him. I trust above all in the American will to defeat him. The value of the shares in his company will decline so quickly that he will be constrained to continue his plans or face financial ruin. His fortune and credibility are now at stake! At first he will claim that the papers are not a forgery at all. He will demand a further investigation. There will be a bitter war of accusation and counter-accusation. Many of the companies in America that once had a hand in building the railroad years ago in Costa Rica will weigh-in to save their reputation as run by honest and upright men. It is possible that even King Leopold of Belgium may enter the fray at some point by buying up declining shares. News reports of that King's activities in the so-called Congo Free-state are beginning to surface. He will wish to appear on the side of those who oppose slavery in foreign regions if only to cover up his own similar practices in Africa. Belgium has no great liking for the more successful Dutch Empire represented by Baron Maupertuis, but strange alliances have appeared before this. I had heard rumors of atrocities committed in the Congo region as early as 1892 when I visited the Sudan to protest against the practices there of the Islamic slave traders. I was made to understand that my mission could not be considered a serious one, since the powers of Europe had conspired to create a region in the Congo where the most atrocious practices were being pursued daily to force the natives into submission in order to obtain rubber and ivory. The tales that I heard then were so ghastly that I did not credit them at the time, but accounts that I have heard since from credible sources, plus my knowledge of the duplicity of the European Empires where such riches are at stake make me begin to believe. I am therefore willing to aid the Americans against all

European interests. Perhaps the hunger for conquest must be its own final corrective. Each power that ventures too far invites retribution at the hands of an opposing power no less greedy than itself."

Such were Holmes' views, as they were expressed to me as we neared New York's harbor. We were about to encounter one of those unique moments of history where the fate of a people is decided. I could only wonder how our mission to America would appear to later reflection when I would return to write of it at my home in Cornwall, a land that has also known many conquests. Even today relics are still found there of the Normans and the Vikings. If Holmes' theory was correct even the Chaldeans had once visited England. All of these early invaders had dreamed of empire and of the domination of trade-routes and yet were now no more. Only their language remains in the vestiges of our conglomerate English language and the epic poetry of vanished days and ages. No race or nation is forever young and the torch inevitably passes in every age to a new power seeking its own frontier and its hour in the sun.

The American torch was bright indeed as we entered New York Harbor. It was truly the hour for America to spread its wings. The famed Statue of Liberty was there to greet us as we rounded Staten Island and made for our berth in the bustling harbor. Holmes had explained to me that the best disguise is to be perfectly average for it is only the unusual that is ever noticed in a crowd. Though the purpose of the feigned attack upon his person in London was to provide a means of exit from England and to confuse any pursuit, Holmes desired that the ruse should be extended as long as possible in order to cover any traces of our abdication from England. He hoped that this might encourage the Baron to proceed with his plans without fear of any interference from us and the need to consider even the remotest possibility that we might be in America and about to expose him.

Though there was little chance that Holmes would be recognized among the many passengers leaving the ship, we still took precautions. Each of us carried a passport under a fictitious name provided through Mycroft's efforts. We carried nothing that would delay us in customs. Inspector Hopkins passed through customs in a group some distance behind ours and we took separate cabs to our hotel. Our plan was to remain only a few days in New York before taking a train from Penn Station to Newport. It was Holmes' desire to sample opinion from many quarters there so as to gage the state of the public temper regarding the possibility of war with Spain. This process would be advanced by hopefully meeting some of the luminaries of the day in the private retreat on the coast of Rhode Island where the wealthy disport themselves in an American version of that great English institution: the country house weekend.

Once beyond the frenzy of New York and the wave of hungry reporters we could drop our disguises and resume the use of our real names. An ethos of privacy was maintained in Newport that would preserve silence about the presence there of England's great detective and his humble friend. Wealth and fame can be great burdens and it was largely to escape both that the wealthy had, as it were, circled their wagons along this small ring of coastline in Rhode Island where they could enjoy the summer months in peace. The dinner gatherings there often included some of the most influential men and women of the day. Holmes could think of no better place to gain an insight into the course that America might pursue in the new century and how the present affair of the war of revolution in Cuba might be resolved and whether American forces would give the rebels any assistance in their struggle to break free of Spanish rule.

Our cab took us from the docks and at Holmes request by a route that would give us a brief tour of the city. Although he often preferred to walk and to use every sense to install the city into his inmost being so that years later he was often able to account for everything he had seen and to bring it freshly forth as though it had been yesterday, on this occasion he made an exception to that rule. New York was, if not as large as London, built upwards to an unprecedented scale. The spires of the buildings dwarfed even the aspirations of the men who inhabited them. The commercial instinct was everywhere apparent and monetary exchange the order of the day. We passed down Wall Street as I gazed at the great marble facades of those temples of mammon. It was here that the great J.P. Morgan, America's Rothschild, executed his own daily machinations. Money for men such as these is simply an abstract series of points by which they measure the extent of their power and not the humble means of obtaining the necessities of life as it perforce is for those who must use money for necessities.

Money in abundance changes its character. The social invention of money has been both a blessing and a curse to mankind. By its very nature it is a social construct, yet it is prone to be monopolized by those who have best devised ways to amass it so that money can make more money. For this reason a graduated tax-structure is essential to prevent the power of money accumulation from gaining control of the laws as well. If the rule of law is not always superior to money a republic cannot long endure, for the masses will then become only cogs in a machine owned by an oligarchy. Democracy demands at least some degree of economic equality or it cannot exist, because the poor will always surrender their rights simply to live. They have no economic choice and where there is no choice there is no political democracy either.

From Wall Street we proceeded through the throngs in the streets to the great Central Park that with great foresight had been preserved from the manmade structures that surrounded it. I could not but remark at the sudden burst of green amidst so much that was brown, grey, or black. How different are the creations of man from those of God. The world of men is about measurement and restrictions; whereas God's original intent seems not to have imposed borders to their enjoyment but to have been entrusted to all equally. Man was created to wander as he pleased in the garden of this earth.

From whence then come so many borders and distinctions? God's clock is the four seasons; from whence then come so many clocks and deadlines? Man desires to measure all things and to allot benefits by degrees, whereas God's world revels in balance and abundance. If there is scarcity and penury upon the earth it is the creation of mankind. We create our own scarcity in a world of abundance.

These reflections of mine were reinforced by the request that Holmes made of our driver to proceed to the area of New York known as Five Points and to tour the region called the Bowery. Our driver expressed shock and I must say disapproval at our choice. It was clearly not the custom of most visitors to the majestic city to request a tour through the bowels of that same metropolis, but so commanding was Holmes' manner that our driver refrained from further protest and we were soon passing through scenes of great poverty and congestion to rival even London. Was this the promised land of which so many recent immigrants had dreamed? If so, it was no wonder that many did not tarry long there but proceeded westward, imagining that their dream was to be found somewhere out upon the great prairies where the herds of bison had only recently relinquished the lands where they had roamed for eons to the farms and ranches. Was New York then but a way-station where immigrants might at least learn the language and acquire the restless spirit of America before pressing onward?

And what of those who remained in New York? Would the seething brew of trade enable some to make their fortune there?

Perhaps they would join those men of influence who controlled the nation. Then they might purchase an estate out on Long Island or travel by rail to the now once again beckoning south and acquire a devalued plantation. The states of the Confederacy stripped of slavery still retained its blight. The region remained a nation within a nation, it seemed to me, and the early plans for equality of the Radical Republicans, such as Thaddeus Stevens, had yielded to mere tolerance of the Negro population as a permanent underclass, while the Indians long since displaced westward were viewed as aliens.

In order to preserve its sense of itself as a source of civilizing influence the white men had forced the Indians even to surrender their children to missionary schools so that they might be raised to be what are termed "productive citizens." This tragic tale might be understood by anyone who cared to make inquiries. The world had been witnessing the course that America was taking all along. It would have shown more concern and outrage at that course but for the fact that Europe was at the time of which I speak a seething cauldron of conquest and depopulation as well. Everywhere there was the demand for new colonies and the wealth they might export to the home nations. Humanity seemed poised for some crisis but what form it might take was for time alone to make manifest.

But I was troubled even then, as was Holmes, by the speed that events seemed to follow. How I longed for the certitude about human nature that had once prevailed in the 18th century among men such as Dr. Samuel Johnson or that sense of immanent reform that had so animated the English Romantics Poets such as Shelley and Byron. But perhaps it is always the truth that the heart of man is an abyss of fear, greed, and jealousy. Nothing comes so easy to man as the struggle for power.

fter our tour of those unsavory regions of the city, we passed back into regions of Olympian splendor as we passed Columbia University whose scholars may yet provide that union of thought and virtue that is the only real education. At last we pulled up before the majestic Waldorf-Astoria Hotel. Our cabman regained his sense of appreciation of our good taste, though he was perplexed at first by the sovereign that Holmes presented to pay our fare. We were soon aided by a team of bellmen who perceived that they were dealing with "rich foreigners." We went through the process of assigning rooms and were soon carried by a lift to one of the upper floors. Our suite of rooms was elegant and the views over the city were splendid.

"After all Watson we shall be in New York for only a day and we may as well sample the best of what it may offer," remarked Holmes.

We dined that evening at the famed Delmonico's though I still believe that Simpsons of London has better cuisine. We were given a quiet table from whence we could observe the plumage of the ladies and gentlemen as they were seated. The entire meal was like a choreographed dance. The food was presented and delivered with such a flourish as to imply that it was not so much to be eaten as observed. I am afraid that I have grown somewhat dowdy in my tastes by living in Cornwall and dining at the local pub so I found the whole demonstration to be somewhat comical. Holmes looked over at me and smiled.

"It is only the amenities Watson, that season life. Of what does civilization consist after all but in just such ceremonies? How many poor pheasants and peacocks have been stripped of their plumage to deck out this scene tonight? Does the humble oyster not yield the pearl? The crowds from the theater will soon arrive for a late supper. We must order dessert and our port soon or forfeit our place. Ah look, they begin to arrive, a new flock displaces the old, and these new entrants are of even greater plumage in fact..."

He broke off suddenly. I followed his gaze towards the entrance. A group of men in top hats had arrived and they were in the process of checking their walking sticks and capes at the door. They surrounded a woman of startling beauty and color whose apparel spoke of Paris and of Milan. She had the immediate effect of riveting the attention of the entire room. Her back was towards us, but her long chestnut tresses fell down her back and over shoulders that were shockingly bare. When she turned to face us it was with a reckless smile that defied censure and her bosom was carried high and proud as she was escorted to her table. Many a lesser beauty eyed her with distaste and envy.

Holmes' gaze had yet to look away from the procession. I turned and looked at her again for her table was only four tables away from our own. Her chair was pulled back and she was seated majestically, the long curve of her neck, swanlike before the immaculate table linen, which now seemed dull in comparison to the whiteness of her skin. She appeared to be of that age when beauty is poised at its summit of grandeur, the face showing the bone structure beneath, with none of the superfluous padding of the rosy flesh of youth. It is the last moment before the features begin to subside quietly into the settled pattern of middle-age and the tides of beauty begin to recede, as at last they must. I gazed at her angelic countenance for she had been placed at the side of the table that caused her to face us.

Suddenly it was as though the years had fallen away. I glimpsed through the residual paint of the theater a slim boyish countenance and swagger as the figure of a young man approached us one night outside of our lodgings in Baker Street calling out as he passed, "Goodnight Mr. Sherlock Holmes." That individual had said this in a pleasant purring accent before passing on down the street. I had not seen that face since, but I knew that there before us sat none other than Irene Adler, known and spoken of by

Sherlock Holmes as "The Woman."

She seemed to be oblivious to the intense gaze of the three gentlemen at our table and was laughing gaily at the efforts of her companions to be amusing and to vie with each other for her attention. I could see though that she was weary and that this night was a repetition of an old routine. She must always appear to be what her public expected of her and to be as happy as they imagined her to be in her fame as an actress of ageless beauty. I could not but wonder if life, which had appeared to bestow upon her all that any woman might desire, had still kept in abeyance somewhere an elusive parallel life that she might have lived, one that might have brought her greater happiness if less fame. The mere absence of ordinary cares is not always a guarantee that life has brought one fulfillment.

I turned again to look at Holmes. His face wore a wistful smile that I had seldom seen upon it. I could only surmise the course of his thoughts. That he had recognized her as well was beyond question; I wondered though whether he had seen her in the years since that evening when they had first met. If so, he had never alluded to that meeting. Yet, here she was again that night. The situation was a delicate one in light of our delicate mission to America. A recognition scene might be fatal to our desire for anonymity.

We could hardly make an exit while she remained between us and the door. I wondered what we should do. I glanced at Inspector Hopkins who seemed to be puzzled by what was happening before him. He could see that both Holmes and I were riveted by the entrance of this woman. He merely smiled and shook his head.

"Well, Mr. Holmes," said he. "New York does have its worthwhile beauties after all."

"Yes," said Holmes, "But this beauty has known the world from Bohemia to London, and yes even in Rome itself."

This was my first hint that sometime during the intervening years they must have met each other again. A meeting perhaps recorded in a section of his journal to which I had yet to arrive in my slow progress, but which I was soon to read in the days ahead. I will produce that part of the journal now in this account, skipping the sections of the journal that continue after the parts of substance that I have already included here. I assure my readers that the omitted section, written in the late summer and fall of 1892 deals only for the most part with the results of his experiments, which he there transcribed, entrees that will make little sense to the general reader.

The section which I will now transcribe takes up with the coming of winter in 1892. Sherlock Holmes had grown restless once again. The summer had passed and the students had returned from their vacation making continued private research difficult in the busy laboratories of the medical school. It had always been Holmes' intent to go to Rome after his travels in Asia. He set off now in November of that year of 1892. I shall take up my transcription of his journal at this point. I shall also take this occasion to comment on the difficulty, which I share with the great biographer of Doctor Samuel Johnson, in choosing how best to choose among so many recollections those events and utterances that best reveal the character of my friend, Sherlock Holmes.

At this late stage of my own life, bearing in mind that my life may soon be over, I have chosen to err on the side of excess. I have always believed that the difference between literature and mere printed-matter of entertainment lies in the leisure of inquiry. We are living now in an age of abridgment. We have lost the hunger for completeness seen in such works as the majestic "Anatomy of Melancholy" by Robert Burton written in the 17th century. Even the great novel-sequences such as "The Waverly Novels" by Sir Walter Scott find fewer readers today among the young. As for the aged, well who wishes to spend the shorter days of their post-maturity in a chair reading rather than seeking out the raw-data of experience while time and health remain? Perhaps I write then primarily for those of middle-years who have yet to reach the adamantine certainties of age or the equally adamantine if untested certainties of youth. Middle-age seems to me to be the peak of one's maturity and good judgment. There is still sufficient life ahead for the acquisition of wisdom to affect one's course in life.

Leisure and reflection are the signs of a well-lived life. Leisure allows one to savor and to sift, to seek as did Montaigne in his famous essays, for the elusive wisdom latent in the circumstantial and to avoid the generalities that hide our ignorance. Such readers will be patient with a poor doctor, one who is writing near the end of Europe's greatest war, when all certitudes seem to have vanished quite away in the general slaughter of these recent terrible years.

From the Journal of Sherlock Holmes

November 1, 1892
All Saints Day

Today is the Feast Day of All Saints and I went to early Mass at the Cathedral of St. Pierre. The choir music was exquisite with a piece by Allegri. This feast along with those of Christmas and Easter are the primary Feast-Days of the Catholic Church and are times of general celebration in the town. I feel in a mood to celebrate. My work in Montpellier has reached its terminus. I have gone as far as I am able to go in my research, as my recent entries of my results have recorded in a somewhat dry fashion of formulae and process notes.

I have discovered certain stains that can be used for microbial study since we may not study what we cannot see. These stains are not a cure for tuberculosis. That agent has I am sad to say eluded me, but to find a stain for gram-negative bacilli is an achievement of rare order for an amateur, which is no mean contribution to the future literature on the subject. I have proceeded as far as I may with my initial insights. Fortunately science is a composite endeavor and another may carry onwards using my published notes and hypotheses. The university has agreed to disseminate my findings. My final meeting with the head of the School of Medicine was cordial. He did me the honor of awarding me a certificate in recognition of my research and the time spent in Montpellier as a fellow of the college that I will hang upon the walls at Baker Street when I return. I have spent the week since then packing in view of my current plan to visit Rome.

I leave here tomorrow. Already a pattern is emerging from the course of the last two years. I can see that I am doing those things that are often reserved until too late in life. Every man and woman has a list of things that he or she must see, hear, visit, or accomplish before his life will seem complete and whole. Woe to the man or woman who is caught up by death before that list of tasks and dreams is in some measure accomplished. The problem of course is that I am always adding to the list. My unread books alone would require a score of lives to read, yet I am always buying more. Robert Browning says that, "A man's reach must exceed his grasp else what's a heaven for." He might as justly have spoken of our earthly ambitions, because they are limitless. There seems to be no end to the writing of books.

I often said as much to Watson when we discussed my own science of detection. I always felt that such a science should be reduced to a single volume thus obviating the need for Watson's many minute accounts of my individual cases. But I have moderated my views since I made those recommendations to him. I now see the folly of seeking a premature simplicity in things. The desire to encompass everything all too often leads one to an attitude of bitterness or intellectual despair. I have long enjoyed that curious volume by Robert Burton entitled "The Anatomy of Melancholy," in which the author attempts to explain once and for all the source and remedy for human unhappiness. That book along with one by Lucretius broadly entitled, "The Nature of Things" sum up the human condition as well as it may be described and contained in a single work. But if they contained everything then no further books would have ever needed to be written. Each generation contains a smattering of people who will add a footnote to all that has preceded them in the way of art, literature, and science. No one man or woman may contain even a fraction of what has been said already. Yet they must do what they can to extend the borders of human knowledge and reflection. Fortunate are those who are granted sufficient time in life to at least peruse some of the great totality of human thought. We tend to encounter just those books that confirm us in what we have always thought and also those books that upset us and cause us to review the course of our lives to discover the validity or lack thereof of our prior convictions.

If even the Bible reposes between two covers and forms but a single volume, then a man shows great temerity if his own account of life must fill multiple volumes. The great French writer, Balzac, exhausted himself with his desire to contain what he termed "The Human Comedy." To aim one's gaze beyond our short course of allotted days and nights does not seem to be merely pride in us, but is rather a measure of our hunger for all things and one proof of our real individual immortality. Our difference from the brute beasts lies in the very fact that we are never satisfied, or as St. Augustine says to God in his Confessions, "You have made us for yourself and our hearts are restless until they rest in thee."

I do not know if God enjoys the spectacle of our many dramas as we blunder about in life, but I often find comfort in the saying of a Hasidic Rabbi who said that God made man because he likes stories. My own story is not yet finished. I propose to go to Rome, which has largely supplanted Jerusalem as the Holy City of pilgrimage for Christians, yet in truth the whole earth is holy from the Sacred Ganges to Wounded Knee. God is everywhere and speaks in the Black Hills of the Dakotas as well as in the Shinto temples of Japan.

We believe that the creedal statement that Jesus Christ is God and the revelation of the Holy Trinity is definitive and true, but it is not for us to gather that unique revelation to our bosom as though we possessed it and were its originators. The Triune God may do as God chooses and if He has spoken to other races in a language that reaches their souls so that they worship Him is it not better that we allow God to enlighten them by our example rather than by our preaching alone? Since St. Paul admitted that we now see as through a glass darkly, surely it is presumption for us to suppose that the full reality of God may be confined to our reduction into doctrine of what is in fact infinite and beyond our total comprehension. Let us be true to what we have received but be satisfied to hear also how God has spoken to other cultures in their own time and place.

The Holy Spirit will discern what may be salvaged from any partial visions of God that they might contain for the betterment of the entirety of the human race the borders of which are set by God alone. My thoughts are trending in this more inclusive direction as I leave behind the beauty of the Languedoc country and the lovely city of Montpellier. The belief that the majority of the human race, one after another, has been condemned to never see the face of God through the mere accidental circumstance of living on an undiscovered continent or following their own best beliefs as inculcated by their own sacred writings is appalling; to believe otherwise seems to me to be a dishonor to God. Doctrinal determinations, even when resting upon Holy Scripture, can only proceed from within the limitations and preconceptions of the culture where such determinations are made. I cannot believe that God is careless with His own human creation so as to make accurate adherence to belief formulae the basis for eternal salvation.

It is natural to use whatever written materials exist to memorialize any event whether sacred or secular in character. There is an inverse ratio between the amount of material in written form available and the value to be placed upon it. Since the invention of the printing press there is no scarcity of written memorials of any significant human event. These parallel sources allow for the correction or confirmation of the historical accuracy of any text. Compare this situation to that facing the early church. We have little data or commentary from an objective point of view to corroborate the circumstantial accuracy in detail of the New Testament accounts of Jesus in the gospels.

These accounts were already theologically infused documents addressed to a believing community and to potential catechumens. The Bible is spoken of as "the word of God" because the living community of the faithful chose to recognize a reflection of its faith in these documents. They were chosen, not for their ability to withstand outside criticism, but for their appeal to their initial audience that included a smattering of people who recalled the events memorialized in these texts.

Within a generation direct experience of Jesus was reduced to oral testimony and these fragmentary accounts. After this period the Early Church Fathers became the primary source material for Christianity, which remained in a somewhat inchoate condition of established doctrine for centuries thereafter; all of which observations are meant to point out that Christianity appears to be a syncretistic religion developed over time where theological reflection provides a basis for further theological reflection.

As each new layer was added century after century to what came before, the Ecclesiastical structure of Catholicism grew in intricacy and in its power to exercise control over individual consciences and over the governing structures of the times, throughout Europe and the known world. Only at the late date of human development in the 19th century has it become possible to adapt a critical stance to the very roots of Christian faith by asking whether Christianity as a belief structure is adequate to leap over and beyond other such writings that sprung up spontaneously in other regions of the world where there was no knowledge that God's "chosen people" even existed, let alone that they had left a literature that claims to be authoritative for the entire human race in its origin and destiny. There is more than my battle with Professor Moriarty at stake here – the integrity of Western Civilization is implicated in the fate of Christianity. These are the very questions that I take with me to Rome. May I now be blessed in my travels and come safely to the seat of the Christian faith where I may explore further some of these questions that trouble my heart and mind.

I go now to Rome not to witness the grandeur there, but rather to seek out the home of the first martyrs who were determined to give up even their lives to prove the sincerity of their utter reliance upon God alone as their portion and their cup. They knew that it is under the Sign of the Cross alone that mankind finds its true destiny. The cross is the final witness to our ability to torture ourselves. We execute those that we deem criminal, but who are the ultimate criminals but we supposed Christians who do not first crucify the worst that is within us so that any virtues that we may possess may shine more brightly forth to illuminate the world?

It is always folly though to question how providence has penetrated events through the ages. For this reason the man of wisdom must leave all final explanations of why and how to God and to another season when all will be explained and everything made whole, with each thing divinely placed in its own proper place. History in the final analysis is inconclusive, neither linear nor cyclical nor even chaotic. History is simply raw data, successive antecedents and consequences. To record it is already to distort it according to one's preconceptions and desires. If history as a theoretical construct then is ultimately an illusion, because we can only trace its contours and not define its ultimate ends, how much more illusory is any idea that we may have of the inevitable progress and evolution of humankind unless that evolution is illuminated and sustained by the guiding hand of God!

November 2, 1892
Journey to Monte Carlo

y train left early this morning for Marseilles and the French Riviera. How good it was to see the sea again and to have it as my companion as the train followed the coastline eastward. I have decided to visit Colonel Moran to explain my plans and to see if he has sensed any impatience from the Professor while I have prolonged my sojourn away from England. The situation is certainly a delicate one and I appreciate the latitude I have been given to pursue my own research and personal odyssey, which I could not in good conscience pursue if I felt that the Professor might cease to honor his part of our wager.

On the other hand I cannot count upon his indefinite delay of his proposed grand plan to destroy the British Empire. But that undertaking will not be a simple one and I can only imagine that he will require sufficient time to assemble whatever infernal device he will use to accomplish that end. I only trust that the chosen mechanism may not be so unstable that events will be initiated on their own accord and without his consent. Even Professor Moriarty is not so powerful that he can assert complete control over the complexity of events. If it is true that even the best of intentions sometimes go awry, then how much more may ill intentions lead to unpredictable results?

I think often of the peculiar courses traced by world history. What is history after all but primarily a series of blunders? Was it destined that Christianity ended up being centered on Rome rather than Jerusalem? Did the Empire of the Gauls under Charlemagne and the prior spread of the great monasteries under the rule of St. Benedict determine the spread of the gospel so that what began as an obscure offshoot of Judaism became a major force in world history that even outlasted the Roman Empire?

Christianity went on to sustain learning despite being called the Dark Ages. By the high Middle Ages gothic splendor reached its apotheosis. But was the supreme power of the Roman Church under Pope Innocent III an age of glory or of bitter triumph leading to the futile crusades and the apotheosis of violence that they represented? Was the building of St. Peter's Basilica in Rome worth the expensive indulgences which represented a sort of celestial tax levied on souls that were used to finance its building? Would Christianity exist as it does today in a hundred discordant fragments if it had always remained in its state of original simplicity and communalism?

At times I have gone so far as to wonder if the universal message of the church was based upon a misunderstanding. Could it be that only a few are capable of partaking in the exalted destiny to share the life of the Trinity in the Beatific Vision? Few people seem to pursue a holy life and to place the commands of God at the center of their every decision, so that it seems that few will be ultimately saved according to the strictures of the narrow gate. The general mass of mankind seems to hope that it may seep into heaven through some obscure crevasse rather than to devote much effort and time towards the goal of seeing God face to face and therefore to prepare for that great meeting by a life devoted to prayer. The result is that even in Christianity one often looks in vain for evidence of the influence of Jesus Christ. The contrary appeal exists to formulate another destiny for mankind such as the fleshly gardens of Mohammed's version of paradise or the infinitely inhuman state of individual destruction and merger into nothingness promised by Buddhist nirvana.

We spend all our lives acquiring the means to sustain a perilous existence with some measure of security in this world, one that so often withholds from us even mere sustenance so that many starve to death daily. And all the time we are bid to keep heaven first in our aims and intentions as we struggle amidst the crowds of our bewildered fellow human beings who jostle and confuse us with their own hopes and dreams of happiness and security.

At times human beings are only loveable from a distance. The hermits can speak of a love for all mankind because they need not deal with people on a daily basis. Still, even the cenobites devoted as they are to solitude meet for prayer and brief common meals. Without the regular clergy and the religious orders to keep Christianity secure in its most pristine forms could Christianity have survived at all? The endless drift of Protestantism into a multitude of contending sects shows that in spite of their personal excesses at times, the church requires some earthly center, some point of focus, and some ultimate responsibility for the entire body of the faithful such as exists in the Catholic Church.

So it is that history blunders on. Who may say how long the Second Coming of Christ may be held in abeyance by the sheer mercy of God? He alone may best judge when the time for His harvest has come? When one considers the geologic ages that preceded the advent of mankind then perhaps all of history thus far has been only the seething brew of an early fermentation. We are perhaps only now just beginning to discern the will of God under the tutelage of the Holy Spirit. If so we must prepare ourselves for a lengthy siege as the forces of materialism gather about us and man imagines that he is his own creation and that he may determine his own final nature and ultimate purpose in life apart from God. It is my opinion that the seeming fruition of the technical advances of this present age will be followed by an age of slaughter such as the world has never known. The high point of our civilization may be so savage that God will intervene at last merely to save us from ourselves.

The ultimate ends of history cannot be evaluated from within history. If there is not a calm and distant perspective from which to view the clamor of events we are inevitably submerged in our own partial visions of the good life and public policy. The eyes of God no doubt view in kindness our simple sphere floating in the infinite silence of space, illumined by the sun, which only shows its light where its beams strike reflecting objects.

Such is also the nature of the operation of Divine Grace; only take it away from the soul and all is darkness within us. Grace penetrates history so as to guide its course even when that course is not evident to us. History is the story of our resistance to the design of God who favors the little ones, the many who are carried along by events that are not of their making.

November 3, 1892
The Grand Casino at Monte Carlo

My train arrived last night in Monte Carlo and Colonel Moran had the good grace to meet me. He even took up my luggage himself after waving away the disappointed porter.

"The porters are like jackals here, Mr. Sherlock Holmes. They imagine that everyone, particularly in the winter season, is here to be preyed upon. They would quickly devour a poor chemist like you. Save your money. I have rented a villa above the sea since my arrival here. You will like it. The view over the city is excellent. My time at baccarat has not been ill-spent as you see. For once the tables of chance have been kind to me and though I have cost the casino a pretty fortune during my time here, my mere presence and reputation draws in trade and my many imitators have more than recompensed the establishment for my winnings."

He continued to speak as he loaded my baggage aboard a fiacre. "I have the good sense to know how best to enjoy Monte Carlo while avoiding its pitfalls. You will be happy to know that I have ceased gambling for the remainder of the winter at least. It is a triumph to me merely to bask for a time in the glow of my reputation. My mere presence has become a talisman for luck and I am usually the guest at dinner or at some entertainment sponsored by some bored count or baronet visiting here for the winter. I am happy to share whatever secrets I may possess with them, but really there are none. Luck is capricious; that is all. You will recall I am sure my primary axioms in what constitutes the Moran Philosophy that this universe has no guiding force or purpose, that everything is guided by fortune and chance and that we walk past occasions of our potential deaths daily. Virtue does not change the odds against us. Once we are dead we cash-in whatever chips we may hold. The only real virtue is to accept death gracefully with at most a look of fond farewell upon the pleasures of the flesh."

I could see that the Colonel was still himself. He was invigorating in his way and even charming, a Falstaff without fat, a Nietzsche with a grin. Yet I could sense a certain tone of desperation this time in his bluff and abrupt manner and there was something in his eyes that betokened the beginnings of doubt in his primordial faith in the visible world. Could it be I wondered that his present victories had brought him face to face with the eternal question of the successful man who must finally ask himself the question: "Is this all that life can offer me?"

Our carriage took us through the lovely boulevards of the town to a point from whence I could view the palace of the Prince of Monaco and the stately harbor where many a graceful yacht lay quietly moored with the expanse of the blue Mediterranean stretching southwards to the coast of Africa, the site of our recent adventures. How distant now seemed our many travels and how strange to me to be speaking English once again to a familiar companion. Soon our carriage passed in front of the circular drive of the Grand Casino.

Upon my questioning Colonel Moran whether he wished to

show it to me at this time the Colonel answered, "Later tonight Mr. Holmes. The Casino is part of a night spent on the Midi when the stars are lit up like crystal palaces and when the ladies appear as one mass of silk and décolletage and when the champagne air of night comes inland with the breezes from the sea. We will walk the grounds then and you will see the lights of Monte Carlo reflected in the still waters of the bay below. For now you must come and see my villa and settle in."

Our carriage ascended by a circuitous route into the rocky hills above the town. The way was steep and our horses strained so that we stopped at various turn-offs so that they might catch their breath. Each level as we ascended higher had its own charming view. The little city lay below us now like a gem in a setting of silver. The sun lay slanting across the bay. It would soon change to burnished gold as the evening approached. I could see why even those who chose not to gamble might see Monte Carlo as one of those places that are always recalled with fondness and to which one longs always to return. I was not surprised now that the Colonel had not been chaffing at me to return quickly to England. I could count on him as an advocate should the Professor grow impatient of my return. Of course it was still the duty of the Colonel still to escort me and he would be in no hurry I could see to leave the site of his present triumphs at the gaming tables.

I must admit here we had grown to trust each other after a fashion during our long sojourn in the east. Our very differences formed a bond between us. Neither hid from the other his true feelings and the intimacy bred of the shared dangers in the course of our travels was such that we were brothers of the desert in a way. I believe that each saw in the other some inverted reflection of himself. I once told Watson, "There but for the grace of God goes Sherlock Holmes." That sentiment was never truer than when I dealt with Colonel Sebastian Moran. We both had a hunger for danger and enjoyed the peril of risk. We both scorned comfort for fear that if we ever yielded to its blandishments we would grow fat and lazy or die like Faust should we ever say of anything, "Stay thou art so fair."

This very characteristic has made me wonder if I shall ever retire from the challenge of the chase. I used to enjoy teasing Watson with the idea that I would potter about among beehives on the Sussex Downs and the poor fellow believed me; but I am one with the sentiments of the poet Tennyson when he says in his poem, "I cannot rest from travel. I will drink life to the lees. Yet always roaming with a hungry heart much have I seen and known of men, climates, counsels, governments, myself not least but honored of them all, and drunk delight of battle with my peers far on the ringing plains of windy Troy. How dull it is to pause, to make an end, to rust unburnished, not to shine in use, as though to breathe were life. Life piled on life were all too little and of one to me. Little remains but some work of noble note may yet be done not unbecoming men who strove with gods."

Perhaps only the restless man may ever know God or at least a God who is as dynamic as this type of man would conceive him to be: a God who creates out of nothingness, a God who revels in the abundance and the fruition of the earth. The barnacle-encrusted image of God put forth by many churchmen seems blasphemous to me. I am not one who knows the peace of Mount Carmel. Though I long for that obliteration of the self in the living flame of love spoken of by Saint John of the Cross, such is not my temperament. I share more theological similarities with the restless Jesuits who penetrated India and China, who made for the virgin land of Paraguay, and created their communal earthy paradise there among the native people, a scandal to the conquerors who wished to exploit the tribal people without religious interference.

The Jesuits believe in an approach to spirituality of contemplation in action. There is a tension between a Christian's anticipation of a better life after death and a commitment to improving the quality of our present existence through the application of the human intellect combined with a commitment to justice and equity between people. An apocalyptic mentality grows out of despair regarding the second goal of religion. I cannot for one cannot despair of achieving some measure of triumph upon the earth, some sense of order, be it only that resembling beehives. My interest in beekeeping is real, buzzing in a quiet glade and giving honey to make life sweeter. This world abounds in vitality and creativity. Life emerges wherever it has an opportunity to take root. Even extinctions leave behind some remnant of former design on which to build new species. To commit fully to life is not an anti-religious attitude.

What does Colonel Sebastian Moran want from life I wonder? I know that I have heard him speak with enthusiasm of the islands in the great Indonesian archipelago. Will he settle down at last with some dusky maiden and leave a legacy of keen-eyed hunters like himself, perhaps sons to lead their land to freedom from the Dutch traders, or daughters to wed a Muslim Prince? Who may say? He is a man who might still pursue a family if his years of dissipation have not incapacitated him for that role. As for Mycroft and me, ah well, we shall leave the duty to carry on the name of Holmes to Sherringford or to those to whom he wills the estate to keep the name of Holmes alive upon the moors of Yorkshire at the Estate of Sigerside. Detection is a jealous mistress. It is no small matter after all to hone one's talents to a razor-edge of excellence. Loneliness is often the lot of anyone who attempts any large ambition in this world.

Such were my thoughts as we viewed the various vistas over the Mediterranean landscape. At last we arrived at a splendid villa that seemed to grow naturally from the hills. It was made of white stone and consisted of two levels: a terrace below and twin balconies above. We descended from our carriage and the Colonel took me on a tour of the premises. A single servant admitted us to the cool interior. He was an elderly gentleman who bowed to the Colonel and immediately set to work preparing a meal of local fish accompanied with a crisp white wine of local vintage and with an excellent soft-cheese for dessert. The villa was comfortable and simple, just such a home as would suit a man of the Colonel's temperament. There were a few paintings by local artists on the walls but few other adornments. The terrace that reached out to the side of the house with a view of the sea was the Colonel's particular pride. After showing me my room, we descended to lunch on the terrace and it was there that we pursued our conversation as the sea gradually turned to a deeper shade of blue below us with the waning sun.

"Our meals may seem desultory here, Mr. Holmes, but such is the custom in Monte Carlo. We will dine later at the casino, but I promise to have you home by three in the morning. Is that too late for a sober detective? Ah I forget the stable customs of the chemist scholar. Very well, we shall dine at eight and I shall have you home by ten, but it is a pity. There will be fireworks at midnight, but we can see them from here as well. Tell me then, how did your research go in Montpellier?"

I proceeded to tell him about the coal tars and of my daily walks. He listened patiently, for despite his often mocking manner, he had come to respect the seriousness of my endeavors. Colonel Moran valued any man with a set purpose in life when so many are buffeted about by every wind. He shook his head when I admitted that a final remedy for consumption had eluded me, but he congratulated me on the cellular dyes that I had managed to synthesize. He also enjoyed my tales of my walks for he was a man who enjoyed local charm and the peculiar virtues of each place: its sights, its wines, and its local customs. We assumed at once that familiarity we had known during our wanderings. His appeal is of another sort than that of Doctor Watson. It is the charm of Dr.

Watson that he forces me to explain what I am thinking and in doing so I make matters clear to myself. This makes Watson of infinite value to a detective. The Colonel's value to me lies in his habit of contradicting me, a trait that would be wearisome in a constant companion and friend. I cannot say that I am in any way growing fond of the Colonel. Our relations are rather those of mutual respect and a certain kinship of temper. As for Moriarty, he is simply the great inscrutable force he has always been to me. I doubt if I will ever really understand him. Even Watson, who I know so well, has his depths and his surprises. How much more does Professor Moriarty have hidden depths?

I did not think to ask Colonel Moran about the Professor and I believe that the Colonel appreciated my discretion. We both understood by our mutual silence that no objection would be posed from that quarter to my continued absence as I continued my own quest and that I in turn would not inquire about any plans being instituted but yet held in abeyance by the Professor. Our wager is evidently being honored on both sides. The Colonel no longer feels that he must keep me under constant surveillance and I feel no obligation to hasten to England to intercept the Professor's plans. I explained that my stay in Italy would continue through the winter at the very least and when no objection was made, we parted to go to our separate rooms.

My room is a comfortable one, sparsely but tastefully furnished. Its window faces the sea, though its shutters were already fastened against the coming chill of the evening. I had purchased a winter wardrobe in Montpellier and some formal attire as well, suitable for Rome and for our visit that evening to the Grand Casino. I was soon finished with my toilet and descended the stairs to where the Colonel awaited me before a fire in the central room on the first floor. He was sitting before the fire reading and I was amused to see that he needed spectacles for that task. He noticed my smile and took off his glasses with a gruff statement that he could still aim a rifle without their aid. It must be difficult for such a man to notice in himself the first signs of age.

Our carriage awaited us outside and we were soon descending the steep grade in the dark lit only by our carriage lamps. I would have found the journey frightening, but the horses clearly knew the way and the Colonel showed no tension but rather chatted away at my side explaining the intricacies of baccarat and the system of betting on roulette devised so many years before by the Professor that he still used but sparingly to recoup any losses incurred when the cards or dice were less than kind to him.

As we entered the casino and checked our hats and gloves I could see that the Colonel was well known and that whatever fears the management might have of his skill, he was at least a valued visitor to those who served in the casino. We were seated at a table that I could see was reserved for the Colonel's nightly use and the Colonel tipped the host who bowed deeply. We were not troubled by introductions, but I could see that certain persons eyed our table and might have come up if it was not evident that the Colonel was not as it were "at home for visitors" that evening. We were therefore allowed to eat in peace. Our table was situated with a view of the lights in the harbor below us. The ceiling was an ornate one with wainscoting of gold leaf in the style of rococo, but I gave it little notice since I was addressing my attentions to an excellent selection of clams, crab, and lobster served on ice with a unique sauce, the secret of which remains with the establishment I am sorry to say. After an excellent onion soup we were served tenderloin of *boeuf en brochette* and finished our meal with a *crème brulee* flaming in cognac. We finished our meal with a fine Madeira and only then did we rise with some difficulty and enter the casino.

I am afraid that the charms of gambling have no attraction for me. My own abstemious habits do not lend themselves easily to seeing money as mere counters but rather as the means to purchase the necessary items for living. I have never lost the frugal habits of my student years or the years of my early practice when Watson and I shared rooms out of necessity and not as was later the case through the enjoyment of our friendship and the professional pursuit of criminals. I could still appreciate though the strange lure of the scene displayed before me. I could see in the avid eyes of the gambler that desire to thwart the laws of chance that makes us court artificial danger and loss out of a need to court excitement in a weary world. To triumph over chance is its own reward for it implies that our powers may be adequate to address those predictable losses dealt out by fate over which there will be no triumph. The gambling instinct or obsession is akin to that of sport and competition. Our adversary is seldom really our nominal opponent but rather the nature of human limitation as such. We struggle against the laws of time and space. We fight for a graceful balance that will lead us through whatever snare exists that would entrap us. So it is that the alpine skier, the big game hunter, the rugby player, and the detective matched against the criminal are really engaged in the same game of danger and of hopeful triumph in the end. Without a possibility of loss no game is worth the candle.

Is it a game that God plays with us? Certainly our love for God would be easier if we were not so distracted by a complex world that appears to deny God's presence, a world in which even the virtuous man is distracted by the sheer number of his needs even if he is not driven on by wanton desire. To whom then should we direct our indignation in contemplating the human condition? Is that condition a result of the sin of man and woman committed in a time so distant that any former estate we might have enjoyed is so dimly perceived or recalled that we only refer it to a mythic Eden or to a divine force that we imagine might have set all to rights in an instant, but instead launched us upon our course of exile?

Is all of creation really a gamble of God that created beings, with flaws inherent in their nature by simply being created beings, can love an all-perfect-being as it deserves to be loved?   Does God call it sin when the innate weakness of so limited a creation fails to be grateful to one who is so much greater that it can appreciate? Is sin itself a surprise to God? Or is it possible that what we term sin is less a fault of the will than it is a misapprehension of our assigned role? If the metaphysicians are correct in saying that the will, which naturally inclines to the good, would of necessity choose its ultimate good if it could only be clearly perceived, then what man would ever choose complete evil?

It appears that our knowledge is clouded and not our wills. The remedy would appear to be clear: for God simply to step out from behind the curtain of this all-too-flawed world would seem to be the answer.   But then I must recall those words of the gospel where the apostles request naively, "Show us the Father and that will be enough for us." Enough indeed! For if we were to see God whose creation alone is more than the senses may bear or conceive, then how would the mind of man bear the complete sight of God? Our tiny brains would shrivel like a moth in a great flame.

Jesus says that anyone who sees Him has already seen the Father. It appears that the person of Jesus is all that we may bear of God in our present state, so that to know Christ is to know God. This reduces the purpose of life then to a contemplation of the perfections of Christ through the derivative means of Holy Scripture and the living means provided by the Holy Spirit dwelling within us. Out of these two contemplative acts proceeds a life that, insofar as it exceeds the normal capacity of man for mere intellectual virtue, is of divine instigation and origin.   For this reason we revere the saints not for themselves, but for the force of God living within them.

Looking about me in the Grand Casino I saw clearly how distracted we can be from God. I witnessed there among other things the total dedication of the gambler to his craft, fixated upon a mere turning wheel. Even should he win he will only place another bet and again watch the turning wheel as though his entire fate depend upon it. And what of the women whose crystalline eyes and parted lips showed the same fascination with gain obtained by chance. It is the very rarity of winning that makes gambling a thrill. It is matching one's chosen number against all of the others on the green felt so that the number chosen seems for an instant to partake of destiny. How foolish the others were to have chosen a different number on which to risk all, for each turn of the wheel is a unique moment in creation and all the world pauses to wait and see into what slot the ball will come to rest and remain!

Is this same desire in play in what we mean by religion? Is the choice of a faith among the many contenders a mere bet placed with one's entire life at stake? Is the beckoning prospect of heaven just a primordial sweepstakes? Some will end in paradise while the rest will plunge downward into hell judged to be blasphemers or knaves. Surely with stakes like these the casinos of eternity should leave the palaces of earthly pleasures empty and the churches full. Do we gather about a deathbed to ask the most important question of all as the last breath is drawn in order to ponder if the soul is about to enter heaven or hell based upon the final disposition of the soul when it has already flown leaving no sign to bear witness behind of its ultimate fate.

Or are we instead, as the atheists claim, mere dying beasts returning to that primal disorder out of which each form arises, but only for a single brief period of life before merging again with the cosmic matter that might once have been elements of a burning star? Are we really no more than the sediment of a cooling universe? Will everything in the universe, according to the law of entropy, become ashes in the end with matter maximally dispersed and all events past, like a clock that has wound down? Will everything remain in that static state forever in utter unobserved stillness with no one to wind it all up again to produce another season of the vanity of all existing things? Or is there perhaps a demi-god somewhere who may restore all things as a whim, a deity in development who swings the world as the poet says like a trinket at its wrist so that all that we imagine of purpose and of high design is as nothing because we can never know that the God of this universe is not in fact an infant God playing random games with creation?

Perhaps there are other universes in which the problem of evil never occurs because it harbors no moral agents. If we could somehow pass over into these then our moral hungers would be resolved in a non-problematic solution so that all absurd distractions would cease and everyone would become saints as naturally as in this world a stone falls at the same rate regardless of its size. Virtue then would not be as rare; but here, ah here, such is not the case. Few indeed scale Mount Carmel or wander as mendicants in the desert in pursuit of sanctity. Mount Athos is not beset by refugees; nor is Cluny or the Grande Chartreuse of the Cathusians.

As I watched the cards fall on this night in Monte Carlo I could see why the Popes had built the great Basilica of St. Peter's in Rome, hoping to show behind the architectural wonders some earthy symbol of the grandeur and the majesty of God, as though a sunrise was inadequate or the simple miracle of one's own consciousness and ability to perceive was insufficient testimony. The only true temple of God lies within us. God is not to be found by excursion to distant stars but by an act of introspection that is at once the losing of self and the emptying out of the particular. The mystics find God within in actual contact, but unfortunately I am not a mystic. My religion is to feel only compassion for humanity, for the poor children of an hour who seek comfort in the triviality of whatever brief joys come their way. I do not blame them for their vain pursuits.

It is said that Jesus looked upon the milling crowds with compassion for they were like sheep without a shepherd and even from the cross asked forgiveness for his persecutors for they knew not what they did. For this reason we are taught not to despair over the human condition or to grow impatient with human failures and vices as Jonah did. How many latter-day self-appointed prophets and judges wish like Jonah or the apostles that Jesus humorously called, "the sons of thunder," to call down fire from heaven to consume sinners. How many Christians seek to preempt God in rendering judgment on their fellow human beings!

I do not believe that God is playing with us callously or that this is a mindless universe. Nor is heaven the result of a lucky gamble by embracing the right faith, while abjuring all others and their adherents. It may be that heaven and hell are mutually exclusive destinations, but that does not imply that the great prism of purgatory will not include infinite gradations between pure light and pure shadow in the final tutelage of the soul. Each soul will find his proper place there and will know it. Time is inadequate to complete so great a task as getting ready for eternity. What appears an end to our lives in death is important then, but not definitive as to the question of our ultimate abode, which we must leave to God in trust that God will spare no pains to explain the furthest parameters of the redemption of Jesus Christ. But let us strive at least to bring at least a feeble lamp still burning to our deaths that God will not quench by a strict judgment, but rather enhance with His mercy. I believe that the Colonel witnessed my distraction as these thoughts assailed me. "Ah, you are off again into one of your brown studies, Mr. Holmes. But the hour is late. Come, we will return to my villa and watch the firework display from there. You are quite exhausted with your labors; you must stay with me for a few days and rest for I perceive that your researches have tired you. You may then leave for Rome. It will surely be the same whether you arrive tomorrow or in a week. Is it not called the eternal city? I will see you to the train then with a clear mind knowing that you are fit and healthy and able to appreciate the full grandeur of the city."

November 5, 1892
A Debate on History

I have accepted the Colonel's invitation to remain for a time in Monte Carlo. Autumn is well advanced, but there are few signs of it here. I seem to have gone in pursuit of summer and to have finally found it. The warm airs of Africa have delayed winter's advance. We are able to eat lunch on the terrace and the few yellow leaves from the trees seem to hang in empty space when a vagrant breeze blows them over the sea-cliffs. I can watch them for a long way as they drift downwards towards the blue waters. I did not realize how weary I was until I was faced with the actual prospect of rest.

I am somewhat surprised by the hospitality that the Colonel is showing to me. Unless it is all some elaborate ruse I can only conclude that he values using me as a sounding board for his own ideas. Our discussion at luncheon yesterday is an example. I shall try and reproduce it as well as I can although I do not have Watson's facility at dramatic dialogue. We had been discussing Rome.

"I do not share your fascination with Rome," the Colonel began. "It has always seemed to me to be a great dumping-ground of past civilizations. Nothing new can ever live there or flourish. Its very vitality is sucked up by its antiquity. It is a land of ancient resentments and vendettas. You have no doubt remarked that I have a penchant for the new. I do not believe in records, genealogies, or heraldry. I prefer a new spin of the wheel with every play, to take my chances on a new throw of the dice."

I could see that he was probing my own beliefs and preferences by his usual abrupt and conclusive manner of speech. "Have you no loyalties then, Colonel?" I inquired blandly.

He paused before answering. "Loyalties yes, but not the undue respect for heritage that stifles new solutions. I suggest that memory is the enemy of innovation. I prefer to be like the eagles and hawks sailing above the plains below. What are traditions to me? You will recall from our recent travels that I was always glad to get out of the cities and to be in the desert again."

"Yet you wanted to return to Europe if I recall correctly as soon as possible," I remarked.

"Yes, to its comforts, not to its preposterous monuments to the follies of yesterday; to me civilization is simply a matter of comfortable living. I value the desert because it has no memory. It is as new each day as through Babylon had never existed, as though no Pharaoh had ever lived or died in Egypt. I feel something of the same spirit even here in Monte Carlo where everyone dreams of a change of fortune for the better."

"If you do not covet the glories of the past, then what do you covet," I inquired.

"I desire what is new and unspoiled, the untried, the virginal buds of spring," he smiled.

After a pause I pressed him further. "But we are both approaching the autumn of all our own dispositions are we not? If your ideas were as original as you suppose them to be, you would be unable to even formulate your ideas in a common tongue, let alone to argue for their validity by appealing to other people to validate them based upon their own experience. I am afraid that the absolute originality that you covet must necessarily elude you, my dear Colonel. Besides, all ideas were new and untried at one time. To reject the past is to reject the very data of history that would confirm or invalidate any opinion you might entertain. I on the contrary I am loyal to the past because it has been found again and again by succeeding generations to be the source of truth."

"It always comes down to that word does it not, Holmes? Truth is a weapon used as a bludgeon to enforce dogma and dogma is simply a formulation of those with the power to define it. Definition is always a matter of choice by someone. Only deny the masses of people a choice and suddenly truth emerges because someone exists to enforce it! The one who is privileged to define the primary axioms and postulates predetermines the results. I on the contrary prefer my data in their raw form to be assembled to fit the unique situation presented by the demands of the moment. We have spoken before of my recognized expertise as a hunter of tigers. The tiger knows how to probe for weak points in any position. The tiger takes nothing for granted, even its own supremacy of tooth and claw. It is always probing the wind for the alien scent of a hunter. In order to be successful against it then I needed to be always in advance of the tiger's own perceptions; to do or better still to be the unexpected, to be where a moment ago I was not, to move while standing still, to be still even while moving, just as the tiger does."

"But Colonel, you have already chosen the paradigm of hunting and thus biased the relevant data," I observed.

"Oh you noticed that did you? Well, I never claim to play fair. I only give the tiger a chance, because I deem myself to be his superior; but against you I use all of my wits, because I cannot be sure that I will win in the end."

"Is everything a matter of contest and struggle?" I inquired.

"Well that is not a question to ask me is it?" answered the Colonel. "Your conflicts are not mine. We live among various dualisms. Nothing can be thought without implying its opposite at the same time. Even your God must have his devil. Show me any conception without boundaries that define the limits where it does not prevail or apply. Everything slides into something else. Every statement exists in a twilight region of supposition and is an incitement to contradiction. I am not happy to find this so, but I must admit what I observe. That is why I seek the new, the pristine, and the integral in all things, because time has not yet worked its oxidation or decay upon it. Its lines are yet un-blurred by the necessary contention that must come eventually to qualify and modulate. I state every observation as though it was like the atoms of Democritus: hard, unqualified, and substantial. I desire no compounds in my universe. Each moment of time should be discrete and insular with no past or future considerations to dilute or to qualify it."

"You sound like a man who wants to merge eternity into time, Colonel. That is a contradiction that dishonors both," I objected.

"But that is just what religion attempts to do, Holmes. You are the last man who I thought would belittle the religious instinct, in me of all people. Religion asks us to abandon our few comforts in order to purchase some vague and vacuous future state that lies beyond our perceptions and hence our values. Why should my particular "dogma of the moment" be anymore blasphemous than the absurd gardens of an uncertain paradise. Most religious conceptions are really non-conceptions, honored as mysterious merely because they communicate nothing substantial. I propose the opposite: that each concrete thing and action should be viewed as sacred and irreplaceable because it is unique and passes away. Apply that morality and see if it would ever yield the same record of slaughter and rapine as the Crusades and tell me which religion manifests the higher morality."

I was silent as I considered what he had just said. I tried to imagine a world without standards, one based merely upon survival and upon present opportunity.

He continued, "But we were speaking of Rome. Let me apply my theory to that so-called Eternal City. Rome is the perfect exemplar of all that desires our admiration. It overwhelms us with spectacle. It shouts when a whisper would be sufficient to impart any real truth. I would be far more likely to believe a rumor of an empty tomb on a barren hillside in Jerusalem than a trumpeted dogma, one so often repeated that it has lost its ability to surprise us with its improbability. Only compare this to naked facts that have yet to be reduced to complex assertions that fit into larger structures of thought or belief. The small things of the world are their own witness. People lament that the gospels were not longer, but look at the mischief caused by the fact that they contain as much as they do. Think of the hairsplitting and web-weaving of the various theological positions that seek their source and substance in what is termed divine revelation! Must I learn Hebrew and Greek to know that I must not sleep with a woman who is not my wife or rob my neighbor? Not because these laws are commanded, but because I encounter the immediate consequences for my actions on the grounds of human reactions. Oh do not smile Mr. Holmes. My prior talk of bordellos was merely to live up to your prior conception of me as a wastrel. I trust that my liaisons follow a stricter morality than that of many Christians who go groveling to God for a forgiveness that finds no remedy in the actual affairs of mankind."

He paused to light a cigar and offer me one as well before continuing. "What I am asserting is that history, which begins as accident concludes with being considered inevitable. We are led to believe that the Kings and Queens were noble in their actions rather than the brigands that most of them actually were. Similarly we are led to believe that God has spoken from burning bushes and in the fragmentary utterances of fevered prophets rather than simply taking what they have said as a working hypothesis for future testing by human experience. Morality is always a generalization and life is often too complex to be governed by general rules."

I objected, "Generalities save us the burden of re-devising rules each time we encounter something. They set up zones of expectation that let us predict results."

He sneered, "If moral rules were that useful, then they would be more universally obeyed. Tell me whether most Christians don't embrace as much sin as the rule allows or venture into forbidden zones and then scurry for cover as quickly as possible. Even children steal as much candy from the dish as they can before it can no longer escape notice. Religion breeds hypocrisy. We condemn others for what we would like to do ourselves. Rome is simply the most egregious exemplar of the poor taste of humanity in its choice of religions. Rome is like the music of Wagner: lacking melody it hopes to succeed by simply increasing the volume of the orchestra and adding a few more helmeted maidens. It was a mistake for the church to have ever left Jerusalem. What Jesus asked of his followers was designed for tiny desert enclaves, not for the wider world. The church leaders should have left the first Roman Pontiffs, the Caesars, unchallenged on their malarial Italian plain. The early church presided over by St. James and his concern for the poor provided a better model. Even today it is not too late. If the Popes could go to Avignon, then why not return to Jerusalem? Of course even the Holy Land has known its excesses. I would extend the prohibition against idolatry and image-making to political structures as well. Cathedrals, temples, and mosques would all alike be prohibited until mankind becomes content to simply kneel on the barren stones of earth among the weeds to invoke their gods and maybe by doing so they will actually find their God at last."

We both sat gazing out into the empty space where a few seabirds disported themselves in the vagrant airs. They would ride one current upward before plunging downwards again towards the sea in pursuit of their prey. After a time the Colonel looked up at me.

"Have you nothing to say, Holmes. I fear that I have been a poor host and have exhausted you with my rambling thoughts. Perhaps you should go in and sleep after dinner. I think the casino can spare me for an evening. My cook prepares an excellent sea-bass."

I smiled over at him. "I have only this to say to you my dear Colonel; it appears to me that you are not far from the Kingdom of God." With this cryptic utterance, one that is still cryptic even to me, I stood up and shook his hand before we both went into the house closing the doors to the terrace and the setting sun.

November 8, 1892
A Brief Reflection on Truth

My discussion two days ago with the Colonel has forced me to deal with the idea that primary ideas are merely a matter of arbitrary definition. I have time to do so today because the Colonel has left me quite alone. He is out upon the waters of the Mediterranean today with several local fishermen and he has promised to bring in some flounder and calamari at least for our dinner. The search for truth is not unlike fishing because one must bait one's hook with some previous truth of which one is certain. The size of the hook determines the size of the catch. There is no doubt that at this time I am engaged in trying to bring in the largest of fishes, the ideas that are termed transcendent. They are termed thus because they cannot be reduced to mere experience. Instead, these truths are what Locke and Kant called categories. These ideas guide perceptions into channels or nets where they can be caught and examined. The human mind works by placing things in groups and comparing similarities and dissimilarities. From this process one develops what might be called the great taxonomy of being in which all things are connected in various relationships existing in space and time. The linkages are similarly examined and refined. But when this process is through there still remains the question of ascertaining whether the resulting whole has any relation to a purpose or design that is beyond itself. It is here that mankind seeks a great analogy to our own partial intentionality: considering all things precisely in their totality.

This question is as simple as the act of addressing a great "Why" to all that is. The answer has always been that there must be a source and end for all things that cannot be equivalent to their mere act of existing. Things exist, according to this view, as a partial manifestation of an ultimate divine intent. Things are insufficient in themselves to account for their own being. Most of the proofs for God can be reduced to this fundamental intuition that all that we know cannot be closed in upon itself and self-subsistent, but must refer its origin and end upon something greater than itself. This "greater than" is more of a direction of course rather than something that is in itself capable of being comprehended. We cannot surround and reduce to an object of thought what is beyond all thought.

This of course creates a gap between our capacities as thinkers and our desire for complete knowledge. For this reason we posit the concept of revelation in which God turns about as it were and comes to us rather than prolonging the infinite chase of humanity to grasp the trailing vestments of God (to use a metaphor). God does more than this "turning about" in the belief of Christianity; He actually enters into the knower by assuming our very limitations of mind and body through the Incarnation of the Second Person of the Blessed Trinity. By union with Christ through Baptism we are made capable of pleasing God and fulfilling our assigned role in creation.

Whether this theistic view makes any sense at all requires that we compare it with the alternative position. If God exceeds his own creation then he cannot be grasped without His prior consent, because we cannot close with him in the chase. God is the beyond in both space and time to any definition that we can ever posit for Him. Since all human truth requires observation or perception as its basis our line must always fall short of the fish that we seek to capture. We are left then with only the alternative, which the 17th century Jewish philosopher Baruch de Spinoza chose, which was to assume that God was simply the totality of things knowable, even if not yet known. This position reduced God to being co-extensive with all phenomena that were at least theoretically observable in their totality if our instruments could make all things theoretically observable.

This totality need not be conscious of itself though as a totality. It was sufficient that man as knower could take a position toward the totality of things even though they are greater than us. This view closes man off from the possibility of transcendent truth because it shifts the responsibility for ultimate meaning to us alone. The possible shrinks then to the measure of our mind or at most our potential mind in some distant hypothesized state of total perception and total cognition of what our minds have perceived. This abdication from a simple acceptance of whatever God chooses to reveal is arbitrary in the extreme because it simply means that we refuse to imagine a realm and degree of being that exceeds all created being, but this is merely an assumption and a decision and can never be proven. We cannot disprove the existence of a transcendent God. To make a choice of denial without persuasive data to support that assertion is arbitrary by definition.

The definition of God as co-extensive with the knowable of course also changes the definition of man. Instead of having a purpose that exists in the transcendent mind of God, man becomes an end unto himself. He becomes a mere vehicle by which being assumes descriptive form in the mind insofar as any individual man cares to exercise this capacity during his short life. The only "transcendence" then available to us is the "transcendence" of the historical enterprise as such, which is none other than the collective memory of mankind in art, science, music, and technology. This means that any ultimate purpose must emerge from within our own nature to simply fulfill our capacities of thought and action in a material universe. The problem with this position of course is that it is doubly unsatisfactory to human needs. If we are only secretaries to all that surrounds us transcribing it into our own cramped script of ideas then who has set us this task, particularly when so few pursue it beyond what is necessary to sustain their animal existence.

The second objection to this view of Spinoza is that even the most ingenious of us will never succeed in grasping the whole. We become then like the ants with each of us carrying our unique grain of sand, but with no conception of how his effort plays a part in the life of the entire colony. Time becomes a prison from which we cannot escape. Any possibility of transcendent thought has its origin in the myth of Eden where we demanded to be like God knowing good and evil and far more we demanded access to the other tree that would allow us to live forever, assuming that an infinite futurity would allow us time to catch up with God and be as gods ourselves. But this we can never do because God is not a subject of objective knowledge using the human knowing apparatus. God is only comprehensible in Himself and to Himself. We cannot reach heaven by using the building blocks of creation, even if we had an infinite future before us in which to attempt to do so. The problem of attaining transcendent truth then is reducible to the humble acceptance of the parameters of our human capacities.

The modality then of transcendent truth can only be grasped by desire and not by knowledge. Our mere desire for God is the best proof of the existence of God, as Soren Kierkegaard has made clear by referring to the ultimate truth as subjectivity or as it might be more clearly expressed to our awareness of our situation as souls encased in bodies with both encapsulated in the chrysalis of time and space.

The first step to God then is to surrender making statements about God and to adopt an attitude of questioning and of supplication, which is a good definition of prayer. Only then does God as God reveal Himself to us. To the God who is more attainable by prayer than by knowledge I am at present concerned, not as a self-sufficient detective, but as a desperate man caught in the web of good and evil. This is merely to say that I am a man aware of my own position at sea bobbing about on the waves and hoping that I may stay afloat until I am rescued or as St. Paul once cried, with no doubt a similar assessment of the human condition, "Who will deliver me from this body of death?"

Colonel Moran returned with a broad smile and with three great flounders and a bucket-full of the purple-mantled calamari for our supper. He inquired how I had spent the day and I explained that I too have been fishing in my fashion. He gave me a quizzical look before going upstairs to his room to change out of his oil-skins, to bathe, and to clothe himself for dinner. I do not quarrel with the comforts of our animal nature. Whether one fishes for fish or for men or for God one does well as a human being. I think I shall close now and rest for an hour before dinner. I already seem to smell the aroma of garlic and vermouth wafting up from the kitchen of the batter-dipped and breaded calamari. I am daily regaining my strength here.

November 12, 1892
Monte Carlo

Today was a day of drenching rain and we were driven indoors from our usual place of discussion on the terrace. The confinement led to a degree of irritability in the Colonel. He returned to his old mocking demeanor.

"I was reviewing some of the old issues of the Strand Magazine this morning and I remarked, not for the first time, the trivial nature of many of your cases, Mr. Sherlock Holmes. You appear to be the court of last resort for confused members of the fair sex or for some befuddled gentleman perhaps who is re-living an old passion. Your Dr. Watson seems to enjoy the thrill of melodrama in recounting such episodes, but I hope that you will not take it amiss if I say that even you seem at times to credit the testimony of persons driven and deluded by the goddess Venus and her daughters who make fools of men."

I made no answer to him so he continued. "Ah, I strike a sore point! Forgive my mentioning it, but as long as we are confined here today you may profit from my own views on women, since you have so little experience with them at close quarters yourself."

"Well I am your guest sir and you must please yourself," I answered.

"I will take that as an assent. Very well, my first point is that no woman is ever to be taken seriously. They do not even wish to be. A woman's opinions are mere toys that she uses tactically to entice a man. Her position on any question is as changeable as her most recent impulse dictates. I take it as my first axiom in dealing with women to only appear to listen to them. To assume any fixed position in trying to agree with them is to fall into a trap for they are sure to contradict themselves upon the morrow and resent your more accurate phrasing and advocacy of the position that they formerly held. Shall I go on?"

"Please do," I answered eager as I was to penetrate deeper into the inner character of the man before me.

"Very well, second then, I always make it a point to maintain a demeanor that will manifest that beyond the throes of a temporary ardent display towards them I can only afford a short span of attention to listen to their inevitable and manifold discontents. Few if any women are satisfied for long because they are always comparing their station in life to that of their friends. Competition among women exceeds even that among men.”

"Third, I make it a point to remind myself constantly that every woman is a mere agent of the will of the life-force to reproduce itself. No woman really ever exists as an individual. She is merely a temporary manifestation of the various throbbing nutrient tissues that are designed to sustain the species. Her time is divided between various processes of gestation and needless tears over the disappointment of her superfluous desire. She will never be satisfied because happiness is to her as oil is to water.”

"Fourth, since she cannot be made happy or faithful I make it my aim to ensure that at least one party in romance will emerge from any encounter with them somewhat better off than he was before. I need not say that I am referring to myself. Women have their own unique utility. They can be light and amusing companions on occasion. It is when they assume that their services are not subject to instant source substitution that they are most vexing. A woman is happiest, note I did not say happy but happiest, when she feels that she has somehow gained an evolutionary edge over her numerous sisters in the choice of a mate whom she will then arduously milk nightly until she has attained nature’s end. After that she will calmly gestate for a time before burdening this sorry earth with another human being.”

"Fifth, I take nature itself as my guide in apportioning my interest in them. Once her childbearing age is past woman swiftly reveals her true inner nature as she metamorphoses into the dreadful harpy or gorgon that she always was beneath her dewy eyes and beckoning lips. Just as nature allows her to dry-up like some blossom of yesterday before dropping off to the earth that awaits her, I dismiss her once the blush is off the rose rather than await the inevitable final metamorphosis.”

"Sixth, if this attitude of mine seems harsh or self-serving I merely ask you to sit and listen to old women around a well in some Italian village. You will find that the toothless hags are still mourning over whichever man treated them most harshly and unfaithfully in life. Women despise men who value them at their own estimation, because only they are truly aware of their own duplicity. Should she find a decent man for a spouse whose actual care for her has made her life possible, she will forget him in preference for the men she was not able to obtain. Her husband's ashes will lie forgotten in his grave, a grave that was no doubt prematurely occupied by any poor devil who desired to please and serve her while he was alive."

Seventh, the primary function and loyalty (if she has any) of woman is directed towards her children not to her mate. She chooses a husband for his utility to her own purposes, the continuation of life. Woman is the guardian of the species; she has little time for anything else. It is men who engage in all the fripperies of this world. It is men who build pyramids to preserve their name and glory. Women know that strength and beauty are temporary gifts and they surrender both in the process of raising their young. Vanity in women is a means to an end. Seduction is their stock in trade. Men are foolish enough to believe in their own charm, forgetting that as men they are mere appendages to a woman's ambition for a better life for her and for her offspring.

I objected at this point. "Certainly, there are exceptions to each of your points," I said quietly.

"If so they are few, and hardly worth the trouble of pointing them out," he replied. "All conflict and disappointment with the female sex ceases when a man simply accepts the fact that most women run true to form. I really do advise you, whenever you return to London, to restrict your practice to cases where the game is worth the candle. Give it over Mr. Holmes. You are far too talented to waste your resources by swimming upstream against what the gods themselves have ordained in the relations between the sexes. Whenever you see a woman, think of some massive and ineluctable force, one that is hungry and insatiable, or think of some noxious tropical plant where the very leaves and spiced pistil lures the questing fly into its secret chamber of death. Remember the fate of the drone bees dropping down like so many flaming sparks after mating with the queen. Think always of the medusa and the sirens. Do this and all will turn out quite well for you. Only reflect that nature would not go to such trouble to enhance a woman's charms with unnecessary accoutrements if she were anything in herself. Woman is a transit point between death and life and man, lest you think that my pessimism is mere misogyny, perhaps even less."

"You do not value life then, Colonel?" I asked.

"I value it as long as it lasts, but in itself life is nothing but a brief respite between two states of oblivion. Death is the only real universal. It is the final destination of all things. Any resuscitation to our former state, unless followed swiftly by a renewal of repose would be a foolish torture. The Buddha was correct in stating the first noble truth, that all is suffering. Buddhism takes the abandonment of hope as its first principle. Dante's inscription at the gate to the Inferno, 'Abandon all hope you who enter here' should not be inscribed over the gates of hell alone but over every cradle for constant contemplation. Whenever I see an infant I say to myself, 'Poor little man, how long you must endure the mockery of fate until you may die at last.'"

We were both silent for a time gazing out over the cliffs to the gray Mediterranean far below. "Then why do you not make an instant end of yourself, Colonel?" I asked. "Since you find life to be so burdensome why haven't you sought nirvana rather than pleasure in this place of earthly paradise, Monte Carlo?"

He smiled at me with his usual mischief, "And leave you here to drink my wine and wire Scotland Yard that one of the greatest criminals of the age has met his justly deserved end? Why you must be mad!"

He laughed at me before pouring us both a glass of rich and deep red wine and smiling at me in a way that was both sad and mocking our conversation drifted off into other topics. Was he serious in all that he had said or was he displaying the technique of baiting the tiger that had made him one of the best big-game shots in all of India?

November 24, 1892
En route to Rome

Reflecting on our conversation during the following days I could see that many people might find in Colonel Moran an example of the charming rogue, but there was also something profoundly lonely in his conception of human life and in the cynicism evident in his views on women. For my part the idealization of the female sex that has held sway since the French troubadours was of the very essence of life and of poetry. Although I am not as romantic as Watson, my esteem and respect for the female sex has never wavered and I still recall my French mother with deep fondness and respect. My love of music and the appreciation of the natural world and even my habits of exact perception I owe to her.

The few days that I agreed to spend with the Colonel have extended beyond my original intentions. I was more tired than I had thought and more pleased with my situation in Monaco with Colonel Moran than I ever expected. I had been losing weight over the summer and the head of the medical faculty had warned me about a persistent cough before I left the university. I assured him that I would be following a quiet regimen in Rome and that the sunny air of Italy and its excellent food would soon revive me. My research work had been demanding and I had spent many hours on my feet in the laboratory each day. My arduous travels had also been a strain to my constitution after my many years of sedentary living in London.

The sea air of Monte Carlo soon worked its magic and I began to improve. The Colonel had a fine cook and I spent my days reading on the terrace that overlooked the city and the sea beyond. After our first day the Colonel pursued the normal round of his life. We would share breakfast and he would then depart leaving me to my own resources. The Colonel has the blessed gift of silence and knows how to respect the needs of a man who is as solitary as himself. Our time together then was both amicable and salutary for me. So when I took the train for Rome today he smiled and wished me well.

"I see that you are not yet ready to take on the Professor and return to London. Instead you are now enroute to Rome where perhaps a few novenas may assist your cause. I appreciate that during our time together you did not insist on pumping me for information about the professor's activities. As a reward I will give you something to mull over, an insight if you will into the Professor's character. He is above all else a man of science and for that very reason objective. A really objective man is a man immune from popular appeal. Principled men are the opposite from the self-interested individuals that you and I encounter each day. These are beyond the usual motive forces for principled action. They adhere instead to the principle of necessity in everything that they do, just as nature does."

"In dealing with the Professor you will not succeed in appealing to the humanity of the Professor for he has none. He is a force, an equation, like a series of numbers reaching into the infinite. He is immune from even possessing a personal history. Indeed, I am not at all sure that even using personal pronouns is apt in his case. Do not attempt then to understand him as though he weighs his actions in the crucible of the affections before determining on a course of action. Instead you must deduce his next move from all that has gone before just as the movement of a mighty glacier may be discovered by the path of the debris that it has left behind."

"So off you go now to that stronghold of your faith, Mr. Sherlock Holmes. No doubt you will see the Pope while you are there. Be sure that you ask him about the crusades and the inquisition, won't you? I am sorry that I will not be able to tag along to compare the Christian Mecca to that of the Mohammedans, but I am sure there will be little difference in attitude with pilgrims everywhere present and the black-clad penguins milling about with all the incense and the bowing at various statues, with tombs everywhere you can look, and a few mummified bodies preserved in wax and adorned with silver, all testaments to survival after death, as though one life is not enough for us."

"You wouldn't care then for one more spin of the wheel Colonel in an afterlife?" I inquired.

He answered at once. "I hope to live with sufficient intensity that when it comes time for me to die, I will be ready to set it all aside and to take my rest in oblivion. Let some other poor fool take my place and run about the globe. Is my consciousness so unique that it should be preserved? There will always be men and women and as long as there are, there will be the same round of human folly, joy, and sorrow. Surely that is its own sort of immortality. The species remains; the type is preserved. The individual embodiment passes. We are droplets in the stream Holmes; we are mere waves upon the shore."

As the train began to move he kept talking. "What difference if the wave breaks as long as the ocean remains? But go along to Rome that great conservator of corpses. Tour the catacombs and ask them if they think the resurrection day is near. It's been almost two thousand years you know and still the great awakening has not arrived. Surely the hour is late and the arch of time should be fulfilled by now. Rome has been shifting bones about and blessing altars everywhere with them for nearly two-thousand years!"

He handed me a note through the window as a parting gift. It read as follows:

The Chinese throw the I-Ching yarrow wands down in order to choose a hexagram by chance. Each hexagram represents a recurring situation met in life. The wise man adapts to the conditions suggested by that hexagram so as to attune himself to the rhythm of the world around him. There is no entity that governs chance in this system. Instead, chance itself is presumed to be more accurate than the most careful of human plans and prognostications. To learn to adapt to a configuration chosen by random throws of sticks serves to break the seeker away from set patterns and the belief that we can control our fate. Similarly, the American Indians when going into battle shout, 'Today is a good day to die' and ride off letting their spirits go free. Christians in contrast have come to despise life and to worship death. They insist on hanging onto relics and dragging up old bodies on a promised resurrection day. Who needs the bodies or even a remembrance of the dead? Human progress is proportionate to the ability to forget and to start anew. Jesus had it right when he said, 'Let the dead bury their dead.' My advice to you is to accept death, Sherlock Holmes, but first for God's sake live!"

Of course I would have pointed out if he could hear me over the sound of the departing train that his last admonition was precisely what I intended to do, to live for God's sake.

Later—

Such was my parting with the man who was still the same old mocking Colonel Sebastian Moran. It would make no sense to explain to him that a glorified body on the Day of Resurrection has special characteristics, such as impassibility, because he would only ask me to produce evidence rather than faith. I am afraid that he is a hardened skeptic after all and that faith for him will not be an easy acquisition. Behind his bluster I sense fear of his loss of identity and power. He would not have labored so hard to build up his own mythos and to alter history with his own version of justice if he held his own individuality in contempt as he pretends. He has his own worship of death.

I am on my own once again. To be distant from one's homeland is to feel the full measure of human isolation. It is one thing to claim to be a social solitary when motherly Mrs. Hudson is downstairs ready to bustle about and bring some food up to her difficult lodger and quite a different thing to see only strangers all about me and never to hear the music of one's native tongue. Daily I miss my good friend Dr. Watson. The dear old fellow has grown to be the echo of my own thoughts so that merely to assemble a case in my own mind, without first thinking through how I will explain to Watson the facts of the case, makes me realize that detection is less the exact science that I always pretend that it is. Perhaps all knowledge is formed through dialogue. We cannot think alone. Even in our most private thoughts we imagine an invisible auditor and witness. The mind of man is therefore already adapted to the presence of God through prayer.

My train passed through Nice and we were soon at the Italian border station where I showed both my passport and my visa. The train then sped southward along the Italian Rivera with its rough seacoast. I caught a connecting train in Genoa for Florence and spent a night in a hotel there with a view of the

Duomo. I woke to sunshine and took a walk along the Arno after breakfast before catching a late morning train for Rome.

Visiting Italy always makes me lighthearted. I enjoy the simple faith of the people, so different from the melancholy musings of the German mind. For the Italians the Catholic faith is as familiar as bread, wine, and children. These are truly the little ones spoken of by Our Savior. Jesus assured us that we would not enter heaven until we accepted heaven with all of the simplicity of a child. Christianity is not after all a matter of books. It is a lived faith.

The face of the Catholic Church is present in its people. The strength of the faith reposes in their unspoken trust in God. Christianity is not a matter of gnosis but of lived charity and of prayer. The Italians know the essentials of life and they concentrate upon them. There is no need here for a Hume, a Kant, or a Descartes but only for wine and cheese and bread and daily mass. I rate a nation's happiness in inverse ratio to the number of philosophers and generals it produces. Knowledge and power are the twin idols of human ambition and ambition seldom yields joy.

Hills and plains dotted with olive groves surrounded my train as it sped through the Italian countryside. The approach to Rome was as always swift and sudden. The brown and ancient houses were no sooner about me it seemed then I was pulling into the great railroad station with its noise and milling people. I managed to alight upon the platform with my luggage intact after the pushing and shoving and to avoid the many vendors as I pushed through the crowds to the great circular drive outside the station where I hailed a cab to take me to my hotel. I have arrived in the Eternal City.

December 1, 1892
Rome

My first days in Rome have been spent in the usual adjustment to its great scale. Rome is so extravagant and monumental that every other city seems by force of contrast to be an exercise in the diminutive. Perhaps it is only in Rome that man and woman are given their full stature as children of God. Others may find this scale to be absurd and bombastic like those laboring figures holding up the columns in the entrance hall of the Hapsburg Emperor in Vienna. I must admit to a preference for the graceful architecture of the French. Paris will always be my choice for the most beautiful city in Europe.

Still, there is a certain masculine vigor in Rome and a substantiality that will not be moved by time. Rome has clearly asserted its claim to the eternal and to the certainty that here is the home of Christianity. It is no wonder that the kings of every nation have guarded what they believed to be their own divine prerogatives against the greatest absolute monarchy that the world has ever known, the monarchy represented by the Papacy. As an office the Papacy was coveted by the great families who vied with each other to capture the office of the Supreme Pontiff who seemed more often to be in his splendor the successor to Caesar than to Jesus or to St. Peter on whom the claim to papal supremacy rests.

This was the scandal that splintered the church in the 16th century, a fragmentation from which Christendom has yet to recover. Why was the authority that had been the bastion of Christian governance for so long suddenly intolerable? Was it not that the full flowering of the Renaissance had placed the individual consciousness at the center of the relationship to God, whereas before that relation was a corporate one between the entire Catholic Church and God? It was not then due to simply the corruption of the Popes that brought about the reforms of Luther and Calvin, but rather that for the first time men dared to approach God as an individual and to read Holy Scripture as a personal address, rather than as one addressed to an entire unified community as an organic whole.

The lens through which man had viewed God changed in the 16th century. Man for the first time entertained the possibility that as a single mind he might hear "the word of God" and discern its meaning as an individual summons. The comforting motherhood of the Catholic Church and the visible mediation of grace conveyed by the Seven Sacraments no longer conveyed the guidance and comfort of spiritual childhood. But in daring thus to approach God directly there was a great terror and a need for an absolute conviction that one was saved. No longer could the soul remain in peace while the collective Mystical Body of Christ engaged in its long discernment of doctrine, a task that extended over centuries. Now all must be certain and complete within a single lifetime and all Christians must agree in a common revelation but one accessible to each man by simply reading scripture. To the protestant mind faith must be formulaic, clear, and accessible. One need only open the Bible and all would be clear.

But of course Holy Scripture is not clear and final and never has been. It took four centuries to settle even the questions regarding the nature of Jesus as both God and man. To approach the questions of faith as though each of us stands alone in the human drama is insupportable and the Catholic Church in its collective wisdom has always known this. Any other questions exist along a gradient of degrees of affirmation and certitude, but the question of religion involves our entire nature as human beings. We are engaged in sawing away at the very bough that supports our own sense of what it means to be a human being at all. If humans are not engaged in some manner of dialogue with God, then our existence as such becomes the blind summons to a transcendent order that exists only within our own conceptions. All transcendent notions then become the mere froth of an excited brain and of the linguistic structures we build to express and to contain meaning. In contrast, the efforts of Zen as practiced in Japan to escape the mind and to create a temporal eternity by suspending our faculties or by treating our ability to make distinctions as arbitrary avails us nothing for always at our back we will still hear the roaring breakers of death that will one day encompass us, a state in which the meditating mind will cease to operate.

Meditation does nothing to reverse or to achieve our efforts to escape death or even to embrace it for the very reason that the discipline required to achieve even that suspended state of consciousness requires effort, an effort to escape our own desire to persist and to endure as individuals. As such Zen mediation only reaches the nadir of human fulfillment by cancelling the very means by which we mediate at all. What is called an awakening to the vanity of thought must then use that very vehicle for one last time if only to deny the very distinction by which it makes that final judgment.

To use mind to deny mind is a contradiction. To this the Zen practitioner would answer that if contradiction itself is the ultimate metaphysic, then so be it. Any means towards the practical end of suspending the froth of thought in order to return to the still pool of being is justified. The problem of human existence is thus solved by assuming that the problem itself is an illusion. A passionless existence thus becomes truth. All things reach a common stasis in a metaphysical equally of non-consciousness: rocks, animals, and humans become one. Thought turns itself inside out as it were and discovers the appeal of non-thought.

Of course this leaves unresolved the question of why we should have been put to the task of thinking our way out of thought in the first place. Surely stones do not experience a similar need and with that realization the problem of our own existence re-emerges in full force for if we can be taught to cooperate in our own extinction by accepting it gladly, we can still not deny that we might have resisted, however fruitlessly, the loss of our individual existence.

Even if our memory is lost and in this way we die before we die, even if one is of feeble mind, or even an infant and as such fail to be able to conceive the loss of what has been, even if one had not been conceived at all, then by proxy as it were those who remain would be able to hope for their restoration and for these limited ones to pursue the quest for God that is still our primal definition as a human-being. The search for an ultimate horizon, or rather that which lies beyond all horizons, is innate in us.

As such the question of God and the question of the human are identical. To think of man without God is impossible without denying what we already know of ourselves and our capacity for good and evil. This means that we must be grateful in a sense to that couple in the Garden of Eden for in attempting to be like God knowing good and evil they bound all of us forever to seek God. We cannot endure our own nakedness and need, nor can we endure the curse of eternity if God does not fill that eternity with His love.

There is no shame then in being in need of God, just as there is no shame for the eye to see or for the ear to hear. There could be no worse fate than to be locked into the prison of solitary thought without God. Even God exists is a Trinity. Stones know the embrace of other stones. The problem of evil then is not an obstacle, but is instead the very road to God. The greatest of all evils, which was to crucify Jesus, who was the Christ and the Son of Man, becomes the ultimate denial of our own constitution as man and as woman.

The Crucifixion of Jesus Christ then was not a mere

historical accident. Evil must attack what is divine in man and in woman. The two-part human nature means that even the human is not one full organism in solitude nor is even a marriage complete without the Holy Spirit to sustain it. Jesus always called himself the Son of Man and even in His divinity did not abjure His human nature. So needy was Jesus in fact that it was a comfort for Him in his human nature to know that others were near for support, even on that last night when His friends would soon abandon him. The cross that followed on the next day of His crucifixion is visible evidence that even when we crucify and deny that vestige of ourselves that is still open to the image of God within us, God will pursue us even into death itself. This is Love indeed!

The Sign of the Cross then is constitutive of the human condition itself. To be human at all is to be in relation to the Cross of Christ even if one is not a Christian. For this reason the final word on man is the Living Word of God, Jesus the Christ. We are born into potential relation with God as revealed in Christianity. Formal Baptism simply acknowledges that fact and begins a lifetime of acting in accord with the human condition by being made more fully human by becoming ever more like Jesus, the image of God in man and woman.

December 4, 1892
The Vatican

During my time in Mecca I was able to see how the Christian concept of the Church differs from the Mohammedan concept of the Ummah. As I watched the crowds milling about the Kaaba I was reminded of a great beehive with the workers dancing about the queen. My little monograph of observations regarding the segregation of the queen, which drew attention from beekeepers even as far off as America, has given me a particular sensitivity to the role of centrality in any authority structure. In a beehive the workers have subordinated their own potential for individual realization to pursue their various functions for the good of the hive as a whole. That interest, when reduced to its most basic function, is to serve the queen. Her role in turn is to produce more bees. No hive can survive the presence of two queens, so that when the hive reaches a certain size the bees must swarm in pursuit of a new queen.

Similarly the greatest struggle in Islam is to clearly define the borders of the Ummah or community of believers each of whom has made an individual submission to Allah. Islam has never resolved the question of the proper successor to Mohammed and has thus been divided since the death of the Prophet Mohammed. The hive is divided so that each believer must discern to which side of Islam he should align himself. In relation to God each believer stands naked to the mercy of Allah. There is no sacramental order or priesthood or sacrifice for sins, no definitive ordained College of Bishops to teach and to interpret, to bind and to loose. The believer is at sea as to which sect to which to ally himself.

In contrast the Christian Church to whom Jesus Christ assigned a role of unity from the beginning in the rock of St. Peter and his successors in the Holy See, the Popes provide a central center as the Vicar of Christ. Even a Church Council is always gathered about the Pope and may not proceed without him. His role is to preserve unity and faith among the College of Bishops so gathered so that the entire body in all its diversity acts as one in its worship and teaching. In his task he is guided by the Holy Spirit of love and by fraternal charity to be exercised so that no soul entrusted to the Church may be lost. The entire Church is ordained toward the salvation of each soul. All of the sacramental activity and prayer form one Communion of Saints. Each member of the Church may draw upon that vast treasury in life and in death for it is the desire of Christ that not one soul, given to Him by the Father, should be lost.

In Christianity then the normal order of precedence is inverted, the Catholic Church is truly a mother who will give all for her child, in which the preferred is the one child who most needs her care. The Catholic is taught never to despair in his solitude, because the entire merits of the Church and the fullness of grace in Christ are at his disposal. The Church exists to save sinners. To be a Catholic though is not to be absorbed into an amorphous mass. The worship of the Catholic is that of a son or daughter of God. God deals with each soul as an integral and unique part of the Body of Christ. Our identity is not lost before God, but subsumed through the mediation of the continuing sacrifice of the Mass into Christ who is both with God and in God. In such an action there can be no division, thus the Church is one through the grace bestowed by the merits of Christ to His Mystical Body, the One Holy Catholic and Apostolic Church.

In all of this, the function of the Pope is to be a servant to the servants of God. The one who wishes to be greatest in the Kingdom of God, as Jesus said, must aspire to be the least of all and the servant of all. The power and the majesty of the Papacy then is a concession to our need to surround what is precious with honor. In Himself the Pope is nothing. He is burdened with splendor solely to honor the Lord whom he serves. The Pope is if anything owned by the faithful, the fractious children of God. To be the Pope is to know the suffering of Christ for sin. To accept that austere office then is to accept the cross at its most bitter. Thank heaven that most people are spared this trial. These were my thoughts as I awaited a private audience with Pope Leo XIII. I was on my knees before the altar in St. Peter's Basilica when a Monsignor came and lightly touched the sleeve of my coat to bid me to follow him. I was led through a maze of immense halls and finally shown into a simply appointed parlor where I was left alone for a few minutes.

I was soon joined by the Pope who suffered me to kiss the ring of St. Peter in homage to his office. He then sat down in a chair facing me. He is a small man with piercing, intelligent eyes. His small stature belies his immense vitality. To see him was like being in the presence of a bright glowing ember. He was from the start friendly and inquisitive, which put me much at ease.

"Mr. Holmes, we are delighted to see you and to express our gratitude once again for the efforts that resulted in the return of the precious Vatican Cameos, an affair that you handled with discretion. They are in their way priceless and the good father who acts as curator of the Vatican Museum was much relieved at their return. They are a part of history, one of the burdens of being a custodian of the artifacts attendant upon our office."

I accepted his thanks, so graciously phrased with a nod, and the Pope continued, "You may imagine our surprise at hearing from you for we had read, in a sad account written by Dr. Watson, that England had lost its greatest detective at the falls of Reichenbach. That you are alive brings us great joy. Your unsigned note to our person stated facts about the case of the Vatican Cameos that only you could have known. That removed any doubts that you are indeed Sherlock Holmes and alive. How did you come to survive Sir?"

I explained briefly the actual events that had occurred and explained that I had been abroad in Asia, Africa, and France ever since and that my survival still needed to be kept secret for a time, since I was engaged in a case the outcome of which would affect all of Great Britain. The Pope nodded at the conclusion of my explanations and inquired about Professor Moriarty.

He said, "This man, who you have termed, the Napoleon of Crime, still lives also. This wager you have made, how very curious it is. One does not usually bargain with the devil as he is a liar and does not honor his bargains, particularly those made at his own expense. Yet you have trusted this man who is your foe. He must then not be completely surrendered to evil."

"That is correct Your Holiness. I may tell you in all honesty that Professor Moriarty believes that he is a great benefactor to the human race. He is dedicated to ridding the world of evil through his own peculiar means of crime. Murder, blackmail, extortion, and theft are his tools and they have been exercised against those who have been most fortunate in the material order, the rich and prosperous of the world. Professor Moriarty was raised in great poverty and obscurity. Yet he is also a man whose great intellectual gifts are of such a unique order that few scholars can follow the range of his speculations in physics. His first and most famous publication, "The Dynamics of an Asteroid," was only a first installment of what he hopes will be a unifying mathematical description of all of space and all of time. He has been willing to grant me this interval to explore and to sound the moral reserves of all of the world's religions, while he in turn is left free to pursue his own course of conduct free of prosecution for his crimes. A conditional pardon has been obtained for him through the agency of my brother Mycroft from Victoria, Queen of England."

"Will he keep the terms of your agreement and the conditions of his pardon?" asked the Pope

After a few moments of reflection I answered him, "I know the Professor as I know myself. His first characteristic is that of curiosity. He must survive to complete his work and towards that end he will direct his every effort so as to display its results before me and before the world. He desires nothing less than to prove that there is no guiding moral force in the universe, that there is no God."

The Pope smiled at this explanation. "Let us hope that he does not succeed for if he does, we are out of a job. Your Professor is not alone in that ambition. It has been one shared by Voltaire and Diderot and in this century by the Englishman Karl Marx. Of course the first two were philosophers and Marx a political economist, whereas your professor Moriarty is a mathematician and physicist. In any case the church has nothing to fear from science. We have quite gotten over the Galileo affair. We even maintain a Vatican observatory. Although one does not find God by scanning the heavens, which are only His footstool. God is to be found where alone he exercises the full order of his dominion, in the hearts of men and women. In contrast it is the function of the devil as personified evil to purify hearts in spite of the vanity of the devil's shallow pretence. There is no equality between good and evil as the Manicheans heretically supposed. The game is settled. What we observe now is only a long and bitter course of retreat back into hell by a defeated foe. It is not that we do not still fear evil, but rather that we trust God more. The Triune God before whom all evil is powerless is our strength. The cardinal virtue of hope testifies that the Catholic Church surrenders nothing to the evil one, nothing."

The Pope gave me time to assimilate the categorical nature of his assertion before continuing. "The intercession of the Church is such that it hopes for the conversion in their last hour and within the mystery of death of even the most hardened of sinners. Making no concession to evil, the Catholic Church desires to use all of the means at its disposal to enhance the rule of charity among all men and women of the earth. Emmanuel after all means that God is with us and in that faith the Church moves forward in every age until Our Lord, Jesus Christ, returns; it is He in whom all fullness of time, space, and even eternity subsist. Of course we respect the effects of evil for they bring great suffering to all people, but we unite those sufferings with those of Jesus Christ so that the merits obtained through His Life, Death, and Resurrection may be completed for the salvation of the world."

Pope Leo had been looking up at a crucifix upon the wall as he spoke, but now he returned his gaze to me as I sat before him. "But you, Mr. Holmes, in your wager, have you not considered that your own victory in your wager may bring about your own death?"

I answered him at once, quite confidently in response. "Professor Moriarty will never kill me because by doing do so he would simultaneously admit defeat. He must press on until he has proven to me that there is no God. He is possessed of a sort of inverse ardor. All the effort that he might have spent in pursuit of wonder and joy is transposed into a hunger for a final triumph of disillusionment. He uses the highest faculty in man, the human intellect, in order to dethrone mankind from any status he may possess as separate and distinct from the rest of creation. Professor Moriarty wishes to think without acknowledging the nature of the thinker. His love of asteroids hurdling through empty space is indicative of the barrenness of his over-arching theory of the universe. One wonders whether he has ever contemplated the living force of nature. He is a hater of life. The sole exception to this is his great love of horses, similar to that of the clergyman Jonathan Swift's satire on mankind, 'Gulliver's Travels.' The Professor was a groom in his youth and he has never lost his devotion to those beautiful if inarticulate beasts. His father was a trainer in my family's stables in Yorkshire. You see, Your Holiness, I have a very long acquaintance with my primary enemy."

"I only witnessed his human side on one occasion. I saw him weep once as a lad. It was when one of our stallions broke a leg and had to be put down. He did it himself because he would allow no other hand to touch the beast with which he had formed a unique bond, the crippled boy and the mighty stallion. He has spilt much blood since then but none I suspect has haunted him more than killing that beloved beast. I fear that he was made to feel ashamed of his own compassion at the time. His father was a hard man and mocked the tenderness of the boy. Some early wounds seem never to heal and who may comprehend the outer limits and effects of such an early act of malice and mockery? I will go so far as to say that even the Catholic Church has its wounds from which it is still seeking a collective recovery. It cannot be easy to serve in the office of Vicar of Christ. I must ask Your Holiness, if I may be so bold, whether you have considered that your own efforts to fulfill your duties as Sovereign Pontiff may not hasten your own death?"

I was surprised at my own temerity in posing such a personal question to such a great man, but my own curiosity of long standing was to know how any man can endure the occupancy of the chair of St. Peter. My hunger for an answer got the better of me at the moment and my question could not be recalled. The Holy Father was silent for a time and I feared that I had deeply offended him and that he would not answer me, but at last he spoke.

"For man, it is impossible, but for God all things are possible. We have often prayed to our Lord to lighten our burden, but each year it grows heavier. It was the third fall of Our Lord Jesus that was the most bitter. Even Our Lord had to ask for the help of Simon of Cyrene to reach the place of his crucifixion. No servant is greater than his master. Were it not for the daily prayers of the entire body of Christ in the Canon of the Mass I should long since have succumbed. As it is, I cannot long continue. May my successors be men of vigor, for I fear that the new century may host horrors that we cannot now even imagine."

After a pause during which I observed the anguish of his face he continued, having assumed the mode of expression peculiar to his office of referring to himself by the use of the plural nominative pronoun, we.

"The path of the Church is a winding one. We do not ascend to God even in our highest conceptions of theology unburdened with the human limitations of earth. Popes must drag the heavy load of the cross over rough ground. We speak of absolute truths by analogy that must always fall short of experience. Theology moves forward by inches. No one Pontificate can contain the whole truth of Christianity. My successors may disapprove of much that we have endeavored to say and do in the course of our pontificate so as to address the needs of the world and to embrace within the limits imposed by the our faith the manifold changes occurring in the world. The Catholic Church may need to rest for a time before moving forward. I pray that the Catholic Church may never lose sight of the times in which it lives. But may it never so embrace the ideas of the historical era in which it finds itself that it will forget its own proper character and unique mission directed towards the salvation of souls!"

"I think often of Our Lord's experience of agony in the Garden of Gethsemane. Imagine if you may the tension between the constant awareness of Jesus of the love of God, an experience that even his Incarnation did nothing to diminish and what he was about to undergo in what the Catholic Church has always called the Passion of his Crucifixion and death. Imagine the sense of knowing all sin for one who has never known any personal sin. Theology can affirm this truth but never convey the experience, the meeting of absolute grace with the totality of human evil and its consequences distilled from all of history focused upon one unique event experienced by a single man in the human nature of Jesus. Try if you will to imagine absolute power confronting complete subjection to its own creation! The sheer disproportion involved exceeds any words that seek to convey the drama that works for our salvation."

I do not think that I was ever so aware of the burden of being the Vicar of Christ than I was at that moment. If it is difficult for any Christian soul beset with temptation and with the added confusion of knowing that other visions of the purpose and ends of human life are possible, how much more must be the burden placed on one who must love God "more than these others do" as Jesus asked of St. Peter and so to confirm them in the faith. For one man to be asked to guide so unwieldy a vessel as the Catholic Church is to ask more than human nature can bear. The failure of so many Popes to be equal to the task merely shows that the need for mercy and forgiveness is not confined to the laity. The sanctity of souls and the interaction of divine grace with free-will are such that the greatest of saints often led lives of obscurity while on earth. It is a testimony to the humility of the Catholic Church at its best in the saints who seek not their own glory but that of their Lord and Savior Jesus Christ. Many of those saints who have been elevated to the dignity of the altar by being canonized were humble and obscure in both their origins and in their lives. In a way the Catholic Church mocks its own worldly grandeur by the rarity with which it has proclaimed so few popes to be saints. Perhaps these men are chosen in order to remind the laity that in the Kingdom of Heaven the last will be first while the first will be last.

For this reason I have often reflected that members of the female sex may hope to enter first into heaven. It must be recalled that the only human being favored by God to be born without Original Sin was a woman. The Virgin Mary is honored by the universal Church as the Queen of Heaven and as the Mother of God. No greater exaltation is conceivable, for Mary is not herself divine. In her then we may perceive the original intent of God for man and for woman. Womanhood is itself exalted by this choice of God. If death came to the world through the sin of Adam then life is restored by a woman. If Eve acted as temptress, then Mary is the refuge of sinners.

The most holy rosary of the Blessed Virgin Mary is the sustenance of souls and its promises are the assurance of aid in the hour of death as is the twin Devotion to the Sacred Heart of Jesus and to the Immaculate Heart of Mary. The twin hearts of Jesus and Mary appear on the reverse side of the Miraculous Medal which is inscribed with these words:

I could not but be aware of this unique opportunity presented to me to ask the Holy Father if my musings as recorded in my journal are correct. I am afraid that I do not possess a humble nature and that I have often not walked in the path that would be most conducive to the health of my soul. I have often known confusion and despair and have presumed to seek understanding to bolster my faith. As a detective I suffer from that irritability of observation that has seldom left me peace. I am one with St. Thomas who would even dare to probe the wounds of Jesus before he would consent to believe.

Even now there are times when I doubt that there is any destiny for man at all. The planet is old and has known so many forms of life. Perhaps the human race is among those peculiar organisms that are haunted by its own nature and doomed to perish. If some future animal should evolve that will study our fossils will they wonder at the dreams of good and evil that floated like some dread miasma in the brain-pans of these ever-curious apes? Yet still I must believe, if only to vindicate my own thought processes.

The very humanism of the Church is a comfort to me. If we were to imagine God as indifferent or as consisting of mere mindless chains of purposeless causality, then we would need to reduce all that is most precious within us to dreams contained in the tiny protoplasm of the skull. What would be the brain of man then but the cranial jelly analogous to a mollusk inhabiting the its shell for a time before that same shell lies empty and dry, abandoned along the sea strand of the ages? I refuse to accept this!

I wonder whether my quest, the one that has brought me here at last to Rome, might be confirmed by the Pope. I thought to submit my writings to him for review and expurgation of any heresy they might contain, since these pages contain only my own efforts to explain my faith to myself.

I might not have that opportunity though so I spoke up, "Your Holiness, as you are the universal pastor of souls I ask you to hear my confession and to leave with you this record that I have compiled in the course of my travels. If only you, I hesitate to ask, would read them and confirm that I am on solid ground then I could do what lies ahead for me and face Professor Moriarty and even the accuser himself, the devil, on my last day."

It was indeed a desperate appeal and his response surprised me. "Mr. Holmes, you mistake our office as Pope. The Catholic Church is one. You need not have come so far to obtain certitude from me. I am not God, nor am I the church. There are many theologians who are brighter than I am and their writings exceed whatever I might tell you regarding your private speculations. Our teaching office is confined to what is certain and approved by the past tradition of the entire church as it reflects upon what it has received. The Catholic Church follows the description of St. Paul who said that, 'Love is patient; love is kind; love is not puffed-up.' If your writings are 'puffed-up,' then pray for humility so that with time and grace you will see them for what they are."

"As Pope I am the anchor of the Catholic Church to prevent the ship as a whole from foundering upon the reefs of heresy and of unbelief. What I speak is constrained by what has been believed always and everywhere. By this means I confirm my brethren in the faith. The Catholic Church has encountered and engaged in battle with many heresies, yet it survives. Our Lord has promised to remain with us in the Catholic Church until the end of time. There is then no cause for concern. Christ will return someday and put all things under his feet. Meanwhile you may encounter the fullness of the church in your own parish in England. Rome is not like Mecca. The sacramental presence of Jesus is everywhere as is the Holy Spirit. Jesus speaks through grace in the universal priesthood and within the baptized person, if that soul is at one with the church in charity, what is usually termed Sanctifying Grace. The Catholic Church is governed by a hierarchy. This much is true, but it is not out of a desire for power, but to make unity in caritas possible in a fractious world."

"If you discover that you are in error, pray for more light. If you are in sin, confess it. If you have doubts, pray that you may be strengthened in your faith. If you wish to find God, then open your heart and keep the commandments for they will save you much pain and remorse later. Recall why Jesus took the sins of all men and women upon Him, it is because we are inadequate to save ourselves. Only do then what you can and leave the rest to God and know that you are not alone but part of the entire church that daily prays for all men and women in every Mass offered throughout the world. Our prayer for you and for ourselves is always the same, "Come quickly Lord Jesus."

That concluded our conversation that day. He did hear my confession though and after granting me absolution said: "We must leave you now, Mr. Holmes. Pray for me." He rose then to give me the Papal Blessing while I knelt and loath I was to forego the comfort of his presence. I dared in parting to ask him for any advice that I might recall when I finally met with Professor Moriarty. I was standing again by then and the Pope was at the door of the drawing room that he had already opened. At first I feared that he had not heard me, but he paused in his departure and turned to me.

"Do not rehearse what you will say but know that in that hour all will be given to you by the Holy Spirit who knows all things." After a brief final bow of his head in courtesy he departed.

I found my escort seated at his desk in an anteroom and I was led to a side door opening into the great Basilica. The immense church was already filling up with worshipers for evening Mass. I joined them with a great feeling of comfort in my heart.

December 10, 1892
Retreat

The days that followed my meeting with Pope Leo were strange ones. I had entered that interview both hoping to hear something that would aid me in my coming struggle with Professor Moriarty while being at the same time secretly convinced that I knew precisely what to do to achieve victory. In looking backwards I can see that this entire quest of mine with its attendant inconvenience and physical pain has been meant to overawe the Professor. I have been lining up the various spiritual authorities of the world on my side leaving the Professor as I have imagined with no allies, since the devil is not loyal to his servants.

Yet now I find myself questioning if every action even in nature produces an equal and opposite counterforce to oppose it. My striving for victory may harden Moriarty into opposition. If I really desire to enlist Moriarty on my side, which I imagine to be also the side of God, then must I not review prior to our definitive encounter the nature of my own motives? Why Mr. Sherlock Holmes must you always triumph? From whence comes this relish in victory at all costs? Is the need for fame and power hereditary?

Why was it that my father (a man of old Anglo-Norman stock) was such a hard man to his tenants and to his sons alike? Each of his sons was influenced to seek out power in some fashion. Sherringford, the eldest, is most like my Father. He has always been a member of the high church faction of the Church of England and a Tory in his political sentiments believing in an ordered society and an ordered church. It is not that this prescribed order ever seems to make him happy, but rather that any disorder is painful and anathema to him. For Sherringford a just order is one where his prerogatives are secure as a member of the ruling class.

Mycroft and I, since we knew in advance that we would inherit at best some share of a trust set up for our education and maintenance as gentlemen, were free to roam the moors and the seaside of Yorkshire and to learn to know the tenant farmers free of the burdens of primogeniture. Mycroft even as a lad was somewhat fat and unwieldy in physical pursuits. The result was that he grew gradually to favor sedentary habits and the enjoyment of his books. I recall that he had a particular fondness for Sir Walter Scott's Waverley novels and for Malory's tales of King Arthur. Even at such an early date he may have imagined a role of centrality, perhaps like Merlyn in service to King Arthur.

I in contrast preferred the works of Charles Dickens, Willkie Collins, Edgar Allen Poe, and the Gothic tradition. Later on I entertained a certain morbid taste for the works of Emile Zola and the English Decadent writers such as Swinburne, Symons and Dowson. I have always enjoyed the sensational and the horrifying, perhaps because if I might keep my horrors before me I might not fear the fiend that softly treads behind me. To conquer fear by facing it head-on has always been my first instinct and it is that innate characteristic that has had a correlative element of never admitting defeat. Humility does not come easy to a mindset such as that which I have always possessed. But surely it is no dishonor to be defeated by God, to yield to grace, and to accept the duty of voluntary faith where one might prefer an imposed certainty. My hope was that I might provide Moriarty with that very certainty and by doing so to disable him, to drag him clawing backwards into heaven, or at least that he might be enrolled in God's service.

Even the Church has at times wished for a similar triumph and used the inquisition to achieve supremacy over the consciences of men. Even in this century it was a bitter blow for the Church to lose the Papal States that had so long protected the Church from the threat and control of overweening monarchs. In this sense Pope Leo XIII is the first modern Pope, because he and his successors must now rely upon moral authority alone. No longer is the use of force in world affairs an option that the popes may consider. Only the Swiss Guard remains as a symbol of that period of church history when the popes were temporal rulers as well as spiritual fathers. God appears to be leading his church through a dark night just as the world is growing in its abandoned wickedness. It is as it was with Jesus in the bitter Garden of Gethsemane.   The church of today appears powerless before the idols of the age.

We live in the age of Empires and of Nation-states. Everywhere statesmen gather about them weapons and the hypocrisy of statesmanship is but the veiled threat of war. How long can it be before a great conflagration breaks upon us all? Against that storm the Catholic Church has only what it has always had, the strength of the Gospel, proclaiming that God so loved the world that He gave even his only Begotten Son, not to condemn the world, but so that it might be saved.

The ways of God always seem to be tinged not by omnipotence but rather by its restraint. The wrath of God is characterized above all else by its sparing use. Even the devil, though his chains are already forged and locked in place, is allowed to rage seemingly unhindered and the helpless and the innocent of the earth bear the pains that should be visited upon the selfish and the greedy who oppress them. God is always with the poor, not as their God alone, but as one of them. It is not that God favors defeat, for His victory is already secured, but rather God makes the same appeal to us by allying Himself with the helplessness that beckons for aid to all men and women whose life circumstances make them more fortunate.

This may be the last hope for sinners. The entire world order is such that the innocent suffer to obtain pardon for the guilty. In this we witness the mercy of God, who will even go so far as to seem to cooperate with evil in order to defeat it from within. If this is the way of God, then how much more should it animate our human actions!

Evil is not defeated by taking up the arms of evil and by doing so becoming like that which we would defeat. Evil is destroyed rather by allowing it so to exhaust its pointless fury so that its final impotence is made manifest. Such is the witness of the saints and of martyrs. There is a difference though between a Christian martyr and the martyr of an Islamic jihad: when a Christian dies it is in imitation of Christ. He takes no other soul with him but bears the cost of death alone.

If all that I have said is true then my entire encounter with Professor Moriarty must be reassessed. In proportion as he is really evil he cannot be defeated by ordinary means, but only by taking up the only armor possessed by the Christian. Moriarty's minions may be stopped by order of law, but if Professor Moriarty is indeed a "king devil," as he was once called by Inspector McDonald, then such a one can only be defeated by prayer and fasting. The greatest of evils may not be opposed, but only endured until they pass away by their own misguided force as they always do.

Where now are such men as Nero, Caligula, or Genghis Khan? The coliseum that drank the martyr's blood is a ruin. The tides of chariots leave no imprint in the dust, while on every altar Christ arises anew each day in the species of bread and wine that are His Body and His Blood. Pilgrimage to Rome is not essential; because the Catholic Church is everywhere in the hearts of believers and the soul's needs may be met at one's parish home. It is God who makes the journey to men and women in the Holy Sacrifice of the Mass. God is both our origin and our destination and He nourishes us in the sacramental life of the church in Holy Communion all along the way towards the salvation that is our destiny if only we choose to avail ourselves of the means offered to us.

December 15, 1892
Recapitulation

I wish that I had dared to ask the pope the question that has haunted me throughout my travels. That question is whether the religions of the world are merely a subset of other cultural phenomena like art and literature. Are we human beings the creation of God or is God a creation of the human societies out of which various religions are distilled in order to help us to cope with experience?

A quick look at Judaism reveals the source of this question for me. The most salient characteristic of the Jewish people has been their abiding sense of political estrangement and their search for a secure homeland, lost and regained. Out of this wandering experience the literature of the Jewish people distilled the need for vindication, renewal, and reward, with these always conditional upon a promise or covenant or upon sacrificial atonement for past offenses.

Could Christianity ever have emerged from any other culture or from a people with a less problematic history than the Jews? The function of any religion is to devise a global solution for a particular and persistent historical problem. For the Jewish people the problem stems from the possession of a unique preoccupation with maintaining a separate identity in an unfriendly environment combined with an apparent inability to successfully assimilate within a dominant culture or set of neighbors.

The history of the Jewish people might be summed up as

either leaving somewhere and being pursued or alternatively as wishing to stay somewhere and being evicted. Exile or the threat of exile is the dominant theme of Jewish existence. For the Jewish people their ultimate fate is always in front of them. Judaism and Christianity alike are always predicated upon an unattained future rather than upon a challenging but sustainable present. Persecution and pain play a central role in both religions and the contemplation of death is never absent. Exile from Eden and the hope of heaven for the followers of Christ, the latter solves the problem posed by the first. The initial sin is the intemperate desire of Adam and Eve to know the difference between good and evil and the solution paradoxically is to make that distinction ever more refined in our discernment so as to live in moral perfection in imitation of God in the person of Jesus Christ. What was at first condemned as premature and forbidden, for man to be like God, is followed by a strange reversal in which God condescends to become man.

As Christianity merged with the world beyond Jerusalem it enabled two thousand years of European history, primarily characterized by Christians killing other Christians all the while praying to the same God for victory. There is a latent strain of justified slaughter in the Bible that can be excavated at will to serve nationalistic ends. The continent-wide decimation of the original inhabitants of America and of Canada demonstrates the utility and the mutability that can adapt Christianity to serve whatever ends that men of power wish to pursue. However much Jesus claimed that His Kingdom was not of this world, His followers are not of the same mind. The immense superstructure that has grown out of the tiny group that witnessed the risen Christ is either a miracle or a monstrous aberration depending on one's point of view. My own conviction is that to use religion for a utilitarian purpose is precisely what was forbidden in the second commandment when God said, "Thou shalt not use the name of the Lord thy God in vain." Religious zeal knows no limits, even those imposed by God Himself.

The prayer given to us by Jesus and thereafter called, "The Lord's Prayer," sets forth a program for the mission of the church. It is addressed to God the Father as the responsible agent for human change. The phrase, "Hallowed be thy name," expresses our subservient status to God and our duty to respect His ordinances. The next phrase after the invocation to God as Father is the most problematic however: *Thy Kingdom come, Thy will be done, on earth as it is in heaven.* As a plea for Divine Grace to provide guidance and a source of strength for our efforts this prayer recognizes our ultimate dependence upon God, but as a practical manual for human action it runs afoul of historical experience. Theocratic rule has proven to be every bit as violent and oppressive as secular rule.

The effort to advance the Kingdom of God by human means or to force the Second Coming of Christ by seeking various prophetic solutions is the height of human arrogance. For this reason the objections that Professor Moriarty will no doubt raise regarding the utility of religion will either force me to mask or dissimulate the historical data or to seek some other way to vindicate an overarching human plan to supplement the glory of God by our own chosen means of moral perfection. While I am not ready to simply surrender any sense of innate human dignity, I am equally unwilling to presume that if certain historical impediments to virtue could only be removed, including the dictates of formal religion, that human beings could simply begin again from a posture of original innocence like the noble savages celebrated by Rousseau or Chateaubriand. I doubt whether the Incarnation and the Sacrifice of Jesus as our redeemer would have been necessary if the Kingdom of God could be advanced by sheer human ingenuity. For this reason I have little confidence that the moral perfectibility of humankind is practically achievable in this life and therefore I take an attitude of skepticism towards any program, whether political of economic, that claims that it can make a better world.

December 21, 1892
A Brief Explanation of the Nature of Evil

The above entry sets the tone for an evaluation of just how far my own efforts may hope to succeed against the fixed position in the mental citadel of Professor Moriarty. I believe nevertheless I have accomplished my original intention in coming to Rome. Insofar as I might have been prepared by research, by travel, and by reflection I have come to the conclusion that the case that I planned to lay before Professor Moriarty is now essentially complete, but still qualified by the tension existing between Christian doctrine and Christian practice. The church is both an avenue to God and an obstacle to faith. It is sometimes difficult to discern God through the fog of clouds of incense or to discern God's simplicity through the veil of elaborate ceremonial observances.

It will be noticed, should this record ever be read by any outside party that my explication contains little in the way of threats. I have proposed Christianity and the prospect of conversion as primarily carrot and little in the way of stick. It must be recalled however that though the rewards of heaven are often painted in vague pastels, the human imagination has never ceased to paint the pains of hell in the most lurid of colors. Perhaps, since happiness on earth is so rarely achieved, it is easier for the human mind to conceive supreme misery than supreme bliss. The pursuit of the latter is so often an occasion for sin. I will go so far as to say that a state of perfect happiness, at least when achieved on earth, would seem to be suspect as judged by the witness of the saints who not content with those ordinary miseries and misfortunes that come to us unsought, would even add to them by undertaking various voluntary penances and by renouncing even legitimate avenues of pleasure, the better to discipline their more unruly passions and to in some manner recompense God for the insult to the deity occasioned by sin.

The idea of vicarious suffering for sin through voluntary penance would seem at first to be an injustice; but what can better demonstrate divine love than to give up one's own well-being for another, particularly for sinners, the most unworthy of any such sacrifices to be made on their behalf. This matter of vicarious recompense reaches its apogee in the phenomenon of certain "victim-souls," individuals of whose personal holiness there can be no doubt who offer themselves as victims to the full fury of preternatural evil as well as often suffering from a variety of physical ailments and often meeting an early death. These persons are to the phenomenon of sanctity what the tyrants of the world are to evil. As such, they are hidden in the mystery of God and any judgment of them and evaluation of their experiences must be tentative. Even the Catholic Church, although it may reach a judgment and proclamation as to their sanctity of life in the process of beatification and canonization, does not demand that their visions, however explicit, must be believed by the faithful. These are private revelations as opposed to public revelation, which ended with the death of the last Apostle. The latter contains all that is required for salvation and any supplement thereto must submit to the collective discernment of the church through the oral tradition of centuries and the current teaching of the Ordinary Magisterium of the living bishops in unity with the pope.

Still, the very horrifying nature of the experiences of such "victim-souls" takes us into those dreadful regions beyond life that awaken terror within us. Death is the *reductio ad absurdum* of all human endeavors. The prospect of hell thereafter is so ghastly that men and women might prefer to forego any version of life that this world offers. We die and are as swiftly forgotten as the mayflies so any sacrifice makes sense in order to avoid hell, a fate that many Christians believe to be that of the majority of the human race. It would seem from this point of view that the true mercy of God would be in favor of the simple act of obliteration of evil souls after death. Why punish when there is no hope for reformation or restitution? Is the infliction of endless pain to be understood as some sort of requirement for God to vindicate His dignity?

In any case such a demonstration of wrath and destruction would appear superfluous after the general judgment of God on all of humanity and the final vision of the Wedding Feast. How are we to ever understand the final wages of sin as death and exclusion? Is more punishment necessary beyond simple separation from God as the source of all that is good and beautiful? Or perhaps hell is the perfect metaphor for self-inflicted suffering. Of what use then is hell beyond providing a sort of ontological parity to heaven? Yet belief in its reality is to be accepted as *de fide* by the faithful although the number of those who are actually condemned to endure the pains of hell remains in dispute.

The better belief it seems to me would appear to be that the existence of hell is a mere ontological possibility for a being made in the image and likeness of God. This fact alone should be adequate to turn the soul to God. Can an image of God deny itself without plunging into misery and fragmentation? But since we know that the devil has established hell as his domain and that certain human lives throughout history have manifested such viciousness, luxury, and lack of repentance that we can easily imagine them to be the human equivalent of the devil and his angels; we may reasonably assume that hell is in fact tenanted by some human souls. Still, this apparent frustration of the love of God would seem to imply that supreme evil, though certainly not positioned as equality with God, can at least claim the sad residual victory of enduring the punishments of hell and thereby implying that God, who could create all things out of nothing, has no similar power of restoring to nothingness souls thus afflicted, or at least that God refuses to do so for reasons of His own.

The net result would appear to be an everlasting chancre on the face of creation when considered in its totality. To say that God is not troubled and frustrated by this end result seems to deny God's omnipotence and to limit the efficacy of the salvation purchased on the cross by the Divine Son of God, Jesus Christ, to a minority of the human race. The conflict between the presumed total efficacy of Divine Grace to achieve its end in redemption and the assumed fact that some souls, though only through their own fault and not by the will of God, are in fact not saved, has led some men such as John Calvin to assume that God actively wills that some souls will be condemned.

To those who prefer and even rejoice in such a theological position God's greatness and holiness is best demonstrated by the eternal existence of pain. Unlike Hegel who sees all metaphysical opposition as leading to a process of reconciliation in a new synthesis in an unending sequence this version of theology sees everything as leading to a final moment where time will be no more. Whatever exists at that moment will be frozen in place and incapable of alteration. To deduce such a metaphysical conclusion from the perspective of Hebrew writings that emerged independently of Greek thought is to presume more than Holy Scripture can legitimately reveal. Modern physics might alter the world-view that posed such theological puzzles in prior eras. To propose the traditional certitudes as the net result of our wager will undoubtedly cause Professor Moriarty to scoff.

I have always been of a different opinion in regard to the ultimate fate of evil. My hypothesis is that if God suffers hell to exist it is only through his residual love so as not to destroy what in creation was found and proclaimed by God to be very good prior to its corruption. This action of preservation sustains the possibility of a return to God even if that offer is never accepted. This would imply that there is some goodness even in hell and that the desire to destroy and to deny that possibility is the very activity towards which hell's denizens devote all of their pointless efforts.

This view of hell implies that it is the love of God, which is perceived in hell as fire. The souls of the damned are unable through an irrevocable and absolute choice made by them from responding to that love by a reciprocal love of their own having abjured forever the enticements of Divine Grace. Since the very source of that love was never ours from the beginning, any lack of God's life within us then is analogous to a dead body no longer animated by the principle of life.

Similarly, it is the refusal of grace, which was always the moral life in the soul that makes any act of virtue in hell metaphysically impossible. The pain of hell then is proportional (and in this its justice appears) to the degree of our sustained resistance to Divine Grace. The theological problem of hell then is actually due to our incomprehension of how time and space relate to eternity. The ultimate identity of a human being, the fate of his or her soul, is thus defined by its degree of responsiveness to Divine Love when we encounter God after death. The spectrum of life in the damned soul would fade into the non-being of eternal death.

The human soul cannot create from within its own ashes the spark of life since that must come from the same God who has been definitely rejected. The hope of all souls then lies in Divine Mercy. Such is the hope of the church and its confidence in God, that if any prospect exists that some residual saving hesitation before the abyss take place within the soul, then Divine Grace will rush in to supplement the many deficits in virtue, to raise some spark of love from any residual fuel that God may find within us. It is the task of "victim-souls" to stand as advocates before the final bar of justice for the deficient souls so that witnessing such a surplus of love in these holy souls, sinners may still turn in loathing from the pit into which they might otherwise have entered only to be entrapped there forever. Hell is the logical outcome of the inability to alter one's state of being. Does this explanation not make greater theological sense than what is so often nakedly proposed for our belief as Christians with regard to eternity? But where shall I look for support for this conclusion? What is the value of any specific content and details described by the visions of many of these "victim-souls?"

Although these revelations are more than metaphorical, these visions may not be accurate in all respects. They should be taken to heart for the pedagogy that they may provide as a source of salutary terror of missing the requisite mercy of God through our own obstinacy in sin. The main effect and value of the witness of heroic sanctity and of voluntary submission to reparation for the sins of others is to inspire us to engage in proportional efforts of our own sanctification. If these unique sacrifices for the love of souls are accepted, the great value of these souls to the collective body of the church is made clear and our gratefulness for these efforts made in behalf of others (that may include us as well) justifies any honor and thankfulness we may express to God for such a great gift. Since the borders of hell do not admit of strict definition, it is enough that the prospect of hell should be present at all so that we may steer clear of any actions or dispositions that would indicate that we are (insensibly perhaps) becoming accustomed to hell's peculiar and noxious climate. The mere scent of evil should be adequate for us to avoid it.

The fruitlessness of evil only manifests how it loathes its every victory; for since it was created good, it is repelled by itself. All being revolts and resists evil, even when that noxious principle is clutched to its very heart. Every denial works a simultaneous affirmation of the glory of God. Evil exists in perpetual deficit that only grows larger in proportion to its own negative efforts. Hell is constantly growing deeper in this sense. It is a falling without cessation, an immobility existing beyond stasis. Beyond these inadequate metaphors language must fail. It is the mystery of iniquity that language cannot grasp it or explain it.

However to return to specifics, I do not intend to threaten Professor Moriarty with hell, but rather to show that goodness is life itself. All sin is in the end mortal only when it is accompanied by despair. Hell is the surrender to another complete order of being in which God is eclipsed. For this reason, to commit one such sin is to commit to their common root which is the despair of God's goodness. All partial change in this direction is the planting of a seed of death; if that partial choice is later affirmed within death so that if one had more time one would persist in that vile aim indefinitely then the sorrow of God would ratify our choice. The validation of that final choice would follow as the last flame of God's life would die within us.

The unceasing prayer of the Catholic Church in the holy Sacrifice of the Mass is the daily intercession for the salvation of souls. It is in this central ceremony, and in other sacramental actions that the church composed of souls who need the very food that these actions provide, that the collective body of the faithful reaches out to God for His promised rewards.

The Blessed Virgin Mary is the mother of the church who crushes the head of the ancient serpent. Already she is clothed with the sun and the darkness is glimmering with the first vestige of an eternal dawn. Evil would not be so frantic if its time was not so short. With each passing day the hours of light grow longer in anticipation of the return of Christ.

December 25, 1892

Christmas Day: A Strange Meeting

ast night I went to Midnight Mass for Christmas, the Feast of the Nativity. I might have attended the Mass presided over by the Pope at San Giovanni Laterno but I chose instead the small Church of Santa Maria della Victoria, where in the Cornaro Chapel rests the famous statue by Bernini of St. Teresa in Ecstasy.

I have always had a particular devotion to the two great Spanish Discalced Carmelite Saints: St. Teresa of Avila and St. John of the Cross. These two great mystics have explored in their writings how the soul in pursuit of heaven may be granted, even in this life, a direct communication with God by focusing our love upon Him alone and clearing away those obstacles that blind us to the Divine Presence.

The famous sculpture I speak of could only portray the suspension of the senses that occurs in mystical ecstasy by a rather fleshly visual metaphor and the lovely figure, wounded by a mischievous cherub, bears little resemblance to the great reformer and eminently practical St. Teresa. But then the worldly mind can only with difficulty portray the heavenly realm of spiritual ecstasy. The religious experience of the majority of believers is confined to the comfort and security rendered by belief in an ultimate ground for our moral being and a remedy in forgiveness for our sins.

The Mass was lovely and sung with quiet dignity. The homilist this year was an English Cardinal who spoke in his native tongue for a predominantly English congregation. The English Catholic expatriate community in Rome had gathered for this unique opportunity. It seemed strange to one who has sojourned for so long in foreign regions to be surrounded once again by my own countrymen. The sermon was one of joy as befits the season and seemed to carry with it the memories of holly and ivy, of roast goose and plum pudding.   I reflected once again that no nation enjoys the celebration of Christmas with equal gusto as the English.   I seemed to taste again the flavor of mince pie and to recall the savor of a tawny port wine by the hearth fire and I longed to be able to toast my good friend Dr. John Hamish Watson and to wish him all the compliments of the season.

In any case, I sent him my prayers and good wishes as I lingered after the Mass while the chapel gradually emptied around me.   I could hear the voices of men and women wishing each other Merry Christmas as they emerged and went their separate ways. The chapel would stay open all night so that people might come to pray or to light a Christmas candle for their intentions in the coming year.

Soon the Church was empty except for me and for a veiled woman in the pew opposite my own.   She seemed a delicate creature and I could discern through the veil in the candlelight that she was what is often termed a great beauty.   I have learned to be aware of faces since precise identification is an essential skill for the investigator to possess.   I perceived as she caught my attention that this night of joy was one of sorrow for the woman in the pew adjoining mine.   She was engaged in silent prayer and her eyes were fixed upon the altar in supplication.   She paused now and again and lifted her veil to dab at her eyes with a handkerchief.   Its veil was such that it covered both her face and her neck.   I could see that she found its presence burdensome, so at last in irritation she cast it aside by temporarily removing her hat to adjust it.

It was then that she noticed that I was gazing at her and that I had been a witness to her distress.   She showed at first some irritation at having been observed and I could see that she was a woman of reticence, grace, and dignity.   Her face softened though after a moment, perhaps recognizing that it was no mere idle curiosity that had motivated me, but a real concern for her distress on such a night as Christmas.   She bowed her head my direction to acknowledge my concern and was about to replace her veil in order to regain her solitude when she suddenly paused. Her eyes looked up at me again and suddenly the years seemed to melt away and I seemed to see a white figure at a similar altar in the London of 1887. She had stood then by the side of a gallant young fellow named Godfrey Norton and at his side, acting as witness to the ceremony, stood no one other than a disguised Sherlock Holmes!

Yes, the woman in the pew opposite mine was indeed the famous alto and stage actress Irene Adler, whom I have always referred to as "the woman" as my tribute to her wit and courage. That I was recognized as well I could not doubt. She had clearly abandoned her original intention of concealment. She seemed even more surprised to see me than I was to see her. Each of us had supposed, I realized at once, that the other was dead. For this mistake I could blame n other person than Dr. John H. Watson whose premature desire to keep his public informed on all matters touching upon the fate of Sherlock Holmes had pronounced me dead in a recent publication appearing in the Strand Magazine entitled, "The Final Problem."

So as not to disturb the other worshipers who remained in prayer she motioned to me to follow her and arose gently gathering her winter cloak and hood about her and replacing her hat from which she had removed the veil. I rose also and we each genuflected and made the sign of the cross before withdrawing to the vestibule where we might presume to speak in quiet tones. We found there an anteroom where we might sit. It was there that I was to hear briefly and in part, what I will no doubt learn more fully in the days ahead, a story that explained the nature of her life since we had last met so many years ago.

I had often speculated about her fate since that evening when she had boldly wished me goodnight in front of my home in Baker Street. She had assumed then the disguise of a young man and as she passed Watson and me she dared to address me showing me that I had no monopoly on dramatic impersonation. I was pursuing at the time a commission for the unworthy and pompous King of Bohemia. I shall relate the tale she told me in my journal entry tomorrow. It is a strange tale and I desire to omit no particular that she may add to what she has already told me. The hour is late though and I have agreed to meet her later today for Christmas dinner at her residence at six in the evening.

For the present I will note here only that it appears that she has long resided in Rome and that what Watson took to be her death, with his usual premature conclusions, had been only her sudden retirement from the opera and the stage. She had feared the vengeful actions of the King of Bohemia and so had covered her traces by an unannounced and abrupt disappearance that had caused wild speculations and chagrin in many circles for she had possessed quite a following prior to her premature retirement. She lived after her marriage for a time in Rome in comfort and even in splendor. But her joy was not to last. Her confession, given to me in a choking voice, was that her dear husband and friend, Godfrey Norton Esq. had contracted cholera on the occasion of a professional visit to Venice. He had died last summer. Since then she has lived in Rome, a broken woman.

Dr. Watson's Narrative Continues

Before continuing my inclusions from the journal I will now present my account of the meeting with Irene Adler in New York in 1898, which came as a great surprise to Holmes since he had assumed that Irene Adler was still in Europe. Just as she had looked up so many years ago in Italy to find the eyes of Sherlock Holmes gazing upon her, so did she look up now and I could see the momentary shock of recognition that was soon followed by a gentle and amused smile. She continued to follow the conversation at her table, but I could see that she was breathing with animation and excitement due to the surprise of encountering Sherlock Holmes once again. Since it now appeared unnecessary to make our departure unobserved, we each ordered an additional brandy and remained at our table. The hour was late and the restaurant was now being abandoned by the early diners. It was clear that the evening hours were reserved for the patronage of the theatrical aristocracy whose bohemian habits and professional duties necessitated a final late meal, which was gladly provided by the establishment.

Since realizing who the charming woman actually was I had applied a greater scrutiny to the one woman who had so long haunted the imagination of my companion. She had arrived at that particular beauty that a woman possesses, who having left behind the first sweet blush of spring, has mellowed and grown in character with time as does a fine sherry. She is no longer one of a crowd of young girls possessed of charming if vapid smiles, but is, in her own right a person of character, substance, and nuance.

It takes time to establish oneself as a unique being, particularly in women whose every gesture is so often choreographed by the strict codes of social grooming. Such refinement often entails suffering and such suffering would not be real if some remnant of its passage did not remain upon the visage. I could see that for the sake of her companions, who no doubt expected it, she maintained the gay and frivolous airs that one associates with the world of the theater, but withal I could see that she was weary and that she would gladly have escaped the necessity of such entertainments were they not a requisite adjunct to her profession.

The performers of opera and the theater must always appear to be more than life and above the natural fatigue that beckons us to sleep. The function of the theatrical arts is to deny and to alleviate the boredom and despair that is the lot of so many. It was a sorry day when the religious pageantry and processions were curtailed as medieval anachronisms. These brought together the need of the people to use their imaginations to envisage heaven through music and dance, the same elements that still reside in peasant and tribal cultures. When religion is reduced to a series of dry propositions to which one is asked to consent, as though one was signing a contract, it fails to animate the entire man or woman and the result is that these unmet needs can only be filled by the secular theater.

I could see that Irene Adler was a senior priestess of that cult of artistry that celebrates the passions. Modern theater is fragmentary and merely serves to amuse. This is not the forum of the great Greek theater of Sophocles and Aeschylus. Once our hunger for the totality of life is lost what else remains?

Miss Adler's appeal was not that of a younger woman, but

rather what is often referred to as an intellectual beauty. Her features, as they lost the plumpness of her early youth, had grown more refined until they seemed almost to be translucent. If I saw so much, I can only wonder what further depths might have been perceived by Holmes that night. He had not taken his eyes off of her since her entrance. I could see a certain sorrow in his face and could only imagine what it might betoken. There are some questions that may never be asked, even among close friends, for they enter upon those regions of the heart where reside the many possibilities of life foregone, which every life contains.

Holmes had never married. In his earlier days I had concluded that this was through a want of feeling in his nature, but in this assumption I feel that I wronged him. I suspect now that he feared to pass on to an heir something of his own melancholy. Holmes, who knew so intimately the many facets and furrows of the collective fate of humankind and who had through his clients seen how often heartbreak and disappointment follow the fond hopes and expectations of youth, did not wish to try his own hand in the game. I believe that his pity and his forbearance of any condemnation of others came from this source.

I have come to see that my early assessment of Holmes as a reasoning machine should have been taken by my readers as a statement of my admiration of the intricate workings of his mind, while all too many may have erroneously concluded that my friend was lacking in the human instincts altogether. Nothing could be further from the truth. His own early loss of his mother had acquainted him with grief from his youth. His habitual restraint indicated if anything that he possessed a passionate nature. His sudden outbursts of energy showed that no neurasthenic temperament was his. Holmes was a student of human nature, but more still he was a student of the actual lives of human beings with their obscure and mixed motives. The truest ethics is the one that comprehends the role of habit, innate capacity, and chance in human affairs.

I recall now that I thought that night of the prejudice that often views all actresses as fallen women. To see Irene Adler that night in New York was to know how wrong any such estimate of her character was. It is no small part of having the strictures of morality passed on primarily by a celibate clergy, whose very office shields them from the necessity to do battle for daily life in the toil of street and factory, that they may too easily define the parameters of morality as though life is lived in a test tube. The great confessors though, whose wisdom since it is sealed by the seal of the confessional is unknown even to moralists, may temper to some degree the hard letter of the law as deduced by moral theologians. It seems to me at times that few people ever die in a technical state of grace and many a man or woman who has done a great amount of good in their life seems, as judged by the mere lottery of death before complete repentance, to be found wanting on the portals of eternity. Shall such people as these be condemned to hell, as the catechism proclaims with such assurance, because of any un-repented sin that remains?

What purpose was served by such clear definitions based upon a presumption of absolute clarity in the texts that served as the base for a religion that emerged out of the determined resistance of the majority of the Jewish people? Does hell contain such a significant number of souls that resemble the very people that we greet warmly each day? If heaven contains only a fraction of God's potential harvest then why sow the seed so widely when the reality is that salvation is as rare as truffles? But then I am probably speaking again as a doctor who never loses a patient without chagrin and a sense that an eternal reward will act as a poultice for the pain of living at all. The very sight of a crucifix should give us pause before condemning others to hell it seems to me. Surely having suffered so much for mankind, Jesus will not bow to the stoic formalisms of his minions who seem so content to imagine that, since they at least are of the elect, that they can accept such prevalent damnation of others with at most an upturned eye and a shake of the head. "They might have repented," they may say, as though that explains all. But I say that any one life, if actually and fully lived, puts one at extraordinary risk of damnation. If the desert fathers were set upon by demons who masqueraded as human beings to tempt the flesh of the hermits, so that every whirl of dust might hide a demon in disguise, then how much more must each street-corner of Soho hide demons in its denizens of the night to our peril.

Holmes would have smiled at my melodramatic presentation here of course but then he hears the confessions that are shared with detectives and doctors sometimes more often than to priests. The doctor is the priest of the body and few die without asking a doctor to do the impossible to save him, as though health was ever ours to bestow. A priest may grant absolution and the soul lives again, perhaps only to sin again, but when bodily death comes at last neither doctor nor priest can perform their usual functions. Thereafter the solitary journey of the soul truly begins.

I have meditated often on death having seen so much of it. When does death really occur? What is death? Might it not take years for the soul to leave its last hold upon the body? Certainly there are tales of ghosts that appear to haunt for years the scene of their life's departure. Might they not be allotted a condition to view in perspective their moral failings now that life is ended and to reach in that twilight world a determination and decision and make their eternal choice? To make of death a mere instant and to imagine that time and eternity are so close as to be crossed in an instant is that not the greatest presumption? Knowing nothing of death as process dare we be so certain of the fate of souls?

Perhaps hell and purgatory lie in such close proximity that a final access of grace may be adequate to reach into the very bowels of hell and snatch from final possession by the devil one or many whom we would assume to be forever lost. I should not care to risk so grievous a fate as to skirt the edge of so deep an abyss, but might it not be that those most ready to consign friend and enemy to precisely that fate might be the ones most deserving to share it?

The function of the saints is to show us how easily we might avoid even the outer heat of those fires. Their admonitions are not to be despised. But they are men and women after all and surely God should not be limited by our own trepidations. It is the function of God to do what only God can accomplish. I should rather assume a universal efficacy of mercy than to restrict the bounds of heaven to a narrow elect when considering the numbers to be saved for the one view gives precedence to God while the other only seems to glorify the devil with unearned victories. If it is an insult to give a party that is only sparsely attended, then might it not be fortunate if the devil alone were to inhabit hell?

Some theologies have recognized a middle station patrolled by the lesser demons. Even the prayer to Saint Michael composed by Pope Leo XIII speaks of these when it says, "Satan and all the other evil spirits who prowl about the world seeking the ruin of souls." But then I have known men who function as devils even in this life. I cannot imagine them in heaven or hell. They seem to be merely bad company.

So perhaps the devil is doing them a service by providing them a place where they may wail and gnash their teeth. These deficient souls that have no other use and would forever be strangers to true happiness may deserve damnation of a sort. If the state of hell is one of legion, this may refer less to the sheer numbers of the damned and more to that iron-clad discipline of evil, which denies all true freedom to a soul encased in sin. The warnings about hell in the gospels may be more pedagogical than prophetic.

The discourses on perdition may also refer to the

fragmentation of evil itself because it is incapable of willing unity in God. Evil has always seemed to me to be analogous to decay. It destroys the integrity of the creature and the order of its sympathies. We call a thing evil because of its inappositeness to any use that is positive or productive. For this reason death seems the greatest evil to me for in an instant a change comes, the limbs stiffen and then grow lax, subsiding into the soft irrelevance of decay into the body's constituent elements. Where then has the life force gone?

To see Irene Adler so animated and so lovely was to believe that death could never touch her. I recall that I was thinking something of the sort that evening. I did not regard her beauty as temptation, but as the very glory of God made manifest.

"I see that Watson is engaged in another of his brown studies," I recall Holmes saying while smiling at Inspector Hopkins. He had risen from the table as had the Inspector. I could see that we must pass Irene Adler's table if we were to exit the restaurant. As we walked forward I could see Holmes produce a small note. We were soon opposite the table and Holmes bowed deeply before Miss Adler and her group of admirers.

"Ah, Miss Irene Adler, is it not? You must pardon this interruption, but I thought that I recognized you. I recall your excellent performance in London in 1887, one that I have often remembered fondly in the years since then. Pray allow me to present my compliments and to express my happiness that you have resumed your career since our last meeting. May I leave my card with you? Thank you very much."

For just a moment their hands met. She smiled up at him with an air of subtle humor saying. "And I in turn seem to have some recollection of you sir. Did we not meet again in Rome some years ago? I recall your courtesy to me on that occasion and I have long hoped that we might meet again so that I might thank you. Your encouragement was valuable to me at the time and as you can see I followed your advice given to me at the time."

She looked unobtrusively at the back of the card while she was speaking and looking up she smiled and nodded. Holmes bowed again and we made our exit. As we entered our cab Holmes murmured, "She will see us tomorrow, Watson." With that our cab jolted forward and we left behind us the gaiety and elegance of Delmonico's. We entered the well-lit streets that were thronged with traffic even at that late hour and a short time later we found ourselves again at our hotel.

Holmes' attitude was one of barely repressed excitement and I prepared a sleeping draught for him. To one who is consumptive even excess of joy may be too much for the constitution to bear. I recall that I was quite as excited as Holmes by the sudden rediscovery of a woman whose early retirement had led me to presume that she had died, perhaps as a victim of the jealous monarch who had first led us into an acquaintance with her. I was delighted that she was alive, because I knew the part that she had so long played in the memory of my friend. I recall that I remained awake therefore and sought in the pages of the journal of his travels some answer to the many questions that thronged my mind and kept all sleep at bay until they were answered. I returned then to that Christmas Day in Rome at the close of 1892, the second year of his long absence from my life.

From the Journal of Sherlock Holmes

December 30, 1892
A Strange Tale of a Great Lady

How strange it is that I should conclude this momentous but often solitary year by spending the last several days in the company of Irene Adler and hearing her extraordinary story. It is only now indeed that I recognize the truth of my early assessment of her character and find that the appellation I have always applied to her as "the woman" was justified. This Christmas evening will long be a memorable one for me. I was greeted at the door of her villa on the outskirts of Rome by a proper British manservant who took my cloak and ushered me into her well-lit drawing room where she awaited me. She was still clothed in black as was proper for one who has lost her husband as recently as last summer, but she had allowed herself a sprig of holly pinned above the bosom. A small gold locket hung about her neck as a memento to her late husband. She rose graciously upon my entering and gave me her hand. She asked if I would care for any refreshment and I was soon seated in an ornate armchair facing her where she sat on the couch. She had served me a thin fluted glass filled with Benedictine. Christmas dinner would be served at seven she informed me. I already could scent the goose and the homely odor of sage wafting through the hall from the kitchen at the rear of the villa.

"I keep a very small establishment here, Mr. Holmes, only a butler, a housekeeper, and a cook, but I shall try to give you a decent English Christmas dinner anyway. I will want to hear an account of your travels abroad, since they must be far more interesting than any narrative of my life since we last met."

I appreciated her demure and courteous welcome and answered her, "Over dinner I shall comply with your wishes Mrs. Norton, but since I have long wondered how you have managed since we last met in London, perhaps you will favor me with an account if it is not too painful for you?"

She smiled bravely and a small spasm of pain convulsed her lovely forehead but she answered me at once, "Of course, Mr. Holmes. I can relate my story best by telling you something of my husband's character, of how we first met, and how it was that our marriage was the sudden and forced affair that it seemed to be on that morning in London when you came to our timely assistance by acting as an impromptu witness of our marriage vows."

She continued after gathering her thoughts together. "I must confess to having been somewhat of an adventuress in my early years. A woman who may lay claim at once to both wit and beauty knows her gifts and feels the power that both may bestow over the hearts of powerful men. I had known a degree of privation as a girl. Not that we were poor, but my father, who was a craftsman was also Jewish and he was made to feel the strictures imposed upon his race even in England. My mother was English and a great beauty and of good family as well, but one I am sorry to say that frowned upon her marriage to a Jew. This was less for reasons of religion than from class distinctions. My mother's father had come over to the Church of England after being raised as a Methodist as his position in the world improved. It is an old story of course, these tiny cruelties that live on in families. After her marriage my mother was never cut off of course; they were not as cruel as that.   But I was never close to my mother's family and I thought of myself as Jewish in blood if not in faith. I was proud of my father's people and could never conceive of the reason for the distaste for them shown by so many Christians, to that very race that after all gave them their Savior. It always seemed absurd to me to believe that the Jews gathered in the courtyard of Pilate on that fatal morning would wish upon themselves and to all of their posterity the guilt that has been so universally applied to them throughout all times and places in the name of Christianity. It was Rome after all that established the first ghetto. I felt an emotion of bitterness as a young girl towards everything called Christian. To make it a virtue to expel and to isolate my race from nation after nation through the ages still seems to me to be a collective sin so appalling that Christians have much to answer for before God and to their victims, the Jewish people."

This flare of spirit brought a blush of color to her pallid cheek before continuing, "I often speculated in my young womanhood that had the center of the Christian Church remained in Jerusalem, perhaps a closer alliance between those who believed that Jesus was the Messiah and those who still awaited Him in another guise might have been formed in a united opposition to the Rome of the Caesars. Perhaps the Babylonian Talmud need not have been written in over the next centuries after the Diaspora. Perhaps the fortress of Masada would not have fallen. Perhaps ... but what is history finally but a series of speculations upon what might have been and a record of hopes dashed. In any case when St. Paul prevailed over even the hesitation of St. Peter and the world of the gentiles was opened to the promises of Christ, so that within a generation all who still attempted to follow the Law of Moses were branded as rank heretics, those sentiments were returned by an embittered Sanhedrin that expelled the early Christians from the synagogues. St. Peter, who had now come over to the vision of the future church entertained by St. Paul, removed to Rome and was later crucified there. Rome then became the center of Christianity. It is of the nature of a faith that sees death and suffering as liberation that it would beard the Roman lion in its very den and come to eclipse the former foundational church in Jerusalem, the very church that was still gripped by the influence of St. James. That tiny community had inherited the concepts of duty, law, and works as evidence of its faith. Rome on the contrary grew more to emphasize the role of the mere act of conversion as dispositive for it anticipated that once the entire extent of the empire had heard of Christ, then Jesus would return at once and the kingdom would be at hand. Alas, it was not to be. Christians might learn much from the endurance of the Jews who are if nothing else accustomed to waiting and hoping even when the wells of hope are dry."

She paused for a moment as though the words that she had just spoken defined her present disposition as well. "I hope that I do not bore you with these thoughts, but they are essential if you are to truly understand my character."

I assured her that I found her observations to be of the greatest interest and that I was currently much occupied with the same issues.

"Very well then, I shall continue. We must remember that those first centuries of the period after Christ were an age of upheaval. The number of cults was numerous. There was Mithraism and its cult of the bull, the teachings of Zoroaster from Persia still exercised influence upon other faiths, and many still worshiped at the Temples of Diana, while the Celtic Druids in our own native England held sway there. Out of this religious soup was spawned heresy after heresy so that it took hundreds of years for even the Roman Church to speak with only a single voice. Heresy and orthodoxy lived side by side then as they do now. The Church of Rome emerged like a rock in a stormy sea and the faithful have always clung to its slippery face lest they be swept again out into the seas of private interpretation and the various sects that expound them. But where did that leave the Jews, despised by Catholic and heretic alike? The Jews had only the Torah and the Talmud and the racial remnant of Israel to sustain the old beliefs. Only two institutions of the western world have survived time and change for two thousand years, the Roman Catholic Church and Judaism, which is even older. The Jews do not accept Jesus, but they are loyal to the Messiah who they imagine has not yet come. It because the Jews still believe that the characteristics ascribed by Christians to the second coming (which will be supreme power and glory) should have been visible at the first coming. Jesus was for the people of my race a bit too familiar, too much of 'God with us' for their taste, a bit too plebian."

She looked up at me earnestly, "No one likes a religion that is too humble, not even Christians. If you doubt this you need only to look about you at the grandeur of Rome. What is Rome but an effort to show the glory of God to man here and now? I assure you I am not impressed."

"And yet you live here in preference to other places," I remarked smiling.

She started at the interruption and looked down in some embarrassment. "You must forgive me, Mr. Holmes, for my extensive disquisition, but I know of no other means to tell my tale."

"On the contrary, Mrs. Norton, I find your observations fascinating. Pray continue since I have always felt that a story should be told in all its particulars before commenting. It is one of my primary axioms as a detective."

She smiled and showed renewed confidence, "Very well then, I will do so. To come back then to my own attitude to my ancestry, it was one of great pride. I was no suet-fed Briton but a buxom and tanned representative of my eastern origins and the combination in my features was exotic to many suitors and guaranteed me quite a following in the theater. My father was not pleased with my choice of acting and singing as a profession, but I assured him that I would become no music-hall artiste, but would tour the continent and be the envy of many grand ladies. He gave his consent and after a year of lessons in voice and elocution I was offered my first roles in the theater and opera. Within two years I had climbed from chorus-girl to prima donna. I toured all of the great capitols of Europe. I became known as the Diana of the stage, for though I favored many with my company, I bedded none of them. The result was predicable. A very torrent of proposals came to me until even members of the nobility favored me with their attentions."

"It was at that time of my greatest celebrity that I met Wilhelm Gottsreich Sigismund von Ormstein, Grand Duke of Cassel-Felstein, and hereditary King of Bohemia. I was later to learn that his liaisons were as numerous as his names, yet I was flattered at first by receiving such attention from a man with so many titles and claims to wealth. He is now as pox-ridden a gentleman as one is ever likely to encounter and a great bigot to boot, who accompanied the occasion of his coronation by having my people expelled from Bohemia leaving their homes and businesses behind.

I set my eye upon him, determined to teach him a lesson. It was said that he might seduce any woman in Europe and it pleased me, Irene Adler, the daughter of a Jew, to tease him and yet remain always beyond his grasp. I hope that I do not shock you, Mr. Holmes, but I have already admitted to being an adventuress and even your friend, Dr. Watson, once somewhat pompously referred to me as quote, 'the late Irene Adler of dubious and questionable memory.' It was not long before I had this man in my grip. But if I had him in mine I was no less in his. He followed me all about Europe and subjected me to his fits of jealousy and rage until I came to wonder whether the game was worth the candle. At last I came to fear for my very life for the man was, if I may so, somewhat unhinged and absolutely ungovernable where his passions were concerned. As I had no intention of submitting to his loathsome embraces even to secure a title and fortune, so I determined at last to let it slip that I was of Jewish origin. But before doing so I intended to extract from him some compromising promises and a picture proffering a degree of intimacy that might serve as evidence, which I might produce as a defense against his wrath and recriminations if he realized fully the merry chase that I had led him and sought revenge or worse still, a forced marriage. I knew that he would then determine to take his revenge upon me, for he was a man with a pride that was equal to his vanity. I will go so far as to say that I feared even violence at his hands or from a paid assassin if I dared to seek my freedom."

"It was at this very time that my life grew even more complicated. While touring with my company in London I came to meet a man who was in every respect the gallant man of my dreams. He was of good family, rich, handsome, but above all he was honorable as the King was not. If women of virtue are hard to find, virtuous men are, if I may say so, even more rare. I had now two things to fear: the wrath of the King and the loss of the man who I swiftly came to adore. You smile, Mr. Holmes, but you cannot perhaps imagine what a beautiful woman knows from her youth, that same capricious nature, which strews her person with unsought favors in youth, soon withdraws her gifts and that her time is short if she would obtain the advantages that her unearned beauty promises."

"But Madame, surely a virtuous woman need fear no such loss of love when she has other more permanent qualities," I interrupted.

"Ah my dear sir, even she must act swiftly, for the age when she may produce the heirs that cement a man's loyalty to her flee quickly even as her beauty does. The best part of fidelity in men is that they often remain married out of mere habit and the loss of their own charms. For this reason wise nature soon despoils most of them of their hair and adds to their girth. Yet the front rows of the theater were filled every night with these vultures gazing lustfully over the footlights at me. It may be that I malign my best patrons; I read your thoughts, Mr. Holmes. You need not smile so. You do not know what it is to be a woman. An actress is not always a courtesan, at least I am not. Though I have used the gifts at my disposal to procure a comfortable place in life, I have for the most part only been a purveyor of illusions that end with my curtain call. I receive flowers and notes in my dressing room, but grant no private audiences. My dresser is a stout and hardy woman named Molly who has on occasion blackened a few eyes in defense of her charge."

I spoke up, "I follow your story completely. Though I come from a household of brothers, I have had many clients whose stories show the peculiar delicacy of a woman's position if her class and family do not shield her from unwanted advances."

"Thank you, Mr. Holmes. To return to my story then, I now wished even more to be free of the King's attentions and at first I thought I had succeeded, for he had returned to the continent and for a time I thought that I should hear no more from him. That alas was not to be the case. He wrote me suddenly and demanded the return of his letters and picture. This of course I would never dare do. I had no intention of forfeiting the only weapons that I possessed against him. It was then that he came to his own absurd conclusion. He imagined that I was retaining the letters to force him to go ahead with the marriage he had proposed to me. He had you see been playing a double game all along with me and was wooing one who, as he would put it, was of his own station all along and matters had reached a state where an alliance was imminent. He must have the letters back. It was at that juncture that the King consulted and received the aid of England's greatest detective, a Mr. Sherlock Holmes."

I must admit to feeling considerable embarrassment at her words. "I could not know, Madame, the true state of affairs. The image you had created in the public mind was..."

"Quite so, but then without bait one does not catch the fish, does one? My male following would not be as extensive if there was not the hope that I would yield, as the public imagined I had done many times before to the frequent solicitations of my male retinue. Yet I was innocent. I came to my husband, a virgin. It is some years now since my career soared to the heights and though I might still choose to resume perhaps a distinguished career, I could never hope to excite again the frenzy of my early years. You see now my plight and the conflicting feelings that prevailed at the time that you and I first met. I had found the man who I truly loved and was beset by a great and possibly violent adversary who would stop at nothing. I didn't know what to do and though my dresser Molly swore that she would guard me from all harm, I assured her that we needed outside help. It was then that I determined to tell Godfrey everything. I did so with many tears and much wringing of my hands. But it was not an act I assure you. My years on the boards had caused many an audience to break into sobs of sympathy at lesser demonstrations of anguish. In the end I was quite prostrate with my grief for fear that he would leave me. You can imagine my joy when instead of hearing the door slam there was only silence. I looked up through my lashes at last to see that Godfrey was smiling down at me beatifically. At first I thought that he was not taking me seriously and in spite of all my fears the color rose to my cheeks and I was about to protest when he placed a finger to my lips."

"'My dearest girl,' said he, 'You have brought me great joy, for though I never doubted your virtue, my father did raise certain objections to our union, which your story shows me are utterly without merit. Your story will go no further than this room of course, but I can now assure him that any inquiry he might care to make would be both impertinent and an injustice and he will take my word for it. As for your King and your present troubles, I have a solution, but I fear that it will cost you your career, for it will entail our marriage. I desire that you make a home with me. I have been appointed as my firm's counsel in Rome to handle all of its legal matters involving our business in Italy. If you would consider becoming my wife, you would both do me a great honor and secure my happiness. I love you Irene. Will you marry me?'"

She was weeping at the memory and was at that moment as beautiful as a woman might ever be and though Watson has so often assured his readers that I am immune from women's charms, I may frankly record here that I am not. A woman has the capacity to double whatever emotions a man feels whether of joy or of sorrow. It is a formidable power and a woman who uses it with any other purpose than sincerity has much for which to answer. There is a sensible fear that a man must have of the ungovernable character of some women, though most women are not like Clytemnestra, yet there will always remain a subtle fear of the powers that lie within womankind. Watson was mistaken in confusing my exercise of prudence for disinterest.

She continued, "I agreed at once of course to be his wife. I could not imagine how he would extricate me though from my troubles, but I was willing to cast all of my cares upon him and to follow his instructions if only I might possess his heart and be free of the King. I asked him how we were to proceed."

"Godfrey answered me, 'We will obtain a dispensation for a swift marriage, Irene. If the marriage banns are published in London we are undone, so we will join a parish in an outlying district where the banns will be read as required by Canon Law. You see that I have already made inquiries in anticipation of your answer. My former intent was to spare you notoriety and unwanted press attention, but now my precautions will also shield you from the King. You must secretly terminate your present theatrical engagement in London so that your last performance will be followed by the day of our marriage and secret departure from London. We will wed before we leave at St. Monica's Church on the Edgware Road. I will have all the necessary arrangements made. You will then return to your lodgings, pack secretly, and we will away to the continent. Your luggage will follow later with Molly after the scent is cold. She will join us in Rome and will act as our housekeeper.'"

"Upon my protesting that the King would have us followed and find us at last, Godfrey assured me that since our alliance was not known, I could not be traced through him. Each of us would leave London by different trains, he to take up his position in Rome while I would at first be presumed to have left England to pursue my career on the continent. Godfrey had devised a means to put the King forever off of our traces by my supposed death in France in a carriage accident incurred between engagements. The public would then suppose me to be dead. But I would be alive in Italy, a married woman, and free at last. It was necessary that our marriage be sudden and secret and we were married in the very manner that you know. Godfrey's plan worked perfectly, but for his rather absurd omission of forgetting the need for a witness at the ceremony, a need which you so happily supplied in your own person and for which I thank you again, Mr. Sherlock Holmes. After that all went well. We came to Italy in safety and our lives were such as admitted no disharmony or lack of joy. We supposed that nothing could change our happiness and interfere with our future prospects until ..."

She burst again into tears and I made so bold as to rise and take her hand for a moment to comfort her. It was then that Molly opened the door to announce dinner. Irene smiled bravely and gave no sign of discomfort at being interrupted at such a delicate moment, but thanked her housekeeper and rose with dignity from the couch where I sat at the moment by her side. She retained a grip on my hand and at her bidding we both left the room where we had been speaking to partake of the marvelous Christmas repast that awaited us in the dining room. It was one of those moments, unforeseen and unthought-of of, where a subtle shift occurs between two people and new prospects, hitherto uncontemplated, open before them.

Later—

Our conversation during the meal was of a lighter nature. My hostess could not have been more gracious. The goose was excellent, stuffed with a dressing of *champignon* and oysters, and served with potatoes and endives with a truffle crème sauce. I told her something of my journey, but did not go into the motivation for my journey. I did mention my chemical research in Montpellier and we compared impressions of that fair city where she had often performed during her years as an actress and diva of the grand opera. I asked her if she missed performing and she told me that she did, more so since her husband's death. It was not the acclaim so much that she missed, but rather the sheer joy of using her gifts and the sense that theater can create a unique sense of magic in this prosaic world. The artist can only be truly happy when practicing her art.

Still she had not been restive in her role as a wife in Italy. The marriage had produced no children so that she was left only with the villa at her husband's death. Her husband had left her a considerable fortune, so she need not be concerned for any necessities. She existed though in a vacuum, unable to imagine what further direction her life might take now that he was gone. The result has been that she goes daily to Holy Mass at the church where I had found her and she often spends hours there, not in active prayer, but simply because she says that she finds there a sense of love and peace that she finds nowhere else.

She asked my opinion about her present practices and I told her that life often has periods of lacunae when the onward momentum of events seems to cease. It is precisely at such times that grace may operate to correct the errors that we retain and to lift our aspirations to a greater joy. She seemed to find some comfort in my words and it gave me pleasure to see her entering into the spirit of Christmas as the meal proceeded. She told me that I had been her first guest since her husband's death. I could see that she had adapted well to the role of hostess and that it was a pleasure to assume again what had become an accustomed role for her during her more active years.

After our feast we adjourned to the drawing room and I was pleased to see a return of color to the face that had been pale in the candlelight on the previous night when I had encountered her after Mass. The evening was well advanced by then and I wished her farewell after a parting Christmas toast. Her own coachman delivered me to my hotel and I have spent the succeeding days since our meeting walking about Rome and wondering what course I should follow in the coming year. Before parting, Mrs. Norton gave me her hand and expressed the wish that I would feel free to call upon her again, certainly before leaving Rome and I promised to do so. I sent her a note the following day to thank her for her hospitality, but I have yet to call upon her again. She is still in mourning after all.

December 28, 1892
The Feast of the Holy Innocents

It is always the innocents who pay the price in this world for the guilty. Yet it is a sin to malign the world that God has created. The Romans see no contradiction between an otherworldly life in their faith and a celebration of what joys may be available in our present state. I have often remarked that the southern peoples remained Catholic while it was the northern Europeans who have embraced Protestantism. The rich sacramental life and the pageantry that have always been the accompaniments of worship and the means of reaching God in a visible way that exist in Catholicism were exchanged for a formal compact based on a text in Protestantism.

After giving up any belief in the actual flesh and blood of Christ as present in the Holy Sacrament of the Altar (which is also living in the members of the Catholic Church through the presence of the Holy Spirit) all that remained to the protestant compact was the mere intellectual assent of faith to a formula for salvation. The figure of the Crucified Christ was taken from the cross in the protestant churches, because the mindset of Protestantism despises images as idolatrous, even if the image is of Jesus Christ. Meanwhile, the written words of the Bible are given a semi-divine nature although the text as merely communicative can never equal the sacramental action of a living God. A living word but one now divorced from the very universal Church that breathes life into the text.

The Biblical texts were recognized and accepted into the canon by the Catholic Church that recognized and assembled certain writings as inspired and as useful to confirm the Christian in his faith. If it is true that man does not live by bread alone but by every word that comes from the mouth of God, it is also true that God knows that we need bread also and has chosen the most prosaic of actions, that of obtaining nourishment, as the figure and means to take us into Himself and to share the divine life of grace through receiving the Holy Eucharist that is the actual Body and Blood of Jesus Christ, the universal source of life for all the world.

It may be a strange thing but all heresy begins as it did with the Gnostics by despising the flesh rather than transcending it.

Beauty is not the gate to destruction, but rather the lust that would deny beauty its proper role in the divine plan by seeking to possess and control what must always be a gift. One need only read Browning's excellent poem, "My Last Duchess," to perceive the difference.

As the Duke points to a picture of his most recent wife upon the wall it becomes clear that she was murdered or perhaps imprisoned so as to cause her death by withering away in loneliness and despair. The reason given is that she valued the gift of her husband's ancient name the same as any other gift; she smiled upon all alike. Her universal joy and charity could not be tolerated by the one who would possess her completely. Art in the form of her painted portrait shows how a person can be made to appear as simply an artifact, an object, and a thing to be possessed for one's exclusive use. The proper attitude of life it seems to me is to see the fullness and the actuality of each unique feature of the earth, to see its integrity and yet to see beyond it at the same time, to see it as a partial revelation of the divine intent in all creation.

This duality is the very essence of the sacramental attitude to life. A sacrament is preeminently an inner reality that manifests itself by an outward sign. Not the least of these outward signs is the simple virtue of hospitality. So it was that I enjoyed the evening with Irene Norton nee' Adler, seeing in her that living fire of light that raises the spirit of youth to imagine that it may do all things. What is youth but the assumption that no other age has ever known its unique fire? That spirit of exaltation is everywhere in the Baroque churches of Rome. Where true joy is manifest in design, evil must give way.

The worst evils always begin as an idea. God on the other hand works as an artist with whatever material is at hand. The carpenter is an artist and even the fisherman shows artistry in knowing where the net is to be cast. The iconoclast always begins by assuming that men and women have no physical needs. We perceive the transcendental by the respect that we show to its temporary forms seen as indicative rather than as definitive. We need images; we need forms. There is something vicious in defacing images and the one who does so usually ends by defacing the image of God in man and woman as well as the objects that the iconoclast scorns. There is something essentially moral in the honest objectivity of the world. The very distinctness of each thing demands that we take its nature into consideration and not to subsume it into some higher genus or order. The nature of the contemplative attitude is to pay attention to the singular and to respect its unique parameters and its right to exist as precisely itself in its limited being.

The end of the year has come. Until now I have been certain and convinced that I was making progress toward the end of giving my life definition. Each of us inhabits a tiny segment of history. The shape of things to come is not, as many would wish, on a straight course, an arrow of progress. In fact history sometimes appears to run in reverse as far as progress is concerned. It may take a century to recover from a cycle of wars or from a religious convulsion.

Over a thousand years separates the high point of Roman culture from the Renaissance. The problem of all historical action is in comprehending whether one's actions are proportionate to the needs of the age in which one lives. It is quite possible that thoughts that seem unique and revolutionary are really the last dying gasp of the present age. How many men whose names were once on every tongue are known to later ages only as examples of the foolishness and fatuousness of a time now past and held in disrepute.

Every man would wish to be a hero in his own time, but the true contributor is most likely to be the one who was then held in contempt, because he was already living beyond the insight of his peers and their collective wisdom. For that reason it is also impossible to know how to evaluate the virtue of our actions in the time when the actions are taking place.

I have feared all my life to reach the point of death and to think that I may have been wrong all along and that my true life ran alongside the one I have actually lived; or that I have missed an essential intersection or nexus somewhere along the way and have ended up in some foreign or frontier region derailed or shunted aside along some railroad siding while the trains of other lives have thundered along past me.

It is then that I have most needed at those times of doubt to fill the hours and days with some measure of success and to have at my side one who would record the adventures lived and the problems solved through my art of detection. Dr. Watson filled that role. Still my life's triumphs seem so little. What are a few monographs on obscure points of detection and the cases solved, often without any personal credit or public acclaim?

Even if I should be offered a knighthood or a peerage at some future date, would it be enough to satisfy my need to have lived a truly useful life? What is this obsession though but mere personal ambition? Is it not enough that I might live a good life in obscurity like the majority of the human race? Why must do I covet more? Perhaps I need first to determine the parameters of the good and then meet those requirements. Would I then be satisfied? Where is God in all of this? Has my real ambition always been that I might someday say with the Pharisee, "I thank God that I am not like the rest of men?"

That prideful prelude is unworthy of any prayer and cannot please God. A proper prayer should begin as follows:

I thank God that I am like the rest of men, that though sharing their faults, I have been favored with hope so that I dare to pray for the following gifts:

First that I may repent of the sins that I know.

Second, that I may repent even more the sins that my

darkened mind does not realize have always been the most
grievous of all, for many of the virtues that I thought were my
own were in fact the mere adjunct of conscience and of grace.
Third, that I may clothe myself in Christ who alone may
cover me though I am naked.
Fourth, that I may offer the suffering of my own
contemplation of my life to the great cry of the church for mercy.
Fifth, that in spite of being blind I may still dare to act in
trust, while suffering providence to correct my course and to
supplant every deficiency at the end of my life so as to take me to
heaven and be with the saints in contemplation of God forever.
Amen.

January 1, 1893
A New Year

Ibegan the New Year with Mass at St. Peter's Basilica. I was pleased to have the company on the occasion of Mrs. Norton. I needed to begin what may be the most challenging year of my life at the very center of Christendom and to feel the suffrages of the Church Universal behind me as I prepare to confront Professor Moriarty. The splendor of the Mass on this occasion was something I shall always remember: the Gregorian chant, the colors of the vestments, the ascending incense, and the aspect of the clear cold skies of Rome when we emerged from the church with the pigeons wheeling in their flight above St. Peter's square while the bells rang throughout the city seemed a blessed augury of good fortune in all that I may undertake this year.

Our walk by the Arno after Mass was one of confidential friendship. I told Irene Norton of the task that lay ahead for me and my fear that I may not be able to accomplish the task that I so rashly assumed at the Falls of Reichenbach. How certain I had been then, fresh from my triumph over the Moriarty organization of crime! I have in many ways grown so much older since then. My birthday is on January 6th and as I was born in the year 1854, I will be thirty-nine years old in five days. I still feel quite young and vigorous, but I read somewhere recently that the life expectancy of a man of my age is forty-five. Of course with the arrogance of youth I have always allocated my various projects on the assumption that I would live deep into the next century.

I believe that my recent frantic effort to reach some final dispensation or summation of my life is not premature, but if I shall be granted a longer life that is all well and good. The approaching prospect of one's death should never be far from our thoughts, but it should not bring us up short and stifle our aspirations. I did not mention these preoccupations of mine to Irene of course, since her own dear husband was not able to live out even those brief years that might have been his expectancy. To die young has the advantage of dying with all of one's powers intact and not to know the ailments of old age, but still I desire that my own poor fire will burn to embers and that I will leave no charred cinders to mock the fire that they once contained. Irene was kind enough to notice my shifting moods of melancholy which, I am afraid, frame most of my birthdays. She offered her home and hospitality to me once again.

"We must celebrate your birthday my dear Holmes," said she. "Dr. Watson would persist in his low estimation of me, if I failed to take his place on this special occasion and to make, this birthday at least, a memorable one. I am at my best when staging things as you might expect from an actress. You must leave everything to me."

I must confess to being pleased by her offer and to have enjoyed the bright eyes and lovely smile that accompanied her announcement of her intentions. It was in a lighter frame of mind then that I took her arm as we continued our walk that ended finally at the Fountain of Trevi. A light coating of ice had filmed the pools within the fountain that morning. The fountain is emptied and cleaned every autumn. It has been filled again and is in operation for the New Year's festivities. We each bowed to the local superstition for the nonce by casting coins into the water. A misty spray was raised from time to time by a vagrant breeze that left its droplets upon Irene's downy cheek. The cold air of morning had brought out all of her color and the broken aspect she had worn a few days ago seemed to have passed.

We shared a lunch together later at a Trattoria that looks out upon the fountain. Her coach met us afterwards and conveyed me back to my hotel before taking her home. I wished her adieu, taking her gloved hand in mine. I had no words at the moment to express what I can only describe as an intermittent sense of profound confusion and embarrassment in her presence. Watson would no doubt diagnose this after his own fashion as romantic feelings. I did not feel the chill in the air when I stood outside my hotel and watched the carriage depart. If Watson should ever comes to read these words I trust that he will not find the situation humorous, for as I have often remarked he possesses sometimes a most pawky sense of humor against which I must learn to guard myself.

January 6, 1893
The Feast of Epiphany (my birthday)

It is dawn and I am writing this entry on the balcony of my hotel as the light breaks in the east and gradually illumines the city of Rome spread out beneath me. I can see the Dome of Saint Peter's Basilica as the sun first illumines the great dome and then descends slowly to Bernini's piazza below. I will spend the day alone until evening in prayer and reflection before joining Irene Norton nee Adler whom I may now call a dear friend for dinner, one commemorating the day of my birth, January 6, 1854.

I have always considered the date of my birth to have been indicative of the course that my life was to take and a prophecy of my choice of a profession. An epiphany is an unveiling, a revelation after a period of being hidden and kept in obscurity. Its celebration concludes the days of the Christmas Liturgical Season with the presentation of Jesus in the Temple for acceptance into the community of Israel. This presentation was accompanied by various prophetic utterances regarding the child's future. For the first time direct words of prophesy are uttered that foretold his future mission, and that he would be a sign of contradiction that would divide Israel. His future rejection was thus foretold as well as his triumph, for many in Israel could now anticipate a greater destiny than ever before: the fulfillment of the promise was at hand and the extension of the universal message from the Jewish people to all of humankind.

The mission of a detective is likewise to make known what has been hidden. In most situations the revelations are minor, but I cannot hide from myself that these last years of exile, arriving now at what I trust will be the third and final year, have been devoted to revealing, if only to myself, the secrets of my own character and what I believe about human origins and human destiny. Events have forced my hand to undertake this great task. I had followed Professor Moriarty for years and suddenly what we have each of us referred to as a slip placed his entire organization into my hands. The question of course was and remains to this day whether this "slip" was intentional. Perhaps Professor Moriarty (who is a man as time haunted as I am) determined not to leave his greater work unfinished while caught up in the pettiness of a criminal enterprise. Realizing the shortness of time, he may have simply reached the end of the natural term of his criminal career and decided to use me to aid in the transition to the final phase of his life's work. The form that the final phase will take though is beyond what I may envision at this time, certainly from such a distance as my present abode in Rome.

I have allowed him time to labor in seclusion and to weave his web to its furthest extent. I have desired to pose no opposition to him, but instead have dared him to do his worst, yet to suspend the final trigger that will set everything in motion, until he hears me present my case and conclusions. I have made him the judge and have made myself the advocate. Surely these are unequal positions. Even if judge and advocate share a commitment to a single set of laws and a recognized set of procedures, there is a divergence of roles. In the present case there is no advance recognition of the rules of procedure for our debate. Indeed we have yet to find a common vocabulary and syntax for truth itself! Have I been rash then to enter upon such a foolish wager, if indeed the word wager may encompass so grievous a contest as the one being played out between us? Perhaps both of our souls are at stake as well as many lives of innocent people should I fail to convince him.

Did St. Paul have something similar in mind to the anguish that I feel when he said that he would even be willing to sacrifice his own salvation in order to win salvation for the souls of those who were receiving his pastoral letters? But even as I ask myself this question I am forced to confront the entire issue of Moriarty's significance to me; why Moriarty of all people to be my judge? Why have I made this one man's judgment the very criterion for the truth of my own faith? Is it not because in attempting to convince Professor Moriarty I am really attempting to convince myself? If so, then it is really not Moriarty, nor has it ever been Moriarty that I have been attempting to defeat; it has been my own perception that I might myself have been as Moriarty but for a singular grace. It is only when we perceive how close evil lies within our own hearts that we fly from it with sufficient ardor. To play with evil, imagining that it can do us no real harm, to listen to the soft murmur of its suggestions and to imagine that we are justified in our acts of indignation toward others and our self-righteousness when we exact revenge upon malefactors is what has brought many otherwise virtuous men to destruction.

Professor Moriarty serves a great function in my life by representing the perfection of intellectual sin that lies so very near to my own door: the desire to be my own God, existing in a state of complete independence, and capable of determining once and for all the difference between good and evil, not through prayerful discernment and revelation as we are admonished to do, but rather as Saint Peter did when he advised Jesus to turn away from the cross and not to suffer to purchase our salvation.

Here is the great underlying appeal of that most sensible position of St. Peter: suffering for sinners is simply not worth it! The final sin of man is to agree with the devil that human beings are simply not worth saving, that the mistake of God was in ever having created anything at all! This great sin is the doubt that love should ever exist, a blasphemy against love that by denying the essence of God who is love itself makes salvation impossible to the one who persists in it. To deny Jesus the task appointed for Him at birth is to deny God. This is not humility but despair. Final impenitence is like saying to God, "Why should you care if I go to hell?" The most complete sin is to be disgusted even with heaven. It is to say to God as it were, "Is this what you had in mind all along: this foolish gift, this wanton excess of love, and for us of all things!"

I believe that the sin of the Devil and the final explanation for evil and its hatred for innocence and weakness lies in the fact of a self-loathing that is so complete that it detests its own being and simply refuses to accept forgiveness for its error. The greatest pride often hides behind self-contempt. All other sin is an invitation to humility, and though misguided, rather invites forgiveness than refuses it. The saint is one who is so aware of sin that he rushes to forgiveness like a hurt child to its parent. The prayer of the saint is not that he or she will be spared consequences, for to be spared them is to risk persistence in delusion. The prayer is that we shall be convicted of sin if only in our own eyes, for only in that conviction and the acceptance of the natural punishment that flows from within the evil action as its spring and source, can the mystery of forgiveness be understood. Forgiveness is the one divine act that severs consequence from cause and by doing so reverses the order of devolution and of entropy that we have come to accept as the natural order of things. We have learned over time to bracket God off from our experience and to accept things as they are, even if it should be our own destruction.

But what is life each day but forgiveness made manifest? Just as the sun returns to witness the destruction and wreckage of so many lives, grace awakens and shines with an opportunity to set everything right once again. What the soul refers to as the temporal punishment due to sin is the residual longing of the soul to still embrace the illusory charms of sin that have so eclipsed for a time the light that in conversion is even now breaking in upon it.

The fruit of forgiveness is a process of gradually letting go of the misguided affection we have for evil. The souls of most men and women are divided if not fragmented throughout their lives. Most enter eternity still in that same division. The wrenching apart of good and evil in death is one that resembles the opening of a vast fissure and at the same time is as sharp as a diamond when cleaving glass. In death everything receives its proper weight and measure. Each becomes at last what it is in complete clarity. A soul, steeped in any evil that it will not then renounce, is simultaneously horrified at the prospect of its own evil and enamored of it, so that only humility will shift (if anything can) its final alliance with an axis for eternity around which everything must turn: self-in-self or self-in-God. Good and evil then exist not so much in opposition, but rather in utter non-relation to each other. To be one is to deny the very principle of the other.

So again I say that vindication is the last thing that a man encased in sin should desire. He should instead thirst for conviction! Only then is mercy possible, when the determination of guilt and innocence has already been made. If I thought that I could convict Professor Moriarty, then he would already be a prisoner at the bar. No, I have made him the judge in our wager so that he can feel what it is like to dare to wish to be like God knowing and determining good and evil by himself!

I have restored him to what might be called the original position of man vis-a-vis God. That position is the one that asks nothing of God, for the necessity of God was the nightmare from which it has always been trying to awaken, ever since the human race first sinned in Eden. The primal temptation was not about our contentment and happiness. In Eden every human need was already being met by God. Our resistance then was that we had been spared evil. Man and woman could never feel themselves to be God's equal as long as they were aware that their own nature and happiness was completely dependent upon God.

But, and in this lies the greatest mystery of all, the final delusion: if man could endure what God alone can endure: -Evil- then we could be equal to God!

The explanation of Genesis is correct: the world in which we exist is in some strange way our choice. The Kingdom of God is at hand, but only if we dare to share the price of evil as born by Jesus Christ. Without God we hoped to surmount both good and evil and instead we came to enthroned evil, and worshiped it in ourselves. If Man has become God and while God in the figure of Jesus Christ is convicted in the folly of His love, then Man must worship Man!

For this reason the death of Jesus Christ on the Cross was,

from the Devil's point of view, both appalling and boring. Boring because God was acting as He had always done, acting mercifully towards evil; and appalling because, what man and woman cannot do alone, God was doing for humankind, working the salvation of the world.

God was winning once again by playing the ace, the God-card that trumps all other suits and cards, by doing what, again from the devil's own point of view, no Supreme Being can ever do and maintain its dignity, to suffer for sinners, to take on a punishment that is not its own but ours.

Jesus said, "No man has greater love than this, to give up his life for his friends." The mystery of the death of Jesus Christ is that He makes friends with His enemies, prays for His persecutors, and by so doing turns the world of evil upside down and empties all the vileness of evil upon God's own head!

It is absurd, unexpected, inappropriate, incongruent...and for all of these reasons I believe it is true, the very truth of God's nature as perfectly and uniquely good. God is Love...

January 7, 1893
My Birthday Celebration

I arrived yesterday at my hostess's villa in the evening and was promptly admitted at the door by her housekeeper and was shown into the drawing room. I was installed before a comfortable coal fire and told that Mrs. Norton would join me presently. The housekeeper, a woman named Molly, was about to withdraw, but instead hesitated at the door and turning back took me by surprise by asking if I intended to remain long in Rome.

"Please do not think me impertinent Sir, but it is my hope that you will remain for my lady's sake. Prior to your arrival in Rome, she had withdrawn even from her friends. But since your arrival her spirits seem to have revived and I do not wish her to descend again into the isolation and sorrow that have encompassed her during recent months."

I answered that my plans were still indefinite, but that I hoped to return to England at least within the year.

"Please do not tell her that I have spoken to you Sir, but you should know that prior to your arrival her spirits had sunk to such a degree that even her health and reason were affected."

I assured Molly that I would do whatever was in my power to encourage her mistress, but that I was confident that time would heal her wounds. At this she shook her head. "You did not know her husband, sir. He was such a man as a woman finds but once in a lifetime. If you could know how happy they were and how these halls sparkled with the wit and elegance of Roman society, and she herself the most beautiful even among these beautiful women of Italy, but still her husband's eyes never left her face. She never spoke of her past and her history as an actress was never known in the circles that she and her husband frequented here in Rome. She was accepted in even the highest diplomatic circles and even by Italian royalty. All of Rome saw her through her husband's eyes and she was loved and now... oh please, Mr. Holmes, you must do what you can to remain here for a time, at least until she resumes something of the vigor and life that she once possessed. I can say no more for I hear her step upon the stair."

She withdrew at once leaving me in some perplexity. If anything I had imagined that this woman, devoted as she was to Irene, must resent my recent visits to a household that still showed the signs of mourning so many months after the master's passing. I had not imagined the extent of the acquaintance that Irene Norton and her husband had maintained. No cards were ever brought in during my visits and even at Christmas, I had been given to understand, there had not been the usual festive callers. I now realized that she had severed all of her former connections after the death of her husband. The condolences, after the first months, must have gradually declined in number as people came to know that the former site of gaiety and celebration had become for her a monument to her husband's memory. The grand lady of the Villa Norton had withdrawn to a life centered upon her religious devotions, because they alone brought her any comfort. The young people of her acquaintance had found new sites of joy and vivacity in the whirl of the winter season and must have remarked in gossip about the melancholy English widow who could only love but once. The Roman mind appreciates tragedy and the orgy of tears, but it cannot understand a woman who in her youth becomes a perpetual widow nursing a private grief.

As I reflected thus Irene entered and I was surprised to see that she was wearing violet for the occasion and not the usual black. The velvet of her gown glistened in the candlelight and though she wore neither broach nor other adornments, she had touched her cheeks with powder and her lips with rouge so that her pallor was somewhat reduced. She blushed as she entered, no doubt realizing that I had noticed the change in her usual appearance and dress.

"I could not celebrate your birthday in mourning, Mr. Holmes. Dinner will I fear be delayed again. The Italians have no idea of how to cook a proper British lamb dinner, and it is being difficult. As you told me that it was a favorite of yours in your youth in Yorkshire, I have obtained a leg of lamb for you and it is cooking with potatoes and a sherry-mint sauce even as we speak. I will do my best to keep you amused though in the meantime and we have a long evening before us."

She was as always most gracious and after pouring me a brandy and herself a small glass of Chartreuse we sat before the cheerful fire ticking away in the grate. It was a scene of great peace and I found myself happy in way that I had not been in years. Her company was such that it conveyed, even in her sorrow, an atmosphere that seemed to make even time itself to pause in its hectic course. There were few sounds in the street and those that remained were shut out by the sable velvet drapes at the tall windows that looked out upon the busy streets of Rome. We might have been sitting in a grotto beneath the sea at Naples. All was candlelight and the richly polished woods and dark satin of the furnishings. It was a pleasure for me to hear her speak. Her voice was such that it's every modulation played its part in the symphony of her presence and I could appreciate how she had once held audiences in thrall.

I asked her finally if she missed the stage. She was silent for a time before answering.

"It may seem vulgar," said she, "To tell you that I have come to miss it of late. You may be surprised that my husband and I avoided the British after settling in Rome. I desired that my former life be dead forever and though dear Godfrey was not embarrassed by my past, he desired that I assume a station in Rome that he felt was my proper place. He always treated me as though I was of the same class as the nobility. I was amused to hear that the matrons of Rome assumed that my station in life in England was much higher than it was and that I was possessed of aristocratic antecedents. Since I had played queens and duchesses upon the stage it was no problem for me to act the part and since it enhanced my husband's career that he be thought the husband of a noblewoman, though I made no such claim overtly, I found myself displaying those airs and mannerisms that convey the impression of noble birth. Besides, in Rome to have some sort of title is *de rigueur*, for the Italians respect even questionable titles. The fact that I did not insist upon an appendage to my name was seen, not as the honesty, which is what it in fact was, but rather as a charming concession to Italian democracy. In a nation that has only recently found itself, this action of appearing less than I was, was found to be charming and I was beloved for it. After a time I began to believe that I was what they thought me to be. I used to sail into this very room and countesses would stand at my entry."

She smiled with amusement at her own daring, "It is extraordinary how fond we become of illusions, is it not? What is the theater but a great shared illusion and what is this vain world but theater on a grand scale? My youth seemed once to me, not a passing gift, but a permanent possession. I thought to myself that I should remain always young through sheer determination. I considered age to be an acquired habit and that mere will could keep the changes of life's seasons at bay. But I was already past twenty-five when I retired from the stage. The world will forgive everything to an ingénue but looks askance at the woman who seeks too long to retain the prerogatives of her debut season in the swift years that follow her coming out. You men are lucky, Mr. Holmes. You may construct a station for yourselves from your own abilities and that station is only enhanced with age. But a woman is defined by her marriage. She becomes subsumed into her husband and when she loses him she becomes what you see before you, a comfortable but deserted ruin."

She pointed about the room. "I live now in the confinement of my memories. I loved my husband. But his loss brought more to me than grief. It brought extinction. What was I to do, an exile in a foreign land? I have become accustomed to my place in Roman life. What am I now but a widow of a professional man and unless I marry some jackal waiting at my door for my period of mourning to pass, what shall become of me? By sustaining my mourning I preserve the afterglow of my connection to Godfrey and thus my respectability and position. I am respected for a degree of devotion to my husband's memory that is rare here. I need respect now, for I remember what it was like to be treated as *déclassé* simply because I chose the theater as a path in life. Only one who has been despised can know what is not to fear the sneer on the lips of men and the hatred in the eyes of women. No country can be more brutal in this regard than England. No, Mr.

Holmes, I do not miss the theater. I have now known the real world and been accepted by it. I cannot return to make-believe." She was silent there in the candlelight. I saw for a moment how cruel life can be even for those who have known nature's favors.

Those whom the gods intend to mock they first make happy. How strange it is that culture after culture has made of woman its dearest idol and it's most despised and wasted resource. It is woman alone who gives life, yet she is so often burdened with the lowest labors. Surely Eve has paid her debt! In Afghanistan I was appalled to see that a woman may not even show her face in public or go out without a male relative at her side. Even in Rome I have often noted the bizarre framing of the faces of the nuns for whom the rules of their order mandates that they shall go about like racehorses with blinders. Men fear women too much, thus their subjugation.

Do even the women of Islam conspire in this subjugation as well? I think not, for what rebel army will come to their aid? Even the familiar figures of the suffragettes are beaten in the streets of London for claiming some ability to influence the laws that govern them by advocating for the vote. Having freed the slaves even America has yet to free its mothers and sisters. Nor has England; nor has the world. Thinking along these lines I nodded and it brought me satisfaction to see her look up into my gaze and to see that I understood.

"What can I do, Mr. Holmes?"

One of the illusions that I fear that Watson's tales have conveyed is that I possess within myself the answer to every question. As I looked into the pleading eyes of Irene Norton I felt my own inability to proceed beyond the experience of life that I have had and the strength of my own prejudices. I have never had much use for society and social position. The mere fact that the great and famous have often needed to consult me in a professional capacity has destroyed whatever awe I may have ever felt in their presence. I have found that the upper classes have their own substantial populations of fools and cads and that the virtues they profess are often a sham. They are frequently held in contempt by those who must perforce serve them in order to obtain a living below stairs. Besides, my own father was a Baronet and although I am only his third son, I am a gentleman by birth.

Although I have no title, I retain the pride of my forebears and I have received an excellent education so that I quail before no man. But I could put myself in this woman's position and imagine how social contempt for her profession, when combined with advancing maturity, might leave her one day soon a wreck upon the shores of middle age. Fortunately, her husband has left her with more than a competent income, a legacy which, if it is carefully managed, may procure her a comfortable living for many years to come. Still, investments can miscarry and she is still in the prime of life. She might marry again of course in due season some suitable man. It might be best to do so because maintaining what is called a comfortable station in life has its own appending expense.

I pointed all of these considerations out to her as well as suggesting that she might pursue her singing on the continent in a less compromising setting than the English stage. France at least is less stodgy than the British and many a chanteuse has been able to pursue her chosen art without the same social censure. I could see that Irene was considering my suggestions, but that neither the suggestion of the possibility of a second marriage or a return to her art had any immediate appeal for her.

"I thank you of course for your advice, Mr. Holmes. No doubt you are right in seeing my situation as less distressing than it appears to me at present, but you must understand that after marrying I had found what I felt would be my life forever after. I imagined growing old with Godfrey and becoming one of those wise matrons who might advise others. I have a friend here in

Rome you see, an American named Mrs. Edith Wharton, who has herself known the strictures of social position to be so oppressive that she spends considerable time abroad. But in her case it has been the even more constrictive custom of being raised in New York's upper class. New York has all the pride and pomposity of a nation that has gone from colonial status to joining the ranks of the great nations of the world. Mrs. Wharton's family prior to her marriage, the Jones family of New York, is among the most influential in New York society. When her mother discovered that her daughter intended to be a writer of imaginative tales, she insisted that she be a debutante a year early; far better to marry her off before she gained too many strange ideas. But the ideas were already there, you see. Edith was raised in Europe and possesses a level of sophistication beyond either her years or her sex. She ended by marrying Teddy Wharton, who is hardly her intellectual equal, but is overall a pleasant sort and one who is content to let her make the decisions of importance in their marriage. I knew that she would understand me, so she alone knows of my background in the theater. Her wise perspective on life and her own rebellious spirit have been a comfort to me, although she is also prey to unaccountable fears at times. I often think that writers must write in order to stay sane and in doing so they convey a sense that they are solving problems that are not their own through mere imagination and not out of a desperate inner need. Perhaps a truly balanced person has no need to write, because they live with such certitude that their inner problems seldom present themselves beyond mere feelings rather than as inner analysis and dialogue. What we do not notice we do not find problematic. For this reason the tortured soul makes the best writer."

She looked up at me suddenly from her distant and meditative perusal of the flames in the fireplace while she was speaking. She smiled and blushed, "Do you find me morbid,

Mr. Holmes?"

"On the contrary, Mrs. Norton, I share your sentiments," said I. "I make one exception though to your observation in the case of my friend, Dr. Watson. He is my one great fixed point. His very lack of imagination is his greatest virtue. He prevents me, in my speculations, from being too fanciful. He draws the balloon of my own thoughts back to earth by reminding me of what is probable, for anything no matter how absurd may be entertained for a time as mere possibility. I am myself prone to a most severe alternation of moods. I dare say that were it not for a lamentable period when I resorted even to drugs to sustain me, I should have been overcome with despondency in my youth. Watson made drugs unnecessary by his counsel and advice so that cocaine became a habit that I gave up under his guidance and care; a course of treatment of my folly began with censure and ended with a practical program of reform. I mention this merely to underscore my own comprehension of how difficult it often is for one of delicate sensibilities merely to survive another day, when all the way before one appears to be one vast expanse of unrelieved grey and black."

"You comfort me, Mr. Holmes," said she, "So perhaps I may take you further into my confidence. My servant Molly has what is often termed an unnatural affection for me. She quite comprehends that I may not reciprocate this affection, but that her company is dear to me and I feel that she is my truest friend. This matter of love within the bounds of a single sex is a difficult one and I fear that society pretends that it does not exist, the better to deny its prevalence among us. It is treated as an occasional monstrosity, when in reality it appears to me to be at least part of nature's design. I hope that I do not shock you. I am a Catholic as are you, but my proximity to Rome itself has given me a sense that the church prefers always to have spoken with absolute clarity on every topic even if our knowledge is incomplete. It does not like any shadows to remain around which opposition or doubt may begin to coalesce. The competence of the church, although supreme in its own realm, does not extend to science or even to the science of the mind of man. Revelation is not a universal testimony of title to the possession of all knowledge, nor does it cover all topics of human thought and research in obscure areas. For this reason there may be gaps that science alone may fill and the wisdom of a later day may reveal certain judgments to have been premature. I will say no more. If, as I believe is the case, the Catholic Church is not capable of speaking conclusively on this matter, then neither can I. I try to adhere to the strictures of the day and season in which providence has placed me. The Catholic Church in its teaching office does likewise. It cannot of course be in advance of itself. This is not to doubt dogma of course, but only its expression and degree, its application to every area of human experience. The distinction is a delicate one, I admit, and a Catholic conscience is often sorely tried just as mine has been. It seems to me that if you are always comfortable in the Catholic faith, then you are much to be envied. I have found that many people are absolutely sure of Catholic truth because they have never troubled to understand the limits it imposes upon people whose lives are different than their own. They are Catholics in culture, but not in fact, because their sympathies are confined to those like themselves. Their faith might evaporate at a single doubt. I prefer the Catholic whose belief is a cross to be borne, a Catholic who is never free from the doubts that it is the business of faith to remedy, but wherein some questions may still remain, not only unanswered but unanswerable. Such a one says, 'I believe Lord, help thou my unbelief.'"

I see now why it is that I have always referred to Irene Adler Norton by the august title of, "The Woman." I proceeded to assure her that I did not find her revelations shocking. I told her that my own quest for faith had carried me from despair to hope and that even now I had thus far found myself entirely inadequate to convince that chief of atheists, Professor Moriarty, to adopt my own views regarding the purpose of life and the existence of God.

As to the affection of Molly for her, I had witnessed already the proof of her devotion and I believed that Irene was safe in her care, although it might be a trial for each of them to keep the relationship within those bounds that may not be crossed without terrible consequences, at least in this time and place. We can only live within the times in which providence has placed us. Universal human nature is a mysterious concept and who may assume that we have plumbed its every depth?

It seems to me that not everything involving the passions is sin as is often supposed by those who do not share them. Indeed I would say that the greatest sins are of intellectual excess. I have for instance never thought of Professor Moriarty as a man of great passions. The devil adjusts his lure to the type of fish he intends to catch. Every temptation is such that it targets the personality at its weakest point. The only exception is that of the saints. When one attacks a citadel, the assault must come from all sides at once. The strategy of the devil is to overwhelm the truly holy person through the sheer intensity of his attack. I will go so far as to say that the devil leaves some people alone because they are such obvious and easy conquests. There is no sport in bagging the sitting bird. For many people, a single vanity, a single favorite vice, is sufficient for the tempter to address his energies in order to triumph. One grows in significance to the devil as one grows in virtue, so that as one grows closer to God, the prospect of a fall grows ever more fearful. The saint looks down from the mountain at the chasms and the swirling mists below and hugs the mountain in prayer. God realizes this truth and suffers the virtuous soul to undergo many trials in order to bring them to perfection.

There is a story about this which I shared with Irene at this point in our discussion. "My dear Mrs. Norton, I know that you share my devotion to the Discalced Carmelite Order of monks and nuns. If so, you may have heard this story already. Saint Teresa of Avila was traveling in a coach on a visitation between convents. Her carriage became trapped in the mud of the road and she was forced to disembark to help dislodge the wheel that had sunken deep into the mire and prevented further progress in the journey. In doing so she lost her balance and fell backwards into the mud and her heavy habit became soaked and soiled. It was in this sorry state that she would now have to present herself to the community of nuns. She was for once at the end of her patience. She heard a voice coming to her from the Lord to strengthen her in her trial, "Teresa, this is how I treat my friends." The great saint looked up and spoke in return, "Alas Lord, if that is so, it is no wonder that your friends are so few."

We were both laughing over the wit of that most practical of all mystics and the familiarity of her discourse with God when Molly entered to inform us that the lamb had at last succumbed to the ministrations of the cook and that an excellent dinner awaited us. With that we both arose and I took the arm that she offered to me. Molly had departed to see to the service of the meal. We proceeded then to the dining room and took our places at the candlelit table where we were to enjoy a most exquisite dinner. The candlelight shown upon her countenance as she sat in her chair facing me; it seemed to restore all the color to her face. Considering the brevity of our prior acquaintance, I find that we have assumed the relation of old and dear friends meeting again after a long separation. I cannot account for this easy familiarity beyond the obvious fact of her charm and my own desire to aid her at this critical time, a task that I often assumed toward others in my practice in Baker Street.

Yet there is surely something more in play here, for what woman does not have her share of charm? My view towards Irene is different. I often think that the creation story is a reflection of the culture of Jewish antiquity out of which it came and that nature, which so favors the female sex in so many ways, may have evolved Eve long before Adam appeared as a remote and lesser possibility, as an after-thought of God. Beauty must always precede utility when one is an artist and surely God is the greatest of all artists.

January 10, 1893
Reflections

It has been several days since I have seen Irene and I have spent them thinking about what advice I might give her that will address her concerns. I quite understand that she may not resume the place that she enjoyed in Roman society because as an attractive young widow she will be seen as threatening by many plump Roman matrons. The pressures brought to bear upon her to marry again may then become overwhelming. The question becomes whether living in Rome is so dear to her that she will be comfortable in the restricted social milieu to which her present state has destined her?

To one who has experienced the celebrity and acclaim afforded to the performers of the theater and the opera, it is no small matter for them to adjust later to the anonymity and indifference that is the response that most of us meet in daily life. I fear that her need to regain the attention that she has known will be such that she will not be able to clothe herself in a comfortable obscurity. She might of course remove to Paris where the social strata are more fluid. There she might play the butterfly for a bit and be escorted in the evenings to various venues by that class of gentlemen for whom marriage has no appeal while still enjoying the company of a woman in public. To such men a woman provides a ready ear to their discourse and even at times a motherly touch free from any drift towards marriage and the awkwardness of setting up a family.

There are women in turn who enjoy the safety of such a relationship, one which spares them the burdens of domesticity and the long series of confinements that come with the bearing of children. To assume that the single life must be selfish rather than an adaptation to responsibilities that one feels incompetent to assume is a harsh and inaccurate appraisal. Many people are married who should never have entered upon that state.

Though I will not go so far as to take the jaundiced view of marriage expressed by Dr. Samuel Johnson, that the definition of marriage is the triumph of hope over experience, I do perceive that any life-long linkage of two personalities, each in constant alteration of needs and of self-perception is such that only sacramental grace and the will to persevere ever makes such a relation possible. To depend upon love alone and the illusions that often feed that emotion is to enter upon a life of struggle to retain as a permanent possession what the experience of the world has shown to be a temporary state of excitation of the nerves.

In any case, our conversation of a few nights ago indicates to me that Irene is not one who falls in love easily and often. She may be among those few to whom friendship is a genius and who make up for the lack of a particular intimacy by the cultivation of an extensive circle of friends, both men and women. Nature insists upon bonding the sexes to preserve the species and the church, that a cynic once said chooses to sanctify what it cannot prevent, has installed marriage as a remedy for concupiscence and the one stable building block of the social order.

The Mohammedans and the Mormons of course have imagined that marriage might be an extended web with many women gathered about a single man. This relation may be a natural outgrowth of a society of social inequality in which women, who may not survive alone in a frontier or otherwise hostile culture, are provided for by whatever man has the most resources.

By the nature of the case though, this situation must deprive some men of any access to a wife at all, assuming that the distribution of the sexes is approximately equal in any population. If to this is added the decline in the number of women available for sustained married life due to an early death in childbirth, it will be readily seen that polygamy yields an unjust monopoly of the privilege of entering upon the married state, which should always remain at least an option for all.

Also, the intense devotion of spouses in a relationship of mirrored affection is such that it provides the unique character that makes marriage the one human institution that excludes the idea of plurality of spouses. The question of what Irene should do then becomes not whether she should be hounded into a new marriage, but how she may enjoy the social swirl that has been her *métier* without becoming again a married woman.

To this there can be but one answer: she must return to her craft and resume her career as an actress, but with the added dignity of having been once married and now a widow. Even the world of the theater grants an aura of respect to the woman who has once assumed those sacred bonds. In addition her age is such that she is now seen as one to whom years have granted discretion. She will be less preyed upon by foolish suitors who assume that the role she has assumed on the stage is in truth her actual identity.

After perhaps ten years of resumed performances, Irene may be able to find value in that same obscurity of a quiet life that now, in the full flush of her third decade, seems premature. This is the advice that I shall give to her. I will suggest that she consider a new sphere for her theatrical life. She may wish to go to America for instance where I trust that she will soon rival even Sarah Bernhardt. She might even tour the western regions of that great country and see something of the majesty of its swiftly vanishing frontier. Surely there is adventure enough in prospect to meet her every need and desire and Molly will prove a faithful guardian to discourage any too avid attentions from the patrons of the stage. She may make a temporary withdrawal from Rome and rent her villa while she renews her former stature. This may take at least a year to accomplish. When she is again hailed throughout Europe she may remove herself to America with the assurance that her fame will have preceded her and thus her success there will be assured.

As for me, I must look to my own prospects and career, for unless I intend to remain forever a journalist of travels under the *nom de plume* of one Sigerson, I must eventually resume my practice as a consulting detective. My personal means are not so large that I am prepared yet to retire. I have I trust at least a decade of practice before me. I must also address this matter of my meeting with the Professor soon and if I may in some way conclude it advantageously, I may resume again the solution of those little problems that present themselves from time to time to me in Baker Street.

Besides, I am growing restive once again. I fear that I shall always crave a home and yet having found it will need to resume my travels. At times all the earth is too small for me. Always there is that thrill of dawn and the beat of the railway wheels beneath my feet or the sonorous drum of the boilers and the churn of the screw as it drives the ship forward. After all, life is short and death is long and whatever my faith in a celestial futurity I do not hold this earth in contempt. These skies and the embrace of this green earth have been at times heaven enough for me. I do not pine for gardens filled with Houris nor seek to clamor upon the dulcet bars of heaven's ramparts. Enough for me at least in this present season of my life is the enjoyment of "this short day of frost and sun" as Walter Pater has so eloquently phrased it in the conclusion of his book on the Renaissance.

January 12, 1893
Meeting with Irene

esterday I returned to the Villa Norton to present my reflections regarding her future to Irene. She listened to me patiently and with a serious demeanor until I had finished. After I had done so, she rose and walking over to the window pushed the curtains aside so that light flooded into the room. Returning, she took her place again, which was located only a few feet from where I sat. She raised her chin and faced the light showing me her profile and then, turning her head, she showed me the other profile. After a pause of some seconds she faced me once again and her great dark eyes stared into mine.

"What you see my dear friend is my medium of expression. My face and my voice are all that I may bring to the endeavor you have outlined for me. When I came to Rome it was with the desire to be able to rest the foundations of my happiness upon more solid ground. I felt that I had left behind the struggle that I had known and placed my fate in the hands of a man who would be a bulwark and protection for me. There is a pleasure for one who has always been forced to allay her fears by struggle to imagine that a warm sea might bathe her tired limbs exhausted in the struggle to stay afloat in this hostile world."

"Rome has become the center of my world, a place where I could re-create myself into the person that I had always dreamed of becoming. I once nursed my imagination on the novels of Victor Hugo and of Alexandre Dumas. It may be a sad delusion, but every woman dreams that she may be overwhelmed at last by a passion that will allow her to yield all of herself, so that she may be encompassed by the flood of love as though a great sea wave had broken upon her. She desires to be the focus of a man's desire, one so impetuous and enduring that she will rise each day, like Venus from the sea attended by her sea nymphs, to face him with renewed joy. It was my custom to spend the day with all of the delightful frivolity that we allow some women and to veil my own intelligence, the better to exist for a few precious hours in ecstasy, to live as body alone and to await and enjoy his embraces."

She sighed deeply and opened her hands in a gesture of irrecoverable loss. "Now there is nothing. I wake and walk to my looking glass and see the first signs of age, just as the fruit that has once grown ripe must be consumed at once in its fullness and at its peak. If I am to return to the stage I must know that the years of my career have been made shorter by the few years of my happiness here in Rome. I know my craft; I know its stern demands. Young women in the theater desire nothing more than the decay of the diva who precedes her because her retirement opens a chance for them to occupy preeminence in the public regard. A following such as the one that I had dissipates quickly. The fickle public finds others upon whom to focus their esteem. Besides, the world has long since thought me dead! I covered my traces well. How then shall I resume even that place that was once my own, let alone to conquer a new land of America where I never appeared on the stage?"

I spoke quietly when I answered, "We are in much the same position Mrs. Norton. The world also presumes that I have perished. To be famous in any capacity is to share a common vulnerability before time. The supposed genius of one Sherlock Holmes has been tempered by my reputation as an eccentric, a drug-addicted recluse who lies about my Baker Street rooms in a dressing gown smoking cheap shag tobacco and conducting strange scientific experiments, hardly a recommendation for respectable clients to entrust their most intimate problems and most convoluted affairs into my hands. I cannot live on what governesses may be able to pay me and whatever fortune I once possessed from my family estate is well nigh dissipated. I have only the rents derived from the cottagers and coal mines in

Yorkshire to provide me with a small annual stipend of secure income from the estate at Sigerside when new cases are rare. The rest depends upon my own endeavors. My moods are such that I often go for weeks when I am unable to muster the energy to go abroad into the London streets. I depend on Watson at such times to provide a setting of stability for me and to undertake missions that for the time at least exceed my own nervous capacities."

"In addition I have a recurring lung ailment that surfaces from time to time that demands periods of rest and retreat if it is not to overwhelm my constitution. I do not therefore speak lightly when I advise you to resume the struggle for life from which none of us is exempt. Let me assure you, that if I did not think that you possessed the capacity to triumph over your doubts I would not have urged you forward into the fray. Your return to the stage will not be the result of a day or an hour. You must work patiently, beginning here in Rome. You will perform first for the Italians who will not, as they are a warm and generous people, withhold their support and esteem."

"After you are recognized as the toast of Rome, you will proceed to Paris where the world will first realize who you are, the former Irene Adler. Your story will be told. The air of tragedy will only make you more beloved and you may find that you have not been as forgotten as you suppose you have been by those who first saw you perform in their youth. It is not you alone who are aging. The world itself grows old. Queen Victoria may not remain for many more years upon her throne. The century itself is about to turn. I think often of how quaint all that we have been will soon appear to be in the new age that is coming upon the world."

I paused to see the effect of my words upon her before continuing. I felt that I was addressing the fears that lay deep within me as well. I could tell that my words touched her deeply. I felt that all my latent affection for her, silent until now, was present at that moment and I could only wonder that my feelings for her had lain so silently within me through the years.

"You must go to America Irene because I feel that it is there that the new century will find its source of energy. The Europe we knew is dying. The new century will be only the long death agony of the great empires established with such care. Our generation is passing, but its death throes will no doubt last longer than our own lives. We may bask though for a time in the golden glow of what has been. It is the function of high art to embody the aspirations of peoples and to enshrine cultures. When all else has passed, only the artists are remembered for their creations and it is their reputations alone that survive time itself."

"We are both artists in our way and though our medium is but the creation of the hours of our actual performance, we will leave a legacy and, who knows, be remembered longer than the rulers of our age. You are still Venus rising from the sea Irene and when the Roman dowagers have been long forgotten, your reputation as an actress will remain. People will recall when they heard your voice. If nothing else, those who may read of you in Dr. Watson's accounts will know that you once had the temerity to beard that old lion, Sherlock Holmes, at the door to his very den and say in a mocking voice, "Good night Mr. Sherlock Holmes."

She had tears in her eyes when I finished and a flush had come to her cheek. We had each said what we had to say that evening and I left her soon after to make her own decision in due season. My words were for myself as well as for her.   I must somehow find the mettle to make my own return to England and to face what lies before me. There comes a time when delay is pointless and when our greatest fears must be faced at last. The great turning may be slow and it may take us time to gather the forces that must be deployed, but the initial orders must be given at last and the army must begin to move towards the frontier where it will encounter its opposition and decide forever the issue of final victory or defeat.

Dr. Watson's Narrative Continues

I must interrupt my transcription of Holmes' journal at this point in its narrative of events. We had both slept well after our festive evening in Delmonico's and as we descended to our breakfast in the hotel served in the second-floor dining room that looked out over Central Park, Holmes was in excellent spirits. We were typically English in feeling that a good breakfast is no insignificant part of the day.

Holmes informed me that he had received a note inviting both of us to join Mrs. Norton at her townhouse on Riverside Drive. Inspector Hopkins had been invited to join the company also, but he graciously declined since he was currently occupied in meeting with his counterparts on the New York police force to explain the delicacy of our mission in America and obtain the requisite aid we may require should any opposition occur here. We did not believe that we had been followed from England, but some precautions were still necessary. Holmes always believed in taking precautions and those who had already chosen to underestimate the scope of the Baron's resources had paid for this oversight with their lives.

There was also the question of Roger Baskerville. Although Holmes appeared to assume that he had taken the money from the sale of the Murillo Papers and used it to abscond to regions unknown, the mere fact that such a resourceful man was alive was a cause for concern. Whatever animosity he bore towards the Baskervilles, Sir Henry and Lady Beryl, was bourn also towards Holmes who had now twice crossed his path. Might he not seek some sort of revenge? Since he might be anywhere in the wide world, we could not assume that he was not upon our traces, thus we were taking every precaution.

The day passed quietly in our hotel and I was able to bring my reading of Holmes' journal to that point in the narrative when his own departure for home appeared to be imminent. It was at three o'clock that we departed from the Waldorf Astoria by cab to travel the short distance to the townhouse where Irene Norton nee Adler, our gracious hostess, awaited us.

The house was an elegant one of three stories, set back from the street by a small garden of low trees and rosebushes. We climbed the steep stairs and were admitted by that very same Molly of whom I had read. She greeted us courteously and led us into a living room, as the Americans call it, where Mrs. Norton awaited us. She was clothed in an emerald green velvet dress with a single strand of pearls at her throat. She rose at once, greeting us with both hands outstretched to receive us. I felt immediately that she viewed both of us as old friends though I had seen her but twice before, the last time as she greeted us that evening so long ago in Baker Street when she passed us dressed as a young man.

How different was the impression made upon me then from the one that her elegant demeanor and bearing made upon me now. Her beauty had if anything mellowed with the years to a refinement and an intelligence that seemed to shine about her in every motion that she made and every sentence that she spoke. I immediately felt at ease. Holmes' reclined his tall form on the settee facing her and I took a comfortable armchair by the fire, which burned in a small and exquisite marble fireplace surmounted by a great mirror that caught the light from the windows that looked out on the busy traffic of Riverside Drive that passed before her door.

Holmes explained our mission in America to her briefly and told her how delighted he was to see her again and to know that she had indeed resumed her career as he had recommended.

"When you departed from Rome I had yet to make any decision," she replied. "In fact it was some months before I was able to accept the fact that my status in the world would always be ambiguous. I believe that each of us has a conception within us of the perfect life in which a perfect congruity is somehow possible. We believe this in utter defiance of our daily observation of the chaos that surrounds us. The goal of a life that will allow us to develop with no opposition or regret seems always to be just out of our reach. When my husband died I found myself condemned again to my own sole self. I could no longer reach out to him and feel that his strength would make my own superfluous. He was the sun and around him for a time I had felt a direction and a purpose that made every day meaningful. Then suddenly he was gone and there was only empty space and me drifting and abandoned, feeling each wave of circumstance as purely random and without any significance. I could do anything and go anywhere but to no purpose. All decisions had about them an aura of sameness. I had lost the chart of my moral universe. There was only time, an endless succession of days and nights, and a sea of faces that might have been masques at a carnival. Even the ordinary sounds in my villa seemed to grate on my nerves, because they were so soft, so quiet. I thought at times that I should simply scream and awaken and all would be alright again until of course I would be forced to stop and the silence would flow about me once again."

"I suppose that I was a bit mad. You have no idea how much I wished that I could have followed you to England, Mr. Sherlock Holmes. You seemed always to be so certain, not unconcerned, but rooted to some source of strength denied to me. You would quote me something from some Chinese sage when we were together and all would be clear again. I am ashamed to say that my confusion reached the point that I consulted an oracle in the form of a woman who believed that tarot cards can provide us with guidance and can read the vibrations of our own thoughts as though we do not live within the prison of our own minds. I suddenly realized that if I believed that cards made of paper dealt out upon a table knew more about me than I knew about myself, why then I must indeed be a hollow gourd surrounding an empty space. Was this what I had come to? I asked myself.

"It was then that I determined to make my own decisions again, even if they were the wrong ones. I realized that it is better to err than to take no position at all. Even faith is an action, however feeble, to reach out towards God. Even the ocean cannot surround us if we remain frozen and motionless on its very shore."

She smiled, "So I took action at last. I attended an audition in Rome for a small part. Within a year I was being offered leading roles in plays again. I played Clytemnestra in the plays of the Orestes cycle. I took all of my madness and pain and became the great madwomen of the classical dramas. I felt what it is to be that terror, that desperation that all people feel exists at some level in their lives. I felt how close theater is to a religious exercise. It purges the clotted feelings that lie within us so that all may flow once again and so that life may continue on its course."

"Soon I was in Paris where I acted in some modern plays by Ibsen. It was then that I finally revealed my past, that I was in fact Irene Adler, so long presumed dead. After that my fame knew no bounds and I undertook my first tour of America. You may be surprised that I am known as far away as San Francisco and Virginia City in Nevada. There I have even been approached to come up to those frontier towns in the northwest, Seattle and Port Townsend. I have not decided of course whether to make the journey west again, because it has been a busy winter season here in New York. I need time to rest this spring.”

She said in a teasing tone, “You seem always to encounter me in a time of crisis, Sherlock. In a few days my present engagement will terminate. I hope that you will remain in New York for a few more days before you pursue your own travels?”

Holmes proceeded to explain that it was his intention to go first to Newport in Rhode Island. He hoped to meet there, among others, the Speaker of the House of Representatives, Thomas Brackett Reed. He had spoken out strongly against any American involvement in the Cuban revolution. Since a nation seldom goes to war until the public ferment is such that the final decision becomes inevitable, there might still be time to ward off an involvement which might forever change America’s posture before the nations of Europe. Holmes felt that we might have a role to play in that decision, to urge America to refrain from what might prove to be a step with unforeseeable consequences to the nation’s future identity and freedoms.

“But, that is perfect!” she cried. “I intend to go to Newport myself. I have been invited by my good friend, Edith Wharton, of whom you have heard me speak in Rome, to join her at Lands End which is the name of her estate in Newport. She will be in close proximity to Theodore Roosevelt who often visits friends in Newport. The man is quite mad I assure you. He is always frothing at the mouth for an American force to assemble and land in Cuba to assist the rebels. If you intend to help to avoid war, you must talk to him. If he can be convinced, you will have no trouble with President McKinley, who is already doing everything that he can do to contain the enthusiasm and the indignation of the American people since the explosion aboard the Maine in Havana harbor.”

I looked over at Holmes and I could see at once that the idea was a congenial one to him. It was clear that an understanding existed between him and Irene Adler. She had resumed her maiden name; for career purposes as she expressed it. I could not say what the nature of that understanding between them was, but it was clear to me that each knew and esteemed the strong character each other possessed and that a real affection existed between them.

Holmes spoke up then at once. "Since you are so kind as to request our presence as your companions, Watson and I will be happy to accompany you to Lands End, if it would work no inconvenience to Mrs. Wharton. I have heard of the woman's social talent and diplomacy. Perhaps in the comfortable setting of her retreat the principal actors on this national drama will unbend so that I can make a sensible appraisal of the national temper at this time."

"I fear that you will not find any unanimity," said she. "Passions are running high on both sides. There are many who feel that America cannot afford war. The nation has yet to recover from the economic collapse of 1893. The farmers have watched the prices for their grain collapse and the recent election, although a triumph for the Republicans and their gold standard, the same monetary base that prevails in Europe, has left many people bitter and afraid of what the new administration will bring. There is a decided sentiment for isolation in many quarters. The country has yet to consolidate and to develop its vast new western territories. Manifest destiny, as it has been called, would appear to have met its logical end upon reaching the Pacific. Still, there are others, including this man Roosevelt, who already cast their eyes towards the Pacific and to the trade with Japan and China."

Holmes looked amused, "How do you know all of this? You have become quite the diplomatist!"

Miss Adler blushed, "One cannot be in the theater and be entertained nightly, as I often am after my performances by men of affairs, without getting a sense of what is happening. The nation seems poised over an issue that will ever after define American policy towards the world. Matters are coming to a crisis, but of course I have no idea what will emerge at last.”

“On the contrary, it is as usual the artists who sense first any change in the wind,” remarked Holmes. “I should rather trust your feelings than the conclusions, of say a newspaper editor, like this voluble man Hearst. It is quickly becoming a question of whether journalists report the news or create it. Do people know what to think until they are told what template shall be imposed upon the naked events that break daily upon us? Journalism is by its very nature it seems to me an interpretation. Facts are not persuasive unless they are perceived to be part of some meaningful pattern of belief. The vast circulation of the daily newspaper can often so sway public policy that the newspapers may be considered, collectively speaking, to be a fourth branch of government. A republic cannot function if it is not guided by an educated public voice, but there is always the danger as well of deception. The press must maintain a great public trust.”

Miss Adler nodded in agreement. “You may be able to share your thoughts with the man himself, for Mr. Hearst often dines at The Breakers, the great Vanderbilt mansion in Newport. The spring season is just beginning and Newport will soon begin receiving guests who desire to escape from the bustle of New York City. I have already declined to accept a tour with the summer players of our company so I will be spared rehearsals. It is high time for me to escape the demands of the theater for a bit to allow me to breathe the ocean air with my face free of grease-paint and to renew old acquaintances.”

She reached over and took Holmes’ hand in hers. “Perhaps in Newport you will be able to share with us the story of your final meeting with Professor Moriarty. I have often wondered since we parted in Rome how you faired at that meeting. I admit that I often scanned the papers to see if some strange tragedy had taken place in the British Isles that would indicate that Professor

Moriarty might have prevailed over you and that you might have fallen as a victim to his schemes. It cannot have been an easy matter to dissuade him from his plans."

Holmes smiled, "You had so little confidence in me then?"

Irene Adler blushed. "Oh no, it was not lack of confidence. But as you presented the matter to me in our short discussion, I came to understand that you had concluded that good and evil do not exist as part of a simple civil dialogue between equally matched opponents. If evil exists at all, true evil that is, then it must by its very nature be beyond the conventions of our speech and even our concepts of it. To utter a word is already to assume some measure of understanding and where understanding exists there must be some sympathy. But evil can have no sympathy with goodness. In fact I should imagine evil to be by its nature uncommunicative and solitary. You see that I have gone far in my own fanciful speculations since we talked of the matter in Rome. I have come to wonder why the devil even bothers with the sordid affair of temptation. If we human beings are held in such contempt, does not the devil demean his dark angelic nature by condescending to deal with us at all?"

"He would not do so, if we were not loved by God," Holmes answered at once. "We are mere pawns upon a chessboard in a game that the evil one is playing with God. It is because we matter to God that we matter to the devil."

"Then why does not God not simply claim victory and gather the pieces up and walk away, for surely the game is His to win? Why are we left, as we are in jeopardy at all?" she asked with interest.

I recall that I turned then to Holmes for I had often wondered about this very question myself.

Holmes looked down at his hands before replying. "There are of course things that we may never know and to speculate about them shows a lack of trust in God. This much may be ventured though. Providence is such that even evil works in some strange way to produce a corresponding goodness over time. It is no small measure of the punishment of the devil that his most cunning tactics are ultimately unavailing. It is a matter to be held *de fide* that the sacrifice of Christ upon the cross meant the final defeat of evil. All of history since then is in a sense only a mopping-up operation. The victory has already been won. But for we who must experience daily evil the battle must appear still to be at the summit of its fury and as regards our own salvation the outcome must still be in suspension."

"John Calvin and many others were convinced that hell holds the advantage and that few souls will finally be found to love God and thus to attain salvation. I have always chosen to be skeptical of this melancholy view. Surely if God is the perfection of all things, then he is loveable beyond all else that he has created (even though they also exist in his love and thus are not independent from Him). I cannot think of any man so evil that he is not devoted to something in this life which must provide within the cavern of his being a small echo of the voice of God. To reject even that tiny remnant of goodness so that a supreme darkness closes like a dark pool over his head must require a final dedication to evil that exceeds the capacity of most men and women. The least thing may serve as a seed of contemplation and wonder and so lead us back to God."

He paused before continuing, "Against this view, for one must give due weight to the warnings of Jesus as reflected in the New Testament, is that God's nature is perfect in being and admits of no degrees. The philosophers and theologians of the church define God as non-composite being. For God to will is for that thing to be. God is unlimited by any contingency, so it is a paradox that God can allow human beings a vacated area not subject to God's will and causality. For the soul in heaven to love God at all therefore is to love Him completely. For this reason every slightest sin tends towards hell for to miss out on goodness in any degree is to be in some small measure in alliance with evil. This means that the soul in dying must undergo a purging that will be such as to rip apart one who has throughout his life maintained divided loyalties. Yet we are assured that what for man is impossible is always possible with God. We must trust then that the grace born of the intermediation of the saints, when united to the manifest will of God that none shall be lost, may prevail against even a sinful life and that we may always hope for some manner of conversion, even in a soul that all human prudence would deem to be lost forever."

These were deep waters indeed and it took me some time to see the sense of what Holmes was saying, because each of us makes judgments every day about who deserves heaven and who deserves hell.

Holmes concluded his remarkable discourse as follows, "This having been said, it is not our business to try God's mercy unduly, for Jesus said that no man should put God to the test, not even Jesus when he was tempted in the desert. For this reason we are advised to attempt to enter by the narrow gate and to rid ourselves of all that may impede our progress through it. Jesus has said that many will try and enter by the wider gate, but be unable to do so. It is not said clearly whether a means may be provided after death by which they may disencumber themselves of all that would bar them from heaven. But if even in our earthly journey that we know to be a short one it is hard to place God first in our thoughts and actions, then who can say that of its own accord and without some extraordinary intervention the soul will have a change of heart when put in the alien realm of death. Will the soul that is about to be damned be able to set aside all that it has relied upon while living to define itself in opposition to God, by then leaving all things behind in preference to God Himself? Or will he not rather gather the rags of his vanity and pride about him and proceed to where the devil awaits him and join the chorus of those who wail and gnash their teeth?"

Again Holmes paused to allow this dreadful image to take root within us before continuing, "It is a fearful prospect! So we are taught by Christ and by His church to take the path of safety. We pray that we are not led into temptation and that we will be delivered from evil and so be spared the test of a last definitive acceptance or rejection of God, a test that we might fail!"

"What is left to us then is the course pursued by the man who stood at the back of the Church and would not even raise his eyes to heaven but said only these words: 'Forgive me Lord for I am a sinner.' To any man who is convinced of his own stature and neediness before God, salvation is always possible. God's grace desires to rush in through even a crevice of remorse. Only the one who feels that grace is a superfluous gilding of the lily of his own independent virtues is immune to grace."

"The church in its wisdom does not judge of degrees of sanctity. It recognizes saints, but judges no soul to be in hell, for it is the task of the church to dispense mercy not justice. When it is said to the Apostles: "Whose sins you forgive, they are forgiven them, whose sins you hold bound they are held bound," what is meant is that the church has met its mandate and fulfilled its obligation by going as far as its mission of mercy allows. It does not withhold its power of absolution through some niggardliness or in order simply to manifest its powers and revel in its credentials, but rather simply to pronounce that it cannot impose forgiveness upon a soul that does not desire it. That soul remains bound in sin by its own choice and not by the church's refusal of forgiveness in the name of God. Any refusal of absolution is only a prudential judgment that the church has reached through its minister when he withholds absolution to one who does not truly wish it. The church then leaves the sinner to God who alone knows the state of the heart. The sacraments do not exhaust the treasury of God but are merely the ordinary means entrusted to the church to ensure the salvation of all and they are entirely adequate to achieve that end."

"As for the rest, it is said that outside of the Catholic Church there is no salvation, but God alone sets the boundary of that inclusion! Who may know how wide is the vestibule of God? It is enough for those of us who have heard the message to enter the Catholic Church swiftly and to procure a seat well within the nave and begin to pray that all will somehow be admitted to share our joy. This is the intercession of the saints for which we pray and who may say what those prayers may accomplish in hardened hearts? God is as great as his mercy and who shall set borders to that mercy without presuming an authority that is not his but God's."

Holmes had the unique capacity to reflect upon Scripture and to see it as a whole and not in parts. In this he showed that he attempted to think with the church. The Catholic Church did not move swiftly, but rather adhered to the admonition of St. Paul to test all things.

Holmes continued, "For all of its reverence for its early history and the teachings of the Early Church Fathers, the Catholic Church as the universal source of salvation is led finally by the Holy Spirit, who cannot be untrue to Himself. Love is inexhaustible. It is not that the church changes its teachings, but that those teachings grow through greater clarity of discernment over time. Any reticence to make premature pronouncements has often saved the church from pronouncing too soon a judgment on matters that exceed its mission. The Catholic Church and each of its members are always in the posture of being 'one who is sent.' It is said in the gospel account that the disciples returned rejoicing from their first mission. They said, 'Even the demons are subject to us in Your Name.' They were like children rejoicing in what they were able to do. Like children though the church has sometimes manifested a measure of frivolity in the exercise of its mission and the church in consequence is often encumbered by many superfluities that as time passes will be seen to have been a passing phase of its history and its maturation before God. What for instance are the gilt-encrusted Baroque cathedrals but the opinion of the church at that time of their construction that God needed or appreciated such fripperies to clothe or celebrate His Majesty. St. Lawrence knew better. When he was asked to bring in and to surrender the treasure of the church he produced not gold but rather a collection of the aged, the lepers and the poor, for these he said are the true treasures of the church."

I could see that Irene Adler had tears in her eyes at this story. I also was deeply moved by this discourse. Holmes had not answered the initial question posed to him as to whether it is possible for evil and good to meet in any discourse, but I felt that I could answer the question myself having heard Holmes speak.

I spoke up at this juncture, "The dialogue then on such ultimate questions as the nature of good and evil, if one is to exist at all, must be in the order of events. It is to actions that all judgment must defer. Yet it is said that God knows the heart and that the heart often proceeds further than the realization of its intentions. How then shall we be judged: by what we have done or by what we might wish to have accomplished in our lives? Our aspirations and highest thoughts usually fall far short of what we actually manage to do."

"Well Watson, we must recall what has been revealed to us, that out of the fullness of the heart the mouth speaks and that it is those who are pure of heart who will see God. There is no doubt that if judged by our achievements we must all be discouraged. Our cooperation with grace is such that much would appear to have been lost along the way in a sort of spiritual entropy. Quite frankly, we are like an old mule that eats more than what would justify its keep. It takes constant application of the stick to his hindquarters or this mule does not move at all. Still, God would appear to bear affection for the stubborn beasts that we are and each day the manger is filled with new fodder."

Holmes eyes twinkled as he said this. It is assumed that the affairs of the soul must always be clothed in proper metaphysical dress. The saints though know that most of the Christians who have ever lived and died were simple people. Still, their faith was adequate and it was not necessary that they know all things or could express them eloquently. Like Mary at the feet of Jesus, they knew that only one thing was necessary, and they would not be deprived of it.

Our hostess excused herself then to see if all was going well in the kitchen. Holmes and I remained together in the quiet room. The afternoon had waned into a still evening. The sun slanted through the windows with its golden light. A short time later our hostess returned to inform us that Molly had been about to summon us and that we might follow now her into the dining room. Holmes rose and walking over to her took her arm in a most natural manner and we proceeded in to dinner.

The course of our discussion over dinner moved from a discussion about the Christian response to good and evil to our present mission in coming to America. I wondered whether Holmes would be open in his revelations to our hostess. He began his answer to what had appeared at first to be a digression from the question he had posed earlier, but I was soon to see that as with all of his comments there was an underlying purpose to all that he said, often by way of obscure allusion.

"The great question now being posed by events to the nation of America is whether it is possible to possess power and at the same time to act morally. One of the advantages of being a private practitioner as a consulting detective is that I was able to refuse cases that for whatever reason might trouble my conscience. It was not essential that my actions determine larger courses of events that might entail unforeseen outcomes. Similarly it is the task of the moral theologian to clarify the general principles of moral norms, but to apply those norms to the individual is the task of the local pastor and confessor who must consider all of the factors that may come into play in any concrete application of a moral norm to a concrete situation."

"Doctor Watson I am sure will recall that we have on occasion engaged in acts that were technically burglary in order to obtain items that we could acquire in no other way. Well, in the case before us we are being asked to attempt to sway events in a way that may defeat a man whose capacity to effect evil and whose past actions indicate a propensity to accomplish great damage in the world. This man's evil is of a sort where dialogue and debate are incapable of producing any change in him. We are left then only with the use of a force of some sort as an option and as the damage that he would do and the means that he will use spans even nations, so our remedy must be tailored to the power raised against us."

"This man's immense wealth is such that he may behave as though he were not a man at all, but rather as a separate sovereign, a nation unto himself. Our actions in this case then are similar to the actions that a leader must undertake when he leads his country into war. The instrumentalities of war are not a scalpel, but more in the order of a scimitar. It is simply not possible to use this means to remedy a great evil without simultaneously causing great harm to those whose nexus to the evil force is often accidental or even so tenuous as not to exist at all. Yet they must suffer also. This means that the responsible agent, who remains after all only an individual, must bear the responsibility for the evil that he does not intend but that he will bring about of necessity in order to address the evil that he does intend to remedy, but at a cost that he deplores."

"What this means, when stated in its most simple form, is

that anyone with power over people must of necessity be caught up in evil's web. Evil is like a cancer. It so invades and commingles itself with healthy tissue that it can often not be extracted without killing the entire organism. This means that the best that can be hoped for when dealing with this type of evil is that when the dust clears, the sum totality of evil will be less. But since evil is such that, as the great Russian author Dostoyevsky has said, the whole world is not enough to justify the killing of even one innocent child; evils are not capable of quantitative analysis as justification. So it is impossible finally to reach a final calculus so as to avoid all evils even when one pursues the good."

"Of course this principle of moral complexity can be misused. Pick-pockets are hanged for trifling thefts in England in order to deter crime among the masses of the impoverished. Great wealth is allowed to accumulate so that great empires may not dissolve into civil wars. Ultimately some moral justification can be trotted out to serve any private interest. The repressive actions of tyrants are always justified as a means to prevent anarchy."

"If the command of God is to do no evil, then all actions must fail in this imperfect world. Even Jesus by the result of his actions might be considered to be a remote cause for the Crusades and for the Thirty Years War with all the suffering that these wars entailed. All of this is by way of a prelude in order to say that I had hoped to finish my life in the moral leisure that my own obscurity in Baker Street once made possible. After, reaching a certain modus vivendi with Professor Moriarty, I imagined that I might return to my private consulting practice for a decade or so and then retire and watch my bees going about bringing honey and new life by fertilization to the world. I had no intentions to ever address the morass of world affairs. But the machinations of Professor Moriarty were such that he presumed that he would be victorious in our Great Wager."

Unfortunately, the train of events that he has initiated has proven to have such momentum that even he, with his complete cooperation, could not stop them in their course unaided. There remained a residual motion to events that we are still attempting to bring to a halt by defeating Baron Maupertuis of Holland. Our task is to bring about the destruction of the Greater Dutch Canal Company and we may only do so by getting the Americans to build the canal instead of the Baron."

"To do this we must use whatever means will so enflame the national pride and spirit of the Americans that they will stand behind this immense and costly project. We have brought with us papers that we believe will aid us in accomplishing that goal. We will require the help of many people though, including men of great influence over public opinion whom I hope soon to meet. This means that we must obtain access to these men of power and must even exercise power ourselves. In the process we may unleash forces that we cannot control and so bear a burden that may deprive us forever of that peace known by those who have never been drawn into the moral maelstroms of this world. If you help us Irene, by using the influence that you possess and that of your friends also, know that it is this responsibility that you will be undertaking."

Holmes went on solemnly, "I dare not form this as a request, for what I would ask of you is more than I would ever wish to ask a friend to bear. Instead, I place before you our case, the one in which we are engaged. If you choose to join us, it must be with clear eyes and only after sufficient reflection. Once engaged we may not in after years change or alter the forces that we may put into play during these next critical months. There is still time remaining in your engagement in the theater. Pray use that time to consider your course of action. We for our part will remain in New York to await your answer before proceeding on our way to Newport."

A few days later we called at the theater and were shown

back to Irene Adler's dressing room. She was still in costume and about to remove the grease-paint that allowed her to project her beauty beyond the footlights. The dressing room was packed with flowers from her many admiring patrons and well-wishers. At our entrance she turned to face us. Her face was solemn and yet animated. She said simply, "Count me in Holmes, I am with you." She could not know then, nor did we, what lay ahead for us all.

From the Journal of Sherlock Holmes

February 2, 1893

A Decision

The time has come for me to leave Rome and return to England. As the time has passed here I have come to realize that Professor Moriarty has ceased to be for me a mere human being like myself. I have come to view him merely as a force. The idea that evil is faceless is one of the devices that evil uses to mask itself. Evil is by its nature always personal. I will go so far as to say that until a man or a woman has some degree of identity and self-possession he or she is to that degree unworthy of sin and perhaps incapable of committing sin, for the ability to sin first of all requires some degree of human dignity. It would be folly to ask for moral improvement if men and women were merely beasts. If we are mere seething cauldrons of uncontainable passions and instincts, then to apply any moral code to us would be absurd. The best that we might hope for would then be the satiation of appetite that makes the lion sleep after sating its ravenous hunger.

It is not that the passions are evil per se. In fact the deepest sins have a cold intellectual calculation about them rather than a mere yielding to the flesh. When I think of the devil I think more of a chill, thin-lipped Scottish accountant then I do of a crass voluptuary. The worst sins are those where malice leaves so little pleasure behind that the sinner is even cheated out of his temporary satisfaction. In fact an honest sinner is closer to redemption than a dishonest man of virtue. For this reason, it is no small task to approach another soul with the intention of converting him. One simply may not judge the inner dispositions of the heart in anyone.

How then may I approach Professor Moriarty when at last we meet? Do latent passions slumber beneath those serpentine and veiled eyes of his? Or should I attempt to use his great intellect to show the flaws that his own reasoning contains? Shall I hold his mind in my hand like a jeweler with a diamond to find the perfect set of planes within and the spot that if hit will reduce the raw diamond to a set of stones that may be further cloven and polished until a set of jewels remains? Or is the mind of Professor Moriarty so set in evil that no change is even possible? Will it crumble to dust at the least blow thus showing that it is rotten at the core or will it be adamantine in nature and resist every word and concept put forward by me as though his mind is encased in its own moral deafness forever?

Perhaps the Professor was correct and we should have simply settled matters by the crude reciprocity of mutual destruction at the Reichenbach Falls. I know that this thought had at least occurred to him. Perhaps he is as weary of the search for ultimate meaning as I am. There comes a time when one would wish to simply emerge from cover, to stand back to back, to walk ten paces, turn and fire. But would our mutual destruction solve anything? Once forces are so nearly equal that both will be destroyed completely the question arises whether a situation like that might imply rather that both should live. Equality in arms makes armed conflict futile. This is the absurdity of the duel existing between us. A duel is finally an obscure sort of perverted love. One is so dedicated to the other's destruction that one forgets one's own desire to live. Hatred then by its nature destroys the self. Do I hate Professor Moriarty? If I do then by that same token I must hate Sherlock Holmes! I have no choice then but to desire that my enemy live and by doing so I assure my own survival.

To broaden this perspective: the only way to defeat evil is not to oppose it but to do, as God so evidently does, to let it have space in which to act. Evil defeats itself through diffusion. It may leave wreckage in its path, but in the process its force is finally spent. Even plagues finally die out when the last victim perishes. Evil can only feed on goodness; it has no being within itself. For this reason evil is an entrapment even to itself. If hell is painful it is not that God wills it so, but rather that non-being claws at its own face, for there is nothing remaining of goodness for it to infect and no other visage than its own to afflict with its talons.

Everywhere evil sees only a reflection of itself, which it finds noxious; not because it retains anything good, but because evil shorn of disguise is always noxious once its core is revealed. For this reason all evil thrives on pretence. The devil will enter even swine rather than return to his own proper nature. Even pigs find his presence within them so intolerable that they will run into the sea rather than endure it.

Yet many men seem at home in their evil; how can this be? I often think that the evil man must be so thirsty for virtue that he would seek every condensation that might gather for even a drop of moisture.   If the poor man Lazarus would only dip his finger into a drop of water...

If there is torment in purgatory it is precisely this, that whereas on earth the opportunities to do good seem infinite with only the will do so lacking, in purgatory one feels all the desire to do good and to suffer any pains to do so, but one is no longer able. If the gates of purgatory were to open for even an instant, the world would be so drowned in a sea of love that it would change instantly.

Does this mean that God is stingy with His grace on earth? Why must we wait until we are beyond life to understand life's meaning? No, I do not think that God is chary of grace but rather that He knows how little we can endure Divine Love. It is said that the heart of St. Philip Neri was so large that the rib-cage of the saint was bowed outwards in order to contain it.

Human beings fear love beyond all else, for love melts away the great glaciers of our vices and our stolid indifference to our own ultimate good. I like to think that when we die we are not so much judged on our lives but rather that our lives become parables to us at that final moment when we stand as it were outside of ourselves and see all things from God's point of view. Until then we are simply too engaged in living to see ourselves clearly. We are like a woman in labor who may not really see her child until the pains of labor cease and the child is delivered and placed at her breast. Our lives are a great labor and what we have produced cannot be seen fully and correctly until illumined by God in the first dawning beams of eternity.

We do but prolong the labor of our soul's birth by our sins. If the world has endured so long and if Christ has delayed his return it is because all of history, even after the coming of Christ and the birth of His church, is still one long labor of injustice. We pray when we cry out the word, Hosanna, for the day of justice to dawn and for the promises of the prophets to reach their ultimate fulfillment and for time to cease. Yet there is still only the heavy plodding of Christ under a greater load of sin as history passes. With each age the cross of Christ grows heavier. We think that we have witnessed all that there is of human depravity, only to glimpse ever deeper abysses with each year. Always the green-wood grows drier. I believe that it will be harder to be a saint in the next century, because the very concept of sainthood will then seem to be folly.

The worst problem of an evil life is that it becomes

gradually tolerable, because we become convinced that true happiness is impossible for us. The wonder of little children is that they assume, for God has implanted this instinct in their very souls, that they should be loved. No disappointment is greater than that of children when they first encounter evil, for nothing prepares them for it. They choose to deny its presence and assume that there must be something evil within them and not their parents if they are not loved.

Only time accustoms us to disillusionment and to the unloving character of the world. For this reason, the saints often seem like foolish children because they refuse to accept this world in any other light than as a place where love is intended to rule. So great is their thirst for God that they feel already what all people may feel in purgatory: that God is love and that love is worth all things.

If the saints seem alien to us and if we feel a certain fear of them, it because that which is evil in us fears what they represent. The saints are like stars in the dark firmament of human life. If even the particle of God's love that the saints contain in varying degrees is a fearful thing to evil, then how must the full intensity of God's love break like a great sea upon the parched lands of hell driving its denizens ever deeper into obscure crevices to escape it, just as beetles scurry to escape the light when a great rock is overturned.

There can be then no real duel between good and evil, for there is no equality in the contest. In the end this great irreconcilability wins out and evil seeks its own proper place. If love is all that really is, then what is not love is condemned to endure in what it cannot share; that is the veritable nature of hell. For this reason the church is the manifestation of reconciliation. It is already the Kingdom of Heaven.

Purgatory in turn is the very eternal embodiment of what the Sacrament of Penance is in this present life. It is a place of reconciliation where the merits of the church are applied to the individual. To seek that reconciliation now is to receive in time the benefits of grace when it most effectual, for it will be a delight to see that each seed planted now will be a great harvest later. The Sacrament of Penance exists then so that our fields may prosper. Though a single part of an acre in bloom with a few sorry weeds may be adequate to get the exhausted and parched soul to Purgatory, it will go easier to the one who enters there and finds already growing there tall trees bearing fruit and watered by a flowing spring.

February 5, 1893
A Farewell

Last night I returned to the Villa Norton to explain my decision to leave for home to Irene. I have grown closer to her in this last month than I have been to any woman since the death of my mother, with the exception of that good Scotswoman, my landlady Mrs. Hudson, who has in many ways played a maternal role in my life. Where should I have been had she not insisted that I eat properly, even in the middle of a demanding case when it was often my habit to rush back to Baker Street for some bread and cheese or perhaps a slice from a joint of cold mutton.

In eating as in all else I have been a creature of extremes. It was Mrs. Hudson then who would bring me up all manner of green things to eat and would insist that I eat a lime concoction "for to prevent the scurvy, sir." Mr. Hudson had been, before his premature death off the coast of Madagascar, a cook aboard a sailing ship and had devised his own remedy for scurvy, that plague of sailors. She plied me with this remedy regularly and I dare say that I often owed my health to her ministrations. I have been on my own for most of my life with the result that I have treated my body with a certain degree of contempt and the assumption that health would endure as matter of course. I have lived my life as though all that mattered was the will to victory and triumph in a case.

I have taken pride in the denial of comforts to myself and lived a Spartan mode of life as though I was merely passing through my body as the home of a transient, rather than making any place or condition a permanent abode. My habit of keeping tobacco in a Persian slipper for instance was never a conscious decision. I simply found it an easy way to force the tobacco into the bowl and was too lazy to procure a proper humidor.

My desire has always been to simply have everything close at hand. There are times when I do not possess the energy to even walk across the room. It was my habit for instance to be always asking Watson to fetch me something when I might just as easily have stood up myself and walked over to the bookcase. It is a peculiarity of men who have lost their mothers early and have lived in a domestic environment devoid of the feminine touch that they often descend into a certain savagery. The only exception to my bohemian ways was in my personal attire. I have always wished to appear professional when receiving clients. These habits of life have been longstanding with me.

My father, whose name in family documents is rendered at times as Sigerson or even as Sigurd was a typical country squire. He was usually dressed in wet tweed and smelling of horses. He was a solitary man by nature and as likely to share a meal with his hounds as with his neighbors. After my mother's death he left my brothers and me to raise ourselves virtually unaided by counsel and advice. Mycroft and I had a French tutor, a legacy from the days when our mother planned our education. We were kept at home while Sherringford was sent off to Harrow. As the eldest son his life was set before him ready-made: public school followed by university and then membership in the House of Lords. None of his particular wishes were ever considered. Fortunately his temperament was similar to that of our father and his imagination confined crops, to rents, and to wages.

Mycroft and I in contrast showed an early spirit that would not brook the discipline of a public school. We would simply not consent to be beaten, nor could either of us tolerate the strict hierarchy in a school that would demand the service of the older boys. We were raised with a certain wild Yorkshire spirit that matched our temperaments. We had each of us a devotion to Dr. Samuel Johnson and we each determined from a young age to match Johnson's scorn of Lord Chesterfield, who deemed himself to be, *"Le vainqueur du vainqueur de la terre."*

We like Dr. Johnson before us would endure no patron. Each of us thought of himself as a knight, a Rob Roy or an Ivanhoe. Our father once said that his best hope for us was that we would fall into some unique and unforeseen situation, "for no man would consent to employ such proud young scamps as you both are." He tolerated our pretentions more out of apathy than approval. He was after all most often busy about his own affairs and unique areas of study, which was unusual for one raised as he was to be a typical member of England's landed aristocracy, the members of which were often as crude in their manners as their station as gentlemen was exalted.

In point of fact he might be considered a liberal of his day. His library contained volumes by Victor Hugo and Voltaire, of Emerson and Carlyle, and he valued the writings of Thomas Jefferson. It was these republican sympathies and the reading of Rousseau's book on education, "Emile," that led to his patronage of the young Moriarty, our stable boy.

The future Professor's own father was descended from the degraded former nobility of Ireland who had been displaced by low-land Scottish Protestants in the home country and he bore the bitterness of that fallen estate, which he unfortunately took out on his son, who was born with a weakened and deformed constitution due to the famine of the 1840's in Ireland. Mycroft and I were each allowed free access to our father's immense library and to pursue our particular studies at home and later, when each of us matriculated directly to university, Mycroft to Oxford and I to Cambridge and then to the University of London.

Meanwhile Professor Moriarty, the son of my father's groom, was sent to the University of London to study science. He did not share a tutor with Mycroft and me, but was instead taught by a local schoolmaster and friend of my father when his duties at the stables were over for the day. He would study at night and I can still recall looking from the window of my room toward the stables and seeing that one light still burned there. I did not of course spend my boyhood hours with Moriarty who was some fifteen years older, nor did anyone else to my recollection. The young man was uncommunicative in the extreme. After his father was fired for drinking and for neglect of the horses, the boy remained with us as my father's ward.

"Good riddance to him!" was his father's last word regarding his stooped and taciturn son. We at the Holmes' estate of Sigerside in the North Riding of Yorkshire never saw the elderly Moriarty again. After graduation the young Moriarty was offered a professorship at one of our smaller English colleges and for a time my father's experiment in reformation seemed as though it would be a complete success. But it is with great difficulty that the wounds of our youth are ever healed and Professor Moriarty soon made the college town too hot to hold him. We never heard details, but dark rumors had begun to circulate. Professor Moriarty, for such he now called himself, took up a position as an army coach, not in athletics but in planning elaborate field maneuvers. Had he had the body and endurance for it, he might have made a fine officer. He showed a genius for tactical maneuvers and some of his field-exercises are used I believe to this very day.

Such was the strange household where I spent my youth. To be now in Rome with Irene is to know again memories of kindness and affection that I recall from the time spent as a child with my mother. I see even a similarity in the eyes between Irene Adler and the dear French mother that I lost so many years ago. It is no small matter to find early happiness in life and to find it necessary to relinquish it; yet that is what I may be doing again now.

But can it be otherwise? I have taken no vow to remain unmarried, yet I have watched as Watson has entered that state of life twice and known the sorrows that it can bring. Today, each of us is alone once more, for I have heard from Mycroft news of a very sad event. The delay in informing me I can only attribute to Mycroft's many responsibilities. Watson's dear wife, the former Mary Morestan, succumbed in November of last year about Michelmas time to complications in the delivery of their first child and both the mother and child did not survive.

I blame myself severely for being absent from London at such a time and the true cost of my perambulations about the world are now becoming clear to me. Mycroft informs me that Watson has buried himself in work and is also engaged in writing up many of our old cases. I am tempted to return at once to London, but since Watson assumes that I am dead and since there is no telling what risks my meeting with Moriarty may pose, I must conclude that affair before informing Watson that I am alive and well, lest he should find me only to lose me once again. Surely Watson has known enough of painful partings. He has lost two wives now, in addition to his dear brother who died a bankrupt in America. It is the losses of those we love that are more fearful to us than the prospect of our own demise. One grows weary as one grows old by the parade of coffins. We do not die at once but are whittled down by the loss of dear friends and intimates. The heart can only bear so much grief before it becomes dry and withered.

It is not that I lack passion but that I feel things too deeply, which accounts for the solitude of my life. My mental state has never been such that I have cared to risk its final unhinging by having happiness in my grasp and then losing it. Each man knows his limits. Where the fair sex is concerned I have known the comforts of distant esteem and admiration to exceed the dull reality of possession. Some men would rather idealize a fancied bliss than to possess it. Such is the nature of all romanticism. If the grail is ever found it would be only another container for wine. To be always in quest though is to see ever before one the shining path to the Golden Fleece or to be always dreaming of a fancied homecoming to Penelope in distant Ithaca.

I confess that I am a romantic after all. To the degree that happiness beckons me, I sense behind its every offering the betrayal of time and circumstance. I am suspicious of relationships based upon the experience afforded to me of human life by my many cases. I have seen, perhaps too closely, the madness towards which all passions tend. It is not that I presume that Irene would be an easy conquest in any case, for I know only too well that her heart remains captive still to her dead husband and may remain so for years to come, to the man whom she has lost, Godfrey Norton. It is rather, that even if I did feel that she might be available and would entertain the prospect of marriage at some day to me, that I would still know that I could not embrace the married state and remain in the only profession that I know, one which is filled with dangers. To run risks for myself is permissible, but to ask another to share my perils ... no, it is unthinkable. So I must do that hardest of all things, to assume again the burdens of solitude when for a time the doors of life have seemed to open for me to imagine something that might have made all of the efforts of my life meaningful at last, for there is nothing we so value as to be invaluable to at least one other person in life. I must be short for the memory brings tears to my eyes.

When I told Irene that I would soon be leaving to return to England she was silent for several minutes. When at last she spoke I wondered at first whether she understood what I had said, for her words seemed about another matter entirely.

"I sometimes think," said she, "That when we are born there is already a life written for us like a drama and that what we call our life is only the process of acting out a role that we never chose, but that was written for us by another hand. But unlike an actress who may lay down the script in front of her and skip ahead if necessary to see how the drama ends so that she may comport her every action throughout the play with that end in view, she is only allowed to act the words just as she reads them with no rehearsal and having spoken the actress wonders if she has read the script correctly, but the words have already left her mouth and they cannot be recalled. She is therefore forced to continue without pause while new words are placed in her mouth before those prior words have had time to return as an echo from the vast and empty theater. The actress looks about her at the other players for a hint as to whether she is on her marks, but they are reciting their own parts and engrossed in what they believe to be the words and actions that are theirs and there is simply no time to stop and to question the stage manager, if there is one, to see if she is playing her part correctly and if the play is proceeding properly. At last the four or five acts are over and the curtain is lowered and the actress waits for the applause and finds that there is nothing but silence. There is only the darkened theater, the empty boxes and the dust-covered seats. It may occur then to the actress that the theater has been boarded up for many years and abandoned and she knows not how she came to be there. Perhaps it is not even a theater at all, for she cannot see beyond the stage where she has been moving and speaking her lines. Maybe she is only standing in the darkness of an empty pit and she has only imagined that the ascending rows will one day be filled, for there are no seats. Then I have gone further and wondered if there is no stage but only a dark enclosure. The actress may have only stood still throughout the play waiting for a cue that was never given and meanwhile time has passed onwards, an entire life in fact, for who may measure time when there is only silence."

She ceased to speak and I told her that I did not understand. She still seemed to be lost in her peculiar vision and hardly to be aware of my presence. She smiled at last sadly before replying, "Didn't you know, my dear, that actresses are creatures of fancy? If we knew who we were, then we could hardly play anyone else with conviction. To act at all one must believe for a time that the part we play is real."

She blushed before continuing, "What I am saying is that it takes an act of faith to be an actress. If all was certain, then our own awareness that we were lying would prevent our performance from being believable. We must fool ourselves then so that while the play lasts we are who we say that we are. The problem is not what we do during the play, for while it lasts we have a duty and a destiny, and we are certain of it even if nothing else is clear. But what about when the play ends, what shall happen then? The lights will come up and the crowd will shout for the author, but what if as in my strange thoughts there is no author and what we have been speaking and doing was only proceeding out of our own visions and dreams. If we alone are the author, then there is no play, no exterior source and purpose. There is only a darkened theater and then comes death and even the theater vanishes with the actress who always assumed that it existed, not as mere empty space, but as a theater."

She paused for a moment of reflection before continuing, "I guess that is why I must believe in God, so that there will be an author after all, someone to guarantee that my life, transient as any role in a play, will have been significant after all. But even having an author is not enough if He has no role for me. Even if I can be sure that there is a theater, I must still wait until the end to know how I have played my part and if the life that I have led was the role written for me, or whether I have been reading someone else's part by mistake."

I began to comprehend her vision. She continued, "You say that you are leaving, and so you must, but I need to ask you if you are certain that you have read your part correctly? To decide upon a course of life is a fearful thing, but far worse is to have missed the life that was truly yours. There are times and places to which we may never return and opportunities that once missed never return. We are both now in Rome, in a time and place that we did not choose, but if you leave now who may say if anything between us will ever be the same again?"

She tuned then to face me. "So I ask you only this, my dear Sherlock, must you leave or is your leaving me only a choice from which even now you may turn aside? If you cannot be certain, at least more certain than I have been in my life, for I have been certain only once on the day that I married Godfrey Norton; then how do you dare to leave me? Are you so certain that it is you alone who must confront such a formidable foe as Professor Moriarty? If all that you have told me of him is true, then you may die and I will never know another such noble man as you and Godfrey are a third time in my life, because that would be too much for one woman to ask of God!"

For a moment her words opened a vista before me of another life, one that might spare me the obligation that I felt was mine. I realized that I might never be able to find a world purged of its evils, a world worthy to be lived in by human beings. Would it not be better to grasp at the fleeting joys of earth before I died? What was Moriarty to me? There will always be men like him in the world. His defeat will only draw down another to take his place. The battle against the world's evils is unending, whereas the prospect of happiness dies with us...

I saw at once though why I have never married and never shall, not because I am, as Dr. Watson has always assumed me to be, immune from the tender emotions, but precisely because I am not immune to them. Nor am I a stranger to those very doubts that Irene spoke of, that the theater is empty after all and that the play, which has already exceeded in length the expected number of acts, will ever end. I understand what she meant, that the actor must continue to speak his lines even if he cannot be sure that it is he alone who has written them; for if he stops to seek in the wings for the author, then the play will cease.

So it goes on and on as it has always done. The play of life endures, but the actors change, and always the same eternal question remains: when shall the curtain fall so that the actors and actresses may take their bows and leave the stage and the audience of God and the devil, each with their separate following and each with a different interest in the drama that is taking place, may leave the theater at last. I had heard her urgent question but I could think of no answer equal to her honest elegance and insight. Our mutual silence grew slowly like a wall between us. I could make her no answer but that which she already knew by my silence. We each sat gazing into the fire that had by then burned low in the grate. The room seemed suddenly to have grown colder and the high walls of the drawing room, reaching upwards remotely to the darkened ceiling, seemed to grow dim about us until there was only the sound of the clock ticking upon the mantel and the soft sound of the falling ashes from the last glowing embers in the grate.

Book Ten

The American War for Empire

Dr. Watson's Narrative Continues

Now time in its strange and merciful turning had brought these two brave souls together once again. The memory of Irene Adler had not vanished. No dance of life could put "her pale lost lilies out of mind" during the intervening years. That much I, who knew Holmes so well, was able to see.

Sherlock Holmes and I left New York at noon on the day following Irene Adler's last performance. The trip northwards was a short one and I could have wished that it was longer, for it took us through the lovely green fields of the state of Connecticut. Our train passed through well-tended villages and through farmlands where placid cows looked up at us from their grazing as we passed. Shortly after this we left the farms behind and our train followed the coastline as we entered the tiny state of Rhode Island.

The town of Newport lies along a crescent-shaped bay. What might have once been a humble fishing village has been transformed in recent years into an American version of the Loire Region of France. It was here that America's new breed of aristocrats decided to create what they call with smug and deprecating irony their "summer cottages." A section of the bay is lined with huge and astonishing mansions in what must be termed one of the greatest and most lavish displays of wealth and indulgence in the history of mankind. If the entire idea of America is based upon the pursuit of happiness through the acquisition of property, then Newport must be seen as a monument to that idea of the triumph of the few over the many. There is nothing about this isolated place that might be construed as redolent of the supposed egalitarian spirit of American democracy. It would seem, particularly in light of the current state of the majority of the American people devastated since the panic of 1893 from which the nation had yet to recover, that the denizens of this frivolous community would be less desirous to expose their contempt for the needs of the many as symbolized here in the gratification of the few.

There will always be something childlike yet no less worthy of censure in any aristocracy. When delicacy of taste is preferred to that substantial fare that nourishes a nation, decadence and destruction must follow in its train. A healthy nation thrives upon a strong and equal economic base. When the masses are kept on the edge of despair, then social evils must multiply and cannot be long contained.

My devotion to the Reverend Beecher, who has spoken in favor of woman's suffrage and equal rights for all, has survived my conversion to Catholicism. The Catholic Church in its desire for social order seems always to be a century or two behind the times, at least it was until the present Pope Leo XIII's pontificate. His marvelous encyclical, *"Rerum Novarum,"* speaks of the duties owed by the rich to the laboring classes. There is an insuperable gap between those whose lives are spent in labor and those who exchange entire factories for profit as though they were merely playing cards or dominoes while remaining indifferent to the effects upon the laborers that their actions have. Their zone of human sympathy is usually confined to those who share their place in the hierarchy of possessions.

Utopians dream of a classless society as a remedy to our narrow sympathies. I fear that only a tyranny will ever succeed in imposing one. But to leave injustices perennially unaddressed and to allow capital interests to grow each year until they are oppressive beyond measure, surely that also is a tyranny. Once again death comes to mankind as the only great equalizer, at least of individuals, since the silent soil of the grave receives everyone in the end. Even the law of property has a limit placed upon the longevity of trusts and estates called, "The Rule against Perpetuities." It prevents the artificial life-forms of trusts from lasting forever. This rule combined with a just taxation system brings back into the commonwealth of all mankind what escapes from the protective shroud of excess private property. I looked over at Irene Adler who shared our carriage. One could not gaze into those lovely brown eyes without glimpsing the fierce intelligence that lay behind them. To deny such a one the vote simply because of her sex could not be other than an absurdity, an injustice as great as to allow the great private accumulation of wealth in the few in defiance of the doctrine of the commonwealth of humanity in a nation calling itself a democracy.

Our train passed onwards and reached its terminus where we were met by a coachman who identified himself as from Lands End, the Wharton Estate. The Inspector and I lent that worthy a hand in loading the luggage aboard while Holmes helped Irene Adler and her servant Molly to board the carriage and we were soon trotting down a wide paved lane bordered by chestnuts, maples, and elms.

In a short time I was able to glance through the trees and to view the facades of the elegant manor houses. I must say that in spite of my contempt at the reasons for their existence, I could not but marvel at the beauty they displayed. The most impressive was the great Vanderbilt Mansion called The Breakers. It stood in monumental splendor surrounded by huge lawns that reached downwards to the sea. We had been informed that one of the largest fetes of the season was to be held there in a few days. We would be the guests of Mrs. Wharton and as such we would be included as guests in the festivities.

A short time later our coach drew up before Lands End. I found it charming, for it resembled more closely a substantial American house without the gaudy transpositions of Europe. It stood, proudly by itself, upon its sturdy plot of shoreline. Its comfort and practicality restored its architecture to a human dimension and in doing so showed the impeccable taste of its owner. Mrs. Wharton was herself at the door to greet us and she and Irene Adler embraced warmly before she was introduced to us. When she heard who her mysterious guests were, for Irene had promised her a surprise, she greeted us with great enthusiasm.

"So I am to have as a guest beneath my roof the great Sherlock Holmes. I am honored to meet you sir," and then turning to me she continued, "And your biographer, Doctor Watson. I have read with great interest your stories that have appeared in the Strand Magazine. Pray come in, gentlemen. I have prepared a small tea in the garden, as is your British custom, which I trust you will enjoy after you are once settled in your rooms."

Several servants were at hand to aid us and to relieve us of our baggage. We ascended a gracious stairway and were soon ensconced in comfort in our rooms at Lands End. We then repaired to the garden for tea. Mrs. Wharton had been to some little trouble for us. A cloth-covered table was laden with raspberry scones, buttered crumpets, and thin slices of salmon topped with dill, as well as the usual cucumber sandwiches, and even a mince pie. All of this was served with a beverage of glasses of cold tea sweetened by an orange liqueur from Curacao in the West Indies. We were made to feel that our host would spare no pains to ensure our comfort during our visit.

The conversation soon passed, after the usual pleasantries, to the purpose for our visit to America. Holmes addressed her questions after first expressing our thanks for her hospitality, extended to us who were only strangers to her.

"No friends of Irene can ever be strangers to me," Mrs. Wharton said graciously. "We have been friends since we met in Rome and we correspond frequently. I know her penchant for the unexpected. You must promise me to stay for the entire season. My husband and I are only recently returned from Europe and have just purchased this estate. We have had very little time to make our bid for notable guests."

Holmes graciously bowed his head in assent and she continued, "I hope that my question as to your purpose in coming to America and being my summer guests will not be viewed as intrusive. We Americans tend to presume upon the slightest chance to make a new acquaintance."

"Not at all Madame," answered Holmes. "I must reserve a few details, for the mission upon which we are engaged is complex and its course is changing even as we speak. Let me begin by saying that you have already made a great contribution to its solution by acting as our hostess and ensuring us an access, which we might not otherwise have had, to men of influence here who I trust we shall meet in the course of the next weeks here in Newport. We are here to sample the temper of the country and perhaps to influence certain events that will be long remembered and may even alter the course of the foreign affairs of this great nation."

"You quite take my breath away, Mr. Holmes," gasped our hostess. "Please know that I will aid you in any way that I can. You know now of course that you will accompany me to The Breakers in a week's time for the Easter celebration. That will be April tenth. Since the guest list includes William Randolph Hearst, Theodore Roosevelt, and Thomas Brackett Reed who is the Speaker of the House of Representatives, you will meet at once some of the most influential gentlemen in America. You come to America at a time when the nation is divided about whether we should aid the rebels in Cuba as they seek their independence from

Spain. I should not have thought that Americans would ever relish the prospect of war again after our own Civil War, but since the sinking of the Maine many are clamoring for intervention and revenge."

"To release the dogs of war is to enter upon dangerous ground, for situations once altered have consequences that may not appear for many years. The affairs of states admit of no return to the balance that may have existed before and he who will change history, even for the good, takes upon himself a fearful responsibility," Holmes replied.

"It is a responsibility then that does not seem to trouble either Mr. Roosevelt or Mr. Hearst," said Mrs. Wharton. "Each of these men is pressing for an immediate American intervention in the struggle. Mr. Thomas Brackett Reed, on the other hand, feels that to do so is profoundly at variance with our tradition as a nation, not to take sides in disputes beyond our own shores. I fear that the table conversation and over their port in the library after dinner is likely to be intemperate and heated. As an Englishman you may be looked upon as an intruder."

"That will serve our purposes well, Madam, for it is only appropriate that matters of such import should cause men of conscience to consider well their courses by open and vigorous discussion. Events in the world seem lately to be spiraling out of control, not merely here but in Europe as well. The tensions in Africa, for instance between the major Colonial Empires are growing each day and I will be very much mistaken if relations between Egypt and the Sudan do not reach a point of crisis soon."

"Irene has informed me that you are about to publish some short stories dealing with the changes in American social life, so I need not tell you that we may be witnessing the last halcyon days of an age that is passing. Our Queen Victoria has extended the period of her reign to the far horizon of mortality. When she passes I fear that the British Empire will have already reached its furthest extent of influence, for all that rises must inevitably fall. Mortality is not mocked by an individual or even by nations. Perhaps, this new ambition that we see in American armament and intentions betoken a desire to assume in turn the laurel of destiny and to take the place in world affairs that England may soon vacate. If this should prove so, America must be warned that in achieving dominion over others the character of a nation may be so altered that it looses its own unique virtues and identity and as a result the citizens may be deprived of their birthright of freedom and prosperity."

Our hostess answered, "I have confined my speculations to the impact of social change on the upper classes and the perennial question of the place of women in world affairs, because these questions lie within the ambit of my personal observation and affect me deeply. I have even thought of becoming a writer, but of course my mother believes that any such occupation, particularly for a woman, is hopelessly *declasse*."

Irene spoke up, "Her mother has at times even disapproved of me, but since I am European all is forgiven."

Holmes then turned the conversation to lighter matters, "But I would not begin our time as your guests in this delightful home of yours with such serious topics. Irene has told me something of your work in garden and household design with a particular emphasis upon the Italian villas. I have traveled in Italy as has Doctor Watson who is only just returned from Rome. Perhaps, you will gratify us with some of your commentary on garden design. We should be most happy to listen."

With that the conversation moved to more genial topics where it remained for the remainder of the afternoon. Later at dinner our discussion at table resumed its course on matters of travel and of design. Champagne was served along with an excellent New England roast beef. I looked about the candlelit room and could not but remark upon the joys of civilization. It is certainly a prerogative of wealth that it may create about itself an air of grace and beauty.

Both Mrs. Wharton and Miss Irene Adler (for professional purposes she had resumed her maiden name) were clothed in silk. The gentlemen wore frock coats. The silver and china sparkled in the mellow glow of the candles that burned upon the dinner table and sideboard. Conversation was lively and interrupted by the discreet laughter and witty observations that make the social graces one of the great ameliorating influences upon the cares of life.

Sherlock Holmes looked healthy and I hoped that months of clean sea air might further secure the advances that he had made upon the course of his chronic respiratory disease. It was my desire to temper any excesses that I might observe and to ward off any influences that might cause his acute illness to return to ascendancy over him.

April is always a lovely month in New England. The spring season was just beginning and the American aristocracy was gathering even now for its yearly summer festivities. But over that gay company was laid the impending shadow of war. Those who advocate wars seldom die in them. Bloodthirsty emotion is usually dependent upon one's distance from the field of battle. The *causus belli* appears to be destiny to those who need do little to ensure actual victory. Certainly any war that is fought from a desire to enhance power rather than to ensure survival as such cannot fail to be immoral it seemed to me. I felt then, as did Holmes, that we must attempt to dissuade American policy from a path of intervention by tamping down enthusiasm for war, even if it was better for our own plan against Baron Maupertuis that the nation should enter into one of those periods of jingoism that leads to wars and might also lend support to the building of a canal in Central America to enhance American trade and power. The onward rush of events soon spared us within weeks of any effort we might have made to turn America away from its precipitous rush to war, for on April 25, 1898 war was declared against Spain. America had taken a step, as later events have shown, that would change its national character forever. America ceased to concentrate upon perfecting the dreams of refuge and equality that had inspired so many immigrants in their journey to America to build a new life relieved of the burdens of history that lead to wars. Even religions are mired in the past and an effort to erase and heal past sins by committing new ones. The very memory of a Garden of Eden prevents the building of a more humble garden requiring human labor. Christianity promises paradise, but it is only on earth that human beings display the ordinary virtues of good sense and good government that make heroic charity less necessary, because each man and woman does their respective duties in the ordinary processes of living a good life.

From the Journal of Sherlock Holmes

February 14, 1893
Zurich, Switzerland

I have left Rome behind me and with it that perennial summer that reigns in Italy. It is as though I have plunged in an instant into the very heart of winter. The great mountains of Switzerland have protected this insular people from ready invasions. The Swiss have learned to tolerate divergence of language and also in religion and to maintain a union based on the practical dictates of survival in this hostile land. The result is a sobriety and reticence that is matched by their thrift. How different they are from the improvident Italians. This land of granite and snow seems immune from passion. It is the very place for me now for this reason.

It was no easy matter to take my leave from Irene. As with all partings that are dictated, not by choice but by necessity, it is easier if farewells are not prolonged. I could wish that we had come to an understanding of some sort, but it is enough that I have the deepest respect for her and confidence that she will succeed in her efforts to re-enter the world. I do not see her remaining a mournful Italian widow living only on the memories of what was. I told her so at our last meeting. She offered me her hand in parting and I held it in both of mine before turning to go.

"I know that I shall hear of you in the future, Mr. Sherlock Holmes," she said, smiling through her tears, "I know that Dr. Watson will soon tell of the return of Sherlock Holmes. I will be able to picture you again in that most comfortable of all retreats at Baker Street. You will resume your posture of judicial rectitude exercised over the affairs and follies of those who require your aid. You will not be burdened there by a mournful diva like me. By then you will also have no doubt met your great enemy, Professor Moriarty. I shall not lose you I know, for God will preserve you until we meet again."

I did not know how to answer her, but I assured her that Covent Garden was not far from Baker Street and that some night she would find me standing in a box applauding with the rest of London after one of her performances. Both of us knew that the future might bring unforeseen challenges, but we dared to express our hopes and in doing so we were better able to face the individual challenges that were forcing us to part, challenges that each of us could only face alone. I did not look back at parting but heard the door close softly on a muffled sob. She turned away at once and was soon lost in the crowd.

I left Rome that same afternoon, knowing that it was only by placing distance between us at once that I could resist the pull of the desire to defer still further the tasks that lie ahead for me. My plans are to take the train from Zurich to Lausanne and from there to go to Lyon and onward to Paris. I am as it were saying farewell to my favorite places on the continent since I do not know what dangers I may face from Professor Moriarty and when if ever I shall return. Perhaps he has spent these years preparing a snare into which I am about to fall. If so, then I consent to the risk. I am determined to honor the terms of our mutual wager at any price. I will inform Mycroft by wire from Paris that I am returning soon.

I will go first to London, so that Mycroft and I may discuss in detail my impressions of the Sudanese leader, the Khalifa. After that, unless something intervenes, I will go to Devonshire to meet the Professor at his estate at Kings Pyland. We have of course not set up a syllabus or agenda for the meetings that will then take place between us. I cannot conceive yet the form that they will take, but we will both at least be spared the absurd indignity of a physical struggle on a cliff-edge above a waterfall.

When I have tried to picture our encounter in the sovereign realm of my imagination, I have seen something in the order of a chess game or rather of a series of games of indefinite number until at last one of us concedes. Beyond this vague image, I have been unable to venture. As a result, I have no strategy prepared, but will rather adapt my every move to the Professor's. Will he be willing to lead the assault or will he also wait for me to make the opening gambit? The situation seems at times to be artificial, but so is any debate over good and evil when conducted from the privileged position of not being forced to make an immediate decision.

Later—

In the stream of events that is our lives we try to do the good and to avoid evil, but seldom do we succeed for long in either endeavor. For the most part a practical ethics in an unconverted world is not a function of religion. The world has yet to find a consistent application of Kant's categorical imperative among the mass of mankind. In the absence of moral consensus most of our actions show some degree of compromise between altruism and self-interest. Especially in politics there is a balance of force between nations that stays short of war but tries the limits of what threats can achieve. Even within nations there is a struggle to find a balance between opposing parties with each pursuing an ideal of rational self-interest in pursuit of an enlightened republic.

The basis of social morality is not the law of charity but the law of contract. Mutuality is nourished by the anticipated benefits to be received by each contracting party and the prospect of future goodwill attendant upon repeated instances of bargained for exchange.

The proposed standard of the cross of Jesus Christ of course knows nothing of this. Heaven is not a reward for many virtuous actions performed. Christianity does not stoop to such low motivations. To follow the will of God for its own sake and to love God as the *summum bonum* of existence is simply to recognize that God is our all in all and the principle cause of all human actions. The principle of evil can never be considered as a viable rival for our affections, if we are adamant in our pursuit of sainthood. For this reason evil is defined as the absence of a corresponding good that ought to be present. Evil is essentially a corruption and a deviation from a corresponding ontological goodness that should have been present.

Evil creates nothing of itself. It is essentially parasitic in nature and cannot exist without preying upon and ordering itself towards the destruction of a preexisting good. This essential servitude of evil makes its presence indicative of a condition of diminishment. For this reason evil cannot be discerned directly until one has already posited something good that will be diminished or destroyed by an evil action. To clearly discern the will of God then is to already know which direction the will should take. The will should always follow the impulse of grace within the conscience and by doing so cooperate with the will of God.

The assumption is that by doing so the human race would be always sailing with the wind and with the tide of God's truth. This is what Jesus meant when He said, "Take my yoke upon you for my load is easy and my burden light." From this same realization we also have the words of Jesus in His admonishment addressed to the devil during the temptation in the desert. Jesus presents it as simply a statement of fact, "Man does not live by bread alone but from every word that comes from the mouth of God."

In this sense then the love of God must come before any virtuous act as the source of spiritual nourishment that is to the soul as basic as bread is to the body. There is nothing mystical or esoteric in this injunction. It seems quite natural, more so even that Kant's rational demand of the categorical imperative to motivate human action. The teleological goodness of the goal exists prior to our action in conformity with what its dictates. One already exists within the Kingdom of God through living in the Holy Spirit prior to any reward whether mundane in origin or divine. From this point of view (and what other can their ever be to the true Christian) the rewards of heaven are not a future event but rather a daily occurrence consequent upon living in the Kingdom of God. This means that Jesus did not come so much to anticipate an apocalyptic event or a reward after death, but to call Israel back to what it should have been doing all along as part of Israel's covenant relationship with its God.

This is a standard of morality of such height and absoluteness that it seems to have nothing to do with human life as we know it. To act according to this standard seems to be too much to ask from human nature and that would be true if Jesus was only revealing what human wisdom itself could have indicated over time and deduced from experience. The Ten Commandments for instance might have been figured out on the basis of human experience alone. Jesus takes morality into unimagined heights by revealing how it is with God in any realm that could be called the Kingdom of God, one that can only lead on earth to the very crucifixion that was to claim the life of Jesus at last. The act of redemption is both atonement for our failures, as St. Paul realized, and simultaneously an invitation to do likewise, if we wish to live even now in the Kingdom of God, a Kingdom not of this world.

It is the perfection of human nature as created prior to Original Sin so to choose that one's every action is done from within grace and for grace. This is what it means to be incorporated within the body of Jesus Christ as the branch is to the vine. For this reason, the sacramental character of our union with Jesus Christ is both demonstrated and actualized by the real and substantial presence of Jesus Christ in the Holy Eucharist as the Catholic Church proclaims.

But lest we lose hope, we remain a church of sinners also. This means that the life of the Catholic is spent in a constant tension between sin, which promises an inverse salvation (and which is only remedied by forgiveness through the sacrament of Penance or its spiritual equivalent as mediated by God alone) and those times when a foretaste of the Kingdom of God is present even now in our actualized union with Christ in prayer and in action.

Properly speaking an attitude of sustained contrition is our best safeguard and protection because it is only then that sin cannot take root within us, when it is constantly washed in the Blood and Water from the side of Our Lord as the perennial sign of the institution of the sacramental order in all its fullness. Our constant prayer as Christians is for final perseverance. This is simply the determination to return to God in all circumstances, an abiding attitude of will that so dominates our thoughts that nothing else can for long prevail against it.

Sin may then be the condition of the moment but contrition is the condition of the hour. From the mustard seed grows the tree. The fever of life waxes and wanes and we pray that our death may find us healthy. This is the course of our spiritual struggle. That it is a struggle at all shows the effects of fallen human nature. We must imagine a state when virtue was the easy course and not the hard one. The fear of death and loss makes us chary in our virtues for fear that having given so much we will be left empty and abandoned at last. For this reason, the beginning of evil is to doubt that God can be trusted, to be more faithful to us than we are to Him.

A proper fear of God is the fear of the loss of God and not a fear of any actions that God might take against us if we displease Him. To fear God in Himself is to believe the devil's suggestion that God demands obedience from man in order to prevent man from achieving his own proper stature as God's equal. For this reason for a man to truly know himself is already to comprehend and to accept that his being is derivative from God and that outside of God he has no being.

God does not require the worship of men and of women to sustain God's own nature as supreme. To say this is to realize that even had we not been created at all, there would have been no gap in God's being as such. Yet it is said that before we were knit in our mother's womb we already existed in the mind of God. To that extent we had a prior claim on being, but that claim was (to use a legal term) merely equitable in nature and not an enforceable legal claim upon God. It is then to the beneficence of God and not to our own sovereign right to existence that we must look if we are to make any claims upon God, even to exist at all, let alone by making subsidiary demands upon God before we will condescend to worship Him.

In other words God's absolute being has as a prerogative the ability to assign whatever meaning and value exists between good and evil. How then can we as contingent beings question any determination of these questions when the answer is set down in a definitive form as "the word of God?" This is the problem of all "revealed religion." It presumes that God's demands can be definitively ascertained by reference to a text. This presumption in turn has a corollary that requires a prior assumption that no extraneous human dynamics have so conditioned the text so as to admit human dynamics such as choice of genre or metaphor or any cultural elements that might shape the form and composition of the text in question or condition how the text was initially to be read and understood by its initial audience. There appears to be no way to purge a text of accompanying elements that may blur the outline of the window into the mind of God provided by Sacred Scripture.

February 15, 1893
Lausanne, Switzerland

If instead we turn to human experience to judge good and evil we encounter a different problem. The history of the world is that moral definitions of good and evil depend upon the results obtained rather than on antecedents. Whatever is judged as good or evil is often determined by whether the results benefit or injure us. The people of Jericho no doubt took an entirely different view of the results of that biblical battle than the besieging army of Israel. Regarding metaphysical evil we must begin with Original Sin. The account of the happenings in the Garden of Eden deal with how human beings were by our own choice plunged into the quagmire of needing to consider the moral results of our actions.

The first question posed is whether God's words to Adam regarding which trees were safe from which to eat was a moral demand made upon a pre-moral being or was it instead a mere statement regarding the nature of things. If a being cannot know the difference between good and evil until after the act in question, then is it fair to hold that being accountable for disobeying a moral commandment? Original Sin then is less about disobedience than it is about a change of relationship between dependence upon authoritative testimony from God as a hitherto reliable source as opposed to independent experimentation before the relevant categories were firmly in place and perceptible.

This is why there always appears to be something a little bit awry in the story of the drama in Eden. Why did God not warn Adam and Eve of the cunning nature of the serpent as an unsuspected risk in a hitherto perfect garden? Was God surprised and dismayed by the outcome of the choice made by Adam and Eve or only angered and chagrined, particularly when a similar experiment with creating contingent being had resulted in the emergence of evil even among angels? In other words, the story as told is unconvincing to an unbiased reader seeking to explain how an omniscient God can be thwarted by the machinations of His creatures. Only by placing the entire story under the rubric of love can we make sense of this anomaly: to love is to be vulnerable to being made the victim of evil, even if the lover is God. In other words God would appear to be the victim of His own nature.

Satan and his angels are in no better position than we are, metaphysically speaking. In fact their position is in fact infinitely worse. The Angels are by their very nature servants of the Word of God. In that sense, all angels are guardian angels. For this reason we can glimpse something of the arrogance of the devil and his mockery of God when he pretends to feel solicitude towards Jesus in tempting him lest He dash his foot against a stone. Had Jesus fallen from the parapet of the temple it would have been the task of the devil to bear him up, for such a delegation from God to the angels was the reason for the devil's entire existence as an angel. For this reason the final temptation of the devil to Jesus manifests precisely the inverted nature of angelic evil, for the devil asks Jesus to pay the devil homage in exchange for all the kingdoms of the world. This is like nothing promising everything to its owner.

Can anything more absurd be imagined? Does the tenant bestow the estate upon its owner? Or was this temptation perhaps more subtle? Perhaps the real temptation was to subvert the mission of Jesus by tempting Him to achieve dominion and success on earth by the devil's own means; that is to say by exercising the subjugation and bribery. Jesus is tempted to use signs and wonders as well as the gratification of human needs and desires to obtain worship. Instead Jesus reveals the Father as the Father actually is and pays the price for doing so by having that love rejected leading to the crucifixion. The entire Christian message is one of salvaging victory from apparent defeat and of the mystery of life proceeding out of death.

February 16, 1893
Lausanne, Switzerland

Our Lord asks for our love by asking us to embrace the cross and not for any reward that we may receive, even if that reward should be heaven, but rather because our nature as made in the image and likeness of God demands it in order to be true to itself. Better the cross than to possess even legitimate comforts, even the prospect of heaven. For this reason the nature of heaven for the Christian is always left undefined: Eye has not seen, nor has ear heard, nor has it even entered into the heart of man what God has prepared for those who love him." Compare this concept to the crude delights of the Moslem paradise as sketched out by Mohammed, a garden of earthly pleasures that however appropriate to convince the men of nomadic tribes, can have little appeal to a reflective mind that is not to be won over by such seductive images.

If however we as human beings can possess no clear idea of heaven, then what may we say of the nature and characteristics of hell? May hell not be best grasped by assuming that it is getting all the things that our folly and greed might suggest, but at the cost of losing God in the process, because that is what hell is like here on earth? In God alone all things find their true meaning. Why is the Devil so generous with his gifts as offered first to Jesus and then to us? All the kingdoms of the world and their glory are ours if we will only worship him.

The offer in the gospel by the devil to Jesus is a sign of condescension and contempt for His humanity. The general scope of this temptation is mirrored in each of us as we each seek our own little kingdom in the realm of sin. To give the devil his due, perhaps for once he was not lying and this bargain at least he will honor. But what if he does? A private Kingdom of our own design will be purchased at the cost of losing the privilege of loving God for Himself alone that can only be attained by giving without counting the cost or expecting any reward beyond God Himself. To settle for anything less is to accept the devil's bargain.

God himself is heaven and there is no heaven that is not in God. Jesus chose the cross because it meant having nothing finally but God. To God who gives all, we in turn must return all, if we are to truly know the depths of love. The nadir of the way of the cross was the horrible and ultimate moment and its eternal significance, when Jesus glimpses what it would be to lose God, for whom Jesus had already renounced all things: if God were then to abandon Jesus, as man and woman had once abandoned God in the Garden of Eden. The words ascribed to God calling out for Adam, "Where are you?" only then manifest for us their true tragic poignancy.

If one moment wrought our redemption it was that moment. Jesus had become sin for the world and as that "sin" Jesus felt what it would mean to lose the love of God forever. All of mankind was derivatively present and subsumed into Jesus at that precise moment and for just an instant God the Father could have justifiably abandoned us to our own devices with nothing but the devil's kingdom and the glories of this passing world to bring us a sterile comfort.

At that instant of absolute emptiness just before death Jesus, turned as He was from the world, but laden vicariously with the world's sin, the Divinity of the Christ breaks forth like the first spark of creation because God as Father did not abandon Jesus but shared His human pain. Jesus was not alone on the cross.

The Crucifixion of Jesus then is a cosmic event of God risking all, of so dividing the Godhead that Jesus Christ is loyal to humanity to the extent of identifying His very being with our sins. St. Paul affirms this when he tells us that Jesus Christ became sin for us. Redemption is effective then precisely because while we were yet in our sins Christ loved us and God the Father so loved the world that He would not turn away from even our sins if those sins were associated and even identified with by the beloved Son of God, because God cannot deny Himself.

The redemption of man and woman involves the cooperation then of the whole of the Trinity. The sacrifice of the Son to restore man and woman to the Father releases the Holy Spirit of love to reanimate a desolate world by finally making available to man and woman the fruit of the other tree, the Tree of Life, from which we may now safely eat for to waken to eternity in the arms of God, forgiven of our sins, is to find the rigors of eternity finally made supportable.

Man and woman cannot endure an eternity of kingdoms of this world even in all their glory. These are left to the devil and his minions and what a poor consolation they are is seen by the fact that the devil would have surrendered them all to Jesus for a moment of worship of the devil in the place of God. The devil is identified with his chosen way. That contrarian aspiration detracts from the devil's own being, which because made for God can serve no other purpose. Made for God, the devil chooses to be like-God, but there is no likeness-to-God that is available to assume without love and sacrifice. No amount of spurious worship can alter that metaphysical fact, which tortures the devil unceasingly and drives him to every degree of degradation, even to creating his own place of torment. Hell for the Devil then is the continuing love of God for him, a love that the devil will never accept.

If man and woman are saved, the devil has no allies in

created reality, except any souls who, in choosing his fate, only invite his contempt. Good and evil then are metaphysical realities and are not confined or strictly attributed to the realm of ethics, but only in a subsidiary way for the ethical is still in many respects the pursuit of self-interest. The moral law was always a favor to mankind meant to re-orient us back to God. It is in the simple realization that the many commands of both law and conscience exceed our capacities that we turn to Divine Grace to grant as a gift to supplement our endeavors. If all of our virtues depend upon grace, then we cannot demand heaven as our just payment, because even the good that we have done, let alone our many sins, must both look to God for validation or remittance. God is our sole remedy and recompense.

Humility then is becoming to us as we turn to God for our every good, knowing that in ourselves we can do nothing meritorious. Even knowing the difference between good and evil, as we do, we still perform the deeds that in our hearts we despise and leave undone that which in our deepest hearts we wish to do.

February 18, 1893
Geneva

My journey to Paris took me through Lausanne situated on its lovely lake and through Geneva. I could not pass through Geneva without thinking of that melancholy legal genius, John Calvin. Whatever his private virtues and abilities, by relying upon a private theology rather than following the collective discernment of the church, he created dissention and schism even within early Protestantism. His dogma of double-predestination that makes providence and the sovereign action of irresistible grace the dictator of all human actions rather than an aid to human freedom had the effect not of glorifying God but of diminishing the dignity of man. Calvin reduced the human drama to a play of shadows without substance, a sort of divine dream in which God is the dreamer. Men and women are, according to Calvin, predestined and thus also predetermined to heaven or to hell by a pre-existing divine decree before they are even born.

If this is the case then why should we as human beings even witness or agree to be players in the drama of life and of history by allowing our virtue to manifest and our reprobation to destroy? But for John Calvin the play has really nothing to do with us anyway, because the drama is intended primarily if not completely to demonstrate before God what He knows already, that He can do to us anything that He wishes without being called to account for His actions before any higher authority.

The more arbitrary and capricious circumstances appear to us, the more we demonstrate our blindness to the celestial beauty of eternal justice. In the world-view of John Calvin the reward for virtuous living is the sign-value that it demonstrates that Reformed Christians are a direct parallel to the Jewish settlement of Canaan, where the Jewish people were unaccountably and undeservedly approved by God and designated as the chosen people.

Nothing in other words is so horrible for the true Calvinist as the thought of universal mercy towards the entire human race. The apostolic vision of St. Paul is seen as essentially contrary to the value of salvation that as in the case of diamonds or gold only becomes rarer and more valuable when it is in short supply. A restrictive God by being more selective in the company He is willing to entertain in heaven, just to that degree even holier and more worthy of worship.

Even the Calvinist Churches were to be stripped of all ornamentation or design because anything human is nauseating to a God who loathes all images. Every source of beauty in nature or in art is disgusting to the Calvinist, because the only real beauty on earth is to be found within the text of the Bible and even then only insofar as it is a text and not an illuminated manuscript. Calvinist theology is the logical outcome of a legalist mind encountering the wonder of revelation without any ability to see through and beyond the mere words and to comprehend the gradually expanding scope of intimacy that God offers to all men and women. Can it be believed that everything that we witness all about us is only the actualization of a script, as though this world was a playhouse with God in the gallery applauding his best lines and hissing at the villains that he has himself created? Was heaven so boring that God must perforce amuse Himself by creating helpless creatures subject to supreme power? Ridiculous!

The doctrine of John Calvin and his followers is the best example of the limits of all theological speculations that try to harmonize the often conflicting words of Holy Scripture without the guidance of the Holy Spirit as promised to the Catholic Church, the Church of the Apostolic Succession, the Church of the Bishops and of Peter's successor as the Pope. The Catholic Church as governed by tradition, which alone can hear the call of God through divine revelation in all its fullness and within its own living tradition is the universal Christian Church from which all others have to some degree deviated in pursuit of partial theological visions. There is no private "inner voice," but rather all things whatsoever must be tested against what has been believed always and everywhere by the Universal Magisterium of the Catholic Church.

Calvin's second mistake was the attempt to create a theocracy in Geneva, an ideal embodiment of his teachings, a sort of weak parallel to Rome with Calvin as the Pope. It is the function of the Catholic Church to penetrate our worldly concerns with both teaching and sacrament, not to assume the duties of civil government and commerce. The civil order depends instead upon the concept of sovereignty. Sovereignty is the right to rule in all matters not mandated by faith to the Catholic Church. The civil order is equally subject to God of course, but the means of execution and the subject matter differ. All civil arrangements must be so designed that the proper rights of the individual are respected, while giving scope for the exercise of the labors of charity and the worship of God.

Just as the Catholic Church may never create a theocracy, so no civil authority, such as a nation-state or a monarchy whatever form these may take whether parliamentarian or not, may presume to assume the functions of the Pope and his Bishops. For this reason the presumption of King Henry VIII of England to be the sole arbiter in all matters, both civil and ecclesiastical in England was heretical and schismatic.

Also for this reason the efforts of Napoleon to reduce the clergy to paid civil servants was rightly condemned by the Catholic Church. It is also for this reason that the efforts of Thomas Jefferson and James Madison to create, out of the popular will alone, a source of natural sovereignty in the people of America, was to assume that the amorphous mass within a designated geographical region has the right to rule itself unhindered in any way by any external authority. But the question of which inhabitants should be counted as citizens of a republic is always an abstraction and subject to manipulation.

The political philosophers Locke and Rousseau were wrong; there is no "general will." The result of such a presumption is the creation of republics where a handful of men end up telling others what to believe and placating the people with toys and baubles while clandestinely serving the rich and the powerful. Republics sooner or later descend into plutocratic rule. There is no justified civil order if that order does not acknowledge that all original sovereignty lies with God and is only secondarily delegated to us. There must be some final and solid source for all derivative authority on which to rest temporal power.

Today, to travel across Europe is to traverse the sites of Christianity's great battlefields waged in the name of differing theological beliefs. There is a direct correlation between heresy from the Catholic Church and the slaughter of people. Only Christian unity can preserve the rule of charity among all Christians and only orthodox belief in the Roman Catholic Church can ensure that unity.

February 24, 1893
Lyon

After leaving Geneva we descended into France. A wind was blowing northwards from the Midi and for a time the air grew warm about us. I disembarked in Lyon and spent two days and nights in that second of French cities writing in my journal before catching my train for Paris. In France I am surrounded by fields of green and brown and the fertile plains reach out all about me giving me a sense of expansion. How glad I am to escape the eternal snows and mountains of Switzerland that for all of their beauty hem one in all on sides. One can not dwell too long among mountains without growing slightly mad. Mountains tend to dwarf a sense of human possibilities by confining our aspirations to the vertical plane. Yet we should always have something above ourselves to excite wonder and show us our proper place in creation.

That being said, a man is never more in tune with his environment than when he dwells upon the fertile lands where crops grow, animals graze, and he may know the joy of a glass of wine at home in the evenings. To care for much beyond our daily bread is to dream of a fevered Elysium that mocks our efforts to attain it. Cities, for all of their productivity in marketable objects are never really independent. Mankind is by nature agrarian. For this reason the folly of power is shown at the beginning of every empire in the creation of a great polis to house the abstraction of the central organizing idea around which each empire grows.

Power always has a shadow side to the degree that some men are exalted by empires, while the majority of its citizens are impoverished and starved of their full-measure of human dignity. We need only to reflect on the spectacle of the squalor of London or of New York or on the slave based-society of ancient Thebes or Babylon to realize and accept this truth. If Paris is an exception to this rule, it is only because the French love life more than power, at least when they are being most true to their national *joie de vivre*. Then it is that even urban conditions cannot remove that languid spirit that will not allow the small enjoyments of life to be forfeited to the clanging demands of the industrial order.

To see Paris is to see life in all of its forms made daily manifest. The reason that no settled form of government lasts for long in France is that the French are by nature so in love with life that they will not allow any form of government to so obsess them that they will succumb like the Germans and the Austrians to whatever autocrat or general may presume to give them orders. The French have a genius for revolution, but also alas for later reactionary regimes. This hunger for novelty and display can cause the French as a people to waste the energy that might have made them the first among Christian nations. Instead that honor has passed to my native England.

The genius of England is due to the British ability to dominate maritime trade ever since the defeat of the Spanish Armada and the gradual supplanting of the Dutch sea-traders by British merchant-men. But there has been a further reason for Britain's primacy in world-trade, its unique brand of jurisprudence and its legal system. Conflict brings about the refinement of laws in an adversary system of justice. The British have shown to the world the virtues inherent in competition and the orderly pursuit of self-interest. In addition, the British throne has been stable since the restoration of the monarchy under King Charles II. The British have been united around a single sovereign, yet that monarch has not been a tyrant but has shared power with the people through an enlightened parliament.

When King Henry VIII proclaimed himself to be the head of the Church in England he attempted an alignment between the civil order and the spiritual order in his own person. It was a wise practical choice for one to whom power had supplanted the rightful demands of his faith. It is always possible in the short-run to justify acts that are sinful and wrong, and even to reap rewards from that choice. This is why Jesus said that the wisdom of this world is folly to God. True sovereignty is always derivative. Jesus said as much to Pontius Pilate when he said, "You would have no power over me at all were it not given to you from above."

But since power is only the rightful exercise of sovereignty and is only rightful when the government acts according to the principle that power may only be rightfully used when it is subordinated to the Divine will, the principle of individual freedom and dignity must be considered first before there is any exercise of power done in the name of the polity. This means of course that government must never exist as an end in itself and that power should by nature be exercised only in the name of the distributive will of the individuals who make up the commonwealth as they in turn are enlightened by faith. This implies a measure of consent in the people to be governed by their collective or majority decisions. Discontent breeds first dissent and then, as popular frustration mounts, to revolution.

Certain tests may clarify this point. If one applies these tests, it will be seen at once how lacking in legitimacy most governments are when they pursue power as an end in itself, whatever accidental form that pursuit may take. The desire of power for its own sake is perhaps the primary motive for sinful conduct. The desire to remain in possession of power is unfortunately the usual experience of mankind in relationship to government.

Instead I would recommend that all forms of government pretending to exercise sovereignty and the right to rule should need to pass a comprehensive test in order to claim legitimacy, a test of service and submission rather than the grandeur and display that are usually used as a mask for tyranny and to impress and arouse fear in the people or alternatively to gratify a collective and vicarious sense of derivative pomp and pride in the anonymous citizen. Only then will the affairs of this world finally be able to show some evidence of a redeemed humanity.

The proper tests for legitimate sovereignty includes, it seems to me, these ideas:

1. Government does not exist to be served but to serve;

2. Government's legitimacy derives from the character of its actions and their conformity to the will of God if it can be ascertained through natural law or from divine revelation;

3. The popular will, the will *en masse* of the people, must be subordinated to and educated by the sovereign in its legitimate exercise of power, which it should be able to meet if tests 1 and 2 are met;

4. The individual retains all natural human rights given to each soul by God, the foremost of which is to possess and be given sufficient means to exercise individual freedom and dignity;

5. These human rights exist in individuals and may never be impaired by governments or by temporary and shifting majorities that would enforce ideological conformity in order to serve the ends of powerful elements within the state;

6. Since creation rejoices in variety and disorder, rules should be kept to a minimum to ensure peace and social order;

7. Since these rights are common and equal in both men and women, no right exercised by an individual may be used to prevent or defeat the same rights in others;

8. Since peace and contemplation, the higher ends of human life, require leisure as shown by the divine institution of the

Sabbath, human activity is not an end in itself but a mode of creating material abundance to secure human needs; when it exceeds its proper measure it threatens the dignity of living and prevents the contemplation of God and the enjoyment life. Production must be curtailed when it threatens these primary pursuits.

These eight principles if more commonly applied to statecraft would advance the general as well as the individual welfare and if universally applied would simultaneously prevent those rivalries between nations and peoples that so augment human misery and frustrate the realization of the will of God and the operation of divine grace among men and women.

That God does not directly intervene to create a more just social order by fiat is due to the fact that we have chosen, in our primordial origins, to define our human nature in opposition to God so that we are given the choice to know the difference between good and evil by experiencing them. We were in fact warned of the consequences of such freedom and might have chosen to abide in that direct conformity of action with grace that was the rule in Eden. What we observe then of evil in the world is none other than the direct consequence of an order of things that we have in some mysterious manner chosen.

That even the manifest evils of the world have not made us as a species fall down in petition and to universally ask God to return us to that former state of innocence, but that instead we act as though what we see about us is worthy to be embraced as a path to happiness has caused men of every religious tradition to wonder at our collective folly. It is as though the world in which we live was the world as God intended it, but this is to wrong God. Who can look about him and not say that life as we live it is appalling?

The first of the noble truths of the Buddha is that all of life is suffering. His assessment is correct. We live in a state that, were it not for grace, would be intolerable. The Bodhisattva is the one who feels the need to turn away from his own entry into nirvana and to help his brothers and sisters towards enlightenment. What motive is this but the Buddhist equivalent to Christian charity, which is the primary fruit of grace? Religions serve God when they execute his will. Our fidelity is less a matter of proper attribution and doctrinal correctness than it is one of practical charity.

Jesus said, "Not everyone who says to me Lord, Lord, will enter the Kingdom of Heaven, but only the one who does the will of my Father." For this reason the pagan who serves God will enter heaven before those who think correctly but fail to exercise their faith by action in accordance with God's will. Grace is not confined by the extent of our understanding of God. The admonition to believe is not so that we may refine our comprehension of God by theology, but so that we might seek to do His will.

God will always exceed even our most exalted concepts. Correct belief, as mediated by Divine Revelation, is asked of us so that we may have the most direct route to grace. Our pretentions as Christians will only raise the standard by which our activities will be judged by God who will no doubt ask of us on the Day of Judgment, "Since you knew so much, why did you not act proportionately better than those whom you called pagans and infidels? Am I not free to invite whom I wish to the Wedding-feast of Heaven? You who thought that you were first will be seated last."

A corollary of the state of the current divisions that exist among mankind is this: the Second Coming of Christ will not occur until all of mankind turns in desperation back to God and with a single voice begs for Christ's return. The process of redemption was designed to mirror that sin called original to which we attribute all of our human ills. To turn the universe back to God requires that the whole world should be aligned with Christ; but how and when that is to be achieved is something that God alone knows.

Salvation is not imposed upon world history; it must be freely chosen. History as the collective experience of the human race is never closer to God though than it is when history resists grace, for where sin abounds, there grace super-abounds. The turning of all nations to God will be sudden and absolute. As the I-Ching recognizes, the rule of opposites is such that alteration is produced by excess in any one direction. Change when it comes therefore is likely to be instantaneous. It is therefore my belief that the rule of human progress is an illusion. In the end the church will witness more martyrdom than even under the Roman Emperors Nero and Diocletian.

The great dawn of the last day will be preceded by a great darkness. Jesus warned us that the end would come preceded by a period of great suffering. This alone will give us the strength to endure that bitter season. But that a new spring of the world will come is certain as faith teaches and our hope sustains within us. Until then the path of charity between all peoples is the task that is ahead for the church to pursue as well as the secular rulers upon the earth, and of course it is also the task to be pursued by each individual soul.

March 1, 1893
Paris

I have been reading over many of my recent entries. I do not know how it is that I feel so convinced of the truth of these bold speculations and definitions, but they must form the basis for my arguments before Professor Moriarty and before the witness of my own conscience. And yet I find the whole matter somewhat pedantic as though these great generalizations on such large matters will always run afoul by the sheer complexity of human events upon which I have based my career. My entire method has been to adjust the general to the unique and the circumstantial. It is Scotland Yard that always fails to grasp the one significant thread that leads to the correct solution of a case precisely because the inspectors of that venerable institution deal with so many crimes. In a similar manner the greatest human institutions fail because they attempt to throw a rope around the largest conceptions, while God if He exists at all, appears in those interstices of our lives where the most significant decisions are made. What are dogmas but a residue of the best guesses of warring churchmen face to face with daily life and its failure to do honor to God? In actuality it is the effort to retroactively lighten the cross of Christ that is the greatest dishonor that we can do to God, for God has all things well in hand and can certainly manage affairs despite our lapses.

I would never claim to be Godlike in any way, yet experience has shown me that I am able by some unaccountable power to solve problems where others have failed to reach a solution. My method is a combination of experience seasoned with imagination. One must always be ready to make exceptions. If the same is true of God, then we must trust that God is adaptable to our needs. Have I been quite foolish wandering across continents in search of theological truth? Might I have done as well by sitting as usual at Baker Street in the candlelight, smoking my pipe and watching as the slight drafts of the room carry my thoughts like wisps of smoke along the walls to float lightly about the ceiling before being dissipated?

Ah well, it is done now. I can think of no more pleasant place to review my journal than in Paris. I have taken a room for a month in a neighborhood occupied primarily by artists, a short distance from the Cathedral of Sacre Coeur, the great white dome of which towers over and guards the city below. I have already settled into my new routine. I wake early for morning Mass and then spend a half-hour in the great cathedral in private meditation. The morning light streams into the nave and when I leave the church, to get my breakfast at a café, Paris lies below me sometimes floating in a cloud of mist rising from the Seine. Gradually the veil lifts. The top of the Eiffel Tower emerges into view and the centrality of the great Cathedral of Notre Dame proclaims the abiding power of the Mother of God in the affairs of her children.

These misty mornings cannot last though, for already I feel a hint of spring in the afternoons. The pink and white blossoms of the cherry-trees will soon be in bloom and after them will come the daffodils and tulips rising from the ground. The penitential season of Lent is upon us, but that penitential season is not a sad one for me; rather it is a period of cleansing preparatory to the rest of the year, a time when the shutters of the soul are thrown wide and the dust and resentments of past years are allowed to disperse, like dust beaten from the drapes that clothe the windows of the soul. At such times of personal review I can even think well of my grim brother Sherringford, a man so possessed by what he presumes to be his duty to his station that he is always the Lord of the Manor-house of Sigerside above all else and aware of his stature as a peer of the realm. To say that he is stuffy would be inadequate as a description of his adamantine conventionality. To him even Mycroft is a bohemian. His view of me is that I am quite mad, flitting about solving crimes and mingling with the criminal classes. I have never given up hope of reconciliation with him, but I fear that Sherringford will never see beyond the interests of the British Empire and the Church of England that seems to have reconciled itself with British colonial policies.

Mycroft on the other hand sees the advancement of the British Empire as a choice between evils. He fears the Germans above all else, while for the French he has only contempt. When I told him by wire that I had taken rooms in Montmartre, but would see him after Easter, his wire in return merely said, "How typical of you." He no doubt pictures me wearing a beret and smock, drinking absinthe with Monet, Degas, or Michelet of an evening and discussing the writings of Zola or the Goncourt brothers. There are men to whom art must always whisper quietly, "subversion and decadence."

For me to be an artist is simply to be alive. The artist is above all one who celebrates the miracle of perception. Watson has always spoken of me as the master of deductive reasoning, but he is quite wrong. If anything I am an inductive thinker. I told him that it is my knowledge of past crimes that has allowed me to formulate rules of criminality so that I am easily able to solve most crimes because of their very lack of imagination. The problem of criminality is that the criminal mind is for the most part so predictable. What crime of passion but takes its roots from jealousy or thwarted love? What crime of embezzlement that does not show pre-existing signs of greed and envy in the criminal? To know the seven deadly sins is already to know how to solve most crimes.

The problem of Moriarty is of quite another order. I realized long ago that the key to Moriarty's character is his pride. Moriarty is convinced that his crimes serve a greater purpose. For this reason he is as dedicated to his criminal enterprise as a missionary is to his mission. For years I have detected a pattern in his activities. His victims are without exception taken from the upper classes or at least are people of influence in affairs of state or commerce. It might not be too much to call Moriarty a private revolutionary. His organization is available for hire to any group that wishes to augment chaos in the present social order. He also acts as a clearinghouse for enmities within the upper echelons and will gladly kill one member of that class at the behest of another, for money of course. To Moriarty wealthy people are fungible. He would kill them all at once if he could or at last destroy the social order that sustains them. But by doing so gradually, he has acquired monetary means of his own, and must no doubt by now have become quite a wealthy man. His estate at Kings Pyland, though not massive in acreage, contains a substantial manor house. It will be interesting to see when I return to England if he has taken up the manners of the class he professes to despise.

The existence of wealth and social inequality may not in itself be an evil, for it certainly opens the opportunity to exercise private charity. Many poor persons are guilty of sins against the tenth commandment, for they spend their lives in envy and covetousness of what they may never possess. In their own fashion they lord it over those who are even poorer than themselves.

On the other hand for the members of any class to aspire to some level of comfort and security seems to enrich the heart. The sour spiritual demeanor of the Puritan seems to me to deny the abundance of God who seems to delight in the abundance and even superfluity of His creation. I have always thought for instance that we have never left Eden. The angel's fiery sword exists only to bar us from eternal life until we are ready to assume it. For the rest, we still dwell in the Garden of Paradise.

Who may see cherry trees in bloom or taste their ripe fruit or that of melons on a June morning and not think that he dwells still in Eden if not in Paradise? But I am not really a Biblical Scholar. I am only a consulting detective. I am not even a typical Catholic due to an innate habit of independent thought that is more typical of Protestants and of various so-called Freethinkers. I might be more sympathetic to the Theosophists and Spiritualists if they were less credulous and were more discriminating in the type of evidence that they are willing to accept.

As for the Order of the Golden Dawn, I am sorry to say that most of the members of that arcane group appear to be out and out crackpots. But I can also not count myself as a scientist because I have not the patience to test everything and advance step by step while submitting all of my conclusions to peer review for confirmation. There is something of the gambler in one like me who enjoys speculating as I do and I am too much of a poet to enjoy living full-time in a laboratory. I enjoy the full spectacle of humanity, even in its squalor and sorrow, because it is real and because I feel an abiding sense of compassion for human frailty that is less charity than the simple appreciation of the full symphony of human life.

For these reasons any conclusions that I reach in theology must be considered tentative and inconclusive. I raise more questions than I can supply answers. Even my short time at Cambridge was spent creating my own curriculum. I was always a source of frustration to my professors. I was always engaged primarily in reading books that were unassigned rather than those that were prescribed by the course syllabus. At last my tutors stepped aside and let me be my own teacher. I was motivated by a desire to follow whatever leads would answer the problem of existence. My interest in the detection of crime was undertaken for the same reason that the farmer studies the diseases and pests that infect his crops. My desire has always been to find a manner of life that is worthy of a human being. All about me I detected waste and blight, weevils in the delicate buds of life. Who can say from whence came this early disillusionment with existence? From what natal spring came the discontentment with the world in which I found myself? Perhaps it was my simultaneous perception that life seemed at times exultant and triumphant so that I wished to comprehend and share that very ebullience with a supine world. It was this passion that led me to desire a general solution to all of life's problems. I would feel at times as a youth a great rejoicing racing along my very blood.

I would gaze out at the moors of Yorkshire with wonder when they would seem to explode in green with the dales dotted with apple orchards making a sea of white like a young bride at her wedding, or when I would gaze in wonder at the sea waves rearing their heads like proud horses stampeding towards the land, whenever I could escape to the seacoast. I would feel then as though all of life could not contain my joy. To return though from such moments was to feel the slowly dripping hours and to see all about me the many faces of my countrymen ravaged with care. This experience always awoke in me an echo of that same bitterness that in Professor Moriarty is an abiding sentiment and the motivation for all of his evil impulses.

Can I now show him a better way? My dispatches as the Norwegian Sigerson have been read widely and been already assembled into a book that I have seen in many bookstalls here, already translated into French. Mycroft assures me that he has, as my agent, assembled a tidy sum from their sale that awaits my return. If it is large enough, I intend to purchase a small cottage in Devonshire near to Professor Moriarty to which I may resort in the years ahead. I have no idea how long it may take to sway him from his course or how elaborate his plans may already be. I can only hope that his great enterprise has not grown to such a state of ripeness that it may be put into instant effect upon my return. May I be granted time to dissuade him!

Ah time, this whole question of time haunts me. Like Professor Moriarty I have also been preparing a vast synthesis of all that I believe, but where is the action? It is this feeling of panic that has led me to take my pilgrimage to Asia. I needed to see if my conclusions were applicable on a world-wide scale. Surely God is not provincial. Can God be satisfied with merely a local effort? What is it to God if the local vicar has a school treat for the students and they go about squealing in paper hats and eating cake while children of the same age are walking about India like living skeletons? What good does it do to sing, "God Save the Queen," if her way of life is a scandal of misapplied luxury? Unless justice spans the globe it is not justice!

But how may one man realize this dream of universal justice and peace, particularly when statecraft and the rules of the market seem designed to concentrate wealth into only a few hands. Thus the need, dare I call it such, for a man like Moriarty, one who by dispensing with the normal rules of ethics has declared war on entire classes and nations so as to at least attempt to create justice by force rather than to await the slow process of the conversion of hearts, the program adopted by the One Holy Catholic and Apostolic Church.

The Catholic Church never loses hope. It endures always as a sign of contradiction, not perhaps in its great Cathedrals, but at least in the most humble of its Saints. One need only think of Saint Peter Claver climbing into the stinking holds of the African slave ships, attempting in his small way to give some measure of comfort to the poor frightened black men and women within that oozing sarcophagus, to know the glory of the love of God extended to men and women by God's saints. To them Jesus Christ is always to be found in aiding the single soul.

Our submission to the institutional church as a whole is not to deny that in it are pockets of spiritual poverty as shown by its often superfluous wealth, but because the Catholic Church as a whole has custody of the treasury assembled in heaven through the individual cooperation of souls with the life suggested and led by Divine Grace. For all its ills, the Holy Spirit still courses through the one great Mystical Body of Christ, the Church.

So whereas Professor Moriarty stands alone and believes that it is up to him alone by any means to create a just world, the Catholic knows that he or she is engaged in a communal enterprise of cooperation with Christ in the slow turning of the world to God. It is this no doubt that accounts for the groaning of the Holy Spirit spoken of by Saint Paul. How very long are the labor pains that shall give birth to a new heaven and a new earth!

It is not my function as an individual then to ask more than what with the aid of grace I can perform. I shall no doubt finish my life with the awareness that the husk is thick and the fruit of my life small and bitter. I can hardly claim that I have offered the first lambs of my flock to God. How sad it is that God must usually be satisfied with the remnant spared of our time and efforts after we have first consumed all that was earliest and best. Perhaps God is like a child who always asks for more than it expects to receive at Christmas and usually has to be satisfied with a few sweetmeats and pinwheels. It hardly seems enough for the creator of the universe.

Jesus once cursed the barren fig tree. The usual course though that God seems to pursue appears to be to water the tree for yet another season and hope for a crop at last. Perhaps my life will show only enough of virtues activated to buy a pennyworth of oil to light my lamp and enable me to accompany the Bride to her Bridegroom. May that be adequate to ensure at least the lowest place at the Wedding-Feast of Heaven!

What man does not entertain doubts at times of his eternal salvation? Only a spurious misreading of Holy Scripture that mistakes hope for actuality may pronounce anyone free of this concern that should always animate us. The function of the cardinal virtue of hope is that it is secure, whereas our confidence in our own achievements is not. It is then that we perform virtuous acts, often late in life in a frantic effort to demonstrate to God our change of heart, but our actions would be only of the natural order without Divine Grace, which alone can transmute the lead of our efforts into gold.

No final measuring stick is provided to assess the degree of moral excellence or good works sufficient to gain entrance into heaven. Many are satisfied merely to weakly confess a favorite sin in the last moments of their lives. The testimony that might aid us in making this calculation, as drawn from passages from Holy Scripture leave room for hope, but also sufficient grounds for anxiety. Neither Pelagius nor Augustine seems to have the final word on the matter although the advantage definitely lies with Augustine.

During our lives we never live in a world where all grace is absent, so that we can never try what we might have done by ourselves alone. This seems to finish Pelagius who assumed that unaided man and woman could work their way into heaven. But to rely upon grace alone as did Augustine is to be caught in the web of predestination entertained by the Calvinists and the Jansenists, both condemned as heretical.

The truth appears to be that God is always supplying whatever is lacking in our virtues at our request, for "what Father gives his son a stone when he asks for bread?" We must believe that providence conserves all that is of value within us. The biblical admonitions of Jesus quoted in scripture are meant to awaken us from moral lethargy and not to plunge us into despair, which is always the devils domain. Even in the final moments of our life a good act of contrition may open the treasury of the Universal Church and allow the contrite soul to draw from the vault of the Communion of Saints.

Each day the Holy Mass sends forth to a dry and dying world a witness of the sufficiency of the suffering and death of Christ to assure us that the wellspring of Living Water still flows. Even in our darkness there is a great light and the night of the world will never overcome it.

March 19, 1893
The Feast of Saint Joseph

After Mass today I took a walk in the Luxembourg Gardens. Spring is certainly advancing upon us. Already there are signs of the coming resurgence of life upon the winter landscape. The trees have budded, the air is mild, and women and children are to be seen in the parks. The homily at Mass today dealt with St. Joseph the Worker. St. Joseph has always seemed to me to be the model of sainthood for the common man. We know virtually nothing of him, but his virtues emerge indirectly. Above all is his humility and trust. Humility, because unlike Jesus, who as the very Son of God was born without Original Sin, and Mary the Mother of God, of whom the dogma of the Immaculate Conception testifies was also born free from that primal wound in our nature, St. Joseph was not so favored by God as to be immune from what may be considered the defining character of human nature, both male and female.

We are born in a state of disorientation in which sin appears as a viable choice to which something within us responds. Original Sin is a flaw and not a fault since it exists prior to any conscious choice on our part as individuals. It is, if put in experiential terms, an innate desire to find our way without God and to assume that we are alone in the universe. This alienation and profound loneliness, this desolation may appear to be the withdrawal of God and not what it truly is perceived as the abandonment of God by man and woman. God's apparent absence, the experience that we exist in a moral vacuum, is not because God has withdrawn from us, but rather that we have in our very nature turned away from God and averted our gaze from Him as the center and solace of our being. The human race has chosen its own path by wishing in some way to stand alone in complete self-determination. Original sin from the first experience of its effects is unfulfilling and in some way alien because we cannot be our own source and goal. Pleasure alone is inadequate to complete our search for meaning. It would appear that our primal parents should then have sought an immediate reconciliation with God rather than compounding their error by hiding from Him.

But since we share that same instinct of concealment their

behavior should not surprise us. To assume that the ontological error of Adam and Eve was immediately reparable is to underestimate the true insight of the tale from which we derive the theological concept of Original Sin. This "sin" was less an action than a disposition. It exists less as a historical event (although the Catholic Church still teaches it as such) than as a present assessment of our position before God, even after the redemption wrought by Jesus. Our estrangement from God is an honest reflection of our inability to see the full consequences even of our morally neutral acts, let alone our sins. Anything less would be to underestimate the totality of the rejection of Adam and Eve implied in gaining the experiential knowledge of good and evil.

Since God is an absolute and because to possess total intimacy with God (that relation that hypothetically our primal parents must once have enjoyed) would be immediately shattered by any lesser desire for contingent goals sought apart from God, rather than being simply awarded to us by God, our ontological status is compromised *a priori* as any of us can testify. To desire anything without referring it back to God as its origin and goal is to desire more of it. Sin was alien to our very nature from the beginning. This meant that sin for a formerly sinless creature required an act of "self-creation" to a degree that man and woman after that act were not only different from what they were before, but radically different, so different in fact that the primal spark of the Godlike within Adam and Eve was extinguished by their act, just as God had warned them it would be.

This new ontological order of existence for humanity changed the entire created order as well, so that death embraced not merely us, but the entire cosmos created to house us. I will go so far as to say that the first sin may have occurred prior to time itself and have been the origin of the law of entropy that governs the physical universe, the laws of the visible cosmos in which we now live. We labor in vain to discover Eden's location in time and space, for its existence is so primal that time and space may be considered its result and not the scene of the commission of that natal sin. I realize how bold such a speculation is, but it is not without support in Holy Scripture if read in its most expansive sense. If it is true as St. Paul teaches that all creation is yearning for the revelation of the sons of God, it is because all of creation, which had been intended by God to serve man and woman, just as the angels were created to serve God, now exists in rebellion against us and against itself because it is wounded by our choice. Theologically speaking, the world that we know teeters over the abyss of complete nothingness, or rather the impotent wish for nothingness, which if allowed to be fully manifest in our "victory" over God would become a hell on earth.

It is as though an avalanche were stopped by some unaccountable force half-way down a mountainside with rocks, trees, roots, all suspended and frozen. The peculiarity of Original Sin then is not that it exists, but rather that its action is still incomplete, in suspension as it were, so much so that grace is operative as a call even prior to our response. This means that though we have turned away from God, God has not turned away from us. God's pursuit exceeds our flight. God remains oriented in love towards his creation.

From the beginning God has intended to recreate us and through us to renew all of creation by an action that would so infuse the Divine Life of the Holy Spirit into man and woman that they would no longer be passive participants in nature, but would share in the very life of the Trinity. We would be infused and merged with that essence that is God, not by our own presumptuous choice to face God as God's equal, for there cannot be a facing off towards God without opposition, but as the Trinity relates within its own Being in which the Three Divine Persons achieve a Unity of love beyond our comprehension.

It will be said, of course, that if the Trinity is beyond our comprehension, so must be any discourse about its character as Divine Love. For this reason all of theology is in way only achieved by way of analogy. Our experience of God is filtered through our human condition and only one born not in Original Sin can be admitted to a more perfect experience of God as the Trinitarian Godhead is in Itself. The mystics of course, such as St. Teresa of Avila, have at times been transported for a time beyond their very natures by a wordless and direct communication with God in which all of their faculties were suspended for a time. Even this though could not be tolerated for long without precluding the possibility of any return to human life as we know it. For this reason it has been said that no one may see God and live.

To know the fullness of grace however, as the Blessed Virgin Mary must, is to carry Life in oneself through the indwelling Spirit of God. So great is this force of Life that even death (unless chosen as it was by Christ's human nature in union with the Divine Will) cannot encompass it. This means that the primal sin includes as its defining characteristic a will for death, not into God but away from Him. Death is nothing else but a futile attempt to evade God, made inevitable by Original Sin.

But God has not allowed death to reign supreme. Death was cast aside by Christ through his Resurrection and Mary was spared it altogether, for where there is no sin there is likewise no death. The transfiguration of Jesus on Mount Tabor was simply a revelation of what Life looks like when it is not veiled by the assumption of Jesus of our human nature, though in His case unmarred by Original Sin.

To be resurrected with Christ on the Last Day will be to see finally what restored human nature truly is in all of the glory once intended for it by God. Even the experience of the Apostles at the Transfiguration was only a tiny filtered glimpse into the Divinity of Jesus as it was revealed after the Resurrection on Easter. Such flesh shines with an unaccountable radiance. The apparition of

Our Lady of Guadalupe is another example of how the life within her might change even the material order so as to leave a lasting imprint upon the cloak of Juan Diego, a miraculous event of the 16th century.

To all of this poor Saint Joseph, a mere man, was alien. St. Joseph was and is one of us and beset by original sin, yet he was no stranger to grace. In fact he was placed in the paradoxical position of protecting the two lives which by their own nature as immune from sin and filled with grace in fact protected him! It trivializes St. Joseph by calling him the foster-father of Jesus. Instead his stature should be estimated by the fact that God entrusted everything to him. His position in the Divine Order is supra-historical in that the fate of the entire cosmos existed in his hands and under his ministration to the needs of Mary and Jesus.

To call his labors earthly then is to forget that to labor for a purpose that serves God is to obtain infinite merit and simultaneously that all labor that would tear down the Kingdom of God is not merely vain but evil, however great may appear its effects. Thus the standard by which all labors are judged is the standard that St. Joseph supplies. Does it further the will of God? If Mary is the lens through which the light of God's Grace is focused upon us, then St. Joseph is the model for the proper response of the soul to that grace when it is offered.

St. Joseph has been proclaimed as the patron-saint of the working man. We live in an age of great labors. Yet it is my view that we often build, not merely without grace but even without beauty. As utility absorbs labor and transmutes it to mere profit, even the comfort of labor, for the experience of the joy that beauty provides vanishes, and we are left with merely the embodied and sordid desire for profits. I fear that we are entering a dreary age of world history. Cities like Paris will not be created again, but rather great Towers of Babel speaking the tongue of commerce will be built in various places until that tongue creates so much competition among the nations that adopt it that they will speak only the language of war that divides all tongues and reduces all to the servitude of death. War is always the handmaid of greed. We never know greater unhappiness than when we labor in vain to create the city of man as opposed to The City of God."

March 25, 1893
Paris

An unusual thought came to me today one, so starting and contrary to my own need for certainty that I must set it down quickly before it is overcome by being clothed in pious language or customary expressions. My entire approach thus far in my thinking and in my preparation for my meeting with Professor Moriarty has been based on the need to clarify my own thoughts and faith, but I must never lose track of the distance that exists between our world views. My own is still mediated by faith in an institutional presence of God to the world, whereas his stems from a sense of difference and alienation that is imperceptible from within that institution even when guided by the Holy Spirit.

Divine Grace must always be discerned rather than being presumed as being always present merely because that conviction conforms to our best image when we view ourselves as servants of God. The New Testament in many ways is a real-life example of the failure of those closest to Jesus to understand the extent of the willingness of Jesus to not merely accompany those who were viewed as sinners but to actually identify with them so that they could know that they were not alone. The impatience of Jesus is reserved for those who in His own time were most convinced that they not only understood God but knew precisely what God wanted of them and were most determined to accomplish it. Spiritual certainty it seems to me is in many if not most cases a sign of the worst sort of pride, the one that sees grace as a possession rather than as a gift that must be constantly renewed through prayer and self-examination.

This is more than an intellectual contest between Moriarty and me. Whatever we are doing we are part of a single process mediated by something bigger than ourselves. I think that the main reason that even after two-thousand years that the reign of God on earth seems to be so distant is that the very people who received the message of the Incarnate God in the figure of Jesus Christ still see God in their own image rather than the other way round. Once God becomes an exclusive possession, then God at least God as He appears to us, ceases to be God.

March 28, 1893
Paris

My time on the continent is drawing to a close. I shall leave Paris three days after Easter. I plan to return to England by crossing from Copenhagen to Whitby in a chartered vessel to avoid any possibility of recognition, perhaps in a Danish fishing-boat. I will use the passport issued in the name of Sigerson that I have used throughout my travels. Until matters are settled with Professor Moriarty I dare not announce my return, because there are no doubt men who have profited by my absence, including perhaps men formerly associated with the old Moriarty organization. They will not be pleased to have me back again, alive and well in England and may take immediate steps to address that problem.

I dare take no chances until I may be certain that I have turned Moriarty from his plans. Until then I must take no unnecessary chances that I may meet with a clumsy but effective retribution visited upon me by some obscure cutthroat. I do not know what dangers I shall run and to put Watson through a repetition of the mourning he has already endured on my behalf would be cruel indeed. He must think me dead until I may rest assured that my life, after my return, promises hope of more than a short duration.

From Whitby, I shall go on to Sigerside, the Holmes family estate on the North Yorkshire Moors, to see my brother Sherringford. Since only Mycroft has known that I am alive, my sudden advent will be a shock for my eldest brother. He is not a man to enjoy the dramas of espionage and may be annoyed at me, but he is still my brother after all and it is only proper that I announce myself first to him upon my return. I doubt whether I have been excessively mourned by that stern gentleman, but perhaps he will be sufficiently gladdened by my survival that he will not assume that a mere desire for play-acting has been behind my actions of recent years. Sherringford will, I am sure, keep my arrival a secret. His servants have been long with the family. They would not have lasted long if they were indiscreet. They have long since adapted to my brother's solitary ways and saturnine disposition that will tolerate nothing less than absolute loyalty and obedience.

From Yorkshire I will return to London and meet with my second brother, Mycroft. Only then will I proceed to Devonshire where the Professor awaits me. I have not been in direct contact with him although I have kept in contact with Colonel Moran, who I am sure sends periodic accounts of my movements to the Professor. Colonel Moran knows that I have left Rome and am now in Paris.

I must confess here that I fully expected Colonel Moran to join me as he had planned to do, but he evidently considers it superfluous to keep me under strict surveillance anymore. I do not know if this is a sign that he trusts me or whether he assumes that my movements are now inconsequential. It has occurred to me that with the passing of time both he and the Professor have concluded that I am simply a harmless madman obsessed with his religious delusions and so one who is not to be feared.

The perception that religion is no longer a force to be reckoned with in world history is not a view peculiar to these two gentlemen, for it is shared by most of the governments of the world. The mighty industries of nations are engaged in creating a balance in armaments. There even exists a body of precepts made of treaty and custom the inadequate fabric of which is termed international law. But there is no balance of religions; each is supreme in its vision of the origin and destiny of the world. I suggest that until there is some negotiation that will reach some sort of agreement or consensus regarding religious truth, more wars will be inevitable. Men do not fight for trade advantages alone. The three great motivators of wars have always been trade advantage, national pride, and religious rivalry. Ethnicity is also a factor of course, but these struggles are more often internal struggles within nations or independence movements within empires.

Religion is the most dangerous of motives for conflict for two reasons: First, religious truth often rests on unverifiable foundations and so does not yield to diplomacy or debate. Second, the sanctions of religion usually include damnation for all opposing parties so that any brutality imposed upon opponents must seem minor compared with the ultimate fate that will be visited upon them after death by an offended deity. The victory promised in religious wars then exceeds any earthly advantage to be gained so that compromise is impossible and even when defeat seems imminent the losing faction will fight on to the very death. Therefore religious wars are the most brutal of all.

For this reason it is a capital mistake to assume that religion in the modern world has ceased to occupy the thoughts of men or that Darwinian science, which has assumed an air of religion itself, has caused any retreat in the tides of religious feeling. For these reasons, even my most abstruse speculations are not to be dismissed lightly, for if they are true and if my adherence to the Christian faith is, as I believe it is, the truth and purpose behind all that has been or shall ever be, then I have assembled a force beyond myself with which to confront the Professor upon my return.

I am always surprised by the eagerness with which men pursue a science that reduces the place and dignity of man to merely a curious monkey on an obscure planet. This attitude has always appeared to me like a man sawing away avidly at a limb on which he is sitting. If the mind of man is nothing more than an elaborate jellyfish of cells contained in a few centimeters of cranium and doomed to die in seventy or so years, then we waste our time with thinking and might be better occupied like the Ottoman Sultans of old drinking saffron scented water surrounded by a harem and smoking hashish or opium from a hookah. What one should not be, if there is no God, is a stooped Professor calculating the regularities that may exist in the movements of asteroids and in an equally fatuous God-obsessed detective!

One need only observe children playing though to know that we are born for wonder. Each child is a sage in the making. We are born open to the infinite. Creation was made to cascade into the mind of man, not as scientists alone but through worship to express the joy that it is to possess the chance to be alive and to give thanks to God that we exist at all.

Being is never an end in itself. Being always points to its source, which is God. Yet the God of religion is not usually contemplated as creator, but rather as the source of some human ethical system or series of dictates regarding human actions and destiny. It would seem then that the latter injunctions are subject to some justifiable inquiry. If the dictates of God seem more petty and arbitrary than the wonder of creation, then perhaps something is amiss in some of those teachings. If there is a science of comparative religion, we may take as its first axiom that the God who creates with such diversity, abundance, and generosity is not to be confused with some image of the dour Scottish moral accountant that many Christians believe Him to be, nor with some obscure absolute force with no care for man as the Deists believe.

It has never seemed difficult when contemplating a Crucifix and there to behold the suffering Christ to proclaim Jesus to have been Divine. This is precisely what a God who is love would look like and do for mankind. For God to create at all and to make possible opposition where there was once only harmony is to take the risk that evil would emerge, as it in fact has emerged in both the Angelic orders and in man and woman. To have taken such a risk would entail absorbing all of the costs that flow from that act of creation within God Himself while not contradicting His own nature in doing so. A God who IS LOVE cannot simply wish evil into non-being, for non-being is precisely what evil, metaphysically speaking, already is. God, if He would create anything at all, could do no less than create everything in the Holy Spirit of love, an irrevocable love that would only contradict itself if it readily abandoned what was created with such care and solicitude.

The mystery of evil then, as willed Non-Being by a creature, attempts to be as infinite as the source of Being. It is as though evil is forever driving spikes into a boat that it is attempting to sink while God does the baling. We are all sailing in that frail vessel and all of time is that strange voyage.

It would seem that evil must win in the end, because the sea of non-being, all that might have been but wasn't, would appear more infinite than God who is kneeling in the bottom of the boat and keeping it all floating with such effort can supply. But I refuse to concede such easy supremacy to evil. This homely metaphor however is not strictly true of course metaphysically because the great sea of the possible is irrelevant to a God who could always create new possibilities.

But to speculate in this fashion, however fascinating to the philosopher, is pointless. To imagine alternative scenarios for creation and to imagine what God might have done had evil never appeared is irrelevant to our present situation. We may only deal with what is and what is appears before us daily. That which the Christian sees God doing is to save the world from evil. If that is so then where else would God appear for us, in the sort of world that we know, but upon a cross on the hill of Golgotha?

March 29, 1893
Paris

As I wander about Paris I encounter at times remnants of the Huguenot past in the various reformed churches that now exist in peace with the Catholic Cathedrals. The Edict of Nantes, signed in April of the year 1598, granted various freedoms to the French Calvinists. It was however revoked by King Louis XIV in 1685 by the Edict of Fontainebleau. Freedom of religion was not restored until the Edict of Versailles of King Louis XVI on November 7, 1787. The wars of religion waged over the centuries are a scandal. That they were waged at all is a testimony to the importance placed upon religious belief and its promise of an afterlife with God. Christianity, strictly speaking, does not admit variations of belief through fragmentation into separate churches. The Pentecost event was one of unification and outreach to the world, in other words it was a sending forth, an apostolic event. The separated condition of Christianity today is therefore an historical accident.

The Christian Church cannot be reformed from segmentation or separation or by protesting; it can only be reformed from within as an integral process of gradual growth and enlightenment over time. This process has usually taken the form of the Church Councils and in the interim through the writings of the saints and recognized doctors of the church. A significant question in any act of Biblical interpretation for anyone who actually intends to practice the Christian religion is whether we should consider God the Author of the Bible or the Subject of the Bible.

For the Catholic believer the primary relationship of course is the experience of being a baptized member of the Roman Catholic Church instituted at the Pentecost event in Jerusalem and existing ever since. The seven sacraments and the Holy Mass are where the Catholic encounters God. In contrast, for the various protestant affiliations the point of encounter is with what is called "the word of God" in the Holy Scripture that was recognized, assembled, and accepted by the Roman Catholic Church during the first centuries of Christianity. In its most specific sense the Logos, or the living word of God, is always Jesus Christ in His very person. Holy Scripture in this sense is always a more general reference to "the words of God" as embodied in the Biblical texts.

The Protestant approaches these words directly and with a minimal of sacramental mediation in order to encounter God directly, but only through the text of the Bible. In other words the Protestant is by the very nature of his or her belief engaged in an interpretive process that in that degree is one step removed from the common assemblage of the faithful with whom he or she shares his individual beliefs.

Catholicism approaches the matter of faith differently. The Catholic does not reduce the point of encounter with God to the text of the Bible, but rather sees "the words of God" as a privileged avenue of approach to the God that can never be reduced to a mere text but is instead embodied and enfleshed in the actual living community of the Catholic Church as nourished by the Body and Blood of Jesus Christ in the Holy Eucharistic celebration of the Mass.

For this reason the Catholic approach to scripture is different than that of the Protestant. For the Catholic who lives within the Mystical Body of Christ in the One Holy Catholic and Apostolic Church, God is the subject of the Bible; whereas, for the Protestant, in their various assemblages, God is the Author of the Bible and as such does not require a church to communicate to the believer who instead enacts an individual covenant with God and is thereby deemed to "be saved."

In short for the Catholic the salvation event is a lifelong process of dwelling within and in relationship to other people within the Body of the Catholic Church; whereas, for the Protestant it is an individualized compact entered into with God directly and without any intermediation and achieved through mere intellectual assent to the words of God. The only residual essential sacramental element remaining is Baptism to formalize that agreement.

To further preserve and to formalize the individual nature of the salvation event for the Protestant, the assemblage of believers for worship is not to celebrate the Holy Mass, but instead is a worship service led by a minister who preaches as opposed to a priest who acts as a celebrant acting *in personem Christi* at the Holy Sacrifice of the Mass.

April 1, 1893
Paris

Continuing with my reflections from yesterday I would like to set down the startling fact that an eternal God should even choose to notice human beings at all, let alone to stoop to relying on a written text as His primary mode of communication with His people. Once any direct nexus is drawn between God and the significance of human life it becomes clear that our human dilemmas will be projected out upon a seemingly insentient universe in the hope that God cares for us.

There is a tension in Catholic theology between respect for

what is called natural law and the awareness in faith that God is able to suspend those laws of nature that govern us at will when they serve a divine purpose. It is at this point that what human reason might expect parts from theology as such. It must also be recalled that all later Christian theology is precariously balanced at its base on the sacred texts that were compiled by the church of its time as acceptable reflections of the lived faith of the early Christian communities. The Bible was not delivered already printed and bound, but was compiled and authorized by the early church. This places later generations in a difficult position as they must adopt these texts as authoritative guides even while addressing other cultures and when reconciling scripture to later scientific discoveries. What might be called the synapse that appears in different methodologies for arriving at truth come into play, particularly as we are about to enter a new era of critical inquiry.

The resulting conflict has led to the wager that is represented *in personem* between Professor Moriarty and me. The search for any all encompassing point or discipline from which every other event or inquiry may proceed puzzles and frustrates any area of human knowledge and imports a degree of relativity where the Catholic Church has hitherto felt no need to be concerned. When any institution, even one with a divine commission, becomes certain that it contains all truth within its formulations a crisis is sure to be at hand when new data seems to reveal prior conclusions to have been premature or in some way misstated.

St Paul once stated that he would be glad to die on the spot to be with Christ. What has been called Holy Indifference embraces God's will in all things. The spirit of readiness for martyrdom and to view this life as comparatively insignificant put a certain premium upon an early death. As technology and commerce have made human life more bearable and as opportunities of human development have expanded this readiness to embrace death has been followed by a more radical desire to stay alive, while never forgetting our ultimate end. Prospects and circumstances must be considered if we are to achieve a balance between life and death while recalling the words of Jesus that He came so that his followers could have life and have it more abundantly.

There has always been a sense in which God respects those who wrestle with an angel and simultaneously honors those who bow down and accept the dictates of fate. The Greeks sought solace in tragedy while the ancient Hebrews sought some point of view from which God could remain justified even when the world He created and its iron-clad laws of causality and chance seemed to appoint that the most bitter costs should be borne by the most innocent among us.

Jesus affirmed that no servant is greater than his master. The solace of the Christian when contemplating the misfortunes encountered in the life of Christ is to recall these words and to press on to remedy what is remediable while looking forward to the general resurrection on the last day. The Apostle's Creed ends with these words:

I believe in the Holy Catholic Church, the Communion of Saints, the forgiveness of sins, the resurrection of the body, and life everlasting.

Amen.

Dr. Watson's Narrative Continues

olmes folded the paper on the morning that carried the news to us that America had declared war on Spain and laid it upon the breakfast linen before him. The entire household was startled at the news and even the placid community of Newport lay now under the grim knowledge that war would mar the coming summer season. Holmes beckoned me out upon the lawn at Lands End.

"We have arrived too late Watson. I did not expect America to take this fateful decision so precipitately. Events must now take their course. Our reports had been that President McKinley opposed the war-fever that was spreading through the country. The journalists who have been beating the war-drums will have much for which to answer. These passions that arise among the masses must be constrained by wise policy or all is lost. I fear that a trap has been laid by the march of events and that what may appear obvious to us, and should have caused all parties to this affair to stop and to consider before proceeding, has now condemned many innocent people to suffer. It is always the people who must bear the costs of war and though they clamor for it, they soon realize that no one ever really wins a war, for the payments are often deferred to a later day."

"What shall we do then Holmes? Should we proceed directly to Washington?" I asked in dismay.

Holmes considered before replying, "No, Watson, we had best adhere to our former plan. We can hardly proceed to raise the question of the canal when the nation is engaged in a war. It is better that we take advantage of our present position to meet the men who may influence the course that the war will take. The President will be much occupied in the months ahead."

"Our task now is one of preparation. We must prepare our brief, as the barristers do, so that when we may present our case it will secure the ends that we have in view. We are spared, thank God, the conflict of conscience that has caused me many misgivings. Since war has broken out, our task is to guide its enthusiasm towards the defeat of the plans that the Baron entertains of controlling the great passage to the east through one of the nations of Central America. We must for the present bide our time and make the necessary contacts that may aid our cause."

After a few moments of silence Holmes shrugged his shoulders in resignation, "Besides, we have the advantage of pleasant surroundings here and yes, my very dear fellow, these will do me no harm. Food and good company may aid me in my own convalescence that has been interrupted by our involvement in this unfortunate Maupertuis business."

As the days passed further news was sparse. There was no sign at first that the nation had gone to war. The first declaration was followed, as is so often the case, by a period of respite, as though the nation looked backwards at the quiet routines of life now made more precious because the effort of the nation was now turned towards the destruction of war. As to our own mode of time, I found myself adapting immediately to the rhythm of the sea and to the surprisingly informal manner of life that existed in Newport. The cliff walk was thronged each day by the denizens of the community and even people from town would come to mingle in the one common area that was open to all, the path that led along the sea. It was as if the sea was able to preserve a measure of democracy even in that most exclusive of American retreats.

The ocean is by its very nature democratic, for at sea all people feel the limitations of human ownership and of dominion. The extent of the great waters diminishes all pretentions and its power makes even the largest ships aware of the forces upon earth that show no care for man. To be a neighbor to the sea is to court the assaults of storm and wave. It is to reside face to face with infinity. To gaze at the beach is to know it to be composed of innumerable grains of sand, each a world unto itself.

Beyond the sand was a wall of granite. I have always been taken with the composition of rocks. What sample of granite that does not demonstrate the crystalline history of its origins? What specimen of lava that does not bear witness to its volcanic birth? The earth is at once old and young depending upon one's perspective. It is old when one thinks of the great ages during which ice swept over the land, scouring moraine and cliff face and leaving great fields of debris. It is old if one thinks of the great deposits of coal, the compacted living matter of ancient plants, or of petroleum made of the organic ooze of vanished swamplands.

But it is young if one reflects that the entire earth is encased in only a thin film to hide its nether regions of fire and of ash, that great earthquakes move entire continents that still flow about each other suffering occasional titanic renderings and collisions. These cause mountain ranges to rear upwards into the sky such as the Himalayas, while the edges of continents are dragged slowly beneath the sea by the movement of tectonic plates.

Time may not even be reckoned for such grand powers, but if at all only in eons. The generations of human life become no more than an hour on the slow clock of the cosmos, so how much less can be reckoned the span of a single human life. We occupy only a second in geologic time. Even the great sphinx is of recent origin. Behind its crouching loins lie vast expanses of silent witness. Our most venerable ancestors possessed a voice for only a short time.

What preceded the Vedas? What antedated the scribes of Mesopotamia? From what source came the earliest civilizations? Did whole communities waken to consciousness all at once? Who was the first to inscribe figures upon clay to record speech? Does literature owe its beginnings to some merchant who merely sought to tally the number of an exchange of skins? When did reflection begin? Did man first gain self-awareness and only after this dream of gods? Or did man once live in daily intercourse with the deity in a communion appropriate to man's and woman's innocence as Genesis records or composes? Did God teach man to speak or was speech born with the need to be like God knowing good and evil? Without speech could God have warned of the dangers of eating from the tree that stood in the center of the garden? Is writing only congealed speech?

What is the Bible but a long discourse? Are the words written by God and are the sacred writers reduced to mere scribes taking dictation? Or is the Bible written out of the intuition of the human heart's effort to imagine what would be appropriate to God and if so are those very ideas implanted as it were within the human soul by God himself lest his intentions towards mankind be otherwise misconstrued? How do event and word work together to envelop history in God's providential care?

To enter upon consideration of questions such as these is to find oneself ensnared in the unanswerable. Sooner or later one must take the great risk of proceeding without certitude because we stand upon the deck of a burning ship. Already the timbers are cracking beneath us and the smoke chokes our view. Our crewmates are falling one by one around us into the unknown. When will our own turn come? Such were the thoughts that thronged my mind since I had begun to read the journal of his quest kept by my friend, Sherlock Holmes.

As I walked the sea path each day and gazed out across the great Atlantic Ocean towards my own humble home in England my mind would seem to traverse the waters and I would see my own quiet bay with my garden slumbering in the sun and the French Windows in my sitting room open to admit the morning air. I found myself longing more than I can say for the restoration of the quiet comfort that allowed me to live like the anemones and mussels along the shore and on the wharfs and piers, with the same insensate peace of slumber and inevitability as they enjoyed, while the waves crashed in and the tides pursued their diurnal course.

But the game was afoot and my companion had led me to return to the land that I had only visited twice before. Once to erect a marker over the grave of my poor brother and once to seek oblivion in medical service in Louisiana after the death of my dear wife Mary. I would return from these long walks to the Wharton estate called Lands End for a late lunch or an afternoon tea and to discuss any developments in the case with Sherlock Holmes.

Holmes was also enjoying the quiet that prevailed at Lands End and the company of Mrs. Wharton and of Irene Adler. Inspector Hopkins acted as our messenger, going often to the telegraph office in town so as to keep us in touch with events in Europe. I in turn was left much on my own to pursue solitary walks by the sea and to continue my reading of Holmes' journal uninterrupted.

Many questions still remained as to the nature of his final parting with Miss Adler in Rome, of his occupations in the year 1893, and his eventual meeting with Professor Moriarty. I did not meet Holmes again until Christmas of 1893, although in my later account I transposed this meeting until we were brought together once again by the case of Ronald Adair and by what I had always supposed to have been an attempt upon Holmes' life by the redoubtable Colonel Sebastian Moran.

I turned to the journal to fill in the missing time that still remained without an explanation in my knowledge of the life and career of my friend Sherlock Holmes. The struggle with Professor Moriarty that ensued I was soon to learn had only reached its conclusion in 1897, the date where my own final narrative begins. The battle with Professor Moriarty was not to be decided it appeared by a single joust. I hardly supposed that the complexity of the Professor's mind and motivations could be sounded by a single throw of the weighted line into the abyss of his darkened heart and brilliant brain. After all, some demons are only exorcised by prayer and a long period of fasting.

It will readily be seen how demanding and enthralling the text of Holmes' journal had become to a mere surgeon and a setter of bones and a dresser of wounds like me. It was tempting at times to think that he had gone quite mad in trying to solve the mystery of the cosmos. Had his years of the abuse of cocaine so addled his brain that he like Don Quixote de la Mancha in the great tale by Cervantes imagined that he could right all wrongs and explain all things, at least during the period during which his journal had been written?

Yet I could not but feel that by a unique effort Sherlock Holmes had managed to weave an intricate thread into a pattern of truth and to connect, much as he had always done in solving his many cases, the many clues of Sacred Scripture into a pattern that while respecting dogma in the Roman Catholic Church had through certain extended metaphors made it more sensible to our experience of life and of what a God of Love would truly be like.

Meanwhile, in between my efforts to grasp Holmes theological reflections, I was also able to take restorative walks with the man himself by the sea that summer in Newport. Holmes had often spoken of the inevitability that we must take the world as we find it and make as much sense of it as we can in the light of our faith even if a perfect synthesis eluded us. Similarly our mission to America had been altered by events as we found them taking place all about us. I had settled into a routine that I had hoped would be continued well into the summer season, a routine similar to the one that I had pursued at home in Cornwall, a routine that might view the larger events of history as irrelevant to my daily life.

But as so often occurs in the case of events of great moment, the forces that seem to govern history had proceeded with such speed that the time for leisurely debate and consideration of alternate courses had vanished. America had turned from isolation to war with a speed that would have seemed incredible only a few months previously. It became clear to all parties that Spain did not intend to surrender its last bastion of empire status without a fight: the Cuban revolution must be put down.

Nations are controlled by the same fear of humiliation that so often leads individual men into folly. The relations between the nations had seemed increasingly to assume a frantic need to retain colonial possessions if their economies were to survive in an era of mass production. The surpluses produced by the newer industrial processes demanded ever new markets and a ready source of often scarce raw materials. Colonies supplied both of these needs. In addition there was the crucial fact to be considered that America was no longer merely an Atlantic power facing the lands from whence vast emigration had fed its remarkable growth as a nation. America was now also a Pacific power facing competition from Japan for hegemony in the Far East, particularly with China. American policy needed to keep the trade with Chinese ports open. This was becoming difficult. England had already begun the process of establishing hegemony over certain key ports there and excluding other nations. It was an open question how long this process would be allowed to continue short of war. History has cruel sanctions in store for nations that fall behind in the pursuit of power. Therefore, the action of one state in pursuit of empire demands that other nations take a similar course or band together to resist hegemony.

Spain, which had once been the dominant trading power in Europe in its union with Austria under Hapsburg rule, had been so diminished after the defeat of the Spanish Armada and later by the various independence movements in Mexico and South America that it had little left beyond the Philippine Islands and its Caribbean colonies to sustain its membership in the society of the great nations of the day. Austria also was beginning to decay. Independence movements were growing in the Balkans. Even Britain knew unrest as close as Ireland. The Irish had never given up their desire for separate nationhood or at least for Home Rule. This continued wound in the side of England had cost the English dearly and the struggle divided British opinion at home at the time. Belgium had long ago separated from France. Only the tiny size of the Netherlands had protected them from similar dissension. The assumption that any nation is a given is fallacious. Nations it would appear are either in the process of growing or they have already entered a period of dissolution through various secession movements. The remarkable growth in size of the United States of America had not gone unnoticed in England. Of the three great external wars that this comparatively new nation had already fought during the time about which I am writing, two had been with England and one with Mexico. I am not including of course the war that the Northern States fought to prevent the secession of the Southern States whose inhabitants began to realize that they were a *de facto* colony of the industrialized North. Nor am I including the wars of conquest waged against the Indian nations.

The English preferred a more subtle policy than overt conquest to introduce colonial rule over aboriginal peoples. Our policy in India had been to allow a certain degree of latitude in the culture, religion, and the internal workings of local government to proceed, as long as trade relations remained securely in British hands. The American concept of conquest on the contrary was one of absolute domination and assimilation of its native peoples. Since the defeat of the last effective Indian resistance at Wounded Knee, Indian children had been removed from their parents and entrusted to various Missionary Schools where they died like flies from measles, scarlet fever, and tuberculosis.

Even when it came to the working poor of Europe, American policy was to quickly subject them to industrial discipline in textile factories and steel mills. Labor organizing among the immigrant working class was forbidden by the courts as a conspiracy in restraint of trade and freedom of contract. After a short period expended in the effort to help the black race through federal enforcement of the 13th and 14th Amendments to the American Constitution, the South was allowed to manage its own affairs, thus showing that the war to free the slaves was more about the threat of disunion to a growing empire and not a holy crusade in recognition of the dignity of all races as is commonly supposed.

The war of the 1860's was immediately followed by two decades of invasion of the Indian lands in violation of the Fort Laramie Treaty and the virtual extermination of the native people in the wars of the 1870's and 1880's. Neither Holmes nor I assumed that in dealing with the Americans in 1898 that we would be dealing with a benevolent power that had forsworn the acquisition of colonial possessions out of a faith in the principles set forth in its Declaration of Independence. If America had yet to acquire colonies it was merely because it had been so occupied by the subjection of its own citizens in defiance of the rights of the formerly sovereign states once secured by the 9th and 10th Amendments to its Constitution and by its wars of conquest against Mexico and the Native American tribes that it had yet to look beyond its own shores, although the Monroe Doctrine had already set the western continent apart as an exclusive zone of interest.

Every nation prefers to maintain a mythos of its own virtue and benevolence in defiance of the actual facts of its history. It may take centuries before the Americans will see that the best historical parallel of their remarkable growth was the conquests of the Mongol hoards under Genghis Khan. That the cruelties perpetrated in America were done under the aegis of Christian missionary efforts merely shows that the Christian religion has often acted as the servant of conquest much as digestive enzymes destroy meat in the stomach by breaking down the integrity of what is to be assimilated. The formula of conquest is always to undermine the leadership of the people to be assimilated, to attack their language, culture and religion, and only then to kill the remnant that resists the complete subjugation of people that was intended from the first moment of contact. The tribes of the island of Hispaniola were extinct through disease and forced labor within a century of the landing of Columbus on that doomed island.

I record these thoughts and convictions here because it might otherwise be supposed that our mission to America was in violation of our plain duties as Englishmen to further the interests of England. If China was to be the prize for which all the imperial powers were contending, then it could only damage British interests if America gained ready access to the east through the building of a canal through Panama. Yet, the building of a canal was the original point of our mission was it not? If Baron Maupertuis were to succeed in his efforts, then his own wealth and influence would grow and he had already shown that he would stop at nothing to secure a Dutch hegemony in the Pacific. Holland controlled the Straits of Malacca already and the entirety of the Indonesian Archipelago. Its favored position meant that it could strike at British interests in China and Burma as well as India.

ycroft had even expressed his fear of Dutch expansion in the region. I will quote here from a letter sent to us in Newport from Mycroft. It was brought to us by special courier from the British Embassy in Washington. It read as follows:

"Dear Sherlock,

The Prime Minister has instructed me to communicate to you Her Majesty's confidence that you will choose the proper course in the mission on which you are currently engaged. While you remain as always a private agent, your actions as my brother must implicate me as well since it is presumed that I have some influence over you. This is the background of understanding against which we both must act in the present instance.

I must say that it is the heaviest responsibility ever placed upon me because I know that some of our views differ. Your faith in the Roman Catholic Church imposes certain obligations upon you, which if I may say so have caused some uneasiness in the highest quarters of our government. Though you are in some ways a national treasure as well as a source of pride to all Englishmen, you are also occasionally, what is commonly referred to as, a loose cannon. You are allowed, as I am not, among other luxuries the privilege of a private conscience.

I am not so favored. My present loyalty remains to the Queen who is the supreme head of the Church in England. This is to say that for me what serves England serves God. It is for this very reason that I urge you to use every measure to defeat the plans of Baron Maupertuis. You have a free hand to strengthen the Americans if it will defeat the Dutch interest in building a canal.

You should know that all nations are in a manner of speaking fictions. In the end there are only men of power who use nations as they use human lives, to acquire wealth and influence. The reason for colonial expansion is simple. With the advent of industrial armaments a general European war would destroy the ruling nations of Europe. It is therefore essential that any impending conflict between the European nations should be kept upon the periphery and that a general balance of power shall be maintained in Europe.

Baron Maupertuis no doubt takes the position that even his own nation's people are expendable. He may even switch his loyalty to Germany. What matters is his personal power abroad. Every nation reaches a point where the fiction of unity at home breaks down before the reality of domestic inequality as plutocrats gain control of the mechanisms of government as they inevitably do. Patriotism exists in order to keep the masses pacified and to provide a source for military conscription in the case of war. No war is ever fought that does not in some way benefit the rich and the powerful. The advent of the modern legal fiction of the corporation allows wealth to transcend time and space. Time because a corporation may potentially live forever and space because ownership may transcend national boundaries.

The reason that Baron Maupertuis is such a threat is because he is a man of the future. We have reason to believe that he will, when the time is right, take his ownership interests with him anywhere in the world. His destiny is not tied to Holland or to any other nation. He is one of those weevils or parasites that bore through the living tissue of nations. He leaves nothing behind but a dying nation. The recent Panic of 1893 from which the nations are only now emerging has shown how delicate is the fabric of international trade that enables the economies of the world to survive. If a deeper or more prolonged depression should take place, then the economic structures that support modern civilization could fail. The medieval world of local economies and commons is no more. Our world depends upon the hierarchies of law and of the commercial order. Men like Baron Maupertuis know that we cannot dispense with them. Their interests have been made the equivalent of the common welfare. This is the source of their power over nations. When the old monarchies shook off the power of Rome, they assumed that the nation-state was the irreplaceable and the natural residue of sovereignty. Alas, they were mistaken.

You will receive this letter in America, a country that began by believing that the people in the separate states and as individuals were sovereign. I expect that you will soon see that this is no longer true. No dissipated French Aristocracy ever had the wealth or power of the new American ruling class. To them the rest of the nation's people are only so many cattle for their pastures. Baron Maupertuis has no doubt realized, as do I, that nations are expendable. None dare call it slavery for the slaves are well kept, for now...

I appeal to you Sherlock to recall that you are an Englishman and that our Queen represents the last living link for us to the belief that sovereignty comes from God. Victoria is an anointed queen. You may look to the Papacy, but the Vatican is no longer a world power. The Papal States are no more. The power of the Pope lies only in the conscience of those who have retained the ancient faith. I am a realist Sherlock and I have cast my lot with my Monarch, not because I spurn the Pope, but because I realize, as did the leaders of the civilized world after the Thirty Years War, the fact that Princes alone can govern. The Peace of Westphalia in 1648 established the principle that the clergy cannot effectively rule over people therefore faith was thereafter to follow that of the King or Prince as sovereign. If the Prince was Catholic, then so were the citizens. If he was Protestant, then so would all be within the national borders. That order has lasted until the present day and nations have ruled and *for the most part kept a general peace.*

The idea of popular sovereignty has changed all of that. The American Civil War made this clear to anyone who was actually observing what was at stake; the American commercial interests are America. Government serves capital. No right may long endure if it opposes the capital interests. Baron Maupertuis was watching this change as was Professor Moriarty who may have been the agent who first pointed out this unique crossroads of history and its significance to the Baron. This degree of individual control that crosses national borders has not been seen since Lutheranism spread across Germany.

As I have said, I am above all else a practical man and I know that the world is in danger of a war or series of wars that may span the next century until power vested in capital, liberated from sovereignty, is brought under control in a new version of the Peace of Westphalia. If I am willing to strengthen America now, it is not because I value American hegemony more than that of the Dutch or the Germans. I only know that the tide is setting away from England and towards America and that our government must make friends with its former American colonies. Besides, the Baron has shown that he is the more immediate threat as you well know after that business with the plague that was intended to ravage our shores, which he tried to import to wreak havoc among us.

I have spoken freely my deepest thoughts because I know that for all of your hesitations about the spread of our own Empire, you know that if we were defeated a new dark age would descend upon Europe. The crowned heads of Europe still retain some distant relation to God. If the Pax Romana had survived it might have been that all would be subject to the Pope acting as the Vicar of Christ, but (and I do not intend to be blasphemous in saying this) Christ waited too long before returning. All that remains then is for men such as me who have blundered into power to use it so as to prevent the general slaughter of a European war.

My trust is that Our Lord will recall his words that blessed are the peacemakers for they shall be called the children of God and reserve some place for me in heaven. Pray for me Sherlock as I do for you.

Your Devoted Brother,
Mycroft

After reading this remarkable letter I could not help reflecting that the fates of entire populations are determined by rivalries that exist between what are after all mere abstractions, creations of the human mind. What are nations, corporations, laws, treaties, but devices conceived by men to control and to guide the exercise of power? What for that matter is power itself but its exercise through these very abstractions?

Yet fortunes are made and lost, people are killed in wars, and material goods are directed to destinations by these abstractions. The entire social and international fabric is stretched to fulfill some human ambitions while denying to others even the food necessary for survival. It is like water being carried in a heavy tub sloshing from side to side with much spilled to no purpose. How much equity is there in these chaotic movements? To find a means of exercising moral choice in such a world the scale must be reduced. For this reason power, whether financial or political, must be abjured. Organizations that pretend to transcend the human become inhuman.

The Catholic Church seeks to avoid this fate by the mutual bond of charity and the unity of the Holy Spirit that dwells in our hearts. The message of the saints is that no two saints are alike. Each soul attains sanctity by doing well what lies close at hand. St. Teresa of Avila was an obscure nun in a cloistered Carmelite convent, while St. Francis Xavier evangelized India, yet both are saints. The hunger to create a system that can contain human greed and aggression has never been created, whereas saints appear under all social conditions. The love of the Holy Spirit is infinitely adaptable. There is always a way to be useful and holy. Even martyrdom does not defeat but rather ennobles and proclaims the faith and love that embraces it in faith and humility.

For this reason, the Holy Catholic Church remains, while empires have fallen. Souls find their way to God through all opposition. The Catholic Church has nothing to fear from defeat. If Jesus fell three times on the way to His crucifixion, shall the Church not fall occasionally to its knees? It is this character of the Catholic Church that allows it to transcend history and to recover from all temporary ills, for it follows its Lord.

Holmes folded Mycroft's letter after I had read it and placed it in a secure place. We were sitting at the time gazing across the ocean and the evening sun was setting behind the trees. The light streamed out across the waters but on the distant horizon clouds were massing for a late spring storm.

"The clouds are darkening over Europe Watson," remarked Holmes.

"Oh, I doubt that the clouds we see stretch so far," I answered without thinking.

Holmes smiled. "Good old Watson, if only the world could share your literal mind. I fear that even nations are subject to strange fancies and dreams. I have seen Mecca's minarets shining in the sun and the sphinx of Egypt that still keeps its own counsel, and now I am here in this playground by the sea where the rich disport themselves by emulating the aristocracy of France. The clouds that you see do reach to Europe though and even beyond. They are the clouds of human vanity and ambition. They surround the Czar in his Winter Palace. They hover over Whitehall. They embrace the Kaiser in Berlin. They have even come to this land, still illumined by the dying sun that shines upon those who once fled to these shores to escape the wars of Europe."

Holmes was silent for awhile and I waited for him to continue. At last he said, "I fear that America has lost its innocence. How bright were those initial prospects that peopled this land with Pilgrims and with those who aspired to land, to quiet farms, and the peaceful life once promised by democracy! What have they now of that early dream? Only a series of demands for sacrifices that will bear only the most transient connection to their actual welfare, and they will make those sacrifices for they will believe, as the people always do, that their leaders are great men, that they would not ask for these sacrifices if it were not necessary. The age of empire may have left the pyramids behind, but at what cost is the pursuit of empire, wherever it rears its ugly head? The price is always death."

Holmes shook his head. We had received our marching orders from home. Our mission was clear and if we were to act as loyal Englishmen then war now between America and Spain was our duty to promote. The Murillo Papers could not be published as we had planned if they would cause embarrassment to the American war effort by casting doubt upon American expansionism by economic means such as building railroads and canals. America must instead appear to be a self-less liberator of foreign people yearning to breathe free and escape domination. We both lapsed into silence and gazed eastward at the darkening waters until the land behind us was also shrouded in night.

From the Journal of Sherlock Holmes

April 2, 1893
Easter

Easter has come to Paris! The bells of its many Churches filled the spring air and I have been reminded that if the grain of wheat falls to the ground and dies it is only so that life may be more abundant. The Church does not rejoice in suffering and death but only in Christ, who by assuming all aspects of the human condition, has bestowed upon even the many evils that we experience, the sign that God is with us.

To comprehend life is to know that it has seasons. The philosopher Leibnitz hoped to explain the problem of suffering by diminishing it. To say that this world that we know is the best of all possible worlds implies that other worlds are conceivable and that God simply chose among a variety of possibilities. This is error falls into the same trap as that of Calvinism. Both make God the victim of his own nature. Calvin concludes that God's omnipotence is such that grace must be irresistible with no allowance made for the freedom of man and woman. Calvin's theology has the effect of making creation and salvation merely the turning of an intricate mechanism for grinding the human race like grain to make flour for a soufflé. From this point of view God ordains human suffering and tolerates evil merely to have the opportunity of manifesting His glory by overcoming it. The image conjured up is similar to a royal play acted out before a captive audience of angels. From the point of view of this faulty theology the sacrifice of Jesus on the cross is a demonstration of callous disregard about the fate of God's Son whereby the Father merely intends to demonstrate the full depth of his anger at sinners.

The effect of all of this is to split the Trinity by assigning power and majesty to the Father and the role of servant to the Son who dares not oppose the sovereign will of a distant and unfeeling parent. This implies a radical difference in status within the Trinity and reduces the Third Person of the Trinity to a mere emanation of the other two with no say in the matter.

The Catholic view refuses to accept a theology that reduces God to an Ogre worthy of Norse mythology. Redemption is the fruit of the common will of the Father and the Son in intimate union. The Gospel message assures us that God so loved the world that He gave his only begotten Son to save a world that was lost. The Holy Spirit emerges as more than a mere life-force and assumes a personal nature equal to the others. The Holy Spirit, that we are told wishes to dwell within us as in a temple, forms a union with humanity that in a sense elevates us into this same Trinity by participation in the love of God.

Although not as noxious as Calvin, Leibnitz makes the same error when he diminishes the force of evil by assuming that the order that we observe in the universe is the best arrangement possible and directed in its every element by the direct will of God. This implies that God actively wills evil. This view requires the same emotional distance towards the human condition shown by Calvin. There is no possible world but the one which we know because God is absolute and as such cannot weigh alternatives; for God to conceive a thought is already to execute it and that execution is not the best of possibilities but the only possibility! In other words Adam and Eve had to sin and Jesus had to die and part of the human race simply must refuse salvation in order for God to be God. From this viewpoint heaven and hell, good and evil, are just opposite sides of the same coin. The roulette wheel spins, but the ball always lands on the number assigned to each of us before the wheel was even spun. The correct view is that of the Catholic Church, which does not seek to imagine a world where sin would have been impossible and then to justify the world that we actually inhabit by positing carefully predetermined Monads all working towards a good but incomprehensible end that resolves all contraries as if by magic.

Instead the Catholic Church follows Christ in seeking unity and solidarity with those who suffer the effects of sin through exercising charity towards them. The faith of the Catholic Church is that to follow Christ is to address the existence of evil in the most efficacious way. To imagine another order is impossible; we must deal with the world as it presents itself to us. This still allows room for the miraculous, which is known precisely because it is exceptional. Jesus enters human fate and shows us a way through it without relying on any excuses to make what we experience as evil to be somehow a mere illusion, because God wants it like this so it really can't be that bad after all. Easter joy is not attained by denying that Jesus died. We as Christians rejoice because though Jesus suffered and died, yet he lives!

April 7, 1893
Paris

Any speculation or determination regarding "the place" that God occupies in the visible realm of our ordinary observations will always be problematic because it is impossible to imagine God as God dwelling within His creation as merely one other object among many.

Similarly the idea of heaven as a "Kingdom" is also only

true metaphorically or analogically, because God is clearly above being confined to a particular human concept of government. For instance we cannot imagine God having a Prime Minister or a Secretary of State. This fact has not inhibited religious structures and institutions from using metaphorical language however while forgetting that these descriptions and appellations cannot be directly predicated of God, but only to our ideas about God.

A most obvious example of this forgetfulness has even managed to get into the creed when we speak of the Holy Trinity. To speak of God the Father and God the Son as being consubstantial is to adopt a metaphysical term in order to distinguish God from all created things and to maintain a basic sense of equality in essence within the Trinity, even though the three "persons" of the Holy Trinity serve different functions within the Biblical account of their interactions with human beings throughout history.

Even that history is presented to us within a Hebraic cultural context. How then is it possible then to ever speak about or conceive of God and if that is not possible, except by means of analogy, then how are we to ever comprehend God?

The answer it seems to me is that for us God is known by the actions attributed to Him rather than by any description of what God is. For instance the usual use of the term "substance" is to describe that which stands under and grounds a particular state of being. A substance in other words provides a metaphysical basis to distinguish one substance from other substances. Substance is the base from which all other attributes must proceed. Without possessing a substantial identity in its substance, various and secondary attributes, characteristics, and properties would have nothing in which to adhere.

So to speak of the three "Divine Persons of the Holy Trinity" as One God and as being of the same substance actually is operational in nature, because it allows us to distinguish God from all things that are not God. It also serves the operational function of preserving equality and integration within the Holy Trinity and prevents Christianity from falling into polytheism as has the Hindu religion.

All of this implies that theology has less to do with what God is than it has to do with what God has done and is doing. The Bible when seen from this perspective becomes a history with the added dimension of the miraculous that is thereafter attributed to a posited entity called Yahweh in order to explain what would otherwise be a mere intuition: that certain significant events in Jewish history carry something within themselves that suggest an underlying moral purpose to the universe. It is that moral purpose that makes human actions significant and meaningful. If that meaning was taken away all that would remain would be movements in time and space, immune from description or validation in any human sense. Our lives as we know and live them would fade into insignificance. This is why Nietzsche's madman (who appears in the book translated as *The Joyful Wisdom*) realized that to deny the existence of God is to erase simultaneously our own existence. We believe in God in order to provide a substrate for our own lives.

The one thing that we do know about God from the gospel is that Jesus said that those who love and dwell in love will by doing so place themselves in the position to receive God and that God, in all God's fullness, will come to him and make a dwelling place within him. This promise is what Jesus undoubtedly meant when He said to his disciples that "the Kingdom of God is within you." We do not find God in a place; we find God in a person.

April 10, 1893
Paris

A further question arises, if the miraculous is possible at all, then why is it not made the universal order? Why does not healing of all ills become the standard for human life? Of course if that was true, then God's occasional interventions would no longer be recognized as miraculous and the testimony of miracles would be lost. So I prefer a position that asks this instead: why is the world we know not even more troublesome and at variance to our desires than it already is? It would appear that this world must resist our will because if it corresponded to our will there would be no need to appeal to God for something better. We might not even be able to perceive God without the contrast provided by an order of creation that so contradicts the fullness that God desires for us hereafter in the Kingdom of Heaven.

Is this world as we know it then a mere balance point arrived at by God that spares us some limitations while leaving others in place and is thus as Leibnitz would say, the best of all possible worlds considering God's purpose in creating anything at all? The answer would seem to be provided by the prayer of Jesus in the Garden of Gethsemane that if it be possible the cup of his suffering and death would pass Him by, but still Jesus asks that the will of the Father should be done. The variance that this implies may sound at first as though Jesus was only operating from His human nature on that fateful occasion, but theologically speaking Jesus is speaking as a representative of the entire human race at that moment. We would all escape pain and evil if we could. The path of redemption seems to irrevocably contain and be summed up in the cross.

This should be our posture towards the evils that we also experience, that we ask God always for a better world, but accept the one we have, not out of resignation that it is the best that God can do, but rather that evil provides us with the opportunity to resist it. Christianity assumes that God is engaged with evil to overcome it from within. In that sense Christianity is neither monist nor dualist. It is not monist, for it does not assume that God wills evil. It is not dualist, because it does not assume that evil has the same primordial existence as God. We are simply shown by revelation that God may transform evil by taking it upon Himself. We are allowed to experience the sparks while God assumes the fire. Beyond this, speculation is useless. Instead we are given only the testimony of Easter, which contains within itself the seed of the new heaven and the new earth where every tear shall be dried and death will be no more. Our ultimate assurance is that in the end "all will be well," as Julian of Norwich said in her writings. These were my thoughts as I gazed out over Paris today and felt that spring is at hand. It is best to recall this always when one is encountering evil: that spring is always near at hand. The optimism of the early Christians was based upon the same trust that sustains us today and will sustain all who will be born after us until Christ comes again.

The season of Lent is over for me and Eastertide is here. Next week, I shall leave Paris. I will travel to Copenhagen and then cross to Whitby in Yorkshire. I am returning home at last. It is only appropriate that my long journey should lead me back to my birthplace. I do not know if my assessment of my life will be different from what it has always been when I have visited my natal home on other occasions. My long-term plans are still indefinite.

If I survive my encounter with Professor Moriarty shall I return to Baker Street and the life of a consulting detective? How will I find Watson when I reveal myself to him after these years of separation? Will he ever be able to forgive me for the great trespass that these last years have been to our friendship? I may only trust that my strange odyssey has been a necessary one. I have tried as best I could to record my experiences and my tentative conclusions.

It is no easy matter to grapple with life and certainly one may ask too many questions. But I am a detective after all and it is a poor detective who does not seek answers. I am glad to be facing my hour with Moriarty at last, prepared or not. At least I feel that I have adhered to the injunction to know myself and perhaps that is the only knowledge possible. We dwell within the caverns of our own soul. The most difficult case of my career has been after all the case of that inscrutable fellow, Sherlock Holmes!

Dr. Watson's Narrative Continues

At this point I must go back a bit in my narrative to explain in greater detail how Holmes and I came to engage with the Americans after our arrival in Newport. I read the above passage from Holmes' journal on the night before the fete to be given at the magnificent mansion of the Vanderbilt Family called The Breakers. We were to spend several days there as guests of the Vanderbilts, a generous invitation extended to us through the ministrations of Mrs. Edith Wharton.

It was a time of high excitement. For the first time the President was asking Congress to declare war upon a nation that had not attacked American troops, nor was there any direct border dispute to act as a stimulus. The incident that had led to the sinking of the Maine was still under investigation. The presence of an American battleship in a foreign port might in itself have been considered provocative considering the delicate situation created by the year-old rebellion of the Cubans against Spanish rule.

The idea that America was obliged to aid any rebel movement there seemed to me at the very least to be presumptuous and to invite Spanish reprisals should the Americans intervene. It had not been the custom for Americans to intervene in foreign concerns. So great was the fear of foreign entanglements that George Washington had warned the nation to beware of all permanent alliances. There was no provision made in the Constitution for a standing army since the founding fathers believed that the state militias could be federalized in an emergency to withstand any aggressor.

Provision was however made for a navy to safeguard American shores, but that America would organize and deploy expeditionary forces was not contemplated. This proves that the concept of offensive war was alien to the original intent of those who had created the nation. As America had been conceived in liberty, it had been conceived also in peace. The country had not broken free from Europe only to enter once again into the cycle of wars that had bedeviled the old world for centuries. Nor was it contemplated that industrial over-production would mandate a constant struggle to expand foreign trade. The mere size and variety of climate present in America meant that it could well subsist on internal trade.

Only the advent of intense industrial expansion since the war with the Confederate States had created the conditions for the collapse of prices from which the country had suffered since 1893. The decline in the prices of farm produce had been particularly severe. This had been hard on the western grain producers. Those farmers had been increasingly forced to sell their land, which was promptly bought up by land-barons and railroad speculators. The big eastern banks and investment houses now controlled the nation's decision makers. For this reason, it did not surprise Holmes or me that America had chosen to follow the tune being piped by the men who now owned a disproportionate share of the productive resources of the country.

The Panic of 1893 had caused a corresponding shortage of "cash money" among the western farmers as they struggled to repay farm debts with deflated dollars. The "gold standard" was strangling them. The Democratic Party's candidate, William Jennings Bryan, wished to convert America to a bi-metallic currency by coining silver to increase the money supply, even at the risk of inflation that would be easier on debtors. The expansion of the money supply through the coining of silver from the Comstock Lode in Nevada would have expanded the money supply significantly and rescued farmers who were being forced off the land because they could not pay the fixed-terms of their mortgages. Declining farm prices coupled with a deflating dollar had made it impossible to repay loans for seed and equipment let alone to pay farm mortgages owed to the banks whose tentacles reached even onto the western prairies.

The farmers, once driven off the land, descended into the cities looking for work. There too they met with disappointment, because wages were low there, depressed by the flood of recent immigrants from southern and eastern Europe. Prices were still high though because of the high railroad fees charged for grain and beef. The most recent waves of immigration created a surplus of foreign labor which allowed for a ready supply of workers and increased competition for jobs. Meanwhile the courts had decreed that unions and collective bargaining were criminal conspiracies in restraint of trade that damaged the huge corporations that now controlled American production. The result was a foregone conclusion: America was now a colony controlled, not by England, but by the small class of men who controlled the corporations and trusts, the railroads and mines, the great farms and factories.

Men like Morgan, Carnegie, Frick, Astor, Stanford, Rockefeller, and Vanderbilt constituted a new aristocracy. The Republican Party that had once cried out to free the black man was now the party that was doing all that it could to bind all men white and black and oriental to a new idea of America. The trappings of democracy were retained, as they often are when democracies become plutocracies, but the opportunities for the majority of Americans were being curtailed daily. The democratic experiment had lasted less than one hundred years.

The states were now mere administrative arms of the

central control exercised from Washington through the Commerce Clause of the Constitution. There was no exit from the union for those who opposed this centralized rule. Lincoln had settled the question of diversity and secession once and for all. Even sovereign states could not withdraw from membership in the Union nor could the Union, as now constituted, turn aside from the world trade that could alone sustain its new industrial economy.

The election of William McKinley, the Republican candidate who was sworn in on March 4, 1897, just over a year ago had done two things:

First it had committed the United States to the gold standard set by England, the richest and most powerful nation in the world. Those without gold must sell whatever they had and at cheap prices. Cotton, tea, and silk from China all flowed towards those who had gold. Gold was the means for oppression of farmer and worker alike.

Second, the election of McKinley meant that America would need to join the other great nations of the world in the rush for colonies. Colonies meant cheap raw materials for factories and markets for finished goods. Colonies like gold were the path to wealth and power. But wealth and power for whom, that was the question?

Certainly not for the working men of England who had yet to see the fruits of their labors. One needed only to visit a factory in Manchester or Leeds or the great port town of Liverpool to see how little of England's prosperity had been shared with the common people. Everywhere in England one could see what the gods of trade and industry had wrought. This was the path upon which America was now to embark as well.

On April 21, 1898, McKinley asked Congress for a Declaration of War on Spain and on April 25th he received it. A dull-witted populace, enflamed by war rhetoric and without any real perception of the abandonment of the ideas that had once sustained the nation, had demanded it. "Avenge the Maine" was a cry heard everywhere. "Aid the rebels! Resist Spanish tyranny!"

I could not but remark that America had only a few short decades ago suppressed its own rebels though those rebels were sovereign states that had at last realized that union was not to their advantage, whereas Cuba was a colony of Spain. If the Cubans as a mere colonial possession had a right to rebel in their own self-interest, then the Southern States had a right as sovereign states to secede. No one at the time seemed to see the contradiction.

I had always deplored slavery with all of my soul and valued all who opposed it, so I had vacillated at the time in my loyalties during the American conflict, although I was only a youth at the time. Only later reflection had shown me what had really been at stake all along, not the freeing of the slaves, but the existence and preservation of the Union and the fate of the western states that had yet to choose between the old agrarianism and the new industry-based economy of the northern states centered in New York and Boston.

I had little doubt that if the Spanish possessions were freed they would soon become the first colonies of an expanded America. America had already taken what it could from Mexico. England protected Canada. Alaska had already been purchased from the Russians. Now American expansion needed one thing, access to the Pacific gateway to China and Japan. The Philippine Islands beckoned as had Hawaii. The doctrine of Manifest Destiny now had developed a trans-oceanic aspect. War was indeed inevitable but I could not but mourn for the nation and its people, for the old America. It would soon pass away forever with this first sounding of the bugle to take up arms on foreign shores.

hen I woke the following day, the day when we were to move temporarily to lodgings at The Breakers, I looked out over the lawns at Land's End to see if Holmes was up early as well. He was already sitting on the terrace that adjoined the lawn below my window. I dressed quickly and joined him and together we walked along the path that led out to the sea. He was wearing his old deerstalker hat, the brim of which shaded his eyes from the rising sun as we walked out to the beach.

It was a lovely day. The wind was blowing in from the sea and violet-colored waves broke in long lines of white foam on the sands below the cliffs. The great mansions, "the cottages" as they are called, stood in weighty masses of stone and timber along the winding cliff path. They were silent, sleeping placidly in the morning sun. Viewing them I could see only their beauty. Wealth demands art to express its power and art is always beautiful. It was as though the great houses had grown organically like some immense crystals from the sandstone bluffs on which they stood at attention to greet the dawn.

The smells of cooking came to us now and again from the kitchens, mingled with the bracing salt-air. It is a peculiarity of good-fortune that while one is privileged to enjoy it, one can imagine for a moment that it is universally enjoyed, just as in one's youth one imagines that the world itself is young and filled with joy and promise. For a moment I forgot my democratic principles in sheer admiration of the scene before me. The connection between this surplus of bounty and wealth and its source was invisible. I could not see the looms turning in the lint-strewn factories or hear the coughs of the young girls breathing the fibrous poisons. I could not see the ships of oceanic trade that did not spare the lash or the seamen subsisting on salt horse and hardtack. I could not see the farmers sitting idle in western towns taking on day labor when they could find it on land they had once called their own. None of these realities were evident along this gracious avenue of splendor shining in the sun.

It was not to be seen in the crisp uniforms of the servants and maids or in the splendid livery of the horses and carriages. It was not to be seen in the gracious bearing of those we had met thus far in Newport or in those famous persons I was sure that we would soon meet. America retained still the memory of its innocence and had yet to show the splendor of the Medici rulers of Florence or the Borgia noblemen of Spain. Empire status would bring all of these things, but they would pass. Holmes broke into my thoughts as we walked along with the sand grains blowing about our feet as the morning breeze caught them up, whipping them along in little whirlwinds and eddies at our feet. "All glory is a fleeting thing," said he.

I looked up startled. "Holmes, I have said nothing! How did you follow the course of my reflections?"

"My dear fellow, a mere dismissive shake of your head is adequate for one who knows your radical sympathies for unions and syndicates, when facing such an opulent scene as this, a scene of marble façade and sculpted statuary. If you will allow me, I shall trace the course of your reflections. Your Methodist roots are showing. You still believe at some level that society improves with sufficiently ardent social action. You have refused to abandon the hopes of your youth, fed by men like the Reverend Beecher. I have even noticed you secreting some of the literature put out by the women's suffrage movement. Do not deny it! Good old Watson, always the friend of those without a voice. How hard it must be for one who has believed in evangelical moral progress to accept what the Catholic Church has always known that human nature does not change *en masse* even over centuries, even in the so-called New World of America. Conversion of heart is the exception not the rule. Though I am not as grim in my views on that score as I found Colonel Moran and Professor Moriarty to be, I am still not an optimist as regards human beings in the course of history.

Freedom from illusions has made many a case clear to me when even hard-headed Scotland Yard inspectors have given it up as insoluble because they could not believe that the innocent young girl before them had poisoned her grandmother for her pearls."

He smiled grimly before continuing, "Do not mistake beauty for virtue, my dear fellow; it is a common error. But to continue, your democratic leanings are well known to me. I have yet to see you smile in anticipation and approval when I speak of the possibility of meeting President McKinley while we are here in America. You will no doubt look with a jaundiced eye at our hosts during the next few days. I need not ask you though to be polite to them, for you are always the soul of propriety. It may help though for you to know that I share your sentiments. I am more in sympathy with the populists of the day than you might suspect. I deplore like you this new aristocracy of America."

"Then why do we not ignore your brother's letter and expose some at least of these captains of industry by publishing the Murillo Letters as we had planned?" I asked.

Holmes considered my suggestion before answering obliquely. "Because this war serves our purpose of helping to defeat the ambitions of Baron Maupertuis, although I also find it deplorable that we must ignore the injustices of America in order to do so. If I possessed freedom to pursue my own inclinations in the matter, I would attempt to point out the probable future consequences of what is at issue here, this absurd war. But we are not our own agents in this matter. The die is cast. We must then proceed with our mission as best we may and attempt to draw some good out of this present evil. We are now in a unique position to influence history. We may not turn aside from the present hour to restore a vanished order. Events press on. The task of the man of conscience is largely consumed in prevention and in reparation. Alas, goodness seldom takes the lead and when it does the temptation to pride and vainglory soon spoils the buds of virtue."

It was clear that Holmes was as disappointed as I was that we could not strike out in all directions at once, like the man who mounted his steed and rode off in all directions. Instead we were being forced to take sides between two sets of malefactors separated by the Atlantic Ocean. Holmes was not ill-humored, but I could not but remark that his stringent realism and desire to live without illusions had already denied him many of the joys of life.

Most men need to believe that life pursues an upward course, that virtue is rewarded and not condemned, and that innocence, wherever it is found, will not be vanquished before the corrupt powers that plot to degrade it. Holmes could not entertain the common hopes of most men and still be useful as a detective. Crime is the rot at the center of the fruit and Holmes in pursuing it had been led inevitably to ask why evil exists at all. It was no wonder to me now that Holmes had grappled so extensively in his journal with the question of Original Sin, since he saw its fruits everywhere about him.

Clarity of mind demands the sacrifice of the illusions that make it possible for most men and women to survive. Sherlock Holmes had often spoken of the charnel-house that is history. Yet he was something of a student of history for all of that. His passion for early English Charters was motivated by a desire to find some instances where the powerful had yielded to the common good by recognizing common grazing lands or peasant homestead rights. He collected any exceptions to the rule of acquisition and consolidation of power, because these minor exceptions to universal injustice surprised him and he cherished the rare treasure of such occasions as landmarks in the long grey night of greed.

Holmes had indeed read my thoughts. In thinking back upon what I had read in his journal, I could see that he had been influenced somewhat by Colonel Moran, whose own character was such as to be a law and destiny answerable to no one but himself. Colonel Moran might have succeeded in attaining to a high colonial office through his force of personality and linguistic abilities. Instead he was barely tolerated in India and though convicted of no crime he was an embarrassment to the colonial leadership who undoubtedly wished that he had perished in his many campaigns rather than emerging, as he had, as a hero if not as a patriot. His crimes of course were known only to Professor Moriarty and to Sherlock Holmes and even I had not been told all regarding the full extent of the power of the Moriarty Organization...

As for the Professor, I had already begun to understand something of his character. He began to appear to me as one who lacks the absolute inscrutability and horror that possesses us when we confront evil at its source. Even the "Napoleon of Crime" possessed only a qualified evil. I began to see that Professor Moriarty was what Holmes might have become had he failed in his religious quest. I had come to that point in the journal where much would soon be revealed that had long puzzled me in the character of my friend. I began to wonder whether Holmes had been so tolerant to the Professor, not merely out of a desire to be loyal to the father of Holmes who had sacrificed to give the stable-lad a chance in life, but also because Holmes saw something of himself in Professor Moriarty!

Few of us can in honesty condemn a man or woman who shares our own imperfections; neither could Sherlock Holmes. Professor James Moriarty and Sherlock Holmes shared a common desire to solve the ultimate mystery of life. This is always a dangerous task and one perhaps beyond what mortal man may prudently attempt. I found myself thinking that morning of the strangely chilling quote from Friedrich Nietzsche, "When you look into the abyss, the abyss looks into you." Were Holmes and I about to look, even in the world of the comfortable and sunlit cottages of Newport, into the abyss?

After our strangely affecting morning sea walk we returned to Lands End. I went upstairs at once to pack a portmanteau with the clothes and other items that I would require as well some formal wear for the evening festivities. I was about to return to my customary daily reading of Holmes' journal when there was a knock on my door. It was a servant who had come to pick up my luggage for transport to The Breakers. I was to find that all my luggage, which I had so carefully packed, was secure and unpacked in my room when I arrived.

Mrs. Watson and I during our married life kept only the smallest staff and my many prior years as a bachelor and my years as a widower had accustomed me to doing things for myself. I have always thought that the institution of personal servants is a peculiar one, however customary it may be. Its primary purpose is to absorb a class of persons into the economy who would otherwise need to find employment in agriculture, manufacturing, or trade. The uncertainty and inequality that pervades the distributive processes of the social order will always mandate that there will be an institution dedicated to personal service. Since human societies inevitably gravitate towards hierarchies, there must be some who are seen as adjuncts to those in a superior social position. Human beings seem to take pride in various distinctions that are the fruit of competition and unequal distribution.

It is difficult to name any parameter that may be measured where some sort of competition and rivalry does not appear. Some of these customary distinctions may be built into nature itself. Variety seems to be the path taken towards species differentiation. Many life-forms seem to prefer extravagance and even ostentation. One need only think of the elaborate mating-rituals of birds for an example of this. There is also the entire matter of sex-trait divergence. Each sex seems to migrate towards a point of maximum divergence so that eventual union of the sexes, in order to be achieved, requires the traversing of a larger synapse. Human beings have taken this matter of display far beyond mere functional differentiation of the sexes for purposes of mating recognition. The result is that human beings seem to rejoice in a tension between opposing positions.

Even politics works in this manner. What would a parliament or congress be without debate and opposition? Even children will fight over some trivial toy or to preserve some advantage so that nothing so disappoints them as strictly imposed equality. They will find some remaining distinction and make that the basis for a new quarrel. Since this is an innate disposition of human nature, it would appear that efforts to establish a lasting peace between nations are vain. Nations will struggle, just as children do, out of envy or spite or simply to establish a hierarchy among nations. To assert the will of one against another and to prevail seems bred within us and perhaps in all of nature. Only the planets keep to their assigned orbits and even they would appear to use gravitational force to dislodge the others from their orbits around the sun.

Christianity deals with this instinct by cleaving to the injunction of Christ that the one who wishes to be greatest must strive to be the servant of all. It would appear that even God the Father acts as a servant to mankind for he sends the sun and rain alike upon the good and even upon the evil and instructs that the last workers of the day are to be paid first. God inverts our normal order of expectations. He aligns Himself with the poor, the powerless, and the lepers and those who lack even that beauty that is bestowed by an intact body. He seeks out the sinner in his sin and awaits even the briefest gesture of repentance to restore all that has been lost. Human nature then seems to be opposed to the wisdom of God and for this reason it was revealed that God's ways are not our ways.

Man and woman untouched by grace turn even love into rivalry and obsession with power over each other. From all of this emerge two types of social order: one based upon monopolization of resources and social subordination and one based upon rejoicing in human differentiation as a sign of God's gifts, coupled with a distribution system motivated by charity that meets essential needs so that variety and some measure of equality may simultaneously exist among men and women. Human history has tried the first and it is well in place. The second has been tried in limited contexts and to its existence civilization owes its existence.

No lasting growth comes from conquest. Conquest must be followed by a period of social growth and order. Even the Chinese Mandarin is advised to treat the people well so that they will follow his leadership. My democratic and Christian sympathies, for the reasons I have just stated, did not make me embrace even the wonder and beauty of The Breakers without causing me to lament that such beauty was the possession of the few rather than a cathedral, which for all its grandeur and expense is at least open to all worshipers.

When our carriage pulled up at the door of the great mansion and we had all disembarked we entered a grand hall that took one's breath away. We had been greeted with courtesy at the door by Alice Vanderbilt and her husband Cornelius, who unfortunately has been confined to a wheelchair as a result of an apoplectic stroke suffered in recent years. He was then only a man in his fifties, an age that should be immune to such attacks, but his many labors as the owner of the great New York Central Railroad had no doubt predisposed him to just such an attack. His wife was a diminutive person of great moral force, but of formerly humble origins. They had met through common involvement with the local Anglican Church. I was given to understand that both adhered to a strict set of religious sentiments, though I found such extravagance as I witnessed about me called into question the actual Christianity present in any belief system that could allow for such excesses and accumulation. Private constructions, such as The Breakers represented should not it seemed to me be possible in a democracy. We were led into the house as I said and taken at once to the drawing room where an early tea had been prepared for us.

I have visited some of the great European palaces and the room where we were seated was equally impressive. It is one of the unique features of baroque architecture that it eludes verbal description. This is because of its very elaborateness and the immediate and total impression that it makes upon the senses that does not lend itself to the linear nature of verbal description. Words must isolate the part and build up the whole by degrees. Baroque architecture is first grasped as a whole with a sense of awe and it is only through careful analysis after the fact that one may see how the parts are combined to achieve that instantaneous effect.

In Gothic architecture everything is subordinated to an idea of light and elevation. This makes the gothic an exercise in simplicity and symmetry. Baroque architecture, in contrast, thrives on excess and variety. If the Gothic elevates one's mind to God through arch, window, and light, the Baroque seeks to reveal God through actual epiphanies glimpsed through the clouds above the apse. Heaven is brought down to earth rather than being the goal of a remote aspiration.

My first impression of The Breakers then was that as with many wealthy persons there was evidently a desire to attain in the present life some measure of a glory that exceeds what is possible to us in our present state. It was not that either member of the Vanderbilt couple was a crass voluptuary, for they appeared if anything to be typical Puritans of a decidedly American type. This

Italianate marvel then was recreated on the shores of New England, not as a native growth, but as a sign of American progress as though the Americans felt that to show their wealth required the emulation of European art and architecture. I could not but wonder whether America might better have used its wealth to create a distinctively American art-form that would celebrate the freedom and equality that were supposedly its fundamental national characteristics. Great wealth and America seemed to me to contradict themselves, because wealth implies the very hereditary nobility and titles that the early commonwealth intended to leave behind in the corrupt Europe from which its emigrants had fled in order to embrace a new vision for mankind in a virgin land.

Mr. and Mrs. Vanderbilt seemed dwarfed by the mansion that surrounded them. Perhaps it was only his afflicted legs, but it seemed that the master of the house had bequeathed a sorrow to the place, so that the grand halls and rooms seemed to be cold and haunted. What may be appropriate to a cathedral is not appropriate to a private dwelling. The Baroque splendor that surrounded me seemed to lack the worshipers that could alone bring the place to life.

My impressions of the time that we spent there are compressed. It was as though I had entered a place where time and space were suspended. Newport was a sort of fairyland where each day began and ended in much the same fashion. The news of the day seemed to be filtered through the class distinctions that would protect Newport's residents from any direct personal confrontation with the stench and suffering of the present war, the impressions of which would be deferred until based upon its historical relevance to a growing empire. It would then be evaluated from the effect it would have upon commerce and the enhanced stature of American interests abroad.

The multitudes might cheer of course at victory, but their

lives would be little changed by it, for despite Walt Whitman's great imaginative epic poems of democracy, America had already come to resemble Florence, Rome, and Venice, at least in the East where the great families had lately consolidated their wealth and power. Holmes was of the opinion that the destruction of even the most civilized eastern Indian tribes such as the Cherokees and the Iroquois Confederation was due to the fact that they manifested a spirit of residual democracy and community that might be copied, which would destroy the utility to be obtained by the employment of the masses to serve the interests of the few. There is nothing as dangerous to a nominal democracy as the potential realization of its elaborate promises.

The Declaration of Independence, a cynic might say, never promised Americans happiness, but only the vain pursuit of happiness. The famous Declaration should have said instead that Americans should learn to be content with what their betters allowed them. The condition of the present American economy made it clear to an outside observer that Americans were indeed an industrious people, but the system of their government had already decreed that the fruits of that production would be used to enrich the few at the expense of the many and to extend American power abroad.

Certainly that was the sentiment that we encountered that evening when we were joined by a glittering company from New York and even from the nation's capitol. The air was filled with talk of the vigor shown by the American response and of the perfidy and tyranny of the Spanish. The battleship Oregon was said to have rounded the Horn and was even then steaming towards Havana. American ships had been dispatched long ago to patrol the waters off of the Philippine Islands. America was ready for war.

It was the exciting event of the season. Even the ladies spoke of little else. War was seen as a great opportunity, a chance for Americans to display their mettle before a wondering world. So great was the festive spirit that even a gentle reminder of war's reality would seem to be a *faux pas* in the face of such heady optimism. Of what use would it be to discuss the ravages of malaria to the very American forces who would soon "teach Spain a lesson."

America did not possess an adequate expeditionary force, so already a call had gone out for volunteers. They were to assemble in Texas and then proceed to Tampa, Florida for embarkation. To the company in Newport these men were grand cavaliers with ribbons trailing from plumbed helmets, lances at the ready, gallant knights of old and not the rag-tag combination of buffalo soldiers and irregular troops that would soon gather in Texas. I recall that I looked over at Holmes during the meal amidst the clinking glasses and the many toasts. He was occupied in listening to the discourse and forming his own impressions of the company. I could see that he would reserve any personal comments for later in the library where the men would soon adjourn for their port and brandy and where more frank discussions of the realities of war might be broached that should be concealed from the fair sex.

I looked across the table now and again towards Irene Adler. I noticed at once certain dangerous signs in her face, as though a thunderstorm was gathering slowly, for her brow was knit and her lovely mouth wore an expression of scorn and impatience. Mrs. Wharton had noticed this also and she gave Miss Adler a pleading glance, which as I was soon to see was to be ignored by the forthright actress.

I had come to understand Mrs. Wharton during our days at Lands End and her unique relationship with Irene Adler. Mrs. Wharton saw in Irene Adler the rebel she would have liked to be. The restraints of her social position had been burdensome to her and she had cast them off as best she could without provoking social ostracism and exile from her class. Her husband was only a lap-dog to her, acquired as a social necessity. Her friends were all artists. I was to learn that she had defied her mother time and again and that she was shortly to begin a career as a writer of novels. In appearance she was distinguished looking, but not conventionally beautiful. Instead she was arresting and intelligent to an extraordinary degree. Her later writings were to reveal her powers of observation and expression.

Irene Adler was then for such a woman the perfect heroine of fiction: beautiful, elegant, and brave. Society had of course no use for such a woman at the time of which I write. She must then always be either an outcast or a tragic figure. Irene was of the outcast class. She was too beautiful to assume a round of domestic duties through marriage to a wealthy man, but too proud to be treated as a mere actress or courtesan. New England society did not know what to make of her, but she had been accepted as in intimate friend by Edith Wharton, so all doors were open to her. Part of the price for that acceptance though was a nominal effort to hide the extensive experience of the world that Irene in fact possessed.

She did not seem to be in a mood to hide it that night. To a woman of intelligence and breeding the subordination of her sex must always be a chaffing experience. To forgive an occasional outburst would seem forgivable and even easy at normal times, but not if it was threatening to a social order that could not exist without that very subordination of her sex into lovely irrelevance. Certainly Irene Adler had seen as much of the world as anyone present that evening and any opinion she might have formed as to the policy that America should pursue was as informed as that of the men who were present. Still, there were certain subjects that were held *per se* to be beyond the provenance of women, so that when she did finally speak up, Irene Adler elicited a general feeling of alarm in all present.

Her hostess looked somewhat censorious and I saw Mrs. Wharton reach her napkin to her lips while her glance was fixed upon her friend with a subtle but alert warning glance. Irene Adler however clearly meant her statement to be addressed to the general company though for her clear and majestic voice was suddenly heard during a general lull in the conversation at table. She looked at no one in particular as she spoke, but rather at her plate where a plump quail in orange sauce reposed still barely tasted upon its bed of wild rice.

"So at last America is making its debut among the imperial powers," said she. "I have performed in Madrid and I found the Spanish to be a gallant and courageous people with a deep national pride. In any case their government has owned Cuba for sufficient time to be considered the legitimate source of sovereignty for that island and the other Spanish possessions should not be in question because there is only a rebellion in Cuba. I wonder, gentlemen, if now that this country is at war whether it will address itself to the point at issue, which is only Cuba, and not use this pretence of aiding the Cuban rebels to attempt to wage a general war against Spain in order to seize its other colonies?" By phrasing her opinion tentatively and as a question and then looking up with her transfixing smile, which she addressed to each male person around the table, she managed to retain that air of uncertainty, which was expected of her sex, while still making it clear that she had grasped the one point at issue.

I wondered as much myself. Would the Americans be content to aid the rebels in Cuba without extending the war further into the rest of the colonial possessions of Spain? Or was the incident of the sinking of the Maine to be used as an invitation to general hostility so as to grab up as much of the Spanish colonies as possible? The Teller Amendment that had accompanied the recent declaration of war was held up as a sign that America had no lasting designs upon Cuba and would not annex it after the conclusion of hostilities; but that amendment did not address the fate of the other Spanish possessions, particularly the Philippine Islands.

There was a general silence after her initial question, but since it appeared to demand an answer from someone and since the former topic being discussed had now faded from everyone's memory, one of the powerful men present that evening must condescend to give her an answer. The entire company expected it. Even beyond the august estate where we were seated America expected it. Would America now take the fatal step to acquire possessions beyond its own shores? This was the question that had divided America during the past year. Two answers had then been forthcoming.

The first position had been advocated in the recent Presidential Campaign by William Jennings Bryan. His position, which some had termed emotional and nostalgic, had been that America had been created to provide for the common welfare, that the resources of the land, particularly those held by the Federal government, were held in trust and could not be distributed to the highest bidder or to favor certain industries without a proportionate public benefit that would show itself by what might be called distributive justice. The eyes of government should be fixed upon the fate of the common man whose growth in freedom and independence would be the measure of the success of the nation as a whole. American policy should be dictated by domestic needs and not by foreign ambitions. Wars were to be looked upon as a misfortune to be avoided at all costs unless American soil or shipping interests had been attacked directly. Even should a war break out then, it was not to be used as an excuse for the standing armies that were the enemies of freedom in the nations that maintained them. Only the states were allowed to keep standing militias, as much to secure their own independence from unjustified incursions from Federal power as to keep other nations at bay.

The opposing viewpoint had been advocated by the Republican Party and their candidate, William McKinley. That view held that the laws of capital investment, industrial production, and free trade were absolute laws and that no nation that ignored the reality of world markets could hope to survive and prosper in the modern world. For this reason it served the nation to serve first its most powerful men. The business of politics was to arrive at a general prosperity by aiding great enterprises that would act as intermediaries between the political power of the government and the laboring masses whose existence would henceforth depend upon just those same great private powers of industry and finance that would run, not merely the nation, but the world. The Republican Party had recognized by its failure to free the black man from the bonds of servitude that it had long labored in the wrong direction. It had decided at last that the fate of the masses could not be elevated through independence and that it was folly to attempt to make the individual sovereign within a limited domain of his own choosing.

That dream still remained though with William Jennings Bryan and with the party that had been founded by Thomas Jefferson, the Democrats. But unfortunately even they would soon be forced to yield to the new vision for the country as later events would show. The Republican Party however had adapted swiftly to the needs of the nation as one of corporations rather than as a collection of sovereign individuals. For this reason it had readily embraced the gold standard and was ready in 1898 to embark upon a struggle with the other great powers of the world for expanded trade opportunities. America, in this view, was at war for its very survival in a competitive world where nations must be either colonizers or colonies. No nation could presume to retain sovereignty by right, for no higher authority, such as the Catholic

Church had once provided, was there to recognize and bless the right to rule.

The idea that the people of a nation are the final source of sovereignty, that their common will institutes government by a collective act, could guarantee nothing as between nations. Here all was to be dictated by what Chancellor Bismarck had termed real-politic, the force of power alone. The defeat of the Indian nations had shown that any government that had the means to do so could defeat any nation over whom it could exercise power. Power alone was the rule of law among nations and power comes from trade and from the military might to obtain its advantages by dominating other nations. This was to be the new world order and all must bow before it. Religion henceforth was to occupy the same realm as any other aesthetic creation of mankind. The idea that God might rule the world and that all sovereigns must look first to God and to the moral order to justify any action or claim to rule by right would be henceforth considered quaint. Religion would be tolerated and even encouraged as long as it had no practical effects upon state policy. Men of affairs should not be swayed by domestic concerns which should be left to women, whose gentle natures might provide a few hours of comfort to the men who alone must make the decisions that would sustain a way of life for both sexes.

It was for this reason (again according to this view) that women must be denied the vote. Nor was it customary for them to be permitted strong opinions or passions that might interfere with their delicately balanced internal organism. Women were prone to hysteria, the internal humors might grow unbalanced, the womb would begin to wander, and days of sickness might ensue. Nor was it becoming to a woman to upset the serenity of the dinner-table by topics that would be found awkward to the company or embarrassing to the men present. For these reasons there was a general air of disapproval and censure about the table when Irene Adler made her pointed observation.

After providing this background to my readers I realize that I have yet to introduce some of the guests who were present around the dining table on this occasion but I shall do so now. It was indeed a distinguished company that was gathered at The Breakers on that memorable night in 1898. Among those present were the owner and editor of the New York Evening Tribune, William Randolph Hearst, Theodore Roosevelt, the Secretary of the Navy, and even the famed American author Mark Twain, who had only recently returned from Europe. Our host, Cornelius Vanderbilt, and his wife, whatever their private opinions, allowed the conversation that follows to proceed among their guests as good manners dictated. I shall therefore attempt to report the dinner conversation as completely and accurately as my elderly memory allows.

I recall that the sun had already set and the electric lights brought out the grandeur of the room and I could not but reflect upon the Olympian splendor that surrounded us there. The sound of the sea came in through the tall windows that opened out upon the lawns and gardens. It was a calm spring night and the storm and clatter of war seemed to reside only in the martial phrases of those who knew that they would survive the bloodshed to come, with the possible exception of Theodor Roosevelt who would soon leave to join a group of volunteers mustering in Texas calling itself The Rough Riders.

I recall that the first to speak in answer to Miss Adler was William Randolph Hearst who cleared his throat and began to speak, quietly but clearly, as one speaks to a child...

"My dear lady, since you have seen fit to bring the subject up, I will ask this company's indulgence to share a few observations with you that may put the matter to rest so that we may discuss other more appropriate topics. My newspapers, as you must know, have taken a severe line with Spain and have encouraged our own government to aid the rebels. This country will always be the friend of those who fight for freedom. Our own struggle to shake off the burdens of our colonial status, with my apologies to those citizens of England who are among us tonight, has left us as a people with an abiding sympathy for any colonial people seeking its independence. Let me assure you that we have no colonial ambitions of our own. The Cubans may freely form their own government should their revolution prove successful, as it is certainly will be with our aid."

He paused before continuing sententiously, "America has never lost a war you know for God always favors the righteous. If we may, with the aid of His mighty hand, enable the Cubans to shake off Spanish tyranny, it is only right that we do so and if we make a general war with Spain it will be only with the end in view that Spain must not be allowed to amass its forces and prey upon a single front but must be forced by us to consider also the fate of the Philippines and of the island of Guam in the Pacific. Besides we must not forget the perfidious sinking of the Maine, which had been sent to exert a mediating presence and to prevent war. By attacking our ship the Spanish have made war upon us and I believe that President McKinley showed remarkable restraint by keeping any countermeasures in abeyance until now."

Mr. Hearst paused and looked around the table for signs of agreement before finishing his discourse by saying, "Ahem, I trust that I have sufficiently answered your question, Madame."

The company was about to breathe a collective sigh of relief, for it was clearly of the opinion that this rather laborious speech had served the dual purposes of clarifying the issue by setting it in its proper context and had also served the salutary social purpose of reminding the daring Miss Irene Adler of her position as a woman, which position entailed that any further words upon the subject from her would violate the natural order that had assigned her to the sex that follows its men blindly into war. Hers was the sex that must bear the costs of war by burying their sons and husbands without expressing any doubts, reproaches, or questions. I cannot say from this remote vantage point of remembrance whether it was her experience as an actress, which allowed her to declaim from the stage or whether it was her own gallant nature, but Miss Adler refused to be satisfied with the speech given by Mr. Hearst, who almost choked on his wine and grew somewhat red in the face when she spoke up again in her clear and lively voice and flatly contradicted him.

"My dear sir, I hope that you do not imagine that I am part of that supine group of readers who believes whatever they read in the newspapers! Do you dare to tell me that America has no eyes on the Philippines? If that be the case, then why did the Teller Amendment not state that intention specifically? Cuba alone was singled out for exemption and dare I suggest that this policy was embraced simply because Cuba's population is largely of African extraction? I suggest that many people even here in New England feel that America has yet to deal properly and successfully with the legacy of domestic black slavery without admitting any new black citizens to this country. Cuba can export its sugar and its rum whether it is in Spanish hands or is independent."

She looked about her before continuing bravely, "The Philippines, on the other hand, would serve as an advance port for an American imperial navy with its eyes on China and Japan. The Philippines were not mentioned by design, because America wishes to retain them for itself! I believe Sir, that is the truth of the matter, is it not?"

"My dear Madame, this is hardly...." gasped Mr. Hearst.

I heard Mrs. Vanderbilt whisper quietly to her husband, "Oh my dear, what shall I do? The fish course hasn't even been served yet..."

It was then that Sherlock Holmes spoke up, after casting an amused glance at Irene in which perhaps only I recognized a glint of his admiration for her. He assumed that judicial air that I had often observed in Baker Street when addressing men whose social position exceeded his own. Holmes' air of impartial observation tended to disarm any criticism combined with his natural superiority of intellect to hold sway.

"Your comments were very interesting Miss Adler. In any case the die is cast is it not? A Pacific war will soon break out and America will have to choose its course should it become the successor of Spain in those lands that were formerly Spanish possessions. If America may resist the temptation of an expanded role in commerce in the Far East, well and good, if not, then Miss Adler's observations, though they may be direct are hardly meant to be indelicate. They will have been quite on point and might well advance the national debate, which must soon determine the role of America for the next century and perhaps beyond."

He took a brief sip of wine before adding, "And since I have spoken this much in Miss Adler's defense, I may as well express clearly my own misgivings as an Englishman, if the company will be so kind as to grant me this indulgence."

He paused for a moment before continuing, "Power once acquired is not easy to relinquish. Those who take the first steps towards empire are usually bound to follow its fatal course to its end. I spent the early years of this decade in Persia and in Egypt where I was able to see what becomes of empires in the end."

The entire conversation might have stopped there as the fish course was brought out to the relief of our hostess, but Mr. Roosevelt then spoke up. "Are we to assume then, Mr. Holmes, that England has a monopoly on empire for this particular age of mankind? Or perhaps it is that England fears a challenge to its own rule of the seas?"

Holmes had already been introduced to the company as the great detective from England who was engaged on a case that required that his presence in America be kept secret. This last request had been directed specifically at Mr. Hearst who looked disappointed at not being able to be the first paper to announce that Mr. Sherlock Holmes was in America. He had murmured assent however to our hostess's request. In return Holmes wished to make the weekend gathering of notables one devoted to comfort and ease and to avoid contention. I could see him pause now before entering further into what might make him the focus of the attention of the company, rather than a quiet observer.

The volatile man before us seemed to thrive on conflict however. He had thrown down the gauntlet personally to my friend. With his high piping voice he had filled the room with his challenge. So, with an apologetic nod to our host and his wife, Holmes answered him at length.

"I assure you Mr. Roosevelt that England has quite enough with which to contend in managing India and keeping the Suez Canal region at peace and open to trade. If your accusation about our English intentions was true, my dear Sir, it may be that England has come to know better from experience that part of the burden of empire is to assume a preeminent place in world affairs. By focusing the ire and ambition of contending powers on itself, England diffuses the energies that accumulate and lead to war. It must also be kept in mind that we are a small nation and one that has learned the value of keeping alert and on guard to protect its interests. It must be recalled that we are an island that has been subject to invasion by many races. Our English blood is itself a conglomeration of the blood of our conquerors. The seas stand as the ramparts of our fortress isle, but they are short seas and not oceans as is the case with America. They present to the invader short passages that are easily traversed by those who would conquer us. England therefore has had no choice but to build up its naval forces to enhance the protection offered us by our own insular situation. We have also have fought the Spanish in our history. We defeated the Spanish Armada, which sailed upon

England in the 16h century. We fought then though for our very survival and not for empire. If England is an empire today, it is because empire was thrust upon us."

Mr. Roosevelt, who was currently serving as Assistant Secretary for the Navy, spoke up again, "Then perhaps England deserves a respite from its onerous duties in that regard, Mr. Holmes. For my part I intend to organize an American expeditionary force to aid the revolutionaries in Cuba. After that we shall see what further exploits may be in store for us."

Holmes replied, "I commend your zeal and courage, sir. There are undoubted advantages to be obtained from dominating the sea. Where would England be if the continental powers were allowed to reign supreme? We would be a nation of coal-miners and sheep-farmers. I myself am from the bleak moors of Yorkshire where my eldest brother lives to this day in the family estate. Though a lord and a landowner, he is only able to keep the family estate together and profitable with great difficulty. Coal from Bohemia drives domestic prices down and wool from Australia competes with Yorkshire wool in our home markets."

"The need to become an empire was thrust upon us by our own humble station among the nations of the earth. England expands so that it may not begin to contract. Yet our role as the center of an empire has cost us dearly. Once having entered upon the pursuit of colonial possessions the cost of their maintenance becomes prohibitive. Wars on the frontiers of empire are required to keep the native populations compliant with British rule. Other colonial powers eye our possessions with envy. The result is an expensive increase of arms at home so that the security and prosperity, which were our initial design, are now compromised and are purchased by the increased costs of unceasing wars. Our profits are used to simply stand in the relative position of power that we currently occupy. A war against us now would not restore us to the peaceful position we occupied a few hundred years ago, but instead would reduce us to complete servitude to the invading power if we ever surrendered our position of sea supremacy."

"Thus we live in continual fear. It is for this reason that we may stand as an example to other nations. The nation that seeks empire covets the eventual impoverishment and destruction of that nation's people. The nation that would instill fear in all others through its excess of arms soon becomes the target of all the others. Nations fear the beast that threatens them. When a hegemon appears they unite against it. Alliances soon appear to defeat that nation that would claim hegemony over all others until its populace, starved to feed its appetite for arms, succumbs to domestic ruin as a remote but certain outcome of its former ambitions. 'The paths of glory,' as our great poet, Thomas Grey has said, 'Lead but to the grave.'"

I could see that Mr. Roosevelt was surprised at Holmes' eloquence, but he could not allow Holmes to have the final word in a matter that lay so close to his own heart. "I am no historian sir, but I believe that I may say that I am a student of human nature. Human nature thrives on vigorous exercise. Meet fear squarely I say and you will conquer it. Nations should never turn aside from conflict. Wars are opportunities to enhance the national spirit. Why do you think that we were able to defeat the Indian nations who once occupied these lands that are now ours? The answer is simple; we wanted it more than they did and were willing to die to obtain it. Our national spirit would endure no opposition and suffer no common ownership of what it might own entirely. We are not a people to share sovereignty with savages. We took them in hand and the result is that they are well along the way from being hunters and horse thieves to becoming good Christians and productive workers. They are wards of this nation, which is taking them from a savage condition to civilization at its own expense. We have taken upon ourselves the task given us by God to improve the world, to apply American courage and inventiveness to a world that needs it if it would stay abreast of the challenge of these times. If we wish to advance commerce it is because without commerce there is starvation and death. Some must take on the choice to rule because they simply know better the way that history must take and the way that disaster is to be avoided."

Mr. Roosevelt paused before concluding his oration on the virtues of the vigorous life. "So my dear sir, if England finds empire a burden as you say, then let it step aside in the struggle and make way for a more ardent nation to take its place."

The table had fallen silent at this display of forensics. Our host and hostess looked distressed and who might say what course things might have taken had not Irene Adler, the very woman whose comments had elicited this contretemps, stepped in to restore somewhat the equilibrium of the evening.

"Bravo, gentlemen," she cried, "You have each stated your position admirably. How I envy your mastery of practical affairs! I trust that we women shall hear tomorrow some report of how matters stand after you resume your discussion in the library over port. It is there that such matters may be best resolved. You must be so indulgent now though as to allow us women a few moments to discuss more domestic concerns such as the recipe for this lovely quiche. My dear Mrs. Vanderbilt, you must convey our compliments to your cook for this excellent repast prepared and served so well in your lovely home."

Holmes turned to me and said quietly, "Now my dear Watson, you know why it is that I always refer to Miss Irene Adler as, 'the woman.'"

As was traditional in such affairs the dinner party broke up and the ladies drifted off to the drawing room while the men strolled casually into the library. Spirits or wines of various sorts were available and before long a measure of geniality returned to the company of gentlemen seated there. Most were of one mind regarding the coming war. It was only later then before a roaring fire that dispelled the chill of the sea mists that had arisen over the lawns at dusk, that we were able to resume in a more mellow and congenial atmosphere, one aided by an excellent port, the discussion that had begun over dinner at the table of our host, Mr. Vanderbilt.

He did not join us in the library though. His health was delicate and the stresses of company could only be sustained by a regimen of rest in the afternoon and an early hour for repose in the evening. His wife had been forced to adjust to a less strenuous social routine as well since his illness had commenced. That illness had already lasted for some years. The result was that The Breakers had known only a single year of festive gaiety in the manner that the couple had once anticipated before their wedded life had descended into a gloom broken only by the occasional house party, such as the one to which we had been invited that evening, which was the inaugural fete of the season in Newport. I could only hope that our boisterous company would not prove too much for the afflicted couple, agitated as we all were by the strenuous events that had recently plunged the nation into war.

I would have been content to have the conversation keep to the tenor of most such gatherings by dealing with the inconsequential topics that make for pleasant social intercourse, for I did not enjoy abrasive speech with my port after a good meal. If discussion must take place it is always easier if the participants share a common world view. On this occasion I could see that the civilized room at The Breakers could not have contained a more diverse assortment of views. I shall for reasons of discretion keep some of the names of the participants in the discussion out of this narrative though their comments will be included here in order to show that there was a general sentiment that reinforced and on occasion took to extremes the opinions of the more famous individuals present that evening.

Conflict often brings to the fore the less reasonable members of the polity and those least likely to compromise in order to achieve the general good of the nation. In just such a manner the leaders of the day emerge and have behind them a group of anonymous individuals whose approbation of their extreme acts and opinions is the source of the power that they exercise over the course of events. It is difficult to recall in the disorder of much that followed the sequence of the speakers, but I can still recall the major points made upon the occasion and I will attempt to do them all justice.

As the evening progressed Mr. Roosevelt was soon surrounded by men with a similar temper and views to his own. Every confidence was expressed that the Americans would soon teach the Spanish a lesson, just as they had the Mexicans in 1849 and the southern rebels at Gettysburg, in the memory of many in the room who had fought in the great war waged between the states. That larger group including Mr. Roosevelt was of the opinion that the right of a colony to independence was absolute so that Spain's desire to keep the people of Cuba as part of the Spanish Empire was tyranny.

The other group I fear consisted of only Holmes and I and perhaps young Inspector Hopkins who kept a prudent silence. Our position was that if a mere territory that had yet to possess any sovereign status in law could withdraw from an empire, then certainly a state with an organized government that had been recognized should possess the same right as in the case of the recent war of the Union States against the States that joined the Confederacy, our position respected the right of secession of those states. Since the war with Spain was to be fought by the Americans whose own civil war had established the principle that a right to secession was not to be allowed under any circumstances it seemed strange indeed that America would now fight a war to deprive another sovereign nation of the right to resist secession by a mere colony. It would appear that one of the wars was thus unjustified; but which one?

I looked over at Holmes who had remained silent since his statement at the dinner table. He was sipping a brandy and gave every indication of being fascinated by the fire in the grate. Darkness had fallen and a brisk land wind was beginning to blow out to sea where the mists now held sway along the shore. An equal storm was brewing in the room. It might have been avoided had not Mr. Roosevelt looked over and noticed that his vociferous pronouncements, delivered in an annoying piping voice, were being ignored by the tall British detective.

"I trust that we are not boring you, Mr. Holmes," said he.

"On the contrary, I have always found the talk of brigands and buccaneers, with their high adventure and romance to be very intriguing. Pray continue your diverting discussion." answered Holmes smiling blandly.

Holmes had hit the mark with this comment. Mr. Roosevelt's mustache appeared to bristle.

"I find that comment offensive in the extreme! Just what do you mean, sir? We are neither of those two categories. You appear to forget that this nation is at war. We are not privateers but volunteers. There is a distinction!"

Holmes turned with a laconic air. He put his glass down on the table and taking out his pipe with a short apologetic look at me proceeded to fill and light it. As the smoke began to circle above his head he continued with the air of having reached a judicial conclusion.

"Your point is well taken when approached in the strict sense. Perhaps, I may make my meaning clearer by frankly stating that this war is simply a war of aggressive intent. America has no direct stake in the conflict. It is a purely domestic affair between the Cubans and the Spanish. The mere fact that America hopes to obtain commercial benefits by intervening does not justify intervention no matter how it is put before the press as a splendid little war. In fact it is a directly contrary position to the one that caused the Union States to resist the secession of the Confederate States. But then to assume that nations act consistently is to deny the realities of national opportunism and we are neither of us ignorant of history. Power finds its own excuses after the fact to justify any actions that it may take."

"You forget sir that the Maine was attacked!" stated one of the gentlemen at Mr. Roosevelt's side.

"Yes, but I believe that the investigation is a continuing one and that a final conclusion may never be reached," answered Holmes while putting a match to his pipe bowl a second time to light it. "Of course there remains a prior question of what the Maine, a foreign warship, was doing in the harbor of Havana in the first place if its placement there was not to invite just such an aggressive act as the one now being used to justify intervention. There are many ways to provoke a war of choice gentlemen. One of the most obvious is to make oneself the aggrieved party by design."

Another gentleman, who I later discovered was an attorney, spoke up. "Your analogy with the situation of the Confederacy may not stand scrutiny Mr. Holmes. The entire Constitutional intent is contained in the preamble to the U.S. Constitution that states clearly that the earlier American Confederation was abrogated. I say abrogated sir, not merely modified by the new Constitution, which was the basis of the new nation to be formed."

He walked over to a bookshelf and chose a volume demonstrating an acquaintance that must have been acquired from prior visits. "I quote the appertaining phrase, 'We the people of the United States in order to form a more perfect union.' Note the wording carefully. The intent was to change the former loose assemblage of independent states into a union in which the states were effectively merged into the new nation. The rights of the states and of the people thereafter were to be a mere residuum of all those rights not delegated in that instrument that gave the new nation birth. However, those rights and powers that had been delegated had been absorbed, encompassed, and were now embodied entirely in the new nation; they could not be withdrawn without the consent of the whole people of that nation, not merely a part thereof. The creation of the union was to be perpetual in intent. No successors could abrogate an agreement so solemn, so noble. No Rule against Perpetuities applies over the creation of a nation. The people had spoken for all time and it was done and binding upon their successors forever. In contrast, the people of Cuba abide in that inchoate condition in which the popular will has yet to definitively speak, but when it has done so, whatever nation is formed shall likewise be perpetual."

Holmes sat smoking calmly with his eyes probing the wainscoted ceiling of the great room. "An excellent presentation of your case, sir; but the point remains a contested one. Surely no nation must be governed forever by the dead hand of those who have preceded them. The compact was signed in any case not by the people as a whole, but by the representatives of the separate states. During the gap of time between the death of one form of government and the new form a termination must have occurred whereby the former representatives would have lost all power to consent in the name of the governed masses. You might point out that the states ratified the agreement but that still cannot explain why the dead should be able to compromise the sovereignty of the living. Besides you must grant me my first assumption, which is that a nation that adopts contrary reasons for its wars must admit that at least one of those wars was unjustified or alternately admit that it acts out of a desire for power and conquest and not from principle."

"Very well," said the attorney, "I will grant your

assumption, but I will not admit that this nation, one which has always pursued the cause of liberty is guilty of any such contrariness in its actions. Least of all are we guilty of it now. Our motive is to liberate the Cuban people. The government that they form shall be of their own choosing. The Teller Amendment has made our intentions clear before the entire world."

Holmes continued to smoke placidly. "Quite so, but I ask you to consider now the case of the Indian nations. I believe that the people's will in that case is clearly discernible. The Indian tribes had no wish to join your union. They had formed tribal governments and had even formed extended and elaborate confederations such as the one that existed among the Iroquois and the five tribes around the Great Lakes Region. These governments were so old as to be primeval and an excellent example of the very perpetuity that you wish your own union to manifest and as such they deserved the greatest respect. Yet these governments were set aside by France, by England, and finally by the United States and Canada as though they had never existed. The result is that America now stretches from sea to sea on conquered land. If these were sovereign governments then they remain so in whatever remnant of their people still survives the predation that took their land away from them by force and oppression. It is not too late to make restitution and to relinquish the lands to which you have never had title from God or from man. If your nation refuses to do so, well and good, but by taking that course it surrenders any reputation or claim it may wish to hold forth that it acts from principle and to protect or aid people to arrive at a national consensus stemming from the common will as in this present question of Cuba."

"I am afraid you are confusing the primitive social arrangements of mere tribes with actual civilized governments. These latter can set down policies, enter into treaties, and form a system of laws. The people you refer to are merely held together by informal rules of association and loyalty, as such they are mere extended familial structures," answered the attorney.

Holmes objected at this point, "So are monarchies familial structures, but let us not belabor that point. I am afraid that you are confusing the type of government chosen with the right to choose it. Your Declaration Independence states I believe that when a people finds that the government fails to achieve the ends for which it was formed and formerly consented to the people may change it. There is of course no record that The Indian nations were dissatisfied with their form of government. Indeed, it had served them well for centuries. It is therefore no business of a people from outside those nations to impose a form of government that they might have chosen were they similarly situated and to replace the one that exists with one that they as outsiders find more appropriate. Once sovereignty is exercised by a people over a certain territory for a sufficient period of time no outside entity may justifiably impose its own will upon them. As an invading force it may of course assert territorial claims based upon a prior right to possess the land, if it has such a claim to make. But since these tribal nations have possessed these lands since long before any European ever even knew of their existence, there can be no question of a prior claim upon the Indian lands. This means of course that no European power could assert a claim to these lands by right, but only by force. I fear sir that your critique of their forms of government is an inadequate basis for a claim to their lands. Unless you are prepared to vacate them and pay some sort of reparation or restitution to its rightful owners you will not be in a position to be heard on this present Cuban question. The equitable maxim is apropos here: one who seeks equity must do equity."

"But this is outrageous," blustered the attorney, "The next thing that you will be saying is that we Americans have no right to be here at all."

"So must any man of conscience and of law admit unless you can show me another basis for your occupancy than theft and chicanery?"

"It was never a question of theft; we have purchased the lands from the Indian Nations. There are several treaties..."

Holmes interrupted the attorney, "Pardon me, but I am afraid that those treaties were imposed under duress and so are invalid under English law. When the fair market price is not paid (and you will surely not have the effrontery to contend that the price paid for this land has yielded to the Indian tribes even a fraction of their fair market value) any court of equity would look askance at the transaction. No, my dear sir, this nation has not paid for the land on which it now presumes to exert a claim of sovereignty. For this reason any claims made by this nation, acting as though it were a sovereign, are void. And the fulminations of a set of mere interlopers may not, in all conscience, be called anything but the braggadocio of brigands and buccaneers. America deserves the opprobrium that its actions to date deserve and to have its right to rule denied by the world community of nations. If your theory is allowed to stand, then it is no crime to move into another's house as long as you may extort from him a bill of sale under threat of force. I am afraid that a nation that begins in violence will have only violence to sustain its future untenable claims. For this reason I am not surprised that you advocate war with Spain in order to extort from Spain further territorial concessions to further augment your national plunder. Americans are simply acting in this matter as they have acted from the beginning."

I must say that I was surprised that Holmes had set off in this fashion to oppose the majority opinion in the room on a matter about which we had not been consulted. I could only assume that he must have some purpose of his own for coming round the headland with intellectual guns blazing.

Holmes had turned away from his opponent to look into the fire again. The smoke from his pipe still curled upwards toward the ceiling where it hung like a shadow over the stunned company. The room was in utter silence. I recalled an old saying of Holmes, which stated, "When you have eliminated the impossible, whatever remains, however improbable, must be the truth." He had just applied that very adage to the entire question of the existence of the American nation. Suddenly, within one hundred years, a nation was formed that reached from ocean to ocean. Even granting the legitimacy of the land-grants of the original Thirteen Colonies, there was surely no valid claim to the lands that stretched now to the west of those colonies.

The Louisiana Purchase was nothing other than a quit-claim deed to lands that the French did not own or control. Removing France as a contender for the future conquest of those lands did not settle the question of the legitimacy of the French claim. It was based on a mere habit of trade and exploration with the resident tribes. Holmes had simply shown that when one eliminates the improbable, whatever remains must be the truth.

At last Mr. Roosevelt broke the silence with a laugh. "Well this is preposterous of course, gentlemen. Mr. Holmes here is pulling our collective leg. The English have no plans to leave Egypt after all. What would you have us do, Mr. Holmes, give the land back to the Indians?"

"Well, that remains your problem does it not?" murmured Holmes with an air of weariness. "I merely suggest what reason and ethics dictate. You might at least pay for the land at some future date. I am sure that succeeding years will add to this nation's wealth. The nation could simply direct some portion of that income stream to be paid over as equity dictates. I suggest though that those payments, if fairly computed, will not allow a surplus to be spent for external adventures of further conquest. Wars are expensive and a nation that adopts them as an alternative to wise policy will certainly pay the penalty one day. I am afraid that America is courting its own ruin by adopting that policy. The present war is but a case in point. You have still time to reverse the direction that this nation is pursuing. I urge you do so and to stop your head-long rush to riches, your greedy desire to possess all over which you may impose your will by force. Should you proceed as you have heretofore done, you will deserve nothing from history but the just condemnation applied to all past marauders and brigands. If you are remembered at all it will be as an example to be shunned and treated with contempt and distain by men and nations with honor."

"Are you speaking as a representative of England, may I ask?" asked the attorney. "If you are, I shall register a formal protest with your counsel when I return to Washington."

"I am speaking only for myself," answered Holmes. "This affectation that the truth must be modulated by one's official status is what allows nations to behave in a manner that is similar to the behavior that a cutthroat in Limehouse or Whitechapel might display. I suggest that if we may not speak the truth because of the organized hypocrisy of nations, then we should simply omit all discussions of right and wrong at all and simply say that we act so in any given case because no greater force can stop us. I believe that Mr. Friedrich Nietzsche came to that very conclusion about human nature. He assures us that we are the will to power and nothing more. I believe that was the point so well expressed at dinner by Mr. Roosevelt when he said that it is the vigor and will of a nation that determines its expanse rather than any pre-existing right of occupancy. The one who may hold the land may keep it and not because he has a right to the land, but because he is capable of denying others that same right of conquest through the threat and use of force. Do I state your position fairly sir?"

Mr. Roosevelt's mustache now quivered with his wrath. "You do not state it correctly. You are forgetting, Mr. Holmes, that we are a Christian nation, that our presence here in America is the direct will of God who has prepared a way for us, just as He once cleared a way for the Israelites to enter the Promised Land. We have brought the benefits of civilization to a people who had occupied an island, an island of savagery sir. This continent was cut off from trade, from modern agriculture, from manufacturing, and from true religion. Were we to allow a few inchoate wanderers, who had always decimated themselves through internecine warfare before we came, to assert claims as nations equal to those of modern states? Was America to cling to a coastline when a continent at its back beckoned us forward?"

"When I spoke at dinner of vigor, I was speaking of a hunger and an inventive drive that lies within the tides that stir in the breast of man. It is this force that quickens life and justifies nations. Extinguish that flame and there is nothing but legends of a glorious past, but no future. The strong survive and the race is enriched and what is lost is soon forgotten."

"How long is an individual's life? Each man has at best thirty or forty years to make his mark on history. He lifts the bar of humanity by a millimeter or so and then he passes. Man was not made for peace but for war. In fact peace is merely the time when resources are built up to sustain the next war. It is a continuing process of giving birth to the new and the one who wishes for peace must step aside and let others put their shoulders to the wheel."

Roosevelt continued to speak passionately, "Spanish rule is over in America. From President Monroe onwards this nation has announced that it will be master in its own hemisphere. If we have delayed this long to oust that final threat of a European power upon our shores it has been because we first needed to set our own house in order. The states know their place, the black men are freed, and the red man is being brought to give up a type of freedom incommensurate with the benefits promised by the progress of the nation as a whole. If we are as brutal as you say we are would we have fought a civil war to abolish slavery? Would we have set aside lands on which the Indians may live and even exercise governments of a type appropriate to their simplicity? If we free the Cubans and the people of the Philippines it shall be to bring them to that level of development when they may join the nations of the world in due time, after they have learned to emulate us. America is in the vanguard of civilization; the century to come will bear witness to this. We shall not resort to arms where the mere threat of force suffices to carry the day. To that end we must have a standing army and after this conflict I trust that we shall always maintain one. It is the price of our freedom and the guarantor of our strength. This is the correct statement of my views and of the America that will shortly liberate the Cuban people."

There was a general murmur of assent in the room. It would appear that the piping voice of Mr. Roosevelt had carried the day. Holmes had looked into his eyes as he spoke, but he had continued to smoke his pipe and the lazy curls of smoke seemed to whirl about the room and to form dim and indeterminate patterns along the darkened ceiling.

The attention of the company then returned to Holmes. The men present seemed anxious to see some sign of defeat and were hungry for the apology that they presumed was to be forthcoming from the arrogant Englishman. When Holmes spoke up at last, it was upon a topic that I at least found puzzling. It did not arise from the battlefield that had been marked out by Mr. Roosevelt. Instead it seemed to come from another quarter entirely. Holmes seemed to be ruminating.

"I spent some time in the desert some years ago," Holmes began. "I found that if I desired to measure the distance traveled in a day, I could not reckon it by landmarks. It was also quite pointless to imagine what the following day would bring, because one day was much like another. I found that I must either surrender my prior concept of time and place or go quite mad. Time was no longer the slow movement of the camel beneath me, regular though that might be, nor was it the scouring sun that made all shade a fleeting resource that vanished like water spilled in the sands beneath our feet. Time was contracted to the instant and the instant became whole days, each inseparable from the others. The nights as well passed in an instant of weary sleep. I was like one condemned each day to lie like an insect before the great eye of God represented by the sun that bore down upon us. I grew to pray for clouds and to rejoice in their variety when they were to be seen. On the worst days sky and sand appeared to be one and I seemed to lose all ability to distinguish anything but direction and even direction was but a compass needle pointing to the dust clouds on a distant horizon. I began at some point to understand in that time and place the way that the Arab sees Allah, not as a person, but as an absolute force, one so beyond us that we are not even insects to God. Only the Koran acts as a bridge between God and man. The Koran, the Moslems believe, is God's great gift to mankind, the reduction to words of all of the wisdom of that vast emptiness that is life in the desert. Land becomes meaningless to such a vision just as does all measures of time and space. Everything is a vast eternity. There is only Allah and the times for prayer to address him. That is life for the follower of Islam."

The whole room was hushed in astonishment at these strange words from the unaccountable Englishman.

Suddenly Holmes turned to face Mr. Roosevelt once again. Holmes pointed towards him and said in an accusatory tone, "Where would your vigor, Mr. Roosevelt, be in such a place? You would march gallantly forth and your foe would always be behind you ... in front of you ... at your side... You would come finally to whirl about like a sand devil, a whirlwind, and ever about you there would be the same enemy, the same fear. To one who has not known that terror, which comes from an absolute awareness of his place in the cosmos, it can do no good to speak. I have been there though and the people whom you have displaced, the American Indians, have been there also."

The room was silent and we thought that he had finished, but Holmes had not. Instead he turned and fixed a piercing eye again on Mr. Roosevelt and said solemnly, "But you in your turn will be there when you have lost everything and all places and times are therefore equal."

The men in the room began to drift away one by one. I was about to make some explanation, to mention that Mr. Holmes had been ill lately, for I could see that some of the company were shaking their heads and smiling at Holmes as if he was mad. Mr. Roosevelt remained however as though he was rooted to the spot by Holmes' gaze. The fire was dying down and the candles in their silver candlesticks burned low; only our long silhouettes seemed to climb the darkened woodwork of the walls.

Holmes continued from the gathering shadows, "My metaphor may still be obscure to you, so I will try another to convey my meaning. To the predator there is ever and always only the next kill. The purpose, even the religion if you will, of the predator such as the lion is always the sweet taste of blood from the still warm neck of the prey. Afterwards the lion will spend hours in grooming itself and then sleep beneath a tree on the savannah. But one day the lion itself grows old and when it dies it is not lamented by the other lions. Only the elephants mourn their dead. America may be like the lion Mr. Roosevelt. It may have many kills ahead of it, but when it grows old, it will not be mourned. It will not be mourned by the Cherokees who walked the Trail of Tears to Oklahoma. It will not be mourned by the Lakota, the Cheyenne, the Arapaho, the Choctaws, the Seminole, the

Apache, or the Nez Perce. It will not be mourned by what remains of the proud land of Mexico. And my dear sir, it will not be mourned by the people who you now intend to free from Spain who will ever after live under your thumb and at the mercy of the American economy. Your empire is one of commerce and not of Christianity. The missionaries that you bring to the people that you absorb act like the enzymes of the great stomach of America. They dissolve resistance by convincing the nations that you would conquer of your beneficent intent. They soften the flesh for better absorption into the empire you are forming with your vigorous intentions. I doubt that you will ever be satisfied. Your Manifest Destiny is in fact your lack of conscience for which you are noted around the world. All nations shall, I am sure, come in time to fear you, but you will never have their respect."

It was just then that a servant came in to light the gas and to clean up. He was surprised that a few men remained in a room that he had thought empty since most of the guests had long since departed. The room was filled with red faces and I am not sure that there might not have been blows stuck had not another servant arrived to announce that our hostess and the remaining ladies were prepared to retire and would appreciate our company for a general good night before they went up to bed. I had retained a good grip on my walking stick while Holmes was speaking. I had caught a few dangerous glimpses of eyes with hostile intent. As it was, I tarried with Holmes as the remaining company slowly withdrew and dispersed until we were quite alone, except for Inspector Hopkins who spoke up at last.

"By Jove Holmes, whatever possessed you? I fully expected at times for a jolly-good donnybrook to break out. I had my whistle in hand to summon aid and was prepared for a bout of fisticuffs in your defense. You singed their fur good and proper, I must say."

"Ah well," Holmes said with a yawn, "A nation about to go to war should be capable of absorbing a few home truths. War is a nasty business as Watson can tell you and as could Colonel Sebastian Moran. I took some of my lion imagery from him. We had many interesting discussions during the course of our travels together. I fear that he left me not uninfluenced by his own extreme opinions. He has never been a great fan of American policy. He once told me, and I quote him as accurately as I may, 'That great brute Andrew Jackson decided to expel the eastern tribes and yielded to the venery of the State of Georgia by defying John Marshall and the Supreme Court. When Jackson escaped impeachment for failure to enforce the judgment of John Marshall that the Cherokee were entitled to keep their lands, America left the rule of law aside and I doubt if it will ever embrace it again.' Thus did Colonel Moran anticipate my words tonight and I have thought of his sentiments often since."

"But you have just offended a man with access to President McKinley," I interposed. "I doubt if he will consent to see us now."

"Oh I think he will. You forget, Watson, that a man like Roosevelt loves conflict. He would hardly have respected me if I had flattered his own conceptions. I think I got under his skin pretty well tonight though and he will be itching for some time. He won't be able to dismiss our conversation easily. It will be remembered and he will see me again if only to attempt to change my views. No, I think we are well along on our mission. I am no longer a mere English detective and finder of pearls and watches. Tonight's contretemps has been a good day's work. But let us rejoin the party now. I would not have these Americans think that we British are a rude people." He knocked out the ashes from his pipe on the andiron and concealed it again in his pocket while our small and embattled contingent returned to the great hall where the ladies awaited us to bid us all goodnight.

e did not see Mr. Roosevelt the next day or on the days following. He had departed to Washington. It is no easy matter for a nation that has been long at peace to assume the stance of a nation at war. Events were moving swiftly now. The Oregon had completed the passage from the west coast around Cape Horn and was soon to assume its station in the Caribbean. On May 1st Admiral Dewey began the Battle of Manila Bay which resulted in the quick defeat of the Spanish forces there. The Philippines were thereafter in American hands. The nation was then free to focus its attention on Cuba. The days following the grand party held at The Breakers were quiet ones. This pleased me greatly. Only the Wharton's, Irene Adler, and our own small party from London remained in that great manor house. I was grateful that no word of our heated discussion in the library had been conveyed to Mr. and Mrs. Vanderbilt. It was understood by the servants and visitors that any excitement could have a most unfortunate effect on Mr. Vanderbilt's health, so no report of Holmes' statements to the company were ever made to our hosts. That there had been a fracas did not escape the notice of Irene Adler however. Her quick observation of Mr. Roosevelt's flushed face that evening had told her as much. She inquired about the matter to us the next morning when she came running up to us dressed in an attractive cotton frock and accompanied us on our daily perambulation along the sea path.

"Mr. Roosevelt seemed distracted when he joined the company last night," she began. "I trust that your defense of my position did not lead you into excesses Sherlock. The Americans are after all a volatile people and Mr. Roosevelt seems a veritable firecracker of a man." She ended with a mischievous smile.

Holmes smiled in return. "I admit that I was a bit severe in my censure of American policies. The discussion touched upon America's treatment of the Red Indians, which has been infamous; though it surprises me that so few Americans thus far take that view. This strange sense of entitlement to use any means to secure national advantage seems to have effaced the conscience of all the Americans. The view for instance regarding the initial inhabitants that Americans have seems largely to consist of a fear of that very freedom that the Indian possesses to live the life of nature without burdensome constraints. There is in addition the nagging guilt of the thief who must disparage his victim in order to justify his actions. It would not be too much to say that the Americans are immune to the sufferings that they have inflicted on others. They view all defensive measures that the aboriginal people have taken as a sign of their savage nature. The result has been a virtual war of extermination, waged through successive Presidential administrations. When a policy is maintained over so long a period, it must be considered to have its roots in the national temperament. Americans seem to suffer from a unique moral blindness. It is something of a national disease for which there is no specific cure. They see themselves as an embattled people, though it is their own desire for expansion that awakens resistance from other nations. Who knows? Perhaps they originally caught that disease from England. Certainly we have been no more generous to the people of the east than the Americans have been to the people of the west. The competing claims of England, France, Spain, and Portugal to the Americas seem to have made no account of the prior existence of those native tribes who occupied these lands prior to their discovery by European explorers."

Holmes sat down upon a log and we joined him there as he continued. "The Treaty of Paris in 1783 that recognized the independence of the American colonies simultaneously dispossessed the eastern tribes by granting to the new nation the British claim to all lands reaching westward to the Mississippi River. England had no right to make such a concession though and no representative of the Indian tribes was allowed in Paris to dispute it. On that basis alone, half of the continent was surrendered to the new government of the United States. What if Germany and France had met and simply given away England, would we not have resisted? Would we have been branded as savages for doing so? It is true that the Americans view the matter as a *fait accompli*, but so great a depredation will leave a stain upon this country that will not be effaced until justice is finally done. Until then America will only repeat its conduct in an ever-widening sphere until it finally overreaches itself. At that time its sins will rush upon it and its defeat then will be the bitterer for its long delay. Nemesis delayed is more violent when it comes. The mere assumption of innocence is no defense. The Americans seem startled by the very fact of resistance as though they occupy the lands that they covet by right and not by conquest. My talk last night attempted to use the present instance as a chance for America to turn about and reconsider its course. It was naturally not well received. I did not expect it to be."

This was the burden of the discourse by Sherlock Holmes given as we walked by the sea that morning, just as we would for many mornings to come during that long and eventful summer season. I could see that Holmes was quite comfortable with Miss Adler and that she in turn had come to relish, as did I, those discourses on method that had now proceeded beyond the mere techniques of detection to embrace wider subjects. There could be no doubt that Sherlock Holmes had become an incurable moralist. I realized that the journey that he had taken in the early part of the decade of the nineties had bestowed upon him a somewhat universal point of view that denied the parochialism and narrowness that sustains national identity. Even his Catholicism was of the universal variety rather than the narrowness that is often associated with that faith. His sympathy to humankind exceeded the borders of those who shared his faith and he was able to see signs of virtue even in traditions that had been condemned as inimical to Christian orthodoxy.

I recalled that he had once shocked me by saying that without heresy to act as a borderline and stimulus, it would be impossible to ever have defined the dogmas of the faith. Good cannot be known without evil. The problem of course was the disputed area where evil and good seem to touch and to an extent seem even to comingle. The price of maintaining, while we are on this earth and in this life as we know it, a rigid religious standard is that such rigidity itself partakes of the evil that it would conquer and destroy. For this reason Holmes seemed to desire a universal compassion that esteemed the sinner even in his sin, because to root it out often left behind only a mass of moral carnage and confusion.

Jesus advised that we pluck our eye out if necessary for the sake of the Kingdom, but that assumes that the evil there has been isolated and restricted to a given part of the body. Alas, evil is far more like a cancer and any attempt to pluck it out or even to surgically remove it, is often as likely to kill the organism into which the cancer has insinuated its tendrils, as to restore the organism to moral health. Goodness works more by changing the balance between good and evil by subtle acts of virtue that become finally habitual. Grace operates as light before which the darkness gradually wanes. Salvation is not the work of a day or an hour. Even conversion must be nurtured and sustained in order for it to set down firm roots.

I could see that Irene Adler shared my own view that Holmes manifested a sustained force, a pressure exerted upon events. It was a strength that exceeded even his great natural gifts. It was born of the experiences that he had undertaken so as to find some clarity where before all had been doubt. He did not come to the faith he now possessed by easy stages. Indeed, there was still something of the pagan in Sherlock Holmes, perhaps a legacy of his Nordic blood strain inherited from his father, Sigerson.

Christianity has, in its way, incorporated elements from the beliefs that it has conquered over its two-thousand year history and development. Jesus promised his disciples that after Pentecost that they would do even greater things than He had done, after Jesus returned to the Father to intercede as Savior on our behalf. Thereafter God is always a God-With-Us and no longer a distant deity, the nature of which we can never know. Jesus asked that we refer to God the Father by the familiar appellation of *Abba.* Surely this should put all doubts that we may still entertain regarding God's universal mercy to rest.

I must admit that my friend was still an enigma to me, just as he had been when we were first introduced by young Stamford at the medical school in London where Holmes was doing some early forensic research. The Journal kept by Holmes during his travels indicated that his father had been a combination of the theorist and the practical man of affairs. He had kept an extensive library while many other Yorkshire squires, in spite of their breeding, cared little for the things of the mind. Yet there was a distance between him and at least two of his sons who had left their native Yorkshire to seek their fortune in London. Both Mycroft and Sherlock had avoided the usual career pursuits of younger sons of the nobility. Neither had gone into the ministry or pursued a career in the regimental service as young officers. Nor had they gone into the civil service or sought to become members of the House of Commons. Instead each had created a unique career for himself that corresponded to their unique talents.

Each of the brothers appeared to have begun their lives with a jaundiced view of human nature. Mycroft had joined the most misanthropic club in London named after the philosopher Diogenes who had once run about with a lantern in broad daylight in order to seek out among those who surrounded him even one who was entitled to be called a man. Mycroft's career was to act as a great central clearinghouse for government data, assigning to each fact its relationship to the diplomatic issues that beset the British Empire daily. His possession of a synthetic perspective allowed him to find the central point amidst the sea of irrelevancy, yet to give each fact its due measure of weight in reaching his conclusions. His very objectivity seemed to be at variance from what is usually termed the artistic temperament, but perhaps this is to misunderstand the nature of art that is always governed by the principles of selectivity and combination of elements in order to create a unified whole.

Then there was my friend, Sherlock Holmes, whose young adult mind was filled with every horror perpetrated in the century. Could his views of human nature be expected to be more sanguine than the views and expectations that his brother Mycroft entertained? If one always confines oneself to the contemplation of evil in others, then how will one recognize virtue when it presents itself to us? It was often only Holmes' own sense of propriety that sustained him and kept him from the natural depression that one must feel when confronted with the squalor of human motives and conduct. My friend seemed to be more capable than most men are of imagining the depths to which he also could have fallen had his circumstances or opportunities differed. Sherlock Holmes seemed uniquely capable of seeing both the sinner latent in the saintly man or woman and the potential saint hidden beneath the darkened aspect of the sinner.

It is a vexed question whether our lives are more the product of destiny or of character, of accident or of a sustained inner narrative. Considering the jars and deformations with which our childhood is often marred, perhaps it is well that most of us do as well as we manage to do with our lives. We do not enter the world as a *tabula rasa* but as part of the hopes and dreams of the generations that immediately precede us. A path is charted for us in every utterance and judgment of our parents in regard to us and who can say how deeply planted and effective may be a parental blessing or a parental curse.

How many people impede or even condemn their offspring lest they might exceed the social station of their parents? Conversely, how many children forget the sacrifices, which have primarily aided and enabled their own success and prosperity? Sherlock Holmes once said that if anyone wishes to understand a person, one must look to his family; for it is the family that works out those primal positions towards life that we term destiny.

There were for Sherlock Holmes instances of both familial blessings as well as familial curses in many of the cases that presented themselves to him for solution in Baker Street. Were they also present in his life as well? If I still did not understand the character of his mysterious father, Sigerson Holmes, I had also yet to solve many of the mysteries presented by the characters of the Holmes brothers. So it was that I returned in the quiet days that followed that spring in Newport to the great journal in search of answers to my many questions. The journal had now become for me an oracle, an immense and comprehensive confession granting access to the heart and even to the soul of my friend Sherlock Holmes, as well as being a monument to the waning world of the Victorian era that we both had shared for the past twenty years of our partnership.

It was both a pleasure and a personal struggle with my own convictions to have such intimate access to his mind and heart as he struggled with the same eternal questions that face us all. It seems too little for God to allow us only a single lifetime out of which to fashion a personal identity and to make the decisions on which our eternity will depend. Perhaps this is why really it is to others that we must look in the Communion of Saints to supplement our moral deficiencies and to show in their individuality what human beings at their best are capable of achieving.

For my part I have never given up on the human race. If

nothing else the beauty of art and of artifice stimulate us to find beauty and meaning in life. I did not know yet how Holmes would fare upon his homecoming, but I reflected that much of the search that had preoccupied him was similar to my own search and I could not doubt that it would be recognized by others, among whom I hope to count the readers of this manuscript, the final testimony of a man who still regards Sherlock Holmes as the best and wisest man that I have ever known.

The long time of preparation was over. I was now at last to read of Holmes' account of his return and of his long deferred and definitive meeting with the Napoleon of Crime, Professor Moriarty.

To Be Continued...

Note From the Author

As one who has always esteemed writers such as Graham Greene, Evelyn Waugh, and George Bernanos (each of whom was Catholic) it has been my hope that my own effort in The Confessions of Sherlock Holmes might be part of a venerable tradition. I would like to point out however that the position of a writer who incidentally is Catholic must be distinguished from that of a Catholic writer whose writings are meant precisely to reflect church teachings as such. There is a tension between these two positions that makes it difficult for a Catholic to be both true to his faith while remaining simultaneously true to the form and literary intent that must accompany any act of composition. It would be awkward and indeed impossible to write a cohesive narrative seeking to capture and comment upon human life and conflict if the writer had to simultaneously ensure that goodness and fidelity always emerged in clarity and triumph while its opposite was equally revealed in all of its inherent malice and folly. Fiction, even when dealing with theological reflection, as is the case with the present work, can never be a substitute for catechesis. The reader is therefore cautioned that in reading the present text no decisive conclusion be drawn that the positions of any of the characters reflect either the final views of the author or the official position of the Catholic Church. Literature embraces life according to its own limited perceptions as it is and even in its suggestions of a better world must always fall short, not only in displaying accurately whatever emerging forces may exist in human history, but in depicting all that has been revealed of a higher purpose and source to illumine us in our beleaguered world.

Thomas Mengert possesses a Masters Degree in English Literature with a special expertise in the complex works of the Irish author, James Joyce. His background in humanities and philosophy are combined in this probing novel. As a final Sherlockian synthesis, The Confessions of Sherlock Holmes is Mengert's attempt to understand the true depths of the best known detective in world literature, a hero to his many fans who find in his character and habits of mind an endless fascination.

www.ingramcontent.com/pod-product-compliance
Lightning Source LLC
Chambersburg PA
CBHW062115290726

48975CB00001B/237